Final or Test Match came from the troops (myself included). And then he was off again, like an Olympic runner, charging straight at it. With force the likes of which I have never seen, the masked marvel delivered a powerful uppercut to the Tiger's front armour, tearing it apart as though it were wet newspaper.

Although the battle was far from over, the belief of victory had been handed to us, and suddenly, we all felt like "super soldiers"...

PART ONE

CHAPTER ONE: RICHIE

*MUD AND BLOOD AND SCREAMS AND FLASHES
AND BANGS AND WHISTLES AND SHRIEKS AND MOANS
AND THUNDER AND LIGHTNING AND BULLETS! A
MONSTER ON THE HORIZON! MEN TORN APART IN ITS
WAKE! THE WORLD EXPLODES!!! THE BLUE FLAMES,
THEY'RE IN MY EYES! OH GOD! THEY'RE IN MY
EYES!!!!!*

"NO!!!!" Richie Spink awoke with a fearful shout. Sweat poured down his face, and his heart raced as he fought to catch his breath. The light in the room was bright, and his pupils dilated rapidly to adjust. A strong hand gripped his. In a panic he tried to pull away, but the grip remained. *It had all felt so real,* and Richie had never felt more terrified in his life.

"Richie? Richie?" the soothing tone of his mother's voice became audible as the pounding sound of his heartbeat stopped thudding in his ears.

The room began to come into focus. The familiar lines of his parents' faces at his bedside finally snapped him back to reality.

Richie looked around the white walled room, trying to get his bearings. The pair sat at his bedside, with 40 years of worry lines all in use. Wearing a red dress, and with her immaculate hair and makeup, his mother was stunningly overdressed for the occasion, and probably would've been in fact for most social events. His Dad was kitted out in his standard attire of tracksuit bottoms, trainers and black Pink Floyd, "Dark Side of the Moon" t-shirt.

Despite the fact that he was lying in a hospital bed, the truly strange thing for Richie was that his parents didn't appear to be shouting. Moreover, it seemed as though they were actually getting on. Richie doubted that it would last. They both seemed far too concerned with his well-being to bother damaging each other's. This felt nice, as at that moment it felt as though Richie's 'being' had been run over by a Double Decker bus. He ran a quick self-inspection.

"Where... Where am I? What happened?" he asked.

His parents sat close at his bedside, his mother gripped his dad's hand tightly, concern etched deeply into their faces. In the far corner of the room, his sister Kathy, stoned on something, sat slumped in a chair, staring glassy eyed at the wall-mounted television. Her dyed black and blonde hair was messy at the back, and as always, she wore too much black eye makeup.

Richie's head swam. His Dad was talking to him, with considerable effort he managed to tune in.

"You're in the hospital Rich. The paramedics found you, and brought you here." he said calmly.

Paramedics? Hospital?

He tried desperately to think back, he was sure he'd been riding his bike, but all he could recall was a flash of blue flame and the screams of the dying. His heart began to race, sweat formed on his brow. *What the hell happened to me?*

"How're you feeling lad?" his Dad asked softly.

"Rough..." Richie responded with a wince, causing his Dad to chuckle slightly. Richie's mother stared at them, annoyed that her husband didn't seem to be taking the situation as seriously as her. She could keep her cool no longer, "How did this happen Richard? Who did this to you? Were you fighting with..."

"Jesus wept Laura! The lad's been awake for like 5 seconds, and you've turned into the Spanish inquisition!!" Richie's Dad interjected.

Her eyes widened and her eyebrows rose automatically, incensed. In the corner Kathy shook her head, and turned up the volume on her Walkman. Just as it seemed World War III was about to erupt, Richie's Doctor stuck his head around the door. "Can I have a word Mister and Missus Spink?" the young man asked. Richie's mum bit her lip and composed herself, the mask of marital perfection slipping back into place.

"Sure thing Doc." Mr Spink replied, instantly getting to his feet and following him out of the room. Mrs Spink gave Richie's hand a kiss, took a deep breath, and followed her husband. From the corner of her eye, Kathy watched them go. She shook her head disparagingly. When their fighting had started all those months ago her moods had swung wildly from despair to anger. With shouting, disagreements and bad mouthing now common pass-times in the Spink household, Kathy had honed her façade of irritated apathy to perfection. Seeing the worry on her baby brother's bruised face, she let the mask slip for a second. She crossed her eyes and stuck out her pierced tongue, its stainless steel ball glinting beneath the fluorescent strip lighting. In spite of how rough he felt Richie let out a chuckle, his ribs were sore and it caused him to wince again. He lay back in his bed and stared up at the square panelled ceiling.

What the hell happened to me?

CHAPTER TWO: WELLS

With more than a little trouble, Neil Wells lowered his 62 year old frame into the garish green, TVR Tuscan. It was parked a good foot and a half from the curb on the street opposite his father's nursing home. A puddle of water distorted the double yellow lines clearly visible in the gratuitous gap between the low profile Pirelli tyres and limestone kerb. His back hurt, and with the vehicles' lowered suspension it was murder getting in and out, not to mention going over speed bumps. Wells remained convinced that the city council were only building them to spite him.

Like the bastards aren't satisfied enough gouging my wallet with taxes and speed cameras, they're going to make me pay out for new suspension AND a new bloody spine!

He started the engine and pulled away into late evening traffic.

Though what are the odds that spinal surgery is covered by the NHS?

Wells was hardly the cheeriest of characters at the best of times, a fact beaten into him by his now ex-wife, but visits to see his father only served to further exacerbate his bad moods. Tonight had been no exception. The past twelve months he'd seen his father's condition deteriorate rapidly. Although Wells had been told by the doctors what to expect; reduced mobility, decreasing lucidity, and of course the memory loss, he found that the words did little to soften the blow of the reality. Despite his borderline draconian upbringing, Wells loved his father dearly, but this evening he'd found the growing dementia too much to bear and had left earlier than usual. The memory skips had been distressing at first, but his grip on reality had really started to twist of late. The usual semi-coherent, fragmented stories from his past had been replaced by delusional fantasies about the war. His tall tales from the frontline were passionate and fantastical but sadly, total nonsense. The most action his father had seen during World War II had been on the Pathé newsreels at the local cinema.

Now with an unplanned extra hour on his hands, he planned on putting it to good use working on tomorrow's hangover. It had taken him a good portion of his 30 year teaching career to figure it out, but alcohol was the best *legal* method of distracting from the abject tedium of marking books, hormonal teenage angst and faculty politics. Like so many things in Wells' life, his passion for teaching and his once-beloved History in general had waned severely.

There's only so many times you can talk about "the Treaty of Versailles", or the bleeding "Munich putsch" before you just feel like topping yourself.

He gritted his teeth as the car went over a speed bump, and the familiar stabbing pain shot up from his coccyx. The underbelly of the car scraped against the tarmac beneath him.

Bastards! Bastards! Money grabbing bastards!

He pulled the car angrily off the side streets and finally got onto the dual carriageway and its blessed freedom from the council's *murderous, money grabbing, humpbacked love children.* He put his foot down, only to immediately see the bright white flash of a speed camera in his rear view mirror. "Bastards!" he swore again, thumping the steering wheel and accelerating once more towards home and his date with a bottle.

CHAPTER THREE: ANNA

Anna Harrison's black pumps squeaked on the linoleum flooring as she strolled down the cold corridor of Humberidge House. Old fashioned, vertically sliding sash windows covered with steel grating ran along one wall, each showed a less than impressive view of another part of the building, complete with its own peeling, white painted, sliding windows. On the opposite side of the corridor were numerous doors; behind each of these were the individual living areas of the Humberidge residents. The old building smelt like cheap bleach and TCP, a smell she feared was slowly seeping into her bones. Anna zipped her black hooded top up a little higher as she walked, and cursed the home's manager Mrs Highton and her penny pinching.

What on God's green earth has possessed her to turn the heating off? It's February for God's sake! Not August!

She felt a little worse for this thought; *she* after all had the luxury of going home shortly, unlike Humberidge's poor inhabitants who would have to put up with it until the place warmed up naturally, which knowing the British weather would be for one day, in about nine months time.

She rounded a corner, and let out a startled scream as she came face to chest with the hulking figure of an elderly man in a bathrobe and slippers. Her big, blue eyes widened in shock, and a loose lock of black hair fell across her face.

"Christ almighty!" she exclaimed, clutching her chest to fend off the impending heart attack.

Calm down girl, you're 15, not 50, take deeeep breaths...

"Mister Wells! What are you doing wandering around?" she asked the man, her voice wavering as she tried to compose herself.

He looked down at her, but beneath the bushy, grey eyebrows, and deeply wrinkled face, showed no sign of recognition.

9

"Are you giving the orders?" he asked conspiratorially, a charming spark of life shining through the fog of dementia.

Anna centred herself and felt her heart rate slow back to a sensible pace. When she replied her voice was assured, and her tone was well measured. Despite her petite frame, it gave her an authoritative edge.

"Yes soldier, I give the orders around here!" she barked.

"Sorry sir" he said, as he slowly tried to raise his right hand in salute. She noticed the pronounced tremor of his arm; lifting it was clearly a real effort.

"No need to salute me, soldier!" she said, taking gentle, but firm hold of his wrist. Clenched inside his fist was a piece of fabric.

"What have you got here, err... *Captain*?" she guessed. During her time working at "The House" Anna had come to know most of its inhabitants well enough, and as far as she was aware, old man Wells was a retired security guard. But she knew better than to burst the delusions of the inmates. So she guessed his rank and hoped that pure luck was on her side.

"Lieutenant sir."

DAMMIT.

"Err... Yes, of course. So *Lieutenant*, what's that you have?"

"Top Secret sir, for the eyes of the top brass only sir" he replied.

If this is used toilet tissue again, I swear to god...

"At ease soldier, hand it over..." she said.

Mister Wells relinquished his grip on the object, and Anna took it from him. She opened up the crumpled fabric. It was a sewn badge, still attached to a rough scrap of thick, khaki coloured cotton. The badge itself was in pretty good condition, and it reminded Anna of the badges they used to give out at Brownies and Girl Guides. The image sewn onto it on it was of a clenched, flaming, blue fist with writing in an unfamiliar language around it. Anna looked at it sceptically.

"What's this Wells?" she asked.

"Top secret sir, top secret…" he replied. His eyes glazed over, the brief spark faded, and he shuffled away up the corridor.

Anna shook her head, and tucked the patch into the front pocket of her jacket.

No, I don't want to work in McDonald's Mum, I want to do something more meaningful for MY part time job.

She let out a sigh, and zipped her top all the way up to her neck. *Roll on summer,* she thought, and continued her walk down the long, cold corridor.

CHAPTER FOUR: BILL

Major William "Bill" North sat alone outside of General Sutherland's office, in an uncomfortable wooden chair. He was furious, but years of training and experience meant that his exterior appearance was one of calm focus. The wood panelled walls, framed photographs and oak flooring would've been of great comfort (or awe) to most, but not he. Bill was a soldier, and a damned good one at that, his place was on the battlefield tackling the enemy head on.

Not wasting time sitting on my arse waiting on the self indulgent "top brass" to get their act together.

The clock on the wall told him that he had been sat there for nearly half an hour. His brand new worn dress uniform was freshly starched, and itchy at the neck. Bill cracked the knuckles of his right hand and tried to work out how many Nazi's he'd killed in the three years since Britain had joined the war. The figure was substantial.

Not enough.

The door to the General's office opened and his young, blonde secretary called him in with a red lipped smile full of white teeth and possibility.

Maybe being office bound has its perks after all.

He admired the sway of her hips as she tottered into the plush room ahead of him. The office was huge, and although this was not Bill's first visit to a Ministry of Defence base, the extravagance never failed to annoy him. He saw the leather bound first editions, priceless works of art, and antique furniture.

I'm sure the lads in the trenches would appreciate the expense the next time they run out of ammo behind enemy lines.

He decided not to share this thought with the General, and instead gave him a respectful salute. The older, rather more debonair gentleman was sitting in a high-backed, oxblood-coloured leather chair, his manicured hands crossed atop his huge mahogany desk. The secretary gave Bill another suggestive smile as she left, but he ignored it, all business now.

"Sergeant Maj… Hrmmph… Sorry." He cleared his throat. "*Major* William North, reporting as requested sir!" he bellowed.

The General nodded graciously. "At ease Bill," the grey-haired, moustachioed man said, "Please, do take a seat." he continued in his perfect, Queen's English. Bill took his offer of the seat, but he was not at ease. He'd become too accustomed to living in battle zones to let his guard down, even in such auspicious surroundings.

"I bet you are wondering why I've asked you here today." The General stated.

There's an understatement…

"Not my job to question orders sir." Bill replied, in his thick Yorkshire accent.

The General snorted, amused at the politeness of Bill's response.

"Oh come off it William, drop the act! I've known you too bloody long! We *both* know this…" The General gestured around the room, and to Bill's uniform, "is your idea of torture."

He laughed, and got to his feet. Bill's brow furrowed.

What's the old bastard playing at?

He was right, they had known each other a long time, but the man had never been this frank with him before. Bill decided to test this out.

"Permission to speak freely sir?" he asked.

The General removed a crystal decanter, and two matching glasses from the bureau. He poured out two liberal measures.

"By all means Bill," he said without shifting his attention.

"You're right Arthur, I *do* hate this. I hate this *stupid*, itchy uniform, I hate this *stupid* office, and I hate the fact that while

13

I'm *wasting* my time talking to *you*, I *could* be on the frontline," He pointed to the window for emphasis, "shooting *bloody* Jerry like I'm s'posed to!"

The General picked up the ornate glasses and returned to the desk. He gestured with one to Bill, who took it in his calloused right hand.

Sutherland sat back down, and with an audible sigh, undid the top button of his shirt. He nodded for Bill to do the same. He was still sceptical but was not going to refuse a Commanding Officer's instruction, particularly one that eased the irritation of the "monkey suit".

The elder gent took a sip of the amber liquid, pleased at its contents. "Ahh… well I'll say this, the Scots do two things right," He swirled the contents, and took in a deep breath, "fighting and whisky."

Bill couldn't help but laugh. He took a sip himself, "Jesus wept!" , he exclaimed, the quality genuinely surprising him. "Bet yer ration book doesn't cover that 'ey?"

The General laughed heartily.

"So, you ready t'cut the bollocks then Arthur? There's no way you've had me pulled out of France and pushed, against my own will I might add, into an officer's rank just so you've got some bugger to drink with."

The General smiled, he found Bill's candour refreshing. It was a rare thing to find someone willing to be so honest, a downfall of rank he surmised.

"Okay Bill, no more 'bollocks' as you say." he said, almost as satisfied with his use of a swear below his station as the whisky. He opened the top drawer of his desk and withdrew a manila file.

"Here," he tossed the file across the desk, "have a look at this."

Without moving, Bill read its title label. "Personnel Dept. Ministry of Defence. Classified Project: "The Eternal Flame". He raised an eyebrow, and looked quizzically across the desk.

"Go on." the General insisted.

Bill shrugged and reached forward to pick it up. Not a man prone to melodrama, he casually opened the file. As he leafed through the pages, what he saw inside caused the other brow to rise.

Bullet and bomb proof, energy projection, 'Alpha' grade tactician... but what does it all mean?

He stopped on a photograph. The picture was of a tall man in basic army issue vest, trousers and boots, oddly enough he wore a mask which obscured the top half of his face.

"It's a... bloke?" he asked in surprise, "Is this a wind up or what?"

A grin slid across the General's aged face, and he got to his feet. He brushed down the jacket of his uniform, refastened his top button, and motioned towards a nearby floor to ceiling bookcase.

"No joke, but I understand your scepticism. Some things just have to be seen to be believed," he took a last gulp of his whiskey, "follow me." he said and put down his empty glass on the desk.

A sceptical look still plastered on his face, Bill did the same. *Well, they've dragged me all this way, the least I can do is see this "special soldier" for myself.*

He followed the General to the side door.

"Why is he called The Eternal Flame?" Bill asked.

"Oh, you'll see..." the General replied, matter-of-factly as the shelves in front of them parted to reveal a simple green metal door. He pulled it open, and slid back the black metallic lattice of the safety gate to reveal a small two person lift. Bill, trying his best not to appear shaken, maintained his composure even as the General beckoned him inside and pressed a button marked B4.

"It's rather curious, you know, this sort of life." his old mentor said, with a playful twinkle in his eye as the lift shook and began to descend.

Twenty minutes later and four storeys below ground level, a slack jawed Bill stood beside the now broadly grinning General. The pair stared through the extra thick glass of the observation gallery down onto the floor below. The area around them was filled with similarly grinning scientists in lab coats. Although they knew what to expect, each of the five present clearly revelled in seeing the response of an outsider. On the floor below, the masked man from the file stood in the centre of the room. Bill was wide eyed as his brain tried to reconcile what he was seeing with what he knew as possible. In his forty one years Bill North had been to the four corners of the globe and seen some incredible sights. But this? This was something else.

For five solid minutes, three British soldiers decked out in full combat uniform had been persistently attacking the masked 'Eternal Flame' from varying angles. Each attack was easily repelled with lightning-quick reflex blocks or dodged with fractional, perfectly timed movements. On occasion, one of the soldiers would land a blow which despite appearing fierce enough, seemingly had no effect on the hulking figure. Across the way from their observation room, Bill noted another similar room containing a film crew, documenting the action.

The propaganda machine in full effect. The PM's idea no doubt...

At the ten minute mark, a short sharp siren sounded. The three sweat drenched soldiers grimaced, gave each other a resigned look and charged in unison. The Flame gave each of the exhausted soldiers an open palmed return blow to the chest, sending their unconscious forms flying to the far corners of the room. In the observation gallery, Bill took a sharp intake of breath, before nodding in grudging approval at the General.

Impressive.

The senior man returned his look with a playful wink, nodding himself to direct Bill's attention back down to the floor.

As the three unconscious men were dragged out of the room by medics, they were replaced by four more. Each of these men drew a pistol from their belt holsters and took aim at the Flame. Bill looked at the General in shock.

Surely he's not going to just let them kill him?!

He gritted his teeth as the four opened fire, and waited for the inevitable. But instead of the blood and screaming that Bill knew to be the standard response to such circumstances, there was... blue flame. He was not covered by the flames, but rather they seemed to flare up in the areas that the bullets struck. The soldiers unloaded round after round into the Flame, who stood there passively as the bullets were seemingly incinerated by the bright flashes of cobalt fire. They emptied their clips, reloaded, and continued to fire, all to the same effect. If anything, the flames were getting bigger. The Eternal Flame, his upper face covered by the pale blue mask, looked up at the observation room directly at the General. Bill turned his head to follow the gaze in time to see Sutherland nod down in approval at him.

With that wordless instruction The Eternal Flame further squared up his shoulders, and spread his arms. Bill looked at the General, who, noticing his change of attention, pointed back at the floor to re-divert it.

The Flame quickly brought his open hands slamming together! The impact sent a blue-flamed shockwave outwards, knocking his attackers from their feet and hurling them five feet backwards to slide across the concrete floor. The glass of the observation room rattled, causing Bill to reflexively take a step back. When he realised that the General hadn't flinched he semi-sheepishly stepped forward again, pretending to adjust his jacket.

The Flame walked over to each of his downed attackers in turn, and picked up their guns and held them tightly together. With slight concentration, he melted them in the grip of his large, powerful hands. The molten slag metal dripped between his thick fingers to the floor, causing steam to rise up in reaction with a satisfying hiss.

Once he had done this he returned to the centre of the room and stood at attention. The General walked over to a nearby console and pressed an intercom.

"Thank you Flame, you may stand down and return to your quarters." he said.

Down on the floor, The Eternal Flame nodded, saluted and walked towards the double doors, as a handful of lab technicians burst past him with fire extinguishers. Without so much as a glance he passed the four soldiers, now being tended to by Ministry of Defence physicians. One of the soldiers cast him a dirty look as he sat on the floor, rubbing the back of his head.

Popular lad…

One of the scientists whispered in the General's ear. He patted the slight, spectacled man on the back, before returning his attention to Bill, who stood there in stunned silence.

"So…" he strolled back over to him, "any questions?"

Questions? Questions?!

Bill's thoughts ran wild, what he'd seen was so far beyond his comprehension! He had more questions than he had the vocabulary to put them into words, so instead he just stood there and waited for the General to continue with his obviously rehearsed pageantry.

"Do you want to meet him?" the General asked.

Bill watched as the four, formerly gun toting soldiers were helped out of the room by the numerous medics. Several scientists made notes, and recorded observations on clipboards. One prodded the pile of cooled slag metal that moments hence had been a pistol, with his pencil.

18

Bill's desire to meet this one man army was being met by a powerful urge to run to the nearest pub and drink it dry. He took another look around him; the feeling of elation amongst the gathered scientists and high ranking officials was tangible. There was no doubt that what Bill had witnessed was incredible,

The man is borderline... superhuman.

He could not share in their jubilation however. Perhaps he was just unaccustomed to witnessing such paranormal phenomena, but there was something about the man's demeanour that chilled him to the bone. He was impressed by the prospect of a seemingly unkillable soldier, for sure, but he just seemed a little *nonchalant*, a little *detached*. From Bill's experience cocky, unfocused soldiers were as much a danger to others as they were to the enemy. Ever the good soldier however Bill decided to refrain from vocalising his scepticism for the moment; he wanted to know more before he cast any judgement.

"Sure."

The General put a fatherly arm around his shoulder.

"He's amazing isn't he?"

"He's *something* alright."

But what exactly, he wasn't sure...

CHAPTER FIVE: WELLS

"The Panzer tank division is perhaps the most enduringly celebrated part of the German War Machine. Whilst the Mark I and Mark II are both well regarded, it is the Mark III that still, nearly 70 years later, captures the imaginations of historians and enthusiasts the world over. The Mark III AKA 'Panzerkampfwagen VI Ausführung E' AKA Hitler's Baby, the most fearsome and devastatingly powerful tank ever created is more commonly known by what name?" Wells, whose enthusiasm for the subject matter had even caught himself by surprise, turned away from his note strewn chalkboard and looked across the sea of disinterested young faces and gawking mouths before him.

"The Tiger, sir?" came a female voice, from the back left corner of the room.

"No, it was in fact, The Tiger, oh, yes quite." He squinted and was pleased, but not totally surprised, to see Anna Harrison give him an awkward smile in return. Several of her wholly more irritating friends muttered something, and the girl, the closest thing he had to an A-star student, shrank down in her seat.

Undeterred, he reached over to his laptop and pressed the spacebar, bringing his Powerpoint presentation to life on the projector screen next to him. He'd forgotten to turn off the ceiling lights, so the image of the vehicle was washed out by the general brightness.

"Yes, indeed, the Tiger Tank, Hitler's birthday present to himself, was a nasty spit in the eye to the Sherman, and unlike its American counterpart, each unit was built by hand, rather than the much vaunted "Henry Ford" method of mass manufacture." He paused to catch his breath.

"With its whopping 88mm gun and 10cm thick armour it was nigh on invulnerable to enemy anti-tank guns. That turret on which the gun was mounted however would take up to a full minute to rotate, and by the quirk of German military officiousness, crews could be court marshalled if it was unlocked whilst in drive mode." Wells smiled, pleasantly surprised that he had stumbled into a thin remaining vane of academic enthusiasm. In the front row, Jackson Sleight let out a deliberately belligerent yawn so large that Wells could see the boy's rotting back teeth.

"Anyway, the Tiger, for all its strength and pant soiling ferocity did have several key flaws that the Allied troops were able to exploit. Firstly…"

The wall-mounted bell rang with the joyous sound of the end of another testing school day, at the end of another torturous school week. Wells' brief annoyance at being interrupted quickly gave way to a palpable sigh of relief as a wave of excitement flowed around his cramped class of highly-strung Year 10's. Weekend plans were passed around, and books were hastily shoved into backpacks. Everyone in the room was doing everything in their power to get the hell out of there ASAP. Everyone but mop topped, gangly teenage boy, whose name he couldn't quite recall.

Spark? Sprite? Swanson?

The boy remained seated at the back of the class, staring vacantly out of the window, his brown eyes glazed over as he idly flipped a well-chewed biro around in his left hand. The last of his classmates, Anna Harrison, a pretty, petite girl with pin straight black hair hung back at the doorway for a moment.

"Everything okay Miss Harrison?" Wells enquired, trying to keep the irritation from his voice.

Trust me to have the only diligent class in the whole school last lesson on a Friday!

The girl opened her mouth to speak, but seemingly thought better of it upon seeing the boy. She stared for a moment longer before shaking her head, slinging a rucksack over her shoulder and dashing off to catch up with her group of loud, brassy friends. Neil Wells, long accustomed to the tiresome classroom "crushes" of his students, ignored her and packed up the last of the papers from his desk into his battered briefcase. Inside was a fresh half bottle of Glenmorangie, which he caressed with the back of the fingers on his hand, lost in a reverie for a moment. The ageing History teacher had been at Shipworth Comprehensive for most of his nearly thirty year teaching career, and although he was nearer retirement than most of the new crop of teachers, it was still nothing like near enough. He snapped back to reality when he remembered that the boy was still sat there, in a world of his own in the back corner. Wells cast a quick glance down at his ever reliable seating chart. "Spink?" he asked tentatively. He didn't respond. Wells closed and locked his briefcase and, picking it up, walked around his desk and across the room towards him.

"*Spink?*" he asked again, more insistently this time. Richie's glance slowly moved away from the window and up to look Mr Wells in the eye. Richie's glazed expression faded,

"Hmm?" he said absently.

Wells looked at Richie as though he had two heads.

"Is everything okay?" he enquired.

"Err…yeah? Why, what's up sir?" Richie responded innocently.

"Well first off it's a Friday, and perhaps more pertinently, school finished five minutes ago, which probably makes us the last two people in the building…" Wells explained with a smile.

Richie looked around the classroom, as if seeing its peeling painted walls and graffiti covered desks for the first time, his eyebrows arched in surprise. He shook his head to clear the cobwebs, and got to his feet. "Sorry sir…"

Wells looked more closely at the boy, taking note of his ill-fitting uniform and the slightly sallow hint to his skin. He perched himself on the edge of the next desk.

22

"Are you sure you're okay? Any problems at home?"

Richie let out an involuntary snort of derisory laughter as he packed away his books.

"It's fine sir, it's just... just got a lot on my mind…"

"Anything I can help you with?" Wells asked, the desire to drink his whisky momentarily overwhelmed by natural concern.

Richie's gaze glazed over again for a moment,

"I *really* doubt it…" he said and opened the classroom door.

Still sat on the desk, Wells shifted around to follow his exit.

"Well, my door's open if you need any help. You can't afford to let things slip now, mock GCSE's are only a few months away, and I know that seems like an eternity, but trust me, it's not…" Wells said in his best fatherly tone.

"Yeah," Richie said as he walked out of the room, "tell me about it…"

When the boy had gone, Neil Wells shook his head ruefully and in doing so found something caught his eye. He leaned over and looked at Richie's desk. Just like its thirty one brothers, the desk surface was covered in many years worth of scrawling, signatures, tags, and the occasional line drawing of a penis. On Richie's desk however was a fresh layer of new graffiti in black biro. A clenched, flaming fist inside a surprisingly well drawn circle dominated the desktop. Wells rubbed his finger across it, smudging the ink and staining his finger tip. He studied the image, a puzzled look forming on his face. He looked back up at the door where the boy had been just moments earlier.

What on earth?

Perhaps it was just the random doodlings of another troubled teen, but something about the design resonated with him, in a way he couldn't quite place. Wells pulled his phone from his inside jacket pocket, and took a few quick photos of the desktop.

A flaming fist...

He stroked the 5 o' clock shadow on his chin pensively for a moment before catching a glimpse of the clock adorned above the chalkboard. 3:35pm.

Bugger!

Wells swept to his feet and grabbed his briefcase as he hurried to the door. He was five minutes into his weekend already, and his Monday morning hangover wasn't going to form itself...

CHAPTER SIX: RICHIE

Although the depths of winter had faded and the sun was out, it would've taken a braver boy than Richie to face February in England without a coat. His backpack swung rhythmically from side to side from his left shoulder as he trudged alongside the busy main road, his thick navy duffle coat zipped up to his neck, and his hands shoved deep into the side pockets. Further down the road a gang of teenage boys hung around at the old metal framed bus shelter. The five of them wore dirty white trainers and tracksuit tops with their school uniforms. They all had varying degrees of short hair from skinhead to crew cut. The shortest of the boys did pull ups from the overhanging roof of the shelter. The other boys, each of varying heights and builds kicked a wrecked football between them, shouting and swearing loudly.

The monkeys are out of their cages...

The biggest of the gang, Jackson Sleight (who ironically was anything but) had the shortest hair and sported a fresh black eye. He controlled the ball neatly on his chest, before volleying it full force at a parked car. The gang roared with laughter as its alarm went off. The ball rebounded up into the air, and was caught by the short, feral looking Mickey Parkinson, Sleight's right hand boy.

Richie stopped dead in his tracks. He looked at the gang, and then up the street at the approaching number 61 bus, the only bus that took him remotely near his house. The possibilities cascaded through his mind, but given the consequences the choice was simple. Richie spun on his heels, and back headed the opposite way. As the rabid gang of lads all hopped aboard, Richie dug his hands deeper into his pockets, further hunching his back and bracing himself for yet another long walk home. As the bus passed him, Richie glanced up as several empty cans and balled up scraps of paper rained down around him. A half drunk can of Fanta struck him on the chest, its contents exploding across his coat, the fur of his hood and splashing the exposed area of his face.

"WANKER!" Sleight roared at him from the thin open gap at the top of the window, as the rest of the gang rushed to the back window, to throw their full repertoire of lewd hand gestures and puerile faces towards him as the double decker accelerated away into the distance.

Richie wiped the drops of sticky orange liquid from his nose with the back of his sleeve and sighed.

"Perfect", he sighed, slumping his shoulders further, before pushing on with the walk home.

An hour later Richie finally arrived back at his parents' house or "the war zone" as he'd heard his older sister Kathy describe it. Although it had been no secret to the neighbours (or most of the street for that matter) for months now, his parents' marital troubles had only just become public knowledge. His mum had posted about it on Facebook, and his Dad had told the fellas down the pub, the 21st century of slipping an announcement to the Town Cryer. This annoyed Richie, private pain was, in hindsight, much more easily avoidable. It turned out that it's harder to ignore or forget about things when every Tom, Dick and Harry wanted to talk to you about it.

"Aww, how's things at home Richie?"

"Everything okay, Rich?"

"Keeping your chin up sunshine?"

The fake attentiveness made him want to vomit.

He reached over the top of the front gate, and unhooked the catch. It was rusty and made a brain aching squeak as it swung open. He wasn't two steps down the driveway, and already he could hear them, the deep bass like bellow from his Dad, and the high-pitched screech of his mother. He felt a headache coming on, and the horrific images from his nightmare began to seep back into his thoughts.

26

Ignore them, ignore them. Just get in, get upstairs. Get in, get upstairs, shut the door, breathe.

Removing his keys from his coat pocket Richie quietly entered the house, and headed straight up to his bedroom. Once inside his decent sized room, he went through his almost regimental routine. He turned on the sticker-covered tower of his PC, kicking the dust encrusted fan into life, before kicking off his shoes, dumping his coat on the floor, swiftly followed by his black and red striped school tie. The sound of his parents arguing easily permeated through the floorboards and the thin, red carpet. Richie found himself listening to it, trying to pick out what it was this time that had set them off. He shook his head and rubbed his temples, angry at himself for getting drawn in.

Just let them get on with it, he thought.

He sat down at the computer, and turned on the scuffed plastic, portable CD player next to it. The opening chords to Smashing Pumpkins' "Siamese Dream" played at a low volume. His parent's voices were still clear, so he turned the music up. Although what he wanted to do was play it full blast, to drown out ALL other sound, it would undoubtedly just piss the pair of them off more. This in turn would lead to them both shouting at him, which was not how he wished to spend his Friday night. He'd rather no-one shouted. No-one shouted at his friend Marc's house, but Richie had long ago learned it was best to dream small.

He double clicked the icon to boot up Command & Conquer from the desktop, hoping that leading a squad of tiny pixelated soldiers to victory might provide some much needed escapism. The shouting downstairs grew louder, and was joined by the sound of smashing crockery. Richie tried to focus on his computer screen, but it fell from focus as tears welled in his eyes.

"No, no, no" he muttered to himself, annoyed that despite being fifteen, he could still be brought to tears so easily.

A louder crash came from downstairs, the sound jarred, like glass on the back of his eyes. He screwed them closed, trying desperately to block out the sound, to regain his composure. He clenched a fist and wrapped it against his temple as his head throbbed violently.

After a few seconds, the sounds seemed to fade and the throbbing behind his eyes eased off. Richie took one more deep breath and opened them. He was standing in a massive, stone walled church.

"What the f…" Richie began to say, but was cut off as the butt of a rifle smashed across his jaw. His head snapped to one side, as he was sent sprawling from the aisle, knocking over several wooden pews before hitting the cold, stone floor. The banging sound of the long benches falling in domino effect drowned out all other sound.

Rolling over, he rubbed his jaw, more out of reflex than pain. He looked up to see two soldiers standing over him, pointing old fashioned looking rifles at him. They shouted and pointed and although he couldn't understand what they were saying, he'd endured enough of Mrs Klein's lessons to recognise the language as German.

German Soldiers?! What the hell is going on? Where the hell am I?

A third soldier stood behind the other two, staring in shocked disbelief at his rifle, the butt of which was cracked in half with wooden splinters jutting out. The other two continued their angry shouting. Richie held his hands up in a defensive posture.

"Whoa, Whoa…" he said, in a deep, masculine voice.

What's happened to my voice? And, my hands?

Richie looked more closely at his hands. They seemed slightly thicker, and more calloused than they should be. He looked down at his body and saw that he wore an old fashioned, Khaki-coloured army uniform, and boots. He felt disconnected, as though he were watching everything through a frosted glass box. He struggled to fully focus his vision. The smaller details slowly began to coalesce. Shifting his weight, he tried to sit up, but the soldiers shouted even louder and brought their guns to bear at his head.

"Okay, okay!" Richie exclaimed, his blood still boiling, and a dull ache now throbbing in his jaw. He ceased his attempts to get up.

Lying down is fine, I like it down here.

Richie looked around, hoping that he would see something, *anything* that might give him hope that this was all just a dream. A beach umbrella, Simon Cowell in a tutu, Anna Harrison from his History class in a Wonder Woman costume, ANYTHING! Instead he saw stained glass windows with numerous pieces smashed or missing, two pigeons on a ledge high in the vaulted ceiling, wisps of his breath forming and vanishing in the cold air, minuscule drops of saliva arcing through the air from the mouths of the shouting German soldiers, tiny veins bulging on their faces, the hairs on the neck of the third soldier standing on end, as he contemplated his broken rifle, and it's myriad of minute cracks and splinters. His vision was shaped in crystal clarity.

Whoa! It's all so real... he thought in bewilderment. *Where the hell is this?!*

Something else caught his eye. Each of the soldiers wore a red band on his right upper arm. On each, a black "swastika" was emblazoned on a white, circular background.

"Nazi's?!" Richie's new thick, masculine voice said out loud in surprise. "You guys are Nazi's?!

Never mind WHERE the hell am I. WHEN the hell am I?!

CHAPTER SEVEN: WELLS

It was early evening by the time Neil Wells bid the rest of his faculty drinking partners farewell and stumbled out of the pub. As always, they'd tried their best not to make him feel out of place. Most of them were more than half his age; fit and full of vitality, and all still believed that their daily public house sojourns were done as a positive social event, not a dire coping mechanism. Neil Wells was fast approaching 60, and though he too was once like them, he knew that his presence made them all a little uncomfortable. Wells had been in education for all but the first 4 years of his life, from school to university, and back to school, picking up all manner of impressive pieces of paper and letters after his name. To this new generation of teachers he was the antithesis of anything they'd dreamt of being as kids themselves. Wells was perfectly placed to judge this having taught several of them himself.

Nothing makes you feel more ancient than your bloody co-workers calling you "Sir".

This was doubly true for the attractive female ones. Wells knew that he drank more to ease the crushing monotony of his life, than out of a desire to socialise and had made his peace with it. The real reasons that he persisted in keeping their company were two-fold. Firstly he didn't like to drink alone when he could help it, and secondly because it amused him to see that little glimmer of realisation in their eyes that they too, would end up like him one day.

Under the streetlamp illumination of the packed pub car park, Wells struggled to find the button on his car's key fob. He eventually located it, and was greeted to an amber flash of the indicator lights of his TVR Tuscan. Its interior lights came on, and he made his way over, making sure to keep his steps as steady as possible. For a man of his age, his receding hairline, and his more than ample waist line, Wells knew that he and the car looked ridiculous together, "like Michael Douglas and Catherine Zeta Jones" a young maths teacher had said. Wells didn't care; he thought the car looked like a fluorescent Batmobile.

Plus, young Adam, the insufferably naive maths teacher rides a bloody bicycle to work, plastic helmet and all, so who's he to judge?

Compared to Adam and his push bike, Wells felt like Steve McQueen. In fact it had become one of the highlights of Wells' day to 'beep' and wave to poor, health conscious Adam on the way to work, as he left him choking on his petrol fumes.

He slipped gracelessly into the driver's seat and, as always, waited for the pain to subside and the spots to leave his vision before he started the ignition. The car came to life with a satisfying roar. Wells reversed it slowly out of the bay. Although he was considerably in excess of the drink drive limit, he was a stead-fast believer in the test. He pulled his sleek, lime green machine around the corner and off into traffic.

If I can get it out of the car park then I'm fit to drive…

Ten minutes later (three of which were spent trying to parallel park outside his house), Wells stepped through his front door. His battered briefcase swung loosely by his side as he turned on the hall lights. Almost immediately, he was greeted by his two lodgers, twin tabby cats Parker and Stacy. The cats both circled his feet, 'meowing' in unison. He deposited his case on the wooden kitchen table. The table, like most of the furnishings in the three bedroomed house, were at least twenty years out of date. He justified this as giving the place "character", though to himself Wells admittedly just didn't see the point in buying new furniture for the sake of it.

It may look horrendous, but it still has four legs and a flat top…

31

He went down the galley kitchen, retrieved two foil pouches of cat food from beneath the sink, and emptied the contents into the twin food bowl by the back door. The cats rubbed against his arm in appreciation and began to contentedly tuck into their food. Wells went over to his huge American style, double-door, fridge freezer. Although he did not see the point in replacing old *furniture*, this ethos did not apply to electrical appliances. Unlike many men his age, Wells was a total technophile, and always made a point of owning the latest gizmos and gadgets. He placed a thick-based, glass tumbler under the dispenser, and filled it with ice. He then removed the half bottle of 'Glenmorangie' from his briefcase, and poured out the amber liquid two fingers shy of the top of the glass. He closed the case and picked it up, and along with his drink took it into the living room.

Wells' living room was a strange marriage between 1960's chintz and 21st century technology. Dusty shelves crammed with books lined the walls beside the chimney breast's electric heater and alongside a multitude of old photographs was a 60 inch plasma screen TV, atop a mahogany, art deco unit in the window bay. There was a sofa against one wall that had been there since he inherited the house, but directly facing the TV was Wells' pride and joy; his high backed, overstuffed, green leather, wing back chair. It was into this chair that he lowered himself upon entering the room, with a deep comforted sigh. On either side of the chair were two knee high coffee tables, he placed his drink on the left, and briefcase on the right. Directly in front was a waist high table, with wheels on its legs, atop which sat a silver laptop. Wells pulled the table towards him, turned the laptop on, and sat back; using his impressive touch sensitive remote to turn on the massive TV. The glow of the screen bathed the room in a pale blue glow as a well dressed anchor recapping the evening news flickered and was replaced by the duplicated display of his computer desktop. Wells took a cool sip of his whisky, placed the glass back down and wiped the condensation from his fingers on his sweater. Next he took out his mobile phone, his pride and joy, an Apple "iPhone", and browsed through the files stored in its memory. He opened a drawer in the coffee table to his right, removed a cable, and connected it to the laptop to transfer three images across. He loaded up the first image, a picture showing the whole of Richie's graffiti covered desktop. Wells clicked onto the next image which was a close up of the "flaming fist" logo. Wells enlarged the picture to full screen, and then sat back in his chair. The logo was, by comparison to the other scrawlings around, incredibly detailed. Of course it was essentially a line drawing in biro ink, but the precision with which it was drawn was what made it stand out. The clenched, left handed fist, with flames licking around it was surrounded by a circle so well drawn that Wells suspected young Mister...

What was the boy's name? S- something? Oh Never mind, I'm sure it'll come back to me...

... That the young *boy* who had drawn it *must've* used a compass. Wells stared at the image intently as he picked up his glass and took another satisfying sip. The image tickled the back of his brain. He sat back and rested the glass on the arm of his chair.

"Now where have I seen you before?"

CHAPTER EIGHT: ANNA

Anna lay atop the covers of her single bed, staring up at the array of plastic stars stuck to her ceiling. With the curtains drawn and the lights in the room dimmed, they glowed mildly in the gloom. Much like the bright pink wallpaper, and the myriad of stuffed animals scattered around the place, they served as a reminder to Anna of how much she had changed in the past year. Although her heartfelt pleas for re-decoration had so far fallen on deaf ears, she was *more* than prepared to take matters into her *own* hands, as her recently dyed black hair could attest. Anna understood that money was hardly in abundance since her step-dad had been laid off...

But I'm fifteen years old, trapped in the fluffy pink hell-hole room of a ten year old.

She sighed, and lowered her gaze to the poster of Bob Dylan adorning the wall above the headboard. Bob looked back behind black sunglasses.

"It ain't me babe..." she said to the poster. On a bedside table, her battered mobile phone buzzed and beeped once to signify a new text message. Anna exhaled deeply, and stretched to retrieve it. Holding the phone at arms length above her head, she opened and read the message. *"WER R U?"* was emblazoned in black writing on the illuminated green display. The phone was far from state of the art, and was brick-like in comparison to the models owned by most of her peers, a fact often highlighted with disgust by her best friend Katie. Anna though was no longer concerned by such things; in fact she took a perverse pride in the fact that it was pretty un-cool. *Plus, if I ever do run into one of those muggers or rapists that Mum constantly goes on about, I know what I'd rather have in my hand...*

She sighed again and tapped out her reply... "C U SOON" and hit send. She looked back up at Bob and shook her head.

Yeah, yeah, yeah, I know. Don't start.

The rest of the gang had been at the shops for an hour by the time Anna arrived. The three girls, whose scantily clad attire would've been better suited to a summer beach party on the surface of the sun, huddled together in the bus shelter. They laughed and giggled as they passed a bottle of cider between them, each wincing in mild disgust as they took a gulp. Nearby, two young lads in dark tracksuits sat astride BMX bikes, whilst a third scrawled his initials onto the side of the shelter with a black marker pen. They all turned to regard the hulking figure of Jackson Sleight as he emerged from the newsagent around the corner. A grin formed on his lightly freckled features as he approached the bus shelter. The gang gathered around as, from the pockets of his parka jacket, he revealed the spoils of his latest "five finger discounted" shopping trip. He handed out the random selection of stolen goods: chocolate bars, sugar sticks, chewing gum, marker pens, cellotape, and his most proud piece of thievery, a copy of The Daily Sport. The other three lads pounced on the newspaper, eager to catch a glimpse of the bevy of topless photos contained within. Katie, with a look approaching adulation on her face, handed the bottle of cider to Sleight. He gratefully gulped it back, finishing the bottle. Wiping the excess from his chin stubble (that he'd had since the day he hit puberty), he tossed the empty bottle over his shoulder and unleashed a massive belch. The gang burst into rapturous laughter at this. Watching the tableau of teenage mediocrity unfold as she approached, Anna let out an audible sigh…

Another fabulous Friday night.

She caught Katie's eye. Slightly unsteady, and obviously well on her way to blind drunk, Katie got up from her seat. "ANNIE!" She shouted, slightly louder and high pitched than necessary. Anna gave a sheepish wave back. The other girls looked her up and down, unable to fathom why any girl would choose to dress in fishnets, and Doc Martens, *especially on a Friday*. Katie walked over to Anna in her best approximation of a sophisticated woman. The cider, and a lack of experience walking in such shoes however made her look like exactly what she was, a drunken fifteen year old in her big sister's clothes. Anna cringed internally, as the three smaller lads cast their salacious glances upon her friend, before returning to their scrap of the now shredded newspaper.

"Annie! Ohhh my *god* girrrrl! It's *sooo* good to see you!" Katie said, an octave higher than normal.

Yeah, good to see you, god, it's been like, three hours!

"Yeah, err.. good to see you too Kate, you look fabulous! Is that a new skirt?"

"No, it's our Cassie's, her *boyfriend* Pete's best mate's *parents* are away, so he's having this *party*, so she went straight over to *his* after *work*, and I *nicked* it out of her *wardrobe*."

Anna detested Katie's tendency to over pronounce pointless words when she spoke, but she let it slide.

"Oh that's…"

"It's not like it *fits* her *anyway*, the fat *cow*." Katie continued, slurring "it's" and "fits" noticeably,

"And you, I like your err…" Her pupils were dilated, she struggled to focus as she appraised Anna's outfit.

Anna rolled her eyes.

Oh, here we go.

A moment passed and it was clear that Katie was having trouble picking any part of Anna's attire she approved of. She scanned her from her booted feet, past her ripped black fishnet tighted legs, to her baggy black hooded top, frowning all the way. When Katie spotted the gold bangle on her wrist, the relief was tangible.

"Your bangle is lovely…"

"Thanks, it was my Nan's, I found it in a box of her stuff in the loft, it's Indian gold. She used to live out there back in the 70's, I…"

"Oh my god, that's so great" Katie interrupted, clearly no longer listening, "So listen I think tonight's the night, I'm gonna let Jackson 'get off' with me" She looked over her shoulder, and let out a barely audible squeal at the sight of Jackson swaggering towards them, a lit cigarette in one hand.

She put a finger to her lips, and made an exaggerated "Shushing" sound.

"Hi, *Jackson*" she said as he reached them, trying to sound coy as she twirled a strand of blonde hair around her index finger.

"Alright Katie," he said rather dismissively, his eyes too were cider glazed, and the stench of smoke was strong on his breath. Anna blinked rapidly, leaning back almost imperceptibly as she fought the urge to fully recoil at the smell. Her experiences in the nursing home had helped build her resistance to foul odours, but only to a point.

"Alright Annie, d'yer wanna drag on this?" He offered the cigarette to her, which she politely declined. She'd hooked up enough oxygen tanks for emphysema patients in work to swear her off them for life.

As an afterthought, he held it towards Katie who accepted it readily.

"So, we're goin' up to the park, you comin'?" he asked with his hands thrust deep into his coat pockets.

Katie, fighting her gag reflex, threw the smouldering filter to the ground, and quickly combined her smokey exhale with her response.

"Sure, the park sounds great Jackson," she said, staring up expectantly at him.

The boy ignored her. He continued to stare at Anna with what she imagined was his best GQ model look, awaiting her answer.

Oh, wow, the park! That sounds simply wondrous! God, what a non-stop thrill ride this life is...

"Sure, why not?" Anna finally replied, barely keeping her dripping sarcasm in check.

Behind them, the other three lads had become increasingly loud and leery. Leaning to one side, Anna looked past Sleight's bulky form.

I wonder what's got the chimps all riled up? She thought, with a quizzically raised eyebrow.

Approaching along the parade of shops was a gangly teenager with a dishevelled mop of brown hair. He wore only a white school shirt, trousers and white socks, bizarrely visible due to his lack of shoes. He walked along in a daze, a puzzled look etched into his face as he constantly studied his surroundings.

She wasn't certain, but she was sure he went to her school.
Isn't he that boy from History?

"Ey, check this out," Sleight said menacingly as a nasty grin spread across his face. Watching his grin become a sneer, Anna couldn't help but notice the faint black eye he sported.

I wonder how someone as big as Sleight ended up with a black eye?

His attention now focussed elsewhere, Anna watched as he began to stride towards the gangly teen, his swagger even more exaggerated than before.

"Alright Pinky!" he bellowed, to riotous laughter from the gang. Beside her, Katie cracked up into a fit of giggles.

The rest of the boys stood by and watched as their hulking leader intercepted the boy thirty yards from the bus shelter. Sleight was probably only half an inch taller than the boy, but his girth made him look far more imposing. They stood toe to toe for a moment, in sight of the gang, but just out of earshot. The boy looked at Sleight quizzically as he was bombarded with what Anna could only believe were Jack's best array of insults, and threatening hand gestures.

The bloody drunken idiot, who does he think he's impressing?

Why the hell is he grinning? He's going to get his head kicked in if he's not careful!

But just as it appeared as though Sleight *would* lash out again, Richie Spink's lips moved, and Sleight's posture seemed to instantly deflate. His hands fell to his sides, and his shoulders slumped. And just like that the escalating aggression was over. Spink crossed the road and walked away, back to his reverie (albeit with a more purposeful gait). Sleight stood there, his back to the rest of the gang who, as mystified as Anna, slowly approached him. Katie relinquished her hold on Anna's wrist, and bearing a look of open-mouthed confusion, joined them in search of answers.

Anna hung back and watched the strange boy as he disappeared past the row of shops and around the corner. In the distance she saw the inquisition begin, and although she was still too far away for the specifics she felt certain that she could easily guess the questions. However, the condition of school meathead Jackson Sleight was not at the forefront of her mind. She looked back to the street corner, with a subtly wry smile of admiration forming.

Who the hell is Richie Spink?

CHAPTER NINE: BILL

The Eternal Flame was sat straight-backed at the desk in his small, but functional living quarters. He was still clothed in his basic uniform of boots, fatigue trousers and vest. On his head he continued to wear the faded blue bandana mask, which covered the top half of his head, and tied back at the base of his skull. The excess material from the bandana ran down his wide back, between his muscular shoulder blades.

From behind the two way mirror that made up one wall of the room, Bill North studied him intently. To the casual observer, The Flame's demeanour was one of calm focus as he took notes from the leather bound textbook open in front of him. But the soldier in Bill could see more than that.

He's like a coiled spring, alert, ready. I bet if someone dropped a pin in there he'd be up in a flash.

The thought stuck with him for a moment.

"Does he know we're in here?" Bill said to the General, stood behind him in the shadows of the small of the tiny observation room.

"Yes, it was actually his idea. The observation is all part of his terms of being here."

Bill made a mental note to find out exactly what that meant later. Right now there was something he wanted to try.

What have I got to lose?

He raised his fists, and sharply banged against glass. In his quarters, The Flame leapt to his feet, instantly adopting a fighting stance. Small blue flames licked around his clenched fists which he held rock steady at shoulder height and Bill immediately noted his solid southpaw stance. A tigerish grin inched its way across Bill North's rugged features.

"Good reflexes, bit jumpy though I'nt he?

"Very droll," the General remarked, "but then again if you had been through what that man has, I suspect you would be too."

41

Intrigued, Bill turned his attention from The Flame back to The General. The masked man glared at the spot of glass where Bill had made contact, his jaw clenched tight.

"Oh aye? What's 'is story then sir?

"Why don't you ask him yourself?"

Bill turned back to regard The Flame, whose form began to loosen as he picked up his chair from the floor. He returned to an air of placid detachment as he retook his seat at the desk, and returned his attention to the book in front of him.

"What? Now?" Bill asked.

"No time like the present Major."

The grizzled soldier shrugged, and made his way to the door.

Let's see what yer made of then masked man...

To Bill, The Flame's quarter's seemed a lot larger from the inside, a trick of the two way mirror along its length. Although realistically the room was scarcely bigger than a prison cell. It was sparsely furnished. An army issue cot (impeccably made) was along the wall opposite the mirror. At its foot was a tall green metallic locker, alongside which The Flame remained sat at the basic wooden pine wood desk. The tabletop was adorned with various writing implements, and text books.

Looks like our man's a bit of a boffin an' all.

"On yer feet soldier" Bill said, his Yorkshire brogue hard and authoritative. The Flame let out an irritated sigh, closed his book and got to his feet. Without looking at Bill, he stepped away from the desk and stood to attention in front of the observation mirror.

"Give me your name and rank soldier"

If he heard him, the Flame gave no recognition.

Bill's eyes narrowed. Not a man used to disrespect, he stepped forward to stand toe to toe. He came up several inches shorter.

Who does this bloody clown think he is?

Bill gritted his teeth, a snarl forming on his lips.

"OY Biggun!" Bill shouted, and snapped his fingers millimetres from the Flame's eyes. For a fleeting moment an abjectly forlorn look washed over the masked man's face. This was quickly replaced by mild annoyance as his eyes regained focus and his gaze lowered to meet Bill's.

"Oh I'm *very sorry*, am I interruptin' summat? Bill said, his words dripping sarcasm.

"No." The Flame said, his gaze returning to the far wall.

"Ohhh, so he does talk! No? No, what?"

The Flame did not react.

"The word you are looking for son, is *SIR.* "

Again The Flame did not react. Not used to being ignored, Bill's blood began to boil.

Why, the arrogant little bastard, I'll show 'im who's boss.

As he would with any soldier who stepped out of line, Bill decided to exert his authority physically. He quickly raised his knee to The Flame's crotch, but with lightning reflexes, The Flame's hand snapped down and *caught* his thigh with a firm THUD. All of Bill's experience failed to keep the look of surprise from his face.

How in the bleedin' 'ell?

Now, bent nearer to Bill's eye level, a firm look of annoyance behind his cobalt eyes, The Flame had left himself off guard. Bill saw his opening, and using his powerful neck muscles, unleashed a ferocious head butt into the Flame's… Open palm of his right hand! Before Bill could react to his situation, The masked man instantly extended both arms, shoving him backwards. Bill slammed into the far wall above the empty cot, but instinct and fury kept him upright. He now stood atop the bed, his teeth gritted and lip curled in a feral snarl. Bill had absolutely no idea how his masked foe had just done, *whatever it was he'd done*, but right now it was the furthest thing from his mind. Although Bill North had gained greater control over his temper as he'd gotten older, the red

43

mist had now truly descended. In one swift movement Bill drew his sidearm, and launched himself towards the Flame. He brought the weapon down butt first, aiming it at The Flame's collar bone. The big man swatted Bill's attack away with the outside of his left hand, clearly hoping to knock the pistol from his grip. This was just what Bill had been expecting. Somehow he kept hold of the gun. The force of the blow altered his momentum and Bill used this to devastating effect, bringing around his left elbow to smash into the Flame's cheekbone. At that moment, The General and two Military Police officers burst into the room, slamming the door into the side of the cot with an ear piercing metallic clang!

Bill and The Flame each with a grip of the other's shirt front, bunched their free hands into tight fists. Miniscule blue flames licked around the Eternal Flame's, as a tiny trickle of blood seeped from the corner of his eye. Gritted teeth and taut neck muscles, both had expressions of bloody murder painted on their faces.

The MPs pointed their rifles at the enraged combatants. Their rage however was easily matched by that of the ageing General; a vein bulged at the temple of his near purple face. "STAND DOWN THE PAIR OF YOU THIS INSTANT!"

The men remained focussed on each other, but after a moment eased their grips and stepped back.

"THE NEXT TIME I SEE ANYTHING LIKE THAT, THE PAIR OF YOU WILL SPEND THE NIGHT IN THE BRIG! DO I MAKE MYSELF CLEAR?!"

"Yes sir." they replied in unison.

"Right! North you come with me. Flame, as you were!"

The General gestured to the MPs who stood down themselves. The Eternal Flame watched with a look of mild disgust as The General led the other three men out of the room. A satisfied smile was etched onto Major Bill North's face, he shot his opponent a wink as he made his way out into the grey concrete corridor.

When they were gone, The Flame's fist unclenched and its luminescent blue flames faded away. He touched a finger to the corner of his eye. When he withdrew it, he inspected the speck of blood with a look approximating surprise. The faintest tinge of a smile formed. Shaking his head, he retook his seat at the desk, and reopened the textbook.

CHAPTER TEN: RICHIE

Richie looked down the thin black hole of the rifle's barrel, acutely aware that, impossible as it may seem, what was unfolding around him was far too real to be a dream. Still lying on the stone floor amidst the toppled pews, he propped himself up on his right elbow, and once again contemplated getting to his feet. The two nearest of his Nazi captors were not so keen on the idea; their shouts became louder, the pointing of their weapons more purposeful.

"Okaaaay, no problem buddy," he said with a wince, holding up the palms of his thick hands. "I'll stay down, that's fine. I kind of like it down here anyway, cosy."

What the hell am I saying?

Richie could feel the tight grip of fear squeezing inside his chest, and although it was far from the most sensible of solutions, babbling senselessly seemed to provide a modicum of relief.

Anyway, it looks like they've got less of a clue than I have...

"You wouldn't happen to have like, a pillow or anything would you mate? No? No, that's fine..."

Behind the two aggressors, the third soldier finally came to his senses. He discarded his smashed rifle, and drew his Mauser pistol from the holster on his hip. He joined the others in taking aim at Richie.

"A Mauser? Oh cool, oh no, wait. I mean, come on!" Richie complained, still surprised at the bass in his voice.

He pushed his palm out further from his face.

"Look, is all of this *really* necessary? If you'll just let me get up" He tried again to get to his feet.

The first Nazi fired a shot. The explosive sound echoed around the stone walls. High in the vaulted ceiling the two pigeon onlookers went into a wing flapping frenzy. The world went black.

A moment passed, and Richie realised that he could feel his teeth firmly gritted together, the pounding of his heart, and the sound of the gunshot ringing in his ears.

OHMIGOD! OH MIGOD! OH MY GOD! They shot me they shot me they... Hang on a sec.

He willed his clamped eyelids open. The three Nazi's still stood over him. The nearest had a slight grin on his face, clearly amused by Richie's fearful reaction. He muttered something to the other two, who afforded a playful laugh at his expense. Richie looked down to see a smoking bullet hole in the stone floor beside him.

Wonderful...

"Yeah, yeah, yeah, okay you got me! Ha, bloody ha! Have a good laugh at the guy crying for his life on the floor."

The moment of levity from the soldiers was just that, the serious looks returned to their faces. The second soldier whispered something in the ear of the first, who nodded and addressed a question to Richie, scowling as he did so. Although he continued to lament having spent his German lessons doodling on his desk top, he felt he should at least try to work out what they were saying to him.

"Warum bist du hier?"

Stupid, stupid desks, what was I thinking?

"Sorry Hans, I've got no idea what you're saying, unless you want me to ask where the nearest swimming pool is? Err... Wo ist das Schwimmbad? Is that right? I think that's ri"

"Was ist dein Nationalität?" he interrupted, more forcefully.

This is pointless... Oh hang about, I think I know this one!

A faint echo of recognition reverberated in the back of his mind. Slowly his under-oiled mental cogs began to turn.

"Nationalitat? As in Nationality, as in... Country? Are you asking me where I'm from?" Richie thought out loud.

The other two soldiers were becoming increasingly agitated. The third, whose finger twitched on the trigger of his

47

pistol, broke his silence and blurted out his frustration in a flurry of shouted words that Richie couldn't follow.

"Wow, easy there Gruber, no need to get your knickers in a twist, me and your mate here are having a nice, civilised conversation and…"

The angry soldier took a step forward, and put the gun inches from Richie's forehead. Richie cowered away slightly, his vision doubled up as his eyes crossed to focus on the weapon.

"SIND SIE AMERIKANER?!" he roared, his face turning a shade of red.

"What?! America?! No, no, I'm just a kid mate, an English kid, not American! Err… Ich bin ein Englischer, err… junge?" Richie stuttered.

"Junge?!" The first soldier bellowed, he turned to his compatriots, half enraged, half pleasantly bemused.

"English boy…" the shortest of them said, with a heavily accented lilt. The three men let out a roar of laughter in unison. Richie, totally lost in the sureality of the situation nervously joined in, and for a few moments, raucous, delirious laughter echoed around the cavernous vaulted ceilings of the dilapidated church. Their levity ended abruptly. His answer, though clearly the funniest thing they'd heard in a while, was clearly not the right answer. Their anger turned to looks of cruelty, as nasty smiles of intent formed on their pale, soot smudged faces. Together, they moved their weapons to bear on Richie's head. The first soldier slid back the bolt on his rifle to load a fresh bullet with an audible CLICK-CLATCH! He barked an order, the other two nodded and then all three pulled their triggers. Once again the stoned walled church reverberated with the explosive sound of gunfire. Richie expected there to be a moment of blinding pain, followed by nothing as his brains and head, or at least the brains and head of *whoever he was* became splattered across the dusty church pews.

But there was no blinding pain.

He felt some pain, sure enough, but it was more like that time when Jackson Sleight, physical comedy genius that he was, had slapped his hand with a ruler in Maths class. It had caused him to recoil slightly, and it stung like buggery for a moment, but that was it. He also felt a warm, tingling sensation running around the three impact spots.

It didn't look like it felt like this when they shot up Murphy at the beginning of Robocop... I think... I think I'm still alive...

Tentatively, Richie unclamped his eyes again. As his pupils dilated, the picture in front of him began to coalesce. And what a picture it was. The three Nazi soldiers stood over him, their eyes wide, and their jaws slack. Struck dumb in amazement, the only sound in the church was of the two pigeons manically seeking solace in the rafters, and the faint sound of bombing in the distance. Richie reached up to feel his face. Confident that it was still there beneath the mask, he looked at his hand to check for blood. At the end of his calloused fingertips, infinitesimal blue flames licked briefly, and faded out.

Ey?! What the hell is going on?

The absurdity of his situation ran like a Waltzer around Richie's head.

How can something so unreal, feel so real? Time to wake up Rich, this dream is properly crap, why can't I just be naked in Geography like normal?

The stunned soldiers began to fumble with their rifles, desperately trying to reload as their confusion and shock melted into terror. Richie watched this happen, but had no clue how to react. The soldiers aimed their weapons in unison, their jaws clenched, yellow teeth grinding together, sweaty fingers tightening on their triggers. Richie instinctively flinched away from the gun barrels.

A loud BANG drew their attention towards the church doors. Richie turned to see another soldier standing in the doorway. The wiry, moustachioed man drew his twin pistols as the splintered shards of the door flew away from the impact of his right boot. The Nazis swung around to face him, each firing off a shot in his direction. The bullets zipped through the open doorway, missing him by inches as the man sprang into a forward roll. The Germans tried frantically to readjust their aim, but it was too late. The man came to rest on one knee. Using his right foot to stop his momentum, he rapidly fired off a hail of bullets from both pistols, striking the Germans in their chests. As their lifeless bodies crumpled to the floor, the man rose easily to his feet, and with his guns still raised, scanned the rest of the building. It was Richie's turn to stare on in shock. A bubble of fear popped in the pit of his stomach, he felt it seeping into his blood, coursing through his veins, his heart rate accelerating out of control. The lone soldier turned his firearms to bear on Richie's prone figure. The panic rose.

Oh my god, he's going to kill me, he's going to kill me, he's...

A wry smile formed on the man's weathered face, as he tucked the pistols into their respective holsters on either side of his hips.

...going to, he's going to...

"What the bloody 'ell are you doin' on the floor there Flame?"

...he's going to... ey?

Like a spiritual slap to the head Richie's panic was replaced by complete confusion. The man had just shot dead three Nazi soldiers, and he was... *smiling.*

"When I said I wanted men who could kill Jerry in his sleep, this weren't what I 'ad in mind." He let out a bawdy chuckle, deepening the lines in his tanned, dirt smudged face.

This, coupled with the prominent flecks of grey in the man's black hair had Richie putting him in his early forties.

Can't be much older than my dad...

He was slightly built, but clearly powerful beneath his Khaki army uniform, and although it was hard to judge from the floor, Richie guessed that he stood around six feet. On the shoulder of his jacket was a circular, sewn patch with the design of a flaming, clenched fist at its centre.

Is that? The thing from my dream???

He shook his head but in doing so glanced at the bodies of his former aggressors. Blood seeped out of their respective bullet holes, their blank eyes staring lifelessly into space. Richie had never seen a dead body before.

Let alone three gunned down in front of him by some Yorkshire Sergeant Rock

Richie realised that he was still gawping. He tried to shut his mouth but couldn't, he felt cold all of a sudden, his head swam, as though he was losing his grip on reality.

The soldier's expression turned from jovial to concern.

"Are you okay Flame?"

Richie opened his mouth to reply, but nothing came out.

The man squinted as he regarded Richie, raising an eyebrow as he leaned towards him.

"Flame?"

Richie couldn't take his eyes off the bodies, and their cold, dead eyes. He'd seen them die.

I'm fifteen years old, I should be at home, stressing about GCSEs, not watching men getting shot...

He felt something else rising in his stomach, it was frightening and familiar. Richie vomited onto the stone floor.

"FLAME!?" The soldier's concern turned up to eleven. He crouched down, and put a reassuring hand on Richie's shoulder. Richie wiped his mouth with the back of his hand.

"Flame, what's up? Are you okay?"

Richie was barely aware of what the man was saying, his attention glued to the Nazi corpses and his racing blood pounding in his ears.

"Richie?" the man asked tentatively, "Is that you?"

The words were like a hammer blow to his skull, snapping his attention back.

Did he just call me… Richie?

Slowly, and still slack-jawed, Richie turned to face him.

The man's green eyes stared intently back at him.

"How did you..?"

"Don't worry son. Everything's goin' t' be okay…"

The growing swell of fear and confusion reached its peak and Richie burst into tears. The man cradled the back of his head, he smelt like cigarettes and gunpowder.

"I don't know what's going on…" Richie sobbed, screwing his eyelids tightly shut, trying to stem the flow of tears.

"It's alright lad, you're goin't be alright." The soldier said in his thick Yorkshire accent. "Breathe son, breathe…"

Richie tried to pull in deep breaths between sobs, but the panic had its claws in deep. He tried desperately to think of better things, of anything but the dead eyes of dead men…

Oh my god, oh my god, oh my god!

Richie opened his eyes, his vision blurred by hot tears. Sunlight beamed in through his bedroom window. He sat up with a start, throwing back the heavy quilted covers of his bed. Still sobbing and struggling for breath, he jumped to his feet. He looked around. It *was* his bedroom.

Just a dream, just a dream, thank god, thank god.

He saw his PC, his Nirvana poster, his portable television, his terrible green wallpaper. It was definitely his room. Richie's breathing slowed. He wiped away the tears with the sleeve of his school shirt, and then stopped. A puzzled look fell across his face as he inspected himself. He still wore his school shirt and trousers, and it was most certainly *him*, but

The others had fallen silent, rapt, straining to listen in.

Oh, yeah, never mind.

She puffed her cheeks and blew a stray strand of black hair out of her eyes.

Sleight began pointing right in the boy's face, both to accentuate what he was saying, and for the added annoyance factor.

The boy began to look bored and annoyed, his attention was visibly drifting, and he began to look around at his surroundings again. This didn't last long. Jackson Sleight, stunned at being ignored, raised a big right hand and SLAPPED the boy clean across the face! Even at that distance, the clap of the connection rang loud. The girls winced, and the lads let out another explosive burst of feral laughter.

Anna felt furious.

"HEY! Pack it in!" she shouted.

Katie gripped her forearm lightly.

"Oh, leave it out Annie, it's only Richie Spink, he's a bloody weirdo anyway."

Anna looked at her best friend, shocked. She desperately wanted to do something, but felt frozen to the spot. These people had been her friends since well, forever. She looked around at their faces, contorted in evil sneers and jeers and finally saw them for who they really were. Her focus returned to Sleight and the boy, poor Richie...

Richie! Of course that's his name!

... who'd just taken a slap to the face from that stupid moron. Poor Richie who was...

Is he... smiling?

Richie Spink had his left hand to the side of his face, and although he still bore a puzzled expression, an amused grin had formed across his pale features. He cocked an eyebrow. Sleight pulled his hand back for another strike but the boy stood his ground, staring straight back at him.

something wasn't quite right. He looked down at his feet, more *specifically* at the grimy, tattered remains of his *formerly* white sports socks. He sat down on his bed and inspected them further. They had been fresh out of the packet that morning. He was certain of this because they bore a red and black stripe on them, and at breakfast his dad had called them his AC Milan socks. His dad had bought them the day before as part of a colour coding plan that would *theoretically* stop his kids from wearing *his* socks. Richie had no idea what AC Milan was, (nor in truth why his dad was so precious about his socks) but he had said it that morning nonetheless.

He pulled them off his feet and held them up in front of his face. He felt tired, shaken, and utterly baffled. The memory of the dead German soldiers rose to the front of his mind again, the crimson blood glistening, their empty gazes looking right at him. Tossing the ruined socks into the far corner of his room, he rested his head in his hands and began to cry again…

CHAPTER ELEVEN: BILL

Bill's blood felt like molten lava, thundering through his veins. Once again he was in the General's stateroom, this time however he was flanked by the two armed Military Police officers, both of whom looked distinctly on edge. With his masked sparring partner now several storeys beneath them, he no longer needed to maintain an air of anything less than the pure rage he felt. What Bill North wanted to do was to head straight back down to the Eternal Flame's quarters and shoot him in the kneecaps for his insubordination. He wanted to pound on his face until his hands were bruised and broken. His lip remained fixed in a snarl, and he took deep, loud breaths in and out through his nose. Two horns and a tail would've made him the raging bull he felt like.

"TELL ME WHAT THE BLOODY HELL'S GOIN' ON GENERAL!" he raged, pounding his fist down hard on the green leather surface of the desk in between them.

General Sutherland looked his usual cultured, serene self. He liberally poured out two more glasses of Scotch from the crystal decanter. Casually strolling over, he handed one to Bill. Bill however was in no mood for social etiquette, nor in fact for the chain of command. He hurled it at the wood panelled wall without breaking eye contact. It smashed in a hail of glass and amber liquid. The MPs, though visibly shocked at the action, each placed a solid hand on Bill's shoulders. The snarl on his lips grew even farther. When he spoke his voice was more restrained, but thick with malevolence.

"If I were you Arthur, I'd tell Doris and Ethel here to keep their hands to themselves."

Only the man on Bill's right removed his hand immediately, the other kept it in place, although he was clearly not keen on doing so. A bead of sweat ran down the young man's forehead. Bill turned his head slightly in his direction.

"I'm gonna give thar *three* seconds to take that hand back, or you're gonna be a very brave soldier, with *very few* teeth."

The man trembled visibly, and cast a glance at the General. The older gentleman nodded his head. With clear relief, the M.P withdrew his hand from Bill's shoulder.

Bill North flexed his shoulders, before tilting his head left then right; his neck produced an audible "CRACK" as he did so.

"Thank you gentlemen, you may leave us." the General instructed curtly.

Grudgingly, they vacated the room, closing the door behind them as they went. The General strolled over to his desk and retook his seat. He gestured for Bill to sit down. Bill remained standing. Although he was regaining his composure, he was by no means ready to retire his indignation just yet. What Bill wanted now was answers.

"Permission to speak freely sir?"

The General cast a glance at the wall, still dripping 40 year vintage scotch, a boyish smirk formed on his face.

"I think we're a little past formalities aren't we William?"

The attempt at levity failed to take the edge off of Bill's demeanour. Arthur Sutherland let out a sigh that seemed to strip him of his youthful exuberance and refined poise. What remained was a tired looking old man at his wits end. He slouched back in his chair staring contemplatively at the glass in his hand, as he sloshed the amber liquid back and forth.

"Please Bill, do tell me what's on your mind…?"

Bill contemplated the man before him. In the twenty years he had known General Arthur Sutherland, he had seen the regal gentleman as many things; soldier, teacher, leader. But never before had his mentor seemed so old, so fragile…

Bill sat down heavily in the chair opposite, the last of the fury fading from his sails.

"Arthur, look, there's a war on and I'm a soldier. I do not do bureaucracy, I do not do paperwork and I do not buy into politics." He paused a moment for breath. "I kill people and not just for King and Country; I do it because it's what 'am best at. As much as I honour and respect any request a superior would make of me, I am what I am, I *know* my limitations. I can't stop bullets, but I *can* stop the men who fire them. For every second I sit here, another British soldier will fall to a Nazi gun!" Bill's anger simmered to the boil once more.

"You've dragged me from the front line, and for what? To pin a promotion I never asked for on me? To see some bleedin' freak show?! The war is out *there*!" he stated, pointing angrily at the window, "And I'm stuck here in this bloody monkey suit 500 miles from the action!" Bill paused again to catch his breath, and reassert his composure. He undid his tie, leaving it hanging loose around his neck.

"Come on Arthur, 'am no Officer, 'am just a soldier. Nar, cut the crap, Tell us why you've brought me here."

The General knocked back the last of his drink, and wiped the moisture from his thick grey moustache. With a little strain he got to his feet. He walked over to the lead framed window casting its broad, bright light over his desk. In the distance a platoon of troops were being put through their paces on a nearby field.

"We're losing Bill…" he said, his voice suddenly seeming shaky, less assured. He placed a hand on the window frame to steady himself.

"But, I thought the Yanks were going to pull their fingers out…" Bill butted in.

"Even *if* Eisenhower finally gets involved, even with those extra troops… the boys upstairs are saying it could be over by Christmas…"

In his reflection in the window, Bill's faded image conveyed a look of shock.

That can't be right, surely we'd've heard something?

"Even with help from the Russians, the outlook is bleak."

Bill couldn't believe what he was hearing. As the good soldier that he was, Bill would go and fight whoever and wherever his orders demanded, his own beliefs, and personal politics never factored into this. However, the thought of a Nazi controlled Europe sent a shudder down his spine.

"But, in our darkest hour, we have been handed the key to the world's salvation." Just saying the words seemed to pick up the old man's spirits. Bill didn't like where this was going.

"You have got to be joking…"

The General turned to face Bill; he was most certainly not joking. He looked focussed, and more like the strong figure that Bill remembered.

"Bill, the man downstairs, this "Eternal Flame" represents our last best hope of turning the tables on the Germans."

Bill got to his feet. "He's a freak of nature!"

"He's an asset."

"He's insubordinate and ignorant and untested!"

"Bill, he's 6ft 4, bullet proof, has the reflexes of a cat, and the strength of a tank."

The General sat on the edge of the desk directly in front of his former protege. A natural smile spread across his weathered features. Although Bill was not convinced, *clearly*, the same could not be said of his mentor.

"And Bill… he's on *our side*…"

Internally, Bill sighed. He could feel himself relenting. He glanced at The Eternal Flame's file, which still sat atop the antique desk.

"But Arthur, he's an unknown quantity," he said, pointing to the file, "it's all well an' good sendin' him against the kids you've got here, but you don't know how he's goin' to react in't field, you can't…"

The General looked Bill straight in the eyes.

"The Defence Minister wants him behind enemy lines by the end of the month."

"HE WANTS *WHAT?!*" Bill was stunned, "That's what, three weeks*?!*"

The General continued blithely.

"Alongside a squad of the best soldiers the Empire has to offer"

Bill threw up his hands, "Oh this just gets better!"

"That's not all Bill"

It never is with these stuck up, pretentious aristo...

"We want *you* to lead them…"

"You're taking the piss" Bill responded automatically.

The General chuckled, though he wouldn't admit it, he had missed Bill's hard edged candour.

"Hardly." was his matter of fact response.

A conflicting mass of roiling emotions overtook the speechless Bill North. Anger, Confusion, Sheer Disbelief…

Bill looked at the file on the desk again. He looked at the kindly face of the General. He replayed the day's events in his head. Annoyance, Rage, Embarrassment. He gave passing thought to walking straight out of the door… But, Bill was loyal to a fault. He had followed, and would continue to follow General Sutherland to the ends of the earth. Both men knew this. That is why despite all of his bluster and protestations; the General had been certain of Bill's response before he'd even made the proposal. He walked around the desk, and Bill raised from his seat.

"I want full control."

"Of course. This is why I pushed for them to make you an Officer."

"I pick the men; I devise the training and tactics."

"Naturally."

"I am solely responsible for troop discipline, even for that lanky freak downstairs"

"I wouldn't have it any other way William."

The General smiled again, and put a fatherly arm around Bill's shoulder.

"Anything else?"

Bill contemplated that for a moment, he was fairly certain he'd covered everything. He was a straightforward kind of bloke, and had no need for extravagances; only those which he needed to get the job done. It came to him.

"Yeah, and I never want to wear this itchy monkey suit again."

The General laughed, and led them towards the door.

"Whatever makes you happy Bill. Now let's get you to your new quarters. You've got a busy day tomorrow. Tomorrow we begin the fight back!" The General said enthusiastically.

As they left the plush stateroom Bill had an uneasy feeling, he thought back to his encounter with The Flame. Something about the man made him uncomfortable, and it wasn't just his bizarre powers.

What 'ave I let me sen in for?

CHAPTER TWELVE: WELLS

Neil Wells' Saturday had been a write off. He'd awoken in his chair at ten 'o' clock to be greeted by the hungry mewing of Parker and Stacy, the empty bottle beside him, and the resultant hangover from hell. His brain felt as though it was soaking in battery acid, and sleeping upright had left his already ruinous lower back in bulk.

"Stupid, stupid old man," he chastised himself out loud.

The effort of this felt monumental, so he decided that speaking would be off limits for the rest of the day.

Never again, never, never again…

The effort of thinking *that* was just as difficult so he'd come to the conclusion that thoughts should also be banned. With that conclusion reached, he took the only option available to him. Armed with a cup of tea, two 'Alka-Seltzers', a bacon sandwich, and with the monotonous voices of the Radio Five presenters as his lullaby, he went upstairs to bed.

His sleep was fitful, his dreams vivid. He dreamt of the striking, flaming fist image illustrated artfully on the desk. Although the classroom was the same, it was *he* who was scrawling the icon. Standing at the head of the class was his father as he was now, old aged and weary, yet wearing, bizarrely, an old army uniform, which was torn to shreds. The old man stared vacantly out of the window. He turned slowly to face Wells, and when he did so, he could see that the old man's eyes were gone, replaced by blue flames.

Wells sat bolt upright in bed, breathing heavily and filmed with sweat. Daylight still broke through gaps in the heavy drapes, on the radio the commentator sang the praises of Birmingham City, who'd just scored the equaliser against bitter rivals Aston Villa. His body and brain still felt wrecked. Satisfactorily convinced that it had just been a dream, Wells slipped back down into the comfort of his pillow and closed his eyes. Within moments he was asleep again. He dreamt of his ex wife driving the car from Thelma and Louise. The red convertible car soaring off the cliff with her inside was of great comfort to him. Thoughts of his father, and the flaming fist icon banished from his mind…

Sunday morning came, and truth be told, Neil Wells still felt truly awful.

It's funny how no-one warns you about the two day minimum for hangovers when you're young.

Of course he had discovered this fact around his mid twenties and having passed on the warning to no-one himself he hardly had grounds to complain. That said, lacking grounds for complaint had never stopped him in the past.

I guess it's the same as how no-one moans about their marriages to you until YOU'RE married, or THEY'RE divorced. Maybe we just get some kind of twisted satisfaction from watching other people make the same stupid mistakes as us. As though the more people who make it, the less stupid the mistake becomes.

Wells was, needless to say, in a fairly philosophical mood. Although this mindset may have done little to brighten his outlook, at least it proved that his brain *was* functioning again.

Not wishing to waste another day in bed, he dragged himself up and straight into the shower. When his back troubles had begun several years ago, he had decided to invest in a Power shower. As much as he loved his TVR, his American fridge freezer, and his big screen TV, it was far and away the greatest purchase he had made in his life. Standing in the shower cubicle, with the various jets of water working their magic on his crippled back and neck, he actually began to feel human again.

Ten minutes later he emerged from the bathroom a new man, *or at least a reconditioned one.* Dressed in his flannel pyjamas and grey, faux-silk bathrobe, he made his way downstairs.

Passing the living room he saw the empty bottle of Glenmorangie beside his chair, pleased to note that looking at it did not induce the feeling of nausea he'd expected. Seeing that he'd left his computer on since Friday night however *did* turn his stomach a little and he made a mental note to turn it off once he'd successfully foraged for some life giving caffeine. As he made his way to the kitchen, he mentally pictured the dial on his electric meter spinning wildly, and the astronomic bill that he would undoubtedly receive at the end of the quarter.

The week before payday no doubt.

He fed the cats, and tipped a hefty spoonful of coffee grounds into the filter of his cafetiere, the rich scent helping to blast away the last of the cobwebs. Whilst the precious nectar percolated, he strolled back into the living room. Stepping carefully over the pile of History books that littered the floor, he collected the empty whisky bottle and accompanying glass. As he turned back, he felt one of the books beneath his toes and froze, too late. He winced at the sound of paper tearing.

"Oh Bugger it!" he exclaimed, as he carefully lifted his foot to reveal the damaged text. It was a book on World War I. A *First Edition* book on World War I, no less. Annoyed at himself for not picking it up immediately, Wells risked further back pain, and crouched down to collect the scattered volumes.

Slowly, slowly Neil...

They were of varying sizes, ages and topics, but there was a concurrent theme to the collection: major wars and conflicts, dating from the Boer War up until the Gulf Crisis. Wells didn't even remember getting them out. He looked over to the book shelf, and noticed that in his stupor he'd even managed to knock his hand painted model of a Tiger Tank onto the floor. A crack ran behind the spare tread on its front up to the main gun.

Silly drunken fool.

He replaced the model to its place of prominence between a Spitfire and a German Messerschmitt, then one by one, slotted the pile of books into their rightful places. The last one was a photo book, the subject matter of which was the Second World War. He casually leafed through the pages. Inside were pictures of the "home front", government propaganda posters on street corners, a Spitfire soaring through the clouds, Winston Churchill at his desk, a British infantry soldier in uniform. Wells paused on the picture for a moment, something about it struck a chord, and brought back a flash from his earlier dream. There was *something* about the uniform, but decided that being bent over holding a stack of books was not the time to be committing oneself to deep thought. With some effort, and an almighty exhale, he stood up. Reaching for the laptop touchpad, he tapped it several times. The TV Screen came back to life and as it faded into resolution, the close-up photograph of the flaming fist icon came into focus. A bolt of inspiration hit him and Wells grabbed his phone, selected a number and pressed the green illuminated call button on the device. After a few rings, someone answered.

"Hello, it's only me. Listen, I need a favour." The voice responded, and Wells grimaced. "Yes, I know how many this will make it, but…"

The person on the other end continued. Wells began to get annoyed.

"Oh whatever Terrance, get off your high horse. Are you going to do it or what?"

There was a brief pause, before the muffled response.

"You're a good man, I shall see you at five sharp."

Wells ended the call, and turned his attention back to the picture of the soldier. A young man, proud as punch in his new uniform.

Probably long dead. No more back pain and world ending hangovers for you young man…

It was ten minutes past five when he pulled his flamboyant green supercar into the parking lot of the local library. With the now standard level of pain and difficulty Wells hauled himself out of his low riding vehicle. He patted it on the roof, still delighted with his purchase.

An entire week without using my breakdown cover, things must be looking up!

It was a Sunday, so he felt justified in choosing the easier of the routes available to him by avoiding the steps and walking the slight incline of the disabled path to the front door. He reached the entrance, but before he could knock, it swung open half a foot. Behind the plain, white door stood Terrance Whittacre, Wells' former student turned career librarian. The long haired young man was of average height, build, *and personality*. His main distinguishing feature; a pair of thick rimmed black glasses, with even thicker lenses perched atop his blackhead ridden nose. Wells thought of them as *Clark Kent glasses*, though more in jest than a creditable observation, and not something that he could've said to Terrance's face, at least not with a straight face. The idea that someone so physically lacking could be a secret superhero was laughable at best. The thick cut of each eye piece served to enlarge his eyes to near comical proportions. On the whole the glasses made his brown eyes seem totally out of proportion with his otherwise average sized facial features, and sadly for Terrance (other than providing sight) they only served to accentuate the slight squint in his right eye.

"What's the code word?" he asked through the open gap.

Wells stood there for a moment and contemplated this. He shook his head, sighed, and firmly pushed the door open, annoyed that he'd even entertained such stupidity,

"Shut up you buffoon" Wells said irritably as he shunted Terrance slightly aside. With an indignant huff, the younger man adjusted his well weathered Pitchshifter t-shirt and pushed his glasses back up his nose.

"The code word is in place for BOTH of our safety!" he stated, matter of factly.

But Wells was out of ear shot. With an audible "harrumph" and one last conspiratorial glance outside, Terrance shut and bolted the door and followed into the Library.

Wells stood in the History section, glancing across the spines of the books. Of course he'd read all of them, he actually *owned* the majority of them. Years ago it had been his dream to have a book of his own, to sit alongside his peers up there one day.

Just as soon as I get the time to sit down and write it.

He held onto that thought for a moment.

Neil Wells had taught History all of his adult life, and though he hadn't lived it all, he certainly felt like he'd taught it all. Over and over. Year on year. Decade on decade.

Nothing new under the sun, sadly...

Terrance walked up behind him, shaking him from his reverie.

"Please tell me you didn't drag me down here on my day off so you could pine over the works of your *published* brethren?" His voice was whiny and nasal, and in large doses grated on Wells' severely. Because of this he made a point to limit his exposure to his former student, in fact under normal circumstances would go out of his way to *avoid him*. In this instance however, he felt the call was necessary. He needed to place that image, and despite his best efforts he still had no idea why it was so familiar.

"Yes, I'm sorry I dragged you away from your doubtless action-packed Sunday evening…"

… The Eastenders omnibus and downloading fake naked pictures of the women from Star Trek…

"I should say so too!" Terrance replied, with all the righteous indignation he could muster.

Wells bit his lip. As a teacher he hated being interrupted, and it was all the more infuriating when he couldn't give an essay or detention to the culprit. He let out a brief sigh and continued.

"But yes, I do have a legitimate reason for requesting your assistance."

Wells pulled out a piece of paper from his jacket pocket. He unfolded the sheet to its full A4 size and handed it over.

Terrance had a sceptical expression on his face that fell away to a completely blank look as he focussed on the print out.

"I don't know why, but I think it's connected to an army division, or…"

"Is this a joke?"

"No, why?"

"Did someone put you up to this?!" Terrance said, his voice nearly breaking. He pointed an accusing finger at Wells' face. Wells was initially taken aback at the uncharacteristic show of aggression. The slight podgy man-child in the coke bottle glasses however was not an intimidating man. Wells however, was. He squared his shoulders and fixed his best teacher scowl down on the shorter, rounder man. His physique (and underlying aggression) had once made Neil Wells a formidable star of his university rugby side, and although time had taken its toll, least of all on his accursed back, for a man his age he carried himself well.

Without another word the deflated Terrance packed away his pointing finger and scurried off across the room with the page gripped in his hand. He turned a corner and disappeared from sight into the stacks. A few moments passed and Wells realised that he was going to have to follow. He sighed.

I'll just follow you then shall I?

He found Terrance sat hunched over at a computer terminal. Beside him was an attached flatbed scanner, a bright line shone from beneath its lid, moving slowly across its length. It was much dimmer in this area of the library, and the pale glow of the monitor screen illuminated his round face. Twin reflections of the flaming fist graffiti slowly appeared on his glasses, as the scanner transferred a digital copy to the PC. Wells leaned on the back of his chair serving the dual purpose of getting a closer look at the screen, and relieving some of the strain from his back. When the scanner had finished working its magic, they both stared at the image in silence.

This did not last long, as Wells' patience ran threadbare.

"So, does it ring any bells?" he asked sarcastically.

Terrance was transfixed, *a little too transfixed* as though he were trying to avoid answering the question. Wells, in no mood for being messed around, decided to press the issue.

"Terrance. Does. This. Image. Look Familiar. To You?"

Terrance began to look stressed, as though he was fighting a moral dilemma. Fortunately for Wells, Terrance Whittacre couldn't fight a cold.

"Err... No...err..."

"What aren't you telling me Terrance?"

"Err... nothing I don't know what you're talking about..."

Wells sighed, deciding to change tact.

They may have banned corporal punishment in schools but...

He reached forward and gripped Terrance's earlobe tightly between his thumb and forefinger.

"Terrance. Tell me."

The podgy man was sweating.

"No, I've never seen…"

Wells twisted his grip sharply. The action caused Terrance to yelp in pain.

"*Terrance?*" Wells asked more insistently, keeping the squirming man's ear locked in a vice-like grip.

"OW! Okay! Okay!"

Wells lamented, and released the traumatised lobe. Terrance immediately covered it with his hand, and swivelled his chair to look up at Wells. He gave him a wounded and accusatory glare, like a punished five year old.

"Hey! That was a bit excessive don't you think?"

"Well I don't *know* Terrance. Do you think it's acceptable to *lie* to me?"

They both pondered their respective questions for a moment, before grudgingly backing down.

"Sorry."

"Sorry."

"So are you going to tell me what you know, or am I going to have to get the pincers out again?"

Wells theatrically made a pincer movement with his thumb and forefinger, grinning maniacally as he did so.

"Sadist."

"Not sadistic, authoritative. Didn't your father ever do the 'old ear twist' when you were growing up?"

"*No*, I'm a child of the 80's, my parents never laid a finger on me, you dinosaur." he replied, baffled at the suggestion.

"Bloody Liberal parenting, it's that kind of hippy inspired B.S that has kids in hooded tops running riot on our streets…" Wells ranted.

Terrance looked down at himself, the dinner-stained tee, brown slacks, and patent leather shoes hardly fit with Wells' belief. He looked sceptically back up at him. Realising the hole in his argument, Wells responded instantly to change the subject.

"Yes, well, anyway, back on topic. Tell me what you know this instant, or I shall be forced to beat it out of you."

It was an empty threat Wells knew, but it seemed to have the desired effect. With a stern expression he watched as the younger man lamented and got to his feet.

"Okay. You're right, I do know something. But I'm not sure you're...*ready* to know what it is" He cocked an eyebrow, trying to look enigmatic.

"What do you mean, *not ready?*" Wells responded angrily. "And what the hell is wrong with your eyebrow?"

Terrance deflated visibly, his eyebrow fell along with the rest of his face. His momentary pomp shattered, he finally gave in completely.

"Okay, okay." He held up his hands. "Meet me in the car park tomorrow at 8pm, and all will be revealed."

This was not good enough, Terrance's 'cloak and dagger' mentality was beginning to grate. Wells felt the tinges of hangover aching his brain once more.

"No, tell me now! Show me what you've got, or so help me god!" He remade the pincers with the fingers of his left hand, and a fist with his right. Terrance shied away, holding his palms out in a defensive gesture.

"You don't understand. I don't *have* anything to show you. If you want to know more, I'll have to take you to see… *'The Order'*."

He said the last words with a degree of theatrical reverence usually reserved for deities, *or geeks referring to the 'original Star Wars trilogy'.*

Wells had never been one for science fiction, nor for organised religion as it went, and normally he would've laughed in Terrance's face. However the severity of the expression on the man's face coupled Wells' own feverish curiosity told him to play along. He could wait another day for answers.

CHAPTER THIRTEEN: ANNA

Anna sat cross legged on her bedroom floor, chewing on her pen lid and wondering why she never had the foresight to do her homework any earlier than Sunday evening. Surrounding her were notebooks, text books and exercise books strewn haphazardly across the thick carpet. The main focus of her attention was on the hand written essay in front of her, but in the background her prized LP of "Blood on the Tracks" played away on her antique turntable. As was her favourite daily pastime she idly daydreamed about teenage life in 60's America.

I wonder if THEY wasted their weekends hanging around in parks and shopping centres with idiots?

Of course she'd seen enough John Hughes films to know that the phenomena was not solely confined to the British Isles. However, for the purpose of these particular flights of fancy, she liked to believe that was not the case. She fantasised about sitting beneath an apple tree on a warm spring afternoon, chatting to cool people about cool, interesting things. All the while, a young Bob Dylan, tousled hair blowing in the wind, serenaded her with his worn out acoustic guitar. Bob finished his song, but when she looked up at him, she was surprised to see the face of the strange boy from Friday night.

Richie Spink? Well that's a new one…

Somewhat puzzled as to why she should be seeing *his* face instead of her beloved's, her puzzlement grew further as, when he opened his mouth, she was greeted by an annoying, repetitive hiss and crackle. Although it took her a moment she recognised the sound and it brought her back down to earth. The needle ran around the last groove of the LP, and would continue to do so ad-infinitum unless she flipped the record and reset it. Anna looked down at her essay which annoyingly, yet not unexpectedly, had failed to write itself during her reverie.

She got to her feet and folded forward to touch her toes and stretch her legs out. Anna had been gymnastics mad, and in fact most-sport mad in her youth, but her dreams of Olympic glory faded as she entered her teens. Katie and the other airheads had decreed that makeup and boys were in, and karate, gymnastics and self betterment in general were out. So she had given up her nightly lessons a couple of years earlier, and although Anna still kept herself in shape, her flexibility was not quite what it was. She tensed and rotated the joints in her ankles and neck with a satisfying crunch and then hopped lightly over the books. With well practiced precision she lifted the arm of the record player and placed it to the side in its cradle. Carefully, she lifted the black vinyl from the turntable, flipped it smoothly and replaced it, B-side up. Lowering her head so that the record was at eye level, she picked up the needle arm. Squinting slightly she lowered it towards the desired groove, holding her breath so as not to… with a loud THUD, her mother barged into her room.

"Have you got any washing Annabelle?"

The abruptness of the entry startled Anna, and the needle slid across the record, with the ear and heart rending SCRAPE that plagued the nightmares of all vinyl enthusiasts. Anna gritted her teeth, a result of the combined annoyance of interruption, pain of the jarring sound and anger at the potential damage she'd just inflicted upon her cherished LP.

"*Yes mother!*" she hissed through her taut jaw.

"Well bring it down now, I'm putting a wash on"

"*YES* MOTHER!!"

"Don't get hoity-toity with me young lady, or you'll be doing your own bloody laundry!" Her mother's well worn face was edged with fresh irritation. In her day she had been quite the looker, but years of chain smoking and drinking had left her looking her age. A fact that all of her trendy clothes,

71

manicures and extortionately priced haircuts failed to hide. Anna had heard her mother referred to as, "a dolly bird," "a MILF," and "a WAG", particularly since her latest boob job. Anna thought "mutton dressed as lamb" covered it best.

The elder woman huffed in dismay at Anna's insubordination and stormed out of the room.

"Five minutes Madam or you'll have no clean knickers for the week!" The last word was muffled as she turned the corner on the landing.

Anna looked up from her wounded record to the door which her departed mother had, infuriatingly, left ajar.

That woman! ARRRGH! She drives me up the wall!!!

Since her older brother Carson had gone to university, Anna had taken the brunt of her mother's growing brand of personalised insanity, exacerbated further as her Step-Dad's job in the military meant he was stationed away for months on end. She'd discussed her perilously maddening mother-daughter relationship with her elder cousin Tracey recently, who, with the venerable wisdom of a 21 year old, had assured Anna that once she moved out of the family home her mother would become her best friend. "Mother-Daughter bonding is inevitable" she'd said with the smarmy, tedious conviction of a Fine Arts Graduate who'd once shared a house with someone who'd studied Psychology. Anna had smiled weakly, hiding what she really thought.

Anyway, as if! The woman's a maniacal, meddling weirdo who makes my life a living hell, like I'm EVER going to be friends with HER!

Anna looked closely at the shiny, fine grooves on the vinyl. Fortunately, there didn't appear to be any damage. She carefully replaced the shiny black disc into its sleeve, before she turned her attention to hunting down dirty clothes. As much as she wanted to ignore her mother's request, more from spite as anything, she knew better than to ignore her ultimatum. From experience Anna knew full well that the threat of dirty underwear was not an empty one, and it would be accompanied by its partner in crime, a solid week of passive aggression. So, with a sigh, she began to gather up the strewn articles from the four corners of her room.

When she was finished the pile in her arms was extensive, but her room looked a damn sight tidier. Through the floorboards her mother's voice struck a nerve again.

"Annabelle!"

"I'M COMING!!!" Anna replied furiously. Only the faint voice of reason stopped her from tossing the pile at the wall. *You're only hurting yourself. Deep, calming breaths. Just go downstairs, hand it to her, plaster on a quick smile, then back to our Bob Dylan fantasy world...*

The plan seemed sound, predominantly because it featured reassuringly minimal mother contact, and of course plenty of Bob.

Her mother was in the kitchen. Clamped between her ruby painted lips was a lit cigarette, her platinum dyed hair (with extensions of course) was tied back high on her head revealing her lined, overly tanned face. Her attention was focussed on filling the plastic wash ball with detergent when Anna entered. Hoping to utilise the moment to her advantage, she quickly crept in, and ever-so-gently placed the pile of clothing on the light oak kitchen table. Satisfied with her stealthy approach Anna allowed herself a smug smile. It was short lived however.

"I hope you've remembered to empty all your pockets. *Someone* left a tissue in with last weeks' wash, and there were white bits over everything..."

Anna of course knew this. Given that most of her wardrobe now leaned towards the darker tones, she had been the hardest hit by the mishap. She wanted to tell her mother this, to tell her that *of course I've checked the pockets, I'm not an idiot.* She *wanted* to tell her this, but of course *she hadn't* checked her pockets. Anna's immediate reaction was to lie,

73

but she figured *once bitten, twice shy. And* after all, it *had* actually been her tissue that ruined the last wash…

So she went through each item individually. When she was done she had a rather nice collection of items that included 23 pence in loose change, three hair bobbles, *and TWO tissues.* She quickly shoved these into the pocket of the checked pyjama bottoms that she wore, hiding the evidence that would spark the unbearable "I told you so," moment and another bout of senseless bickering.

"What about that black jacket you wear?" her mother asked, her tone conveying how much she disliked the item in question.

"*Which* black jacket?"

Anna knew full well which one she meant, the black hooded top in question was amongst her favourite clothes, but she fancied making her mother work for it.

"The one hanging on the bannister, the one I've told you to move TEN times already this evening!"

That was of course an exaggeration, *it was no more than six.* With an overstated sigh Anna went and fetched it. She threw it on the pile with the others.

"Have you checked the pockets?" her mother said in a sickeningly sweet, and condescending voice. Anna could feel her blood boiling.

Did you SEE me check the bloody pockets!!!! I mean for Christsakes! I've never put anything in these pockets in my whole entire… Oh…

She pulled out a patch of thick, green cloth. It was roughly square shaped, and no bigger than five inches on each side. She regarded it with a puzzled look on her delicate features, all semblances of irritation vanished. She ran her fingers across it. The material felt coarse, and the edges were frayed.

What the hell is this, why is it in my pocket?

The underside felt different again, bumpier. She turned it over, and recognition came flooding back. In its centre was a circular badge, with an intricately stitched clenched fist surrounded by blue flames. It was worn, and faded, and some of the stitching had become frayed, but the words "THE ETERNAL FLAME SQUADRON", and some other writing in a language she didn't recognise were still visible running in a circle around the circumference.

Oh, d'uh, of course it's what old man Wells gave me...

"What's that you've got there?" her mother asked quizzically.

Dammit.

"Oh nothing, just a patch I picked up from that new vintage shop in town."

Anna actually surprised herself with how easily the lie rolled off her tongue. There was no need for it, she knew, but somehow, keeping her mother in the dark over things gave her a slight sense of satisfaction.

"Well it looks filthy, I hope you didn't pay much for it."

"What*ever*"

"Have you done all your coursework?

"YES," she lied again.

"Good, because your mock exams...

Are only a few months away...

"...are only a few month away"

...and if you mess around now...

"...and if you mess around now..."

"You're just throwing your future away" Anna said in unison with her mother.

"Don't get smart Annabelle," her mother said sourly. "If you want to make a success of your life you have to work for it, things aren't just going to drop into your lap..."

"Yeah, yeah, I know mum." Anna replied, as she stuffed the patch into her pyjama pocket, and stormed out of the kitchen.

It's not like you haven't told me SIX THOUSAND times already...

75

Having had more than enough maternal meddling for one evening, Anna retreated back upstairs to her room. As the proximity between them grew, she found herself instantly more relaxed. Carson had described her as Anna's "Kryptonite" on one of his all-to-brief returns from uni. Anna missed her big brother, he always knew how to put things into perspective.

Back in the relative safety of her room, she flopped down onto her bed; the accursed homework effectively abandoned for the night, and decided to focus on more pleasant things. Anna stared dreamily up at the poster of Dylan over the headboard. Once again however the face of Richie Spink came to mind. She thought back to the other night, and the calm, controlled look on his face as he stood up tall and spoke down to Jackson Sleight. She had never seen the arrogant bully taken down a notch so easily. The thought brought a smile to her face.

They'd been in the same school for four years now, and although she recognised his face she really would've struggled for his name had Katie not said it. From what little she knew, Spink was a quiet boy, not particularly a high flyer in anything. He was taller than most, but in all truth was hardly the most handsome boy she'd ever seen, hard as it was to tell behind his mop of hair. Of course he was by no means ugly, he was just… *a boy*. Anna may not have known a great deal more about him, but she *did* know that his confrontation with Sleight was more than a little out of character, and really *that* was more of a general assumption. After all, it didn't really fit the profile of *anyone* in that school to stand up to that meatheaded menace.

She got to her feet, and emptied her pyjama pocket, depositing the laundry-rescued content onto the cluttered dressing table. The flaming fist patch sat amongst the balled up tissues and bobbles, and a myriad of random earrings, jewellery and half used nail varnishes with crusted tops. She gathered up the school books from the floor, and piled them on the dressing table chair, before picking up her school bag. The once smart, maroon and navy Jansport rucksack was now covered in a patchwork of indie band logos and her own (actually pretty good) scribblings of anime characters. Anna looked again at the Eternal Flame patch, and then again at her bag. She shrugged.

Meh, why not?

Pulling out a small velvet box from the dresser draw, she removed a small pair of scissors, and a needle and thread.

I wonder what it was he said to Sleight?

Anna pondered on the mysterious boy as she elegantly went about the well practised stitching process.

I wonder what he's into?

Yes, it was fair to say that she knew next to nothing about Richie Spink, and that would have to change…

CHAPTER FOURTEEN: RICHIE

"In our modern world of satellite televisions, microwaves, and Super Tin-ten-doo's, the value of organised religion has never been more important a subject!" ranted Mrs. Lord, Richie's frighteningly aptly named Religious Education teacher. The portly, middle aged woman had been on this particular rant for about ten minutes now and Richie had switched off from it several minutes before that. It wasn't that he was being *deliberately* ignorant, but Mrs Lord was far from the most charismatic of orators and he had heard this rant before. As evidenced by the sea of glazed expressions around the pokey classroom, so had the other 31 members of his class. Today it had been the turn of Richie's best friend Marc Townsend to pose the key question.

"Why do we need to study R.E Miss?" he'd asked, trying his best to convey a genuine interest in a question to which he had heard the answer *every* lesson, *without fail*, since they were thirteen. Whilst she passionately rattled through her response with all the conviction of the devout Catholic she was, Marc pretended to make notes. Sat next to him, Richie could see that those detailed notes were in fact surprisingly detailed doodles of himself hanging from by the neck from a gallows. His best friend was far from the most morbid of people but these R.E lessons would've driven Mister Motivator to an early grave. He and Marc had been inseparable since joining Shipworth Comp; Richie found his confident demeanour, dry wit and sarcastic attitude constantly entertaining. In return, Marc liked Richie's dependability, and of late, having someone with criminally bad dress sense to stand near him, thus elevating his own air of style.

Probably likes having someone with him who can reach the top shelf at the supermarket too.

Friday's "incident" remained etched nay, *burned* into Richie's consciousness. The sights, the sounds and the smells were all as vivid, as *real* as his graffiti covered desk, the shrill tone of Mrs Lord's voice, and the scent of the horrible pine disinfectant used on the plastic coated floors. What Richie found just as troubling was that he was unable to remember anything else between the time he'd arrived home from school, and waking up in his bed Saturday morning. Fortunately he'd had no pressing homework to do, and for that small mercy he was grateful. The thought of trying to do his science homework *on top* of dealing with what had (or had not) happened to him didn't bear thinking about. After sleeping for pretty much 24 hours straight, he'd then spent what little was left of his weekend trying to fathom things out, but to no avail.

Richie had seen enough of Spock on "Star Trek" to have a reasonable grip of logic, and *logically speaking* he must've simply fallen asleep, victim of some sort of nasty superbug. The whole World War II themed dream probably represented the ongoing conflict between his parents, *or some other similar psycho-babble.*

Sounds great in theory.

The theory did not however throw any light onto why *this* dream had been so much… more, than any he'd had before. Richie Spink usually had nightmares about getting a bad haircut, or missing his bus, or asking out Anna Harrison, only she turned out to be Mrs. Lord.

Eurgh!

Richie threw up a little in his mouth, the act forced him to tune back into her ongoing sermon.

"*AND* a good, solid, *moral* basis for young, growing minds…" Mrs Lord continued.

Marc nodded with an Oscar winning representation of interest, meanwhile adding "blood" to his picture with deep scribbles of red biro.

And most certainly, for as good as the theory sounds it certainly doesn't explain the state my socks were in. Unless… I sleepwalked..?

He tossed that thought around his head for a few moments. Again it *sounded* like a very reasonable explanation, however there remained a nagging thought buried somewhere in the back of his head. He just couldn't shake the feeling that the real reason behind the "incident" was something far less straight-forward.

The bell rang to signal the end of the lesson, and the rest of Richie's classmates breathed a collective sigh of relief. Although they each knew it was better than *actual* work, listening to that same rant week in, week out was long past tedious, *particularly* for a subject that was only worth half a GCSE. As always, the ruddy-cheeked woman was shocked at how the lesson had passed so quickly.

"Oh, well, I hope I managed to answer your question Master Townsend?"

"Oh yes Miss, *most* enlightening…" The dripping sarcasm of Marc's response went unnoticed by the woman. She adjusted her green cardigan, and squinted down at the hand written notes before her.

"And now that we've cleared all that up, I want you all to complete exercises 1, 2, 4, and 5 for next week. Is that clear?"

"*YES MISS*" the class droned in unison. It was only half eleven in the morning, but Religious Education really had a nasty habit of draining a person's natural enthusiasm for life.

Richie and Marc gathered up their things. His friend, a good half a foot shorter, packed away his horrific doodle along with his expensive fountain pen, replete with his initials 'MT' monogrammed onto the silver plating. Across the room, a pensive looking Jackson Sleight stared at Richie and Marc as they left the room. Long used to avoiding eye contact with the brute, Richie was oblivious to this fact.

"What have we got next?" Richie asked.

His friend withdrew a small, cardboard timetable from his top pocket, around its worn edges were more graphic doodlings.

They both studied it for a moment, before dejectedly vocalising the answer, "Games…" They exclaimed this with a deep, sorrowful sigh.

"How is cross-country ever, EVER classed as a game?" Marc said.

"Run? For *fun?*" Richie replied in a southern American drawl, effectively aping the line from Back to The Future III.

The pair chuckled, happy in their geekishness.

Ahead lay the locker corridor, hundreds of head height, gun metal grey containers ran down one side, opposite large sash windows looking out onto the empty school yard. Further down the corridor, Richie admired the petite frame of Anna Harrison as she withdrew several books from her locker, grateful that the school's liberal enforcement of the uniform code allowed the grace of… *varying* skirt lengths. On the tip toes of her black Converse All-Stars, she pulled out another book from the very top shelf of the locker. Used to stealing glances whilst she summarily failed to notice him, Richie nearly choked on his tongue when out of the blue, she looked his way and smiled. His heart began to race, and probably would've leapt out of his mouth had his stomach not jumped up to strangle it.

Oh. My. God. She's smiling, she's smiling, she's smiling at me. At ME!!

His knees felt weak and his face flushed, all of a sudden his hands were too big for his body, and his vision began to blur. Panic began to set in.

"Oh no, not now, not now!

He felt a firm hand on his shoulder.

"Come on Rich, we're gonna be late."

Marc's familiar tones brought Richie back to reality. Behind his overgrown fringe, Richie risked a glance back up the corridor, Anna's attention was now focussed on her irritating friend Katie Styles.

"Yeah, yeah, let's go…"

The last thing he needed was an essay or detention, there was nothing on Earth more embarrassing than being reprimanded by a PE teacher. Richie glanced back one more time, the heat in his cheeks beginning to cool. He watched as Anna and Katie bounced off towards their next lesson arm in arm. As she went, his usual bout of appreciation was jarred by the sight of a newly stitched patch on her backpack, it was tough to make out as she moved further away, but the sight of it sent a cold shock up Richie's spine.

The flaming fist?

Richie's mind flashed to the mustachioed soldier. The deafening bang of gunfire. The dead eyes of the Germans. A patch of a flaming blue fist on their killer's shoulder…

"Rich? Where's your head at?" Marc laughed, as he dragged Richie down the bustling corridor. As they walked, he looked his gangly, dishevelled friend up and down. After completing his 'assessment', he grinned sardonically.

"You're sweating mate! Oh no, you haven't forgotten your P.E kit again have you?"

Richie's face fell, all thoughts of Anna, the flaming fist and the church banished. He stopped dead in his tracks, and brought the palm of his hand to forehead. In his mind's eye he could see the kit bag sat by his front door. With all that had been going on, his brain was at peak scattiness. Bringing in his games kit had been low on his list of priorities.

"Oh for f…"

Fifteen minutes later, as he stood alone in the changing rooms, he was beginning to question his life priorities.

Give me a crazy war nightmare any day…

He was dressed in "lost property kit", which on the social acceptability scale, sat just below having your mum cut your hair, and buying your trainers from Tescos. The wafer thin vest was dirty, smelly and had clearly belonged to a sixth former, *or a bear*, Richie thought, based on how it hung on his slender frame. The blue shorts were entirely the opposite, a relic left behind from the 80's, and what his Dad often chucklingly referred to as *John Barnes shorts*. These dictionary definition 'short shorts' served to highlight Richie's pale, gangly legs. To top off the humiliation, he still wore his grey school socks and his scuffed Doc Martin shoes. Richie looked himself over in the mirror by the door, the parallels with what had happened on Friday were unavoidable.

A horrible, vivid nightmare I can't wake up from.

Just as he was coming to terms with his garb, Mr. Leeson the P.E teacher emerged from his office. The athletically dressed, diminutive man took one look at Richie and let out a snort of laughter. Repressing full blown hysterics, he shook his head and pulled open the door. A cold blast of air from the corridor shot across Richie's shin like icy thorns.

"Right, off you pop Slink, go and catch up with the rest of the class…"

"Err, it's Spink sir."

"What?" he replied, although he seemed far more interested in the contents of his coffee mug. He drained the last sips.

"Nothing sir" he lamented with a weak sigh.

"Good, now hurry along, and tell the class to get started on the course, two laps of the field, I've just got to," he cast a glance casually at his empty mug, "fill in some paperwork, and I'll be over shortly."

He retreated into his office, leaving Richie alone again in his trauma-inducing kit. The lanky teen felt like a complete tosser.

For Christ's sake, even the teacher knows it.

His thoughts turned to what he had to do next, and he felt the fear rising in his gut. The rest of the class, with their staring eyes, angry laughs, and barbarous jibes awaited him on the school field. Richie closed his eyes, and took a deep breath, trying to remain calm.

As he left the changing rooms, beginning his walk towards humiliation, he bumped into Marc. Still dressed in his uniform, he looked Richie up and down.

"I didn't know "Mister Muscle" went to our school…"

Richie was not amused.

"Ha, bloody ha."

"Hey don't take it out on me, I've got a serious" he pulled a handwritten letter from his pocket, and scanned it quickly, "knee injury, that would only be further aggravated by such a high impact athletic endeavour as Cross Country…"

"You mean you *HAD* a knee injury? A *bruised* knee you got when you fell over after drinking all that Bucks Fizz at your Dad's New Years party. LAST YEAR!"

Marc shrugged nonchalantly.

"Is it *my* fault if I've got the foresight to… *retain* a certain number of sick notes over the years?"

He patted his top pocket.

"Like I always say; 'If teachers don't ask, they don't receive.' You're just annoyed because you're too bloody honest to do it yourself…" Marc finished his statement with another sly chuckle at Rich's expense.

"Oh this *cannot* be happening." Richie exclaimed.

It felt as though he was having heart palpitations. The thought of jogging around the playing fields would normally have been reason enough for stress, but this was just gratuitous.

Down the corridor Mr. Leeson emerged from the changing rooms, sporting a thick, red and black bench coat and carrying a fresh mug of coffee. Richie knew the inevitable was approaching.

Today's life scarring humiliation is mere moments away…

"Oh God… I can't do this" Richie moaned.

Marc seemed to be enjoying Richie's dilemma.

"Come on, I thought Mister Muscle loves the jobs I hate…"

Normally this kind of banter would've washed straight off Richie's back, but now was not the time.

"Drop dead Marc…" he said venomously, through gritted teeth.

Mr Leeson reached them, but before he could say anything, Marc chimed in.

"So Richard, remember to get your breathing right, and when you hit the wall, just plough straight through. Oh hello sir…" he said, plastering on the plastic enthusiasm for the teacher, "just passing on a few words of encouragement. It's such a shame, I'd give anything to be able to get back out there, but…" He tapped his right knee, with a slight wince.

"Oh no, you need to keep it rested, I tore my knee ligaments as a teenager and if you're not careful it'll never heal right." he said before turning his attention to Richie.

"Come on then Slink, let's get you over there and stuck in" He gestured towards the fire doors that lead outside.

Shoulders slumped, a picture of utter dejection Richie made his way towards them, and his destiny of degradation.

"Yes, knock 'em dead *Slink!*" Marc shouted after him, clenched fist raised in the air in salute, a cheesy grin on his handsome features.

Behind his back, out of sight from Mr Leeson, Richie stuck his middle finger up to his smirking friend.

Marc watched them leave, before inserting a set of small, black earphones, and strolling off down the corridor. In time with the music, he danced a little jig on his "injured" right knee.

On the field, Richie's forty-eight other class members were split into their rough social groups. The less physically inclined huddled for warmth. Those in the athletics team warmed up using various stretches. Members of the football team hung together, laughing and play-fighting. Amongst them was the hulking figure of Jackson Sleight and his diminutive crony, the rat featured Mickey Parkinson. With the exception of one or two of the athletes, the rest of the group detested Cross Country. For them, running around a field on a wet, Monday morning was a diabolical sacrifice made so they could *pick* their sports on the Friday double lesson. For most this meant a double lesson of football sandwiched between break and lunch, as close as it got to heaven for Shipworth Comprehensive's alpha male students.

Richie had been sport mad as a kid, but had found his interest dwindling in recent years to a point where he'd only taken it as a GCSE option to keep his dad happy. As he walked through the gates of the school playing fields, Richie was seriously wondering whether he would eventually acquire enough experience or intelligence to actually *make* a good decision. For some reason, in spite of his racing heart beat, the calming words of his history teacher Mr Wells ran through his head,

"There are no such things as wrong decisions… Poor, stupid and misguided decisions however are all too commonplace".

He quickly banished this thought as it was wasting brain power better spent willing the earth to swallow him whole. In the distance the others milled about, as yet unaware of his presence.

If only I can keep them from noticing me, then I might just get through this…

Behind him, Mr Leeson blew a huge lungful of air into his whistle, shattering Richie's hopes and brightening the mornings of the assembled students. In unison they turned to look at the catastrophically attired Richie Spink.

For a moment there was silence, as their brains processed what they were seeing. Slowly, smiles began to form on their faces. All except for the bruised Jackson Sleight, whose expression actually seemed to go the opposite way.

This is it, this is the moment, I'm dead. Here lies Richard Thomas Spink. Forgot his games kit. Died of the resulting shame...

And then, like a tidal wave crashing onto the sea wall, the laughter came. Forty eight delighted voices roared as one. Richie felt the tears welling, the heat rising in his cheeks, sweat forming on the back of his neck. He couldn't look at them. His jaw tightened, he balled his fists, he turned his eyes to the muddy floor, and his dirty army boots...

Hang about...

Richie lifted his head and looked around, struggling to place his surroundings as his equilibrium did a backflip. His blurred vision began to sharpen. All about him, soldiers were engaged in hand to hand combat. Fists and feet slammed into flesh and bone. In the distance smoke billowed from a demolished gun placement. The sounds of violence filled the world around him. In spite of the gut spinning nausea, and the horror that surrounded him, Richie could only feel one emotion... Utter elation. He thrust his clenched fists in the air in celebration.

"GET IN!!!"

Boy Facing Life Ending Embarrassment Pulls Incredible Disappearing Act!

His elation was short lived however, as amidst the fighting, a grenade landed at his booted feet.

"OH SH...!"

All of a sudden, Cross Country didn't seem so bad...

CHAPTER FIFTEEN: BILL

"Is this the best that this great country has to offer?!" Bill barked as he walked down the line of assembled troops. His scuffed boots echoed off the cobbled floor as he inspected each recruit in turn. The sun was out, and the air was mild in the courtyard. As per his agreement with the General, he had exchanged the dress uniform for the second skin of his combat fatigues, though the formality of the situation however still required that he was clean shaven. The thin black line of his neatly trimmed moustache bore no signs of the grey that grew from the temples of his slicked back hair.

The men were fifteen strong in number, but despite their athletic physiques and stern expressions, the eldest of the bunch was barely a week past his 23rd birthday.

"I'm being asked to lead a dangerous mission into occupied territory. All I asked for in return was a comfortable uniform and a selection of *combat ready* soldiers to help keep me from getting killed..." Bill continued.

He came to the end of the line and turned to face the General. The older gentleman stood ten yards back from the troops, flanked by his secretary Ms. Summers, resplendent in her tight white blouse, and Captain Frederick Willerton-Smythe, his sour-faced Chief of Staff, who looked as uncomfortable in field gear as Bill did in his dress uniform.

"... And what you've given me instead is a bunch of bloody snot nosed kids!" Bill's rant continued. "How old are you son?" he asked the nearest of them.

"Eighteen sir!" the fresh faced young man replied, just managing to keep the nervousness out of his voice.

"Pathetic..." Bill snarled, shrugging his shoulders and opening his palms out as he walked towards the General. The elder man, almost regal in his freshly pressed uniform, had known Bill too long to rise to the bait, instead he folded his arms and waited. Bill North took his place alongside him. A wry smile formed on the scarlet red lips of Miss Summers, who herself was dressed in an even less practical, albeit infinitely more appreciable way. Her figure hugging blouse and pencil skirt provided a pleasant break from the sweaty men in Khaki norm.

Having allowed Bill a few moments to calm down, General Sutherland cleared his throat, breaking his silence.

"You asked for the best Captain, and these young men are just that…"

Bill's eyes narrowed as he continued to sceptically scan the line.

"And will I be expected to take their mothers along with me to continue their breast feeding an' all sir?"

Miss Summers tried to stifle a giggle and failed spectacularly. Willerton-Smythe was typically unimpressed. Below his heavily receding hairline his brow furrowed and his nostrils flared in a picture perfect rendition of outraged disgust. As well as being a decade younger than Bill, the two came from completely different worlds. Whilst Bill, the son of a Sheffield Steel worker had clawed his way up through the ranks the hard way as a soldier, Frederick Willerton-Smythe was quite the opposite. Eton and Oxford educated and Sandhurst trained, he had been groomed as Officer material before he hit puberty. Lacking the passion for combat present in his peers, no-one was more pleased than he when a freak training accident took the end of his trigger finger. The incident not only cut short the finger in question, but his manoeuvres in North Africa. The result was an expedited return to his beloved Blighty. His excellent education plus the money invested in his training, with no small input from his rather influential father, culminated in him landing his current position. Although his seniority commanded respect amongst the cadets and staff, his lack of field experience made him a target of ridicule from combat veterans. Bill had taken an immediate dislike towards him. The feeling however was mutual. Willerton-Smythe held nothing but disdain for men of his ilk, a fire stoked by now having to serve under a man he deemed his social lesser.

"These young men are a credit to their country they are shining examples of…" he argued.

"Keep your hair on Willy, I'm only saying…" Bill interjected, not taking his eyes off the soldiers.

"*Willerton.*" he corrected, through gritted teeth. "*Major Willerton-Smythe*".

The General gave Bill a stern look, a casual reminder for Bill to play nice.

"Yes, of course, my most humble apologies *Major*." Bill said, unable to keep the edge of sarcasm out of his voice.

Realising that it was the best he was going to get, Smythe opted to press on.

"Would it not be wise to, at the very least, see them in action before dismissing them out of hand?"

Bill tilted his head and shrugged slightly, *of course* that had been his intention all along. The grousing was merely part of the front he was creating for the recruits. 'Dismissing them out of hand,' as Willy had put it, was his way of laying down the gauntlet.

No-one rises to low expectations.

"Raight then children, report t' training ground immediately!" Bill barked.

The troops' faces all changed from stoically set to puzzled, one or two of them looked down at the heavy kit bags on the ground behind them.

"Is there a problem boys? Do you perhaps require your nannies to wipe your arses first?"

"No sir!" they replied in unison. In unison but for one cadet, who clearly wasn't happy. Bill spotted him and scowled.

"Do *you* have a problem son?"

The young man in question was easily 6 feet tall and broad shouldered, his sandy-brown hair was straight out of a "Brylcreem" advert, slicked back and side parted. His bright blue eyes stared insubordinately back at Bill, holding his glare.

Who does this toe rag think he is? Bill thought.

"What are we supposed to do with our kit bags sir?"

"What's your name lad?"

"Green sir!"

Bill approached the insolent youngster as the rest of the recruits stared on aghast.

Green was a couple of inches taller and wider than Bill, a fact emphasised when he rolled his shoulders back and straightened up to his full height. Bill stopped an arms length away, staring a hole into the younger subordinate. Still Green refused to break his stare.

This lad's got balls

"Where are you from son?"

"Up North, sir."

At least that explains the attitude.

"Well Mister Green, you're a long way from home now son"

Bill paused for dramatic effect. The silence in the courtyard was deafening. When he spoke again, the volume of his voice, and the broadness of his Yorkshire accent increased with each word.

"And unless you want you and it to be part of the Third Reich by Christmas, I strongly suggest that you pathetic, nursery nurse suckling, nappy needing, molly coddled mummy's boys get your arses AND your bloody kit bags t' training ground NOW!!!"

The others didn't need telling again, and quickly gathered up their bags and headed off apace. Green held Bill's gaze a moment longer.

"Do you have a problem with that Green?"

"No sir"

"Magic."

Green finally looked away. He hefted his bag onto his broad shoulder, and jogged to catch up with the rest of the recruits. Bill watched them go.

Although he did not *like* people disobeying him, it happened so rarely that he couldn't help but feel a slight respect for those with the strength of will to do it. In fact 'The Flame' was probably the only exception he'd met to that rule.

Maybe they're not ALL stupid kids after all...

Ten minutes later Bill stood alongside the Major, and a pile of overstuffed, muddy kit bags on the training ground. The rain had started minutes earlier, and was becoming heavier by the second. The weather didn't bother Bill who had been in worse, but it was doing nothing for Willy's already sour demeanour, as the rain drops bounced from the top of his balding head.

Before the recruits had begun tackling the obstacle course, Bill had challenged them all to prove his assumptions about them wrong. As he watched them being put through their paces, he had to admit that, thus far, they were performing adequately. Of course he had expected as much, General Sutherland was a shrewd man and an excellent judge of talent. If he said that they were "the best of the best" then that is what they would be. But physical prowess, and expert soldiering skills were not all that interested Bill. The qualities that he was looking for could not be seen in a file, or even in the recommendation of a seasoned veteran. The kind of fire and passion displayed by young Mister Green in their brief encounter earlier was far more impressive to him, than say, a soldier who could run 100 yards in full gear in under fifteen seconds. Although in a perfect world, what Bill wanted were men who could do both.

This was where his real problem with the much hyped "Eternal Flame" lay. As a physical specimen, he doubted that there was a soldier on the planet who could best him, but it was the lack of drive and seeming detachment that worried him. A desire to fight, to win and to live was vital on the battlefield. So far he had seen the blue flames on the outside, but had only seen the barest spark of fire in his belly. Once again, he would have to trust his mentor's assessment and hope that the coming weeks would present a solution.

Bill watched in silent appreciation as he saw young Mister Green give up his lead to help up a fellow recruit who had fallen badly. At Green's insistence another of the men dropped out to assist him.

Bill's attention was jarred by the shrill, piercing sound of Willerton-Smythe's' whistle.

"Leave the injured recruit, and finish the course post haste!" the balding man shouted. "This is a race not a game of doctors and nurses!"

Bill shook his head in annoyance. He honestly couldn't decide which irritated him more, the sound of the whistle or his second in command's voice. Green was clearly ignoring the order, and with a strong few words (and threateningly raised fist) encouraged another to do the same. Between them they chair lifted their prone compatriot, and continued on with the course.

The Major, still standing in the same spot some thirty metres distant, blew once again on the tin whistle even harder this time. Bill sighed, he had been working alongside Smythe for 3 days now and he was already wishing he'd saved a spot on his list of demands. He was happy to be able to have final say on who would be joining his squad, and he *hated* wearing that god-awful dress uniform but just being in this man's presence was enough to drive him up the wall.

I think I'd rather lead a battalion of clowns into battle wearing an Iron Maiden if it meant being rid of this whiny Toff.

Smythe continued on with the unbearable screech of the whistle, all the while, Green trudged through the mud with a deepening scowl and continued to ignore him.

This kid just gets better and better, Bill mused then winced as the whistling went up another ten decibels.

"Knock that bloody whistle off Willy, or you'll be chokin' on it!" Bill said through gritted teeth. A nonplussed Willerton-Smythe lamented, and let the whistle dangle from the string around his neck. Bill shook his head before jogging over to the stubborn soldiers.

"What's the problem lads?"

The soldier helping him looked worriedly at Green. Having already disobeyed a senior officer's order at his behest he was clearly not sure how to proceed.

"No problem sir," Green said, not slowing his trudge or taking his determined stare from the course ahead. Bill strolled alongside and looked at the injured soldier held between them. He gave a pained, sheepish grin, and again Bill was shocked at just how young some of these "men" were.

"I went over on my ankle sir, I think it's," he winced in pain as he tried to move his foot. "I think it's broken Sir."

"Okay. Hold it there a second Gents. That means you too Mister Green."

They came to a halt, the exertion of carrying the boy showing in heavy breaths as the rain beat down. They continued to hold a leg each, with the boy putting an arm around each of their shoulders. Bill knelt down by his feet, and tentatively reached to inspect the afflicted ankle. He barely laid a finger on him, and the boy cried out in pain. He withdrew his hands, pleased to see that at least there was no signs of blood seeping through the thick green fabric of the uniform above the boot.

"What's yer name son?" Bill asked, his face giving nothing away.

"Parkinson, sir"

94

"Okay Mister Parkinson, you're going to be okay, but what say we leave the rest of the obstacle course for the day ey?"

Relief washed over Parkinson's baby face.

"Since they've already got you, Mister Green and Mister…?" He looked at the other young man.

"Welsh, Sir." he said nervously.

"And Mister *Welsh* here might as well run you to the infirmary. That is, if that's okay with you Mister Green?"

Green, who had been watching the remaining recruits going round the course turned to look at Bill. His stubborn edge appeared to have worn off, and if anything he looked a little disappointed that he wouldn't get to finish the course.

"Sir, yes Sir!"

Bill walked with them as they carried Parkinson back towards the Manor, its limestone, ivy-covered walls no less stately despite the downpour. As they passed Smythe he looked as though he were about to say something. Bill shot him a look that could stop a bullet, and continued straight past.

"Tosser." Bill muttered under his breath.

As far as he was concerned money could buy you the best education, the best training and the best weapons, but there was nothing on God's green earth that could buy you a shred of common sense or decency.

No amount of schooling can teach a rat the value of honour..

He turned his attention back to the young soldiers in front of him.

Or valour for that matter…

CHAPTER SIXTEEN: WELLS

The subject of Wells' dedication to the job was one often bandied about the staff room. A number of faculty members were of the opinion that he was suffering from burnout at best, and at worst alcoholic depression. While he would admit that his enthusiasm had waned somewhat in recent years, he would be damned if anyone were to question his commitment. Yet as his mind hazily wandered through yet another student's copy and pasted, barely literate presentation, it would be lying to say that he was currently on anything other than autopilot. Well, autopilot *and* the several sizable gulps of Glenmorangie he'd snuck in at break time.

As another nameless, plain faced student rattled parrot-like through his interpretation of the events leading up to the Liberation of Belgium, his attention remained focussed elsewhere. If Neil Wells had learned anything about himself in his near sixty years, it was that he *hated* not knowing things. He simply *detested* mysteries he couldn't solve. For a man who could finish the Times crossword *and* the daily Sudoku on his lunch break, it was simply not a feeling he was accustomed to.

The image of the flaming fist would not go away, it was burned into his brain. More annoying than not knowing what it stood for or where it came from was the maddening question.

Why do I even care!?

He felt like he was trying to put together a jigsaw without all the pieces.

Who am I kidding? It's like trying to put a box-less jigsaw together without all the pieces… upside down.

In complete honesty, all Wells really had was a solitary piece, and an irritating itch at the back of his mind. It was like an intangible whisper that promised answers, only to vanish into the ether upon approach.

He had decided that the best option was to switch off from the problem, and allow the answer to come to him naturally. The fact that he had no idea what class he was currently teaching was firm testament to the fact that it was proving easier said than done. Aware that his negligence was only going to get him in trouble he decided it was best to get his bearings. Wells looked up, and allowed his vision to focus. The boy still robotically delivering his report had fair hair and freckles, and Wells had absolutely no idea who he was. He cast a glance around at the sea of bored faces, hoping to spark recognition. None came. He tried to place their year group hoping to narrow it down.

Year 7? Year 8 maybe?

Screwing his eyes closed, he rubbed the bridge of his nose between thumb and forefinger. When his eyes opened, he noticed the piece of A4 printed paper on the desk. It was the lesson plan, *his* lesson plan. Like a smack to the head, the blindingly obvious hit him:

MONDAY- 13:00-14:00- YEAR 9 – "WWII-THE LIBERATION OF BELGIUM- KIDS TO READ WRITTEN ESSAYS.

Year 9? My god... All these bloody kids look the same.

He looked around the room again, hoping that with that revelation, he might be able to put a few names to the bored faces. He couldn't, and although it should've, it didn't concern him.

Maybe the others are right about me after all...

Several hours later Wells was sat awkwardly in the hard, racing seats of his car waiting for his clandestine meeting with Terrance. He was showered and changed into his more casual attire of blue jeans, shirt and well-worn brown leather jacket. His "Indiana Jones" jacket he'd once called it. The name was met with such scathing derision from the ex-wife, that it was the first and last time he'd done so. At least out loud anyway.

The library car park was recessed below street level, with an "in" and an "out" ramp at both ends to the left and right, opposite Wells' parking space. In the evenings it also served a number of small restaurants across the street and as such it was near enough full. Wells' irritation had been steadily growing since arrival. He checked his battered old watch for the time, and was further annoyed that, despite the fact that he had been waiting nearly a quarter of an hour, Terrance was only a couple of minutes late. Of course his anger at having to wait was fundamentally caused by his own obsession with punctuality which, like his precisely ordered sock drawer and mirror polished shoes, were symptoms of his draconian, almost militaristic upbringing. So ingrained in this way of thinking was he, that it was of course *never his fault* for being too early, merely everyone else who were not early enough. Being a career teacher of thirty plus years and having an IQ of around 145 meant that his "I'm right, therefore you are wrong" mentality had not been questioned enough by others to encourage Wells to question it himself.

As he shifted in the TVRs ludicrously cushion-less seats for the umpteenth time, cursing Terrance for his failure to grasp the basic concept of meeting times, a young couple walked down the ramp and into the car park. The man was skin headed and built like a tank. Wells couldn't help but admire the woman on his arm, and admire her he did, until the couple became aware of his casual voyeurism. He quickly, and he hoped casually, pretended to wipe some dust from the dashboard.

The young man with the tree trunk neck glowered at him, until the woman whispered something hilarious in his ear, and the pair cracked up laughing. Wells groaned.

Oh my god, check out THAT sad old tosser, spends his evenings hanging around in car parks perving on the women of young meat-headed males.

Still laughing, the couple got into the man's black VW Golf, and drove off.

Not for the first time, Wells looked around at the cramped interior, felt the twinge in his lower back, and wondered whether the old man in the petrol guzzling, AA cash cow, lime green sports car *might* have looked a little ridiculous. It was at this point that Terrance appeared, and instantly put his mind at ease.

A sad old man I may be, but Christ it could be worse…

Wearing a battered, tan trench coat with black jogging bottoms and scuffed black shoes, Terrance looked like a vagrant Columbo. His outfit was set off by the wide-rimmed, brown fedora hat atop his head coupled with a ropey looking red rose pinned in his lapel. Wells watched on as he pulled out a cigarette case from his inside coat pocket, revealing a flash of black t-shirt underneath, withdrew a cigarette and put it to his lips. He then, in what one imagined was a well mirror practised manoeuvre, pulled out a Zippo lighter from another pocket and flicked open its lid with a 'click' of his fingers. Sadly the power of the 'click' was too great for his grip, and the brushed-steel lighter flew from his hand. With it went Terrance's composure. He flailed wildly trying to catch the object, but succeeded only in knocking it further away. It hit the gravel floor and skittered along another few metres. As Terrance bent over to retrieve it, the hat fell from his head knocking the unlit cigarette from his lips on its downward arc to land in a small puddle.

Wells stared on aghast, his mouth literally hanging open as he regarded the human train wreck unfolding before him. He began to slide down in his seat, hoping somehow that his former student might not see him. However, with space at a premium, Wells inadvertently knocked the horn. It BLARED OUT in response.

"Bugger!" he exclaimed under his breath as the sharp sound immediately drew the dishevelled young man's attention. Terrance, who was now resetting the old fashioned hat upon his lank, unwashed hair, gave him an enthusiastic wave. Sheepishly Wells gave a slight wave back, hoping to god that no one of any import was around to witness his admission of collusion. To say the least, he was beginning to regret his decision to arrange this meeting.

Still, it can't get much worse... he thought as his unfortunate guide slipped awkwardly into the passenger seat.

Half an hour later, as he regarded the ceremonial opening to "The Order of The Flame's" weekly meeting, Wells pondered how a man of his age, intelligence and experience could have allowed his expectations to spiral so wildly out of control. Had it been the reverence in tone used by Terrance when referring to "The Order"? Or had it just been blind optimism? Either way there he was, standing in a dingy pub function room watching seven overweight men in black robes sit in bean bags chanting.

The situation was so ridiculous that it had even shorted out Wells' usually scathing inner monologue. The only reaction he could muster was a raised eyebrow as the comically clichéd events unfolded before him.

The group sat in a circle in the middle of the scuffed dance floor. The eldest amongst them was sat back slightly from the others in a larger, plusher bean bag. He was heavy set and bearded. Although he was clearly going bald this had not deterred him from keeping what hair he had left long, and tied back into a ponytail. Like his beard, it was shot through with grey.

"We shall now recite... *the oath...*" he said, with theatrical emphasis before clearing his throat. "We pledge ourselves to the Order of the Flame."

From their seated positions the men, who ranged from mid twenties to early fifties, each sparked a blue candle with a brushed steel "Zippo" the same as the one Terrance had juggled earlier and began to say the vaunted oath in unison.

"We pledge ourselves to the Order of the Flame,
To hold the truth,
and to guard the name,
That he might return from whence he came,
To burn forever,
The Eternal Flame."

Neil Wells' eyes rolled so far back in his head they threatened to dislocate.

Oh, a rhyme, how delightful.

By now he was well aware that this had been a complete waste of his time. He was beginning to formulate his exit strategy, when the leader of the group, or "The Chairman of the Chapter" as Terrance had explained on the way, spoke again.

"Now we move on to new business."

Leaning over he pulled out a mauve, leather backed book from a Tesco carrier bag, followed by an ornate gold fountain pen from his pocket. A quick inspection of the book was enough to remind him to put on his reading glasses, which he pulled out of another pocket.

"Our youngest member and recent inductee Brother Whittacre has, as you can see, brought along an *interested party*."

The group all turned to look at Wells. Caught slightly off guard, he returned their gaze with a sheepish smile and a half wave from the hip.

"Mister…" He made an exaggerated point of consulting his book. "Wells is it?"

"Yes indeed. Well at least until the operation anyway."

The seven faces failed to react to the joke and Wells cringed internally as his attempt at levity fell flat on its face. From the looks on their faces it was clear that he was as welcome as Patrick Stewart at a Star Wars convention.

"Brother Whittacre informs us that you have some questions regarding an *image* of some sort?" he said with a puzzled expression, as though it was all news to him.

Wells found this a little strange, surely Terrance had pre-mentioned his arrival?

He quickly dismissed the thought, subterfuge seemed beyond them.

By the looks of it these bloody idiots need mummy to tie their shoe laces. Oh well, in for a penny, in for a pound I suppose...

"Yes, I saw this image recently..."

He pulled the print out from his pocket and unfolded it to show the room.

"And although I have this feeling that I've seen it somewhere before, I can't for the life of me seem to place it."

The five other members of the Order's faces gave away their recognition, but the Chairman remained impassive.

"What makes you think you've seen it before?"

"I really don't know. I thought it might have something to do with an army regiment, but I can't find reference to it anywhere..."

"What made you think it was army related?

"I, I really don't know. I mean I'm a career historian and Modern British conflicts are something of a specialty of mine. The fact that I haven't been able to place it *should* have been enough to dissuade me from that line of thought, but still my instinct tells me otherwise." Wells thought about his statement for a moment and shrugged.

"And what made you think that we, the benevolent Order of

The Flame, could help?"

Wells furrowed his brow sceptically.

"I had no such thoughts, Chairman. After all I *was* invited here. If I have managed to draw any parallels between the image in question and yourselves then I can assure that I have come to them via the bare facts presented to me."

The Chairman looked on, as stoic as a brick wall.

"Go on."

Wells felt certain that explanation was totally unnecessary, but having taught some of the dimmest kids ever to grace the public school system he took a deep breath and did it anyway.

"Well first of all, there was Terrance's *clear* reaction to the image. Secondly was his *insistence* that I approach you for more information. And then finally," His expression deliberately fixed to show just how ridiculously, pathetically stupid they must be, "there is the fact that the image that I have presented to you." He gestured an open palm around the room "…is quite clearly embossed on the backs of all of your robes…" He pointed at Terrance who was aimlessly fiddling with his floor damaged lighter. "AND not to mention those rather spiffy looking lighters you all have."

Morons…

The Chairman's eyes widened slightly, and he cast a glance around the embarrassed faces of the circle. The older man, aware that his strong stance had been eroded, hoped to use the momentary pause to gather his thoughts. Wells however was done waiting around, and decided to go on the offensive.

"Now quite clearly you know *something*. Given your glaring ineptitude at keeping that fact a secret, I can't imagine that you would know anything of any value. But all the same, what say we draw a line under events thus far, save ourselves any further embarrassment *or annoyance*, and let me know what it is. How does that sound?"

Wells folded his arms across his chest and fixed a stern gaze upon the Chairman who was shuffling uncomfortably in his seat. Across the room, Terrance's head fell down into his hands. When he'd approached the subject of bringing in an "outsider" this was pretty much exactly as badly as it could've gone. He felt certain that his membership to the Order would be revoked. Given that his seat was hereditary, that would be unprecedented.

The Chairman finally lamented beneath Wells' withering gaze.

"Inductee Whittacre," he said with more than an edge of displeasure, "fetch the projector. We wouldn't want to keep your *guest* waiting would we?"

Terrance apologetically, awkwardly, got to his feet. Amid the glares of his fellow members, he shuffled off to fulfill his master's command.

Having successfully established his dominance over the room, Wells was feeling as happy as he had in months. Although in truth it was like waving fire in the faces of cavemen. Far too smug did he feel to notice how much his presence was annoying his hosts, nor how he had potentially damaged Terrance's reputation.

Now it's time for some answers.

Terrance wheeled in the projector on an old canteen trolley.

The Chairman produced a small, black, lock box from the carrier bag at his side and placed it on the floor in front of him. The box was old and damaged, as though it had been through hell and back. There were several cuts and in particular a deep gouge on one of its surfaces that appeared to have been caused by attempts to gain access to the contents. It was no bigger than six inches on any of its sides, and on the top facing of these were seven small keyholes. The Chairman nodded regally to his followers. In turn they each struggled to their feet, and removed a small silver key from around their necks. Their keys were each placed into a corresponding lock before it was handed to Terrance. With another nod of his sweaty, ponytailed head, the Chairman instructed Terrance to continue. Visibly nervous, Terrance began to turn each of the keys individually, following the corresponding click of the key turn, he moved on to the next. With all seven locks open, the tubby young man wiped his hands on the back of his robe, followed by the film of sweat from his top lip.

Oh for god's sake hurry up!

Wells shifted his weight from foot to foot, the only man in the room not taken in by the auspice of the occasion.

When Terrance reached for the lid of the box, his hands were trembling. Wells' euphoria at getting his way was fast returning to boredom and annoyance. Or *normality* as it had become in recent years. He watched Terrance's squinted eyes widen in anticipation as he opened the box and reached inside. Despite his bitter demeanour, the suspense even began to put Wells on tenterhooks. He waited to see just what was so special that it required such time consuming reverie.

Judging by the aged condition of the box it must be something very rare and valuable…

The bespectacled youngster reached in, and produced… A small disc. The assembled men inhaled in unison, a physical rendition of awe. Wells' eyebrow instinctively shot up, and he fought the urge to blurt out the first words that came into his head.

Is that a bloody DVD?!!!

Terrance examined the shiny disc, which reflected the overhead lighting in a rainbow pattern on his face. From his position Wells was sure that he could see "ASDA Value" branding on it, along with "The Eternal Flame Footage" scrawled loosely in black marker pen.

Oh you have GOT to be taking the pi…

Terrance inserted the disc *very carefully* into a DVD player beside the projector. Blurrily, Wells could make out the DVD Video logo slowly bouncing off the sides of the screen. Terrance again wiped his hands, before adjusting the focus on the device. The Chairman turned to face Wells, a grin forming on his face.

"Now Mister Wells, we are ready to divulge the information you so seek. But I must warn you, the footage you are about to see is not for the faint of heart. Are you prepared to bear witness to the raw power of The Eternal Flame?"

Christ this bloke should be going toe to toe with Widow Twanky, he is the living personification of Christmas Pantomime...

"Yes Mister Chairman," he let out a sigh, knowing that further sarcasm at this point was unproductive, "I believe that I am ready."

"Very well then, Brother Whittacre, you may proceed."

Terrance bowed slightly then turned off the main lighting and began the playback. As a five second countdown began, with accompanying beeps, the entire room, Wells included, watched on intently.

The footage was old, black and white, square. It reminded Neil Wells of the Pathe news footage that was commonly shown in cinemas in his youth. From a high vantage point, a well built masked man in army fatigues defended himself from attack before his counter attacks sent three soldiers flying across the room. Several more entered, drew their guns and began firing. The masked man barely flinched. He then made short work of his attackers. The camera shakily zoomed in as he picked up one of their guns and watched as fire erupted from the man's hand and melted it to slag...

The footage jumped around, like old film melting in the gate, and ended abruptly. Though it was played on DVD, it seemed as though the original stock it had been copied from had been damaged beyond repair. As Terrance brought the house lights back up again, The Chairman, a smug grin settled on his fat face, turned towards a flabbergasted Wells.

"So." The Chairman began, raising a cocky eyebrow. His smug grin spread to his cohorts in the room. "I trust that you have… *questions?*" He let out a solitary chuckle, and gestured to the others, who like good little lemmings followed suit.

To say that Wells had questions was the understatement of the century. Like a hurricane, questions ran riotously around his brain, so many of them that it was hard to know just where to begin. But like the calm, collected and cultured man that he was, Neil Wells BA, MA, and seeker of knowledge decided upon his first question.

"IS THAT IT?!" he blurted out. Judging from how the conceited faces in the room dropped at his reaction, The Order clearly put a great deal more value into the footage than did the sceptical Historian. The Chairman's confusion at Well's response was quickly replaced with irritation. From his beanbag vantage point the switch in mood was highlighted by the bulging vein in his forehead, his venerated stoicism finally cracked.

"What? What do you mean '*Is that it'!?*" he blustered.

Well's momentary shock however was now long gone. With his brain back firing on all cylinders and the realisation of just how much of his precious free time had been wasted on these jokers, he was through pulling his punches.

"What do I mean?!" he said in sheer disbelief. "I have just wasted an hour of *my* life watching a bunch of grown men chanting stereotypical, self obsessed, self deluded nonsense, ponce about in robes and then FINALLY show me some much vaunted footage that looks like it was lifted from the cutting room floor of some piss-poor Ed Wood science fiction film!!!"

Wells took a deep breath, his heart was racing, his blood boiling. In this mood he could've kept up his tirade all night, but a glance at his watch was enough to make him change his mind. It was just after ten, and with last orders at his local pub fast approaching the possibility of salvaging a thoroughly pointless evening remained in reach. But, with each passing moment spent in the company of the intellectual black holes that made up "The Order" that possibility slipped away. After some quick mental time, speed and distance calculations Wells turned his attention back from his antique watch to the sea of irritated faces. The Chairman had been staring at Wells' battered time piece, but quickly turned his fascination back to indignation. He pointed his finger, about to make another "regal decree". Wells beat him to it.

"Well thank you very much gentlemen for a thoroughly *spectacular* waste of my valuable time." Wells' venomous sarcasm was masked behind a bright, almost cheerful delivery. Eat your heart out *Basil Fawlty...*

"Thank you for the insight into your homoerotic little cult, and what will doubtless make an outstanding anecdote in the future..."

He span 180 degrees on his heel and strode towards the door. "Bloody Super powered, gun melting soldiers, absolute poppycock!"

Behind him the maligned Chairman got to his feet and shook his fist in the air.

"The Power of The Eternal Flame should not be mocked, *outsider*! YOU HAVE BEEN WARNED!"

Wells shook his head as he walked through the doors and headed down the stairs.

"Morons..."

As much as tearing a strip off deluded fools was a real mood booster, he knew the feeling would fade. Once again he was back to square one, no closer to the answers his own stubbornness demanded.

Wells stormed through the double doors at the bottom of the stairway and out into the car park. The instant bite of the cold, night air felt good, cleansing even, after being confined in a room thick with the scent of sweat and idiocy. He gingerly lowered himself into his car, playing back the footage again in his mind's eye. A massive hulk of a man wearing a mask and army issue vest and trousers standing up to close range gunfire without so much as blinking. He had to admit looking back that the special effects were quite good, particularly for something so old. But regardless of the production values, or the reverence those idiots gave it, Wells was not buying it.

Secret Army divisions and magical soldiers. What a load of old tosh.

He started the engine, and roared out of the car park at top speed.

I mean really, who in their right mind would believe in that?

Back inside the function room. Terrance sat, hunch backed and devastated, the ire of the members of the Order turned towards him. The silence, thick with anger, was broken by the generic Nokia ringtone of the Chairman's phone. Shaking his head, he pulled it from the pocket of his robe, his eyes widening as he read the display. He closed his eyes and took a deep breath before answering the call.

"Yes Grand Leader…"

Though the voice on the end of the line was muffled by the excessive flesh of the chairman's round face, the reverence he held for the speaker was clear.

"Yes sir, I agree, he knows something. Yes, Grand Master, of course…"

With an audible bleep, the Chairman ended the call. With a look of intense focus, and a hint of dark purpose he fixed his gaze upon the crestfallen Terrance.

"Keep an eye on him. The Grand Leader," he said, nodding towards the red blinking eye of a CCTV camera high in the corner of the room, "believes this Neil Wells character knows more than he is letting on…"

Wiping away tears from his eyes, a look of almost innocent joy swept across the young man's face.

"Yes Chairman, it will be done. Praise be to the Order"

"Praise be to the Order!" chanted the rest of the gathered men.

Terrance looked down at the beaten old container in his hand and lifted the lid. Inside was the charred remnants of a Flaming Fist patch. He gently caressed it with his fingertips and allowed himself a smug smile as the Order's chanting rang around the room.

CHAPTER EIGHTEEN: ANNA

Having survived the weekly torture of R.E, Anna knew she only had to face the equally torturous double French before heading home for a quick shower in preparation for her even more torturous shift in the nursing home. Of course she actually *enjoyed* French, and despite the stingey use of central heating she also liked her job, but half an hour in Mrs Lord's R.E lesson was enough to take the shine off a diamond.

Still, it's an easy half GCSE, and it's better than actually having to work.

That mantra had helped maintain her sanity throughout the year, but although it remained true, her patience with the repetition was wearing thin.

So far her attempts to find out more about Richie Spink had fallen flat. Her "in depth investigations" had thus far uncovered a generic, photo-less "Myspace" page that listed his birthday and revealed that his religious affiliation was to the "Watcher's Council". As the only girl in her form class who owned the entire Buffy the Vampire Slayer DVD collection, the last piece of information was encouraging to say the least.

A geek, but a geek who knows Buffy. As long as he's not into that 'dice rolling' crap, we might be onto a winner!
Annoyingly the only lesson they shared on a Monday was the aforementioned R.E. In which Spink sat directly in front of her. Half an hour of staring at the back of his head had revealed little, other than he had reasonably sized ears, a good head of hair, and no dandruff.

More annoying than this however was her daily battle to cram her mass of textbooks into her stupidly high locker.

You'd think they'd have the common sense to assign the low ones to us short-arses, she thought as she strained on the tip toes of her black converse high tops. Aware that her precarious position left her open to the lecherous glances of

111

every teenage boy on the corridor, she looked around, and nearly choked on her chewing gum when her eyes met with those belonging to the gangly, stooped shouldered form of Richie Spink.

Ohmigod!

Anna fought against the horde of rampaging butterflies in her stomach. Never in her life had she been the kind of person who lacked confidence, but all of a sudden it felt as though she'd lost motor control. For that moment time stood still. Their eyes remained locked for what seemed like an eternity.

You're staring, Anna, do something, do something quick or you'll look like an idiot.

Nothing.

Do ANYTHING Anna. Smile. Yeah, smile, that's a good, simple solution, do that.

Still nothing.

Dammit Anna SMILE! Nice and easy. Raise the corners of your mouth, and SMILE!!!!

Finally after staring vacantly for an hour she managed to convince her lips to curve into the most pathetically weak smile ever seen on God's green earth. However, when she went to check what effect it was having on its target, Anna was dismayed to discover that his attention had been diverted elsewhere; the floor to be precise.

Oh that was just brilliant. Bravo Anna! You've gawped at a lad, a lad who probably doesn't even know you, for a whole week and THEN scared him so much that he'd rather check out the floor!!!! Bra-bloody-vo!

In the midst of her mental self flagellation, she saw a hand from the crowd place itself on Richie's shoulder. The body it belonged to brought such a bolt of recognition that Anna would've slapped palm to forehead, had she one to spare.

Marc Townsend! Of course! Why didn't I notice sooner?!

She had known, or at least known of, Marc since Nursery School. They had been in the same class at Junior school,

112

where the fact that they had held hands for a couple of playtimes had once made them "boyfriend and girlfriend". The memory nearly made her giggle out loud.

God! I'd forgotten all about that!

Image-wise Marc was the stereotypical John Hughes school rebel, a fact that made him extremely popular amongst the tween girls in the years below. He was witty, handsome, intelligent, *and* he had a cool, American-influenced wardrobe. Whilst Anna could see the surface attraction, she also knew that it was all a carefully constructed front. Marc Townsend *knew* he was good looking, and *knew* that his image was a vital part of that. *Anna* knew that he was a self obsessed egotist, with the emotional depth of a paddling pool.

At that moment, Katie's all too chirpy voice finally pierced her introspection and Anna forced herself to tune in to her friend's frequency in case she missed anything important. She needn't have bothered.

"…Oh my god wasn't that *so* funny getting Missus Lord to answer that question *again!*"

"Oh… Yeah, it was…" she sighed, "…*hilarious.*"

Although Anna patently couldn't disagree more, she didn't wish to pointlessly trample Katie's enthusiasm for the mundane. After all, "Whatever floats your boat" as her Dad would say. She loved her Dad dearly but did not share his perma-positivity. As Anna closed the door to her locker, and with Katie continuing to witter away, her mind drifted back to Richie Spink. She glanced back down the rapidly emptying corridor she caught another glimpse of him and Marc in the distance. The more she thought about it, the more it occurred to her that if he was friends with Marc, then she actually *had* seen Richie about over the years. As she saw them disappear through a set of red double doors, something else about Richie struck her as odd. Something she couldn't quite put her finger on.

Overhead the bell rang to signal the start of the next lesson, and Anna again remembered that Katie was still standing next to her.

"What have we got next Annie?"

"French, Kate."

Same as last Monday, and the dozens before that.

Not wanting her annoyance to show, Anna plastered on her dimmest, Barbie-esque smile, and linked arms with Katie.

"Come on, let's go before we end up right in the '*merde.*'"

Katie looked at her blankly, and Anna realised that she should've known better. Throwing French witticisms at Katie, even easy ones like that, was like asking her mother to find her spam folder… pointless.

"Never mind, come on let's go."

As they quickly hurried off, once more Anna let her attention drift back. Where only minutes earlier she had nothing, suddenly things were beginning to look up. Sure she'd made an unforgivable idiot of herself with the smiling debacle, but at least she had her first, solid "in". Okay, so under normal circumstances she would have no desire to put herself in the company of 'the walking ego' Marc Townsend, but if he was friends with Richie Spink then that made all the difference. If they were friends, then Marc would know things about him, what he was into, where he hung out, yadda, yadda, yadda. Although she didn't quite know why the answers to these questions were important to her, they *felt* important, and that was reason enough. Now she had something to work towards. The first step was to get hold of her "ex"…

CHAPTER EIGHTEEN: RICHIE

"...AAAARRRGGGGGGHHHHH!!!"

Richie began to realise that his screaming was having no effect on the grenade at his feet. Normally his internal monologue would be working overtime, but his brain felt as frozen as the rest of his body. As the terrorful instants passed, the tiny fraction of his brain that still operated could ask only one question:

How long IS the fuse on a Nazi grenade?

Not a question he thought he'd ever have to postulate, but there you have it. It felt as though he'd lived a lifetime since it had landed at his oversized, dirty boot covered feet. Impossibly long, *too long*. Still bellowing his fearful exclamation, he managed to crane his neck upwards. He was in the ruins of what he imagined to have once been a picturesque little town. Now, as the gruesome ballet of a military skirmish unfolded, he saw the tolls of war taken on his surroundings. Stone buildings bore gaping holes in their walls, floors and ceiling; rubble piled waist high and higher along the torn up cobble stoned streets. Craters of varying depth and circumference pock marked the earth. The soulless button eyes of a child's doll stared back at him from a dusty gutter.

Over the bassy tones of his guttural roar, Richie became aware of another similar sound. He tried to trace its origin. Like moving in treacle he turned his head towards it.

"GGGGGGGGETTTTTTTTTTDDDDDDDOOOOOOOOOOW WWWWWWWNNNNNN!!!!!"

Before he could register the voice's owner, he was struck in the waist by a human freight train. The world snapped back to normal speed. The deafening roar of the exploding grenade thundered in his ears. His world was blinding light and the physical force of being slammed into the dusty, cobbled floor. Whatever had knocked him down was up in a flash. The sound of gunfire rattled his teeth. As his vision cleared he saw a slender figure crouched over him, silhouetted against the glaring backdrop of the afternoon sun. The figure fired off several shots from a handgun at four separate targets, after which the overall volume of gun fire dropped dramatically. As his eyes slowly adjusted to the light, the features of the man came into focus. Five o clock shadow, pencil moustache, face smudged with dirt, greying hair at the temples…

"Oh my God! It's you!"

The man's expression was one of stern detachment, his movements fluid, almost mechanical. He picked off his last shot, and snapped his piercing gaze to Richie. He found that the intensity behind the moustachioed man's green eyes scared him even more than the bloodshed going on around him.

"Gerrup. Now!" The man barked in a thick Yorkshire brogue. Despite the fear that gnawed at his insides, somehow Richie found himself on his feet and moving. The man took a grip of his lapel.

"Keep yer head down!"

Again Richie did as told, and was immediately rewarded as a bullet zipped through the space his face had occupied mere instants earlier.

Jesus Jesus Jesus!

The pair headed quickly over the rough debris strewn landscape. Ahead, despite its blown-out windows, and absent door, was the closest thing that remained to an intact building.

"Gerr' inside. Stay down!"

As they ducked through, a bullet embedded itself into the wooden door frame. The man shoved Richie into a corner, and fired another precise shot back out of the doorway. Richie remained sat, stunned, his mouth hanging open like a gawping idiot. The man was unbelievable. To Richie the entire world around him was like some sick, twisted, horrifying nightmare,

116

and at the centre of it was this… guy. He was the calm, quartz-precise centre of this murderous military bizarro world.

He's like… Batman…

Despite all of the ambient sounds of the battle outside, Richie became aware that he felt far calmer just being in the man's presence.

"Is this a dream?"

He looked around the room, at the broken wooden furniture, and the lone blood covered shoe and knew the answer. The man answered without turning his focus from the raging battle.

"This is *not* a dream, no."

Oh well, it was worth a go.

Richie gleaned no satisfaction from the knowledge as it only left the more unfathomable, and frightening possibilities.

"So. This, this is all… Real?"

The man's attention again remained unturned.

"'Fraid so lad."

Damn.

"Okay, so, if this isn't a dream, and it's all real…"

Richie could feel his panic returning. "… then where the hell am I? What the HELL is going on?! And WHO IN THE NAME OF ALL AND HOLY THE HELL ARE YOU?!!"

Richie started to hyperventilate. But, with total nervous breakdown due to set in, he had one final gambit, he closed his eyes...

Come on, we can do this Richie…

"There's no place like home. There's no place like home. There's no place like home." he said, clicking the heels of his muddy boots together as he did.

After repeating his mantra ineffectually several more times, he opened his eyes again.

Bugger…

The world around him remained the same, but he had at least succeeded in attracting the man's undivided attention.

Richie watched as he fired off one last shot, and quickly crouch- walked across the room towards him.

"There's no place like home. There's no place like…"

The soldier slapped Richie hard across the face.

The effect was like, well, a slap to the face.

"Ow! Ey! What did you do that f…"

"Knock that off now, or the next one's a bullet! Clear?"

The man's proposition was acceptable. Richie nodded in agreement as he brought his hand up to his cheek. It didn't *actually* hurt, he realised, the "Ow" was as much an instinctive reaction as anything. He'd never been slapped before. Slapping was something that heroic masculine types did to hysterical women in old films…

Oh, yeah, right.

"Sorry." he said earnestly, trying his best to quell his hysteria.

The man nodded, the barest hint of a smile at the corners of his mouth.

"It's okay, but if you can just stay focussed for a second I'll be able to tell yer what yer need to know." he said, putting a firm hand on his shoulder. The calming effect he had came off him in comforting waves.

"We are currently behind enemy lines in Northern France, in what is left of Orchies. My name is William North, *Major* William North, but you can call me Will… Richie."

The noise outside was getting louder again.

"It *was you* in the church then?"

"Yes."

"How did you, I mean, how *do you* know my name?"

"Now that's a longer story, and not one we've got time for now."

"But."

"No buts lad, just remember, call me Will next time you show up."

The increasingly raucous noise outside began to drown out the sounds of battle.

"But who am I?"

"You're the Eternal Flame of British Resistance."

I'm the what?!!!

"I'm… What does that mean? What do you mean next time? What the hell is going on????"

Will responded, but his words were drowned out by the noise. Richie winced as the noise began to hurt his ear drums. He closed his eyes, trying to focus, to block it out.

What the hell is making that noise? Is that… cheering?

When he opened his eyes Will was gone, and so were the stone walls of the building. In their place were legs in blue shorts, socks and running shoes. He felt desperately short of breath, as though his lungs had been set alight, then put out by having a herd of elephants jump on them. A firm hand fell on his shoulder, patting him frantically. It belonged to his PE teacher, Mr Leeson. The man's tanned face bore a look of starry eyed astonishment. Still fighting for breath, Richie looked around to see that the cheering came from the owners of the legs, shorts, socks and running shoes. A collection of his classmates stood in front of him, sweating and tired. Many of them stared at him in disbelief through their fatigue, as they wiped the perspiration from their brows.

Richie struggled to get his bearings, and the strange twist on the familiar locale made this no easier.

What are they all gawking at?

"SLINK!" Leeson exclaimed jubilantly.

"Err, it's Spink sir." Richie retorted, but just barely as he struggled for air.

"Sorry. Of course, *Spink*. That my son, was absolutely incredible!"

Oh my god, he KNOWS! He must've seen me disappear or something! Good god, what must they all think?

He looked up again at the astonishment on the faces around him.

"Strange boy vanishes during Games lesson". They'll think I've...

"I've never seen a Cross Country performance like that in all my years!" Leeson exclaimed seemingly on the verge of tears.

They'll think... WHAAA?!!!

"Sir?"

"Come on, up you get."

Mr Leeson helped Richie to his feet. His legs felt like jelly, and without the arm of his teacher he would've slid straight back down into the mud.

What the hell is going on?! You'd think I'd just won gold at the Olympics, but I wasn't even here... I was...

He thought back to only moments earlier, the dusty room, the bloody shoe, the age worn creases of "Will's" dirt smudged face. Each and every part of it was as vivid, as real as the damp turf beneath his mud caked school shoes and the burning sensation eating his lungs. As his breathing threatened to return to normal, and the oxygen supply to his brain resumed, the surreality of his situation became all the more evident. It was as though his brain and body had become completely detached from one another. His body felt as though it had run the London Marathon, but his brain, that had struggled to cope with being dropped in the middle of a battle, simply couldn't fathom how it was possible. Richie felt weak, and his head swam, like stepping off the Waltzers with the flu.

"I'm going to be sick."

Still beaming, as he helped Richie off the field, Leeson was too lost in his own world of PE teacher pride to take in what Richie had said.

"What did you...?"

120

But it was too late. As he fell to his knees, violently relieving his stomach of his packed lunch, he prayed that the PE department would have the good sense to wash the lost property kit, before forcing it on the next poor soul to leave theirs at home…

INTERLUDE:

The roaring fireplace in the second floor study cast dancing shadows around the room. The vast collection of leather bound books filling the floor to ceiling cases became dark, rich blocks of burgundy, jade and navy in the dim lighting. A high backed leather armchair cast the longest shadow in the room, bisecting the antique rug before blending into the dark mahogany of the doors. The chair itself was occupied by the thick, muscular frame of Director Christian Kessler who contemplated the flickering orange flames as he took another sip of 40 year old single malt scotch. He placed his crystal tumbler down on the ornate side table beside the bottle and adjusted his robe. The robe and the whisky, like the stately home that contained them, were lavishly expensive; all perks of a life that had come with many sacrifices, and carried the intense burden of responsibility. It was a life he'd been born to, a role he'd been bred for.

The grandfather clock on the far wall rang its declaration of one in the morning, and although Christian knew that he would be rising at 6 he had no intention of heading to bed just yet. He rarely slept more than 4 hours a night, and from experience knew that he could function perfectly well on just an hour. 'The Grand Leader' had called it a gift, but in truth the real gift was in the peace and quiet that a late night existence brought. Unfortunately, that peace was broken by the tinkling of a small brass bell hung above the dark, heavy doors. It informed him that someone was at the main entrance, what he didn't know was who.

With the staff all signed out for the night, Kessler got to his feet and smoothed down the front of his robe. Beneath it he wore thick, dark flannel pyjamas and slippers on his feet, adequate defence against the coldest corners of the mansion. Although he couldn't be certain who would be foolish enough to disturb him at this hour, the person in question knew the

122

code for the main gate, which narrowed it down to seven possibilities. Of course he could immediately discount himself, as well as his young counterpart Nathaniel Greymalkin, and of course 'The Grand Leader' himself; both of whom had retired to their respective wings for the night. Of the remaining four, Kessler calculated the likelihoods. Knowing the men in question, their personalities, dedication, and in the end, out and out fanaticism there was one who stood out.

He descended the wide central staircase into the main hallway which served as the access hub to the entire building. To the right of the main doors were another set leading to Nathaniel's wing, whilst those on the opposite side led to The Leader's. Behind the staircase on either side were two more sets, one to the main dining room, ballroom and kitchens, the other to the main library and rear gardens.

Kessler paused for a moment beside the towering doors of the main entrance to study a large flat screen television. The screen was as out of place in its auspicious surroundings as a digital watch on a suit of armour, but was merely one of many such technological anachronisms added in recent years. On the doorstep a rotund man stood with stooped shoulders, hugging himself against the bitter cold. The picture only confirmed the conclusion he'd had already reached. Not a man who suffered fools gladly, his disgust was clear to see as he opened the heavy door. Though he was easily 6 feet tall, the doors dwarfed him. Behind them the pale, pudgy, bearded face of local chapter chairman Keith Cowley looked up in nervous expectation. Christian Kessler returned it with a stern glare, like an owner finding his dog defecating on the front lawn.

"What are you doing here Keith?" he asked in his silkily flawless English accent.

The paunchy man shivered before responding. "Apologies for the late hour of my arrival Director Kessler, but I come bearing news of *critical* importance."

Kessler opened his mouth, about to interrupt, but Cowley continued.

"I know that I should've called ahead, but I am simply following the rule of 'Directive Seven'."

The Director's anger was suddenly put to one side, to cite 'Directive Seven' meant...

"You have found a link?" he asked with genuine, but guarded interest.

"I believe so." Cowley replied, withdrawing a folded piece of paper from his coat pocket and handing it across.

Christian opened out the sheet. His eyebrows raised instinctively when he focussed on the picture printed upon it.

"Where did this come from?"

"A teacher. Inductee Whittacre brought him to me."

"Did he now?" Kessler asked rhetorically, unable to keep an edge of surprise out of his voice. An icy gust of wind blew through the door but he refused to pull his robe tighter around him. One did not display weakness in front of one's lessers.

"What is this *teacher's* name?"

Cowley withdrew another piece of paper from his pocket. He unfolded this one himself and handed it to Christian. Printed in Arial type was some basic information on Neil Wells. Christian glanced over the information, committing it to memory instantly. He handed the page back.

Puzzled, but unquestioning Cowley stuffed it back into his pocket.

"What does he know?"

"I showed him my Chapter's film segment, he was..."

"Sceptical?" Kessler offered.

"Unimpressed... and rather rude to be honest." Cowley finished, there was a hint of upset in his tone.

Kessler weighed his options, coming to an almost immediate decision.

"Does inductee Whittacre share a bond with this, Wells?"

"Tenuous, but I believe so…"

"Good, ensure that their relationship continues. In the meantime, have him followed and report back daily. I want solid proof, not speculation."

Cowley made a mental note of his orders, stopping just short of sounding them out, when he was done he nodded.

"As you command Director Kessler."

The cold had worked its way through his clothing, the core warmth provided by the fire finally dissipated. He had what he wanted, and was in no way looking to invite Cowley inside, so brusquely moved on.

"Is there anything else Chairman?"

Cowley, who had clearly harboured the vain hope of sanctuary for the night, seemed a touch dejected. Ever the faithful servant, however, he hid it quickly. Just being in the presence of a Director was reward enough.

"No Director, but I was hoping to see The Grand Leader about this matter personally." he stated, nervously.

Kessler shook his head.

"The Leader is sequestered in his quarters."

"But, surely information such as this should be passed on immediately?!"

Kessler frowned in growing annoyance, but kept his tone even.

"Oh I feel certain that he knows already…"

Without further explanation, he shut the door, in the sniveling man's face and turned towards the stairs. High up near the ceiling, a surveillance camera was bolted to the wall. A red light blinked beneath its all seeing glass eye.

Inside his personal study, The Grand Leader took a deep breath behind the transparent oxygen mask strapped to his face. On one of the myriad screens in front of him he saw

Kessler walking back up the stairs towards his living area, the sound of his footsteps filled the room, amplified through several floor standing speakers. On another screen Cowley trudged his way back towards the main gate.

The frail old man pushed a controller on his wheelchair, turning it 25 degrees to the right to face another screen. On the flat monitor was a picture of Neil Wells' driving licence, beneath it a picture of his National Union of Teachers registration card. On the screen above, his vital statistics were listed. His age, Date of Birthday, Place of Birth, Family, Next of Kin, Addresses past and present. The Grand Leader lifted his pale and shaking, bony hand to click a mouse and zoom in on Well's photo. An unremarkable person with an unremarkable life, like most in this pitiful world. There was something there though, a familiarity that the wizened old man couldn't quite place. With a mechanical whirr, The Leader turned his chair again, and with a technological dexterity that belied his advanced age and wider physical condition, dug deeper into the teacher's family history, clicking through page after page of information until he settled on medical reports from Humberidge House nursing home. The medical reports of Frank Wells scrolled before him. He double clicked to open an image, so that the two central screens bore passport style photos of Neil Wells and his Father side by side. The Grand Leader studied the images, breathing in and out with slow, wheezing breaths. He ran bony fingertips across a deep scar on the side of his head, and closed his eyes tightly in focus. So many of the details of that fateful time in his life were lost to him, what remained was but a feeling, an instinct. A dry lipped smile stretched across his sunken cheeks.

"Perhaps..." he croaked, fogging the mask with his breath.

He had waited sixty years for a link to present itself, faced so many dead ends. This felt different. A lifeline cast out of the darkness. Perhaps his long set plans would finally come to fruition…

PART TWO

CHAPTER NINETEEN: RICHIE

"You have got to be kidding me!"

The incredulous look on Richie's face barely did justice to the sheer disbelief that he felt. Marc Townsend stood in front of him, hands on hips in an overly stagey, heroic pose. He blew on his finger nails and with a rakish grin, rubbed them on the lapel of his jacket.

"She?" Richie said.

"Yes."

"Asked?"

"Uh-huh."

"To meet *you*?"

"No word of a lie Richie baby."

Richie's incredulity turned to a look of raise-browed scepticism.

"Why the hell would she do that?

"Clearly the tasty minx can resist my devilish charms no longer." Marc said with a wink.

Whilst he couldn't deny that Marc Townsend was a good looking guy, what with all his white teeth and groomed eyebrows, this all seemed a little out of the blue. After all, hadn't she been smiling at *him* in the corridor yesterday?

All of a sudden the voice of doubt reared its ugly head.

Maybe she'd been smiling at Marc.

Richie's stomach dropped. The thought that the lovely Anna Harrison had actually been smiling at him had been the only bright spot amidst his recent troubles. To have it taken away by that explanation; *by that wholly more realistic explanation* was, in a word, gutting.

Marc was preening in his full length mirror, one of his friend's more time consuming hobbies. His cosmetic obsession was one that Richie didn't share. Marc's image was crafted to perfection. His faux bed head, trimmed "Johnny Depp" tuft and goatee, and all his pseudo-retro Americana clothing gave the impression that looking cool was effortless. In truth it was Richie's look that was truly effortless. An ill-fitting, oversized t-shirt and baggy jeans hung off of his skinny frame. His unbrushed and often unwashed hair crept below his eyes, framing his pale face. Sadly in Richie's case, effortless did not translate to cool. Although it had begun to bother him in recent months, particularly when he noticed the attention his friend received from the opposite sex, it still didn't concern him enough to enact any change.

Anyway, it's not like anyone's going to notice me…

Marc gave himself another pearly white smile in the mirror.

…Not with Captain Vanity around anyway…

Marc winked at himself, and turned 90 degrees to face Richie, who was perched on the side of the bed, staring miserably into the middle distance.

"What's up with you? Did those handsome pills you bought out the back of FHM turn out to be a hoax again?"

No, you preening idiot, I've been randomly jumping into the body of some World War II soldier, well that or I'm very rapidly losing my grip on reality…

"Ha, ha, bloody ha." Richie said dryly, opting out of spilling his true concerns. Getting locked up in an asylum would be an even crumbier way to end an already crumby week.

"I know," Marc said, clicking his finger into a point with an accompanying wink, "I'm hilarious… hilarious, *and* devilishly handsome. In truth, it's just a surprise that it's taken the delectable Miss Harrison this long to come to her senses." He cast another quick glance in the mirror.

Richie sighed.

"You forgot modest." he added dryly.

Marc opened the doors of his wardrobe, and began flicking through the contents.

"Modesty is for people who are too afraid to admit their own brilliance Richard." he said, as he withdrew a brown leather bomber jacket with a flourish, and slipped it on. It must've cost more than everything Richie had on put together... times fifty. His friend withdrew a pair of aviator sunglasses from a small rack and put them on with a winning smile; A young Tom Cruise height and all.

"A bit, err, Top Gun isn't it?" Richie asked.

"Got it in one Ricardo." He readjusted the collar, unsure whether to wear it up or down. "I got it from Macys in New York last summer, cool isn't it?"

"If by cool, you mean camp, then yes it's a winner."

The ever so slight deflation in his friend's demeanour was a small personal victory for Richie. Marc gave himself another once over, and as if seeing what Richie was saying for the first time, hastily took the jacket and shades off. The former had barely settled in the bin before he had withdrawn an alternative from the tall oak wardrobe. In truth Richie *did* think Marc looked cool, but at the back of his mind the green eyed monster of jealousy had reared its ugly head and was pulling all his strings. What he wanted was for Marc to make a complete tosser of himself, which given his natural gift of the gab would have to be achieved by other means.

Maybe I should've let him keep the camp pilot look...

An hour later, having borne witness to a further five outfit changes and an intolerable amount of self congratulatory bragging, Richie was walking home. Normally Friday evening was Marc and his video game night, where Richie could experience a world of next generation gaming that would make his decrepit PC at home explode. With that out of the window, he made his way back home, *on foot,* because at some point since his accident, his trusty mountain bike had vanished off the face of the earth.

Yet another mystery, yet another kick in the teeth.

His brain was fraught with too many things that he really did not want to think about. As if dealing with his current "identity crisis" AND loss of transport hadn't been taxing enough, now came the thought that his best friend was going on a date with the girl of his dreams…

Oh yeah, life is good…

Richie sighed as he listlessly kicked a flattened Coke can into the road. He felt yet another headache coming on. The doctor back at the hospital had warned him to expect them in the weeks following his mystery accident. There was that word again. Mystery. Right now Richie had more mystery in his life than Scooby Doo and the gang, which made his situation sound far more pleasant than the reality of it all. Realising that this train of thought was heading to nowhere but depression, he decided to switch back to his more pressing, though no less cheery problems.

His last time shift had raised more questions than answers, but however vague those answers were, at least they were something. The man with the moustache, Will, had called him "The Eternal Flame of British Resistance." Of course he had no idea just what that meant. Then again when he'd been set an essay question in Design Technology about Adi Dassler last year, he'd had no idea who *he* was either.

But that's why God invented the internet!

Buoyed by the possibility of getting *more* answers, Richie's walking pace increased, there was research to be done.

To the Batcave Robin! he thought, and immediately winced at the notion that he'd referred to himself as Robin, and not Batman.

Christ. Even in my own head I'm the bloody sidekick…

He turned a corner and walked straight into a barrel-chested wall. He instinctively flinched, stepping back to avoid further contact. His stomach leapt into his mouth and then scurried down into his ankles as he came face to face with

Jackson Sleight. Although the two were of comparable height, the bully's freakish girth and Richie's trademark stoop made him seem all the more massive. Richie felt like a little boy facing up to a heavyweight boxer.

Oh sweet Jesus, can I please just get a break?!

With a beating the exact last thing he needed, short of a beating whilst watching Marc and Anna kiss, Richie decided that retreat was the better part of valour. Without making eye contact he bowed his head, sidestepped the walking slab of beef and carried on towards home. He felt his skin crawl with tension as he did, expecting his plan to be scuppered by a good solid kidney punch, or slap across the head at any moment.

This is NEVER going to work! I'm going to die, I'm going to die... I wonder if they have bullies in heaven?

One step was followed by another. Then another. Then ANOTHER! Six more followed, and Richie's neck muscles began to relax.

Holy hell! It's working. Maybe all these years of totally worthless anonymity have finally turned me invisible!!!

His delirious delusions were short lived, shattered by Sleight's shout from back down the street.

"Oi Spink!"

Richie had three choices. Turn and fight; Stand and cower; or ignore and walk. At least *he would've had those choices* had his legs not, in an act of instinctive self preservation, continued to carry him away.

He rounded the street corner, and once out of Sleight's line of sight, broke into a sprint the entire way home. Richie Spink had dodged a bullet, a metaphorical one this time to be sure, but dodged it he had. Of course he would love to know what the hell had just happened, either way he was not sticking around to find out the "how's and whys."

When the hell did my life become an episode of the Twilight Zone?

133

Richie only stopped when he reached his front gate. He gripped it with both hands, gasping for air. He felt absolutely exhausted. Thank God it was Friday. Of course it was not every week that you dealt with the embarrassment of forgetting your games kit, fought in a World War II skirmish, seemingly beat your entire class in cross country AND fast walked your way out of a beating from your school yard nemesis. He was more than shattered, even his bones felt tired.

His limbs felt like dead weights as he trudged up the stairs and collapsed face first onto his bed. His home life had been falling apart for months now, so it seemed stupid to dream that the rest of his life should be any more stable. For a few moments, every crazy aspect of his ludicrous existence bounced around the four corners of his brain. Marc, Anna, Sleight, Will the moustachioed killing machine and The Eternal Flame of British Resistance all ran through his head, before gradually fading into the warm, comforting abyss of deep sleep.

Beside him the green LCD of his bedside alarm clock turned to 6:36pm. In the doorway of the room, the troubled face of his sister Kathy peered in at the snoring Richie. Although a weight of the world expression had become an increasingly common part of her facial repertoire, there was something more there this time. Behind her tired blue eyes was worry, confusion and a hint of fear. In her hand she thumbed an ageing piece of paper no bigger than A5 in size. From its overall condition it was clear that this gesture had been repeated many times before. Despite her concern, Kathy Spink thought better than to disturb her brother's slumber. With concerns unappeased and questions unanswered, she closed the door gently and left the comatose boy to his slumber…

CHAPTER TWENTY THREE: ANNA

It had been twenty minutes since Marc Townsend had swaggered through the glass doors of the local McDonalds looking like an extra from The Matrix. Had it been a movie, he would've entered in slow motion with his full length leather jacket flapping gracefully behind him, as the late afternoon sun glinted in the lenses of his Ray Ban sunglasses. Had the magical movie camera focussed on Anna's slim figure in the booth across the restaurant it would have captured her eyes slowly rolling to the heavens, paired with an annoyed sigh escaping from her pursed lips.

Christ... What has HE come as?

Over in another corner, a small group of tween girls with unbrushed hair, stripy tights and too much eye make up nearly swooned at his arrival. Their besotted looks turned to snarls in Anna's direction as he smoothly slipped into the vacant seat in front of her. For Anna's part, she was classically decked in her finest work clothes- black trousers, slip-on pumps but, sadly, minus the currently radiator-drying-at-home, black hoodie.

The thin metal chain that attached Marc's wallet to his belt loop clanged lightly against the metal frame of the chair. He raised his sunglasses to the top of his head, and gave Anna a wink designed to make her go weak at the knees. Just to be thorough, he dropped his voice half an octave, and let loose his dulcet tone upon her.

"The lovely Miss Harrison, to what do I owe the pleasure of this..." He paused for dramatic effect. "...invitation?" The emphasis on the final word, along with the addition of his trademark eyebrow raise, was executed to perfection.

Anna frowned.

"Err... Are you doing an Austin Powers impression?"

"What? No, I..." Realising that he was still using his deeper tone, he cleared his throat to return it to normal.

"I was just y'know, being funny." he continued, slightly flustered.

Amused at knocking him from his clearly well rehearsed stride, Anna was tempted to press the advantage. But animal cruelty wasn't in her nature, so instead she bit her lip and tried to put him at ease.

"Oh… Hahahaha." she replied, approximating a genuine laugh as best she could. It seemed to work, and Marc's aura of confidence returned. Not sure how to proceed, and too nervous to get straight to the point Anna decided to ease herself into conversation.

Just get the ball rolling, ask him a few general questions, and then coolly steer him towards the desired topic.

"So, was school okay?" she asked and almost cringed herself inside out.

Genius. "How to open conversation with questions only ever asked by parents" by Anna Harrison, available soon in all good bookstores.

Marc didn't seem phased by it.

"Oh y'know, just another day at *Shit*-worth Comp." he smiled, clearly delighted at working such a masterful witticism into his answer.

Anna smiled weakly, Noah had been passing *that* line around the ark. Not wishing to let conversation die off, she frantically tried to come up with another topic.

"So, I err… I like your coat."

Marc straightened the lapels with the thumb and forefinger of each hand. "What, this old thing? I picked it up in a boutique in L.A. The assistant told me that the Wachowski brothers bought all the coats for the third Matrix film from there. In fact…"

As Marc prattled on about the wondrous history of his one colour dream coat, Anna felt her attention begin to drain away.

Five minutes passed. Then ten. Then twenty. Twenty minutes of brain numbing self congratulatory posturing and "label chasing". The vast majority of Anna's wardrobe came from supermarkets, and in fact the only label she readily *did* splash the cash on was down to her fanaticism for Converse trainers. Showing such concern for the price and name of clothes was much more Katie's cup of tea.

Twenty *one* minutes.

God, doesn't he EVER stop!?

Anna was beginning to think that she'd made a mistake. In truth she'd begun to think that about four seconds after Marc's arrival, and as she mentally counted down the wasted minutes until she had to go to work the thought had become a concrete certainty. She was at the crossroads of sleep and storming out when Marc's self indulgent ramblings finally turned her way.

"...and I had this jacket that was just like the one Tom Cruise had in Top Gun, but Richie said I looked camp in it..."

Wait a second! Ooh ooh this is it!

"Richie?" Anna enquired innocently.

"Yeah I know, he wouldn't know fashion if it slapped him in the face, the poor, tasteless sod. I don't know why I even listened to him, I'll probably go back to wearing it, it is a cool jacket..."

"Yeah, the err... Top Gun is super. So what's HE into then?"

"Rich? God he couldn't tell Converse from Reebok Classics that boy. I've been banging on at him for years to take a bit of pride..." he continued.

"I don't mean clothes, I mean what is he into? What does he do for fun?"

"For fun?" He paused for a moment as though he was really considering the answer. "Well he usually comes over to mine to play computer games. I've got this MASSIVE monitor and the picture is..."

Keep going, stop him talking about himself...

"What type of games is he into?"

Marc shrugged, the line of questioning was not holding his attention. "Whatever's out y'know? Not big on sports though," he paused again. "In fact I think he's still playing those old 'Command and Conquer' games on that dust box he calls a PC".

Small, probably inconsequential facts, but all duly added to Anna's mental Richie Spink scrapbook.

"Does he ever... hang out anywhere?"

"Hahaha!" Marc slapped his thigh, and mock wiped away a tear from his eye. "Are you messing? Richie? Nah. He used to but, he's scared stiff of your mate Sleight and his cronies.

"He's not my..." Anna tried to interject

"Bless him, Jackson has been tormenting since Year 7. I keep saying he should just stand up to him. I mean for Christsake, have you SEEN the size of Richie, he's not exactly Jimmy Krankie is he? If he ever actually stood up straight for a change and worked up the bottle to go all George McFly and take a swing he'd probably knock that pituitary moron on his arse. God, what a day that would be. But nah, he'd rather hide in his bedroom, cryarse about his mum and dad's divorce and wear hand-me-down clothes. Still, at least he gets to bathe in my reflected glory..." Marc gestured to himself, half jokingly, but also three-quarters seriously.

Divorce?

Suddenly, Marc's finally insightful diatribe was halted by the soul crushing sound of Anna's mobile phone alarm. She let out an overly pronounced sigh as she withdrew it from her well-graffitied, maroon shoulder bag.

Just when he was FINALLY getting interesting...

Mobile phone alarms meant one of two depressing things, and as she'd already been to school it could only mean the other. It was time to go to work.

Oh well, plenty to unpack, even if it took an ice age to get there.

"Urgh, got to go to work." she said with an apologetic smile.

Marc's smile vanished momentarily, clearly not expecting this turn of events.

"Oh, really?" he said, checking his watch. "Already?"

"Yeah, sorry." she said, truly meaning it, though only because she'd have liked more time to grill him further. "As much as I'd love to stay and chat there is a building full of old people who aren't going to bathe themselves." she continued light-heartedly.

Marc's face contorted at the statement.

"Oh my god! *Really?*"

"Oh yeah, hundreds of 'em, festering away just waiting on my arrival." she said, wiggling her fingers in front of her wicked smile. Of course Anna had never bathed one of the residents before but it was fun to watch Marc squirm. In fact, at fifteen, it wasn't even technically work, just volunteering, but calling it work seemed to stop most of the questions about why she'd actually want to spend her time there.

Anna got to her feet and swung the black strap of her backpack over her shoulder. Marc looked it over, seeing that his date was coming to an abrupt end he sought out options. Mild relief washed over him when he picked out the hand drawn "Foo Fighters" logo amidst a ton of others scrawled on its surface.

"Hey, you like the Foo's?" he said as she stepped towards the door.

"Huh? Oh yeah, Dave Grohl, yummy."

"I've got a signed copy of their first album, you know? If you'd like, you can come round to mine tomorrow and I can show it you"

Anna mused over the proposal. The prospect of looking at a signature (even if it was from her second favourite musical

139

crush), was nowhere near enough a reward for putting herself through more of Marc's torturous company, but...

"Yeah, I'm not sure, will.. Richie be there?." she replied, seeing an opportunity presenting itself.

Elated with his last ditch save, Marc's smile returned, this time even wider than before.

"Huh, oh yeah probably, I mean it's not like he's got anywhere better to be..." he replied, oblivious to Anna's ploy.

He smoothly got to his feet, and in an equally smooth action took her hand, and brought it up for a gentlemanly kiss.

Anna heroically fought both her gag reflex and the instinct to snatch her hand back, run to the toilet, and scour it clean with bleach. Instead she returned it with a weak smile, and a shuffle towards the door.

"See you tomorrow then?" Marc beamed.

"Tomorrow." She nodded in confirmation and quickly made her way out, shuddering as she did.

Bleaurch! What a creep! Damn you Richie Spink you'd better be worth this!

Anna arrived at "work" a full hour before her shift. Her well intended plan of having her alarm go off early had been put in place to rescue her from terminally boring conversation. In true Wile E. Coyote fashion it had only served to blow up in her face. Now she was left with the choice of sitting in the freezing cold staff room with only a ten year old copy of "Chat" magazine for company, or seeking out the company of one of the "inmates", otherwise known as starting her shift early. Ten year old gossip about long past celebrity couples (Shock Affleck and J-lo split!!!), or more unpaid work. She sighed.

Sophie's choice...

Remembering her secondary mission for the day she opted for the latter. Standing in front of the beige staff room lockers, she slid off her back pack and held it up to examine the sewn patch that had been forced upon her by old man Wells. It was attached centrally, sewn tight below the zip. With the blue stitched flames licking around the clenched fist, it fit in really well alongside the ocean of rock and metal band icons. It was absolutely the kind of thing that she'd buy from the local goth shop, and even better, it was free! But if there was only one thing her wacky upbringing had brought her, it was a strong set of morals and taking the possessions of dementia suffering patients most definitely brought those morals into conflict.

Clutching the bag to her chest, she mindlessly rubbed the patch with her fingers as she strode down the corridor, postulating its origins. Although Anna had been volunteering at the nursing home since the summer she was really only now getting to know each of the fifty-two residents. Of course more than half of those were or had become "un-knowable," such was their mental and physical health. Over the past few months Frank Wells had gradually slipped into that category to the point that, as with last week's episode in the corridor, it was tough to get much from him at all. Anna found it very sad, particularly as she knew him to be the father of one of the teachers at her school, but also because when she had started there he was easily one of the most fascinating people she'd ever met. In those early weeks, when the culture shock of the working world was still frying her brain, Frank (as he'd insisted on her calling him) had really helped her through. None more so than the first time she'd had to deal with the passing of one of the residents.

Frank was kindly, charming and world wise. Whilst many of the other guests would prattle on endlessly about the most mundane of topics (*oh wow, another new grandchild Ethel!?*), she would sit for hours listening to his fantastical army stories. Of course she knew that he embellished his role in them, (according to her line manager Brenda, he had been a museum guard in a past life). Most of his yarns sounded more like something from one of those American comic books her brother used to cherish. But Frank Wells was nice and fun and

141

roguish at times and she didn't have the heart to correct him. Despite being in his eighties, he had remained in good physical shape, and though she doubted that he had really fought alongside some kind of real life World War Two superhero, she certainly believed that he'd been a hit with the ladies. He wasn't the only dementia sufferer under her care, but he was the one whose decline Anna had really taken to heart.

I wonder if Katie deals with this kind of stress at sweeping up hair at her Mum's salon?

Anna remembered how horrendous those places could be with all the Mum wags fighting for their curly blow time slots, decided that life was tough all over, and banished the thought from her brain.

With a little effort, she pushed through the heavy double doors of the corridor that lead to Frank's room. She had a mental list of questions for the elderly man, and hopefully more than enough time to get the answers she was looking for. Her reverie though was broken by the sounds of struggle and breaking glass reverberating off the painted brick walls and linoleum floors. Thirty yards down the way, a slender man in a grey trench coat and matching suit burst out of the door of Frank's room. Under one arm, he clutched a collection of small items. He wiped away blood from his lip with his free hand and spat a thick cob of it on the floor.

Anna stood frozen.

What the hell? What the hell!???

Without thinking, Anna reacted with a swell of anger.

"HEY! WHAT THE HELL DO YOU THINK YOU'RE DOING!?"

The man caught eyes with Anna briefly. They were dark and cold and sent a frozen chill down her spine. He winked at her and broke off into a sprint, clattering through the doors at the far end of the corridor and out of sight. As the doors swung shut she heard the sounds of commotion as the fleeing mystery man collided with one of the orderlies. The loud clanging of metal bed pans on the floor intermittently dampened as the doors swung back and forth, before settling closed.

Anna swung her backpack over her shoulder and charged towards Frank's door. It hung loosely off its hinges, splintered wood crunched under her feet as she entered. The room was a mess. Book shelves had been cleared, broken picture frames lay under foot amongst strewn pieces of yellowing paper and various trinkets. In the middle of it all, Frank Wells sat against the side of his bed, one arm clutching his ribs, the other lay limp, the elbow turned at an impossible angle. A giant welt was forming below his right eye, blood streamed from his nose and mouth. His breathing was shallow and strained. Anna recoiled at the sight,but managed to catch a scream before it reached her lips. Instantly composing herself, she threw her bag to the floor, and slid on her knees amongst the detritus alongside the wounded man.

"FRANK! Oh god, FRANK! Are you okay?!" she said, wanting to comfort him, but too scared to touch him for fear of aggravating his injuries.

The old man, struggling for breath, convulsed into a violent coughing fit. Speckles of blood stained Anna's white smock top. With clear effort, he looked up at the young girl, her pale face etched with concern.

"Don't…" he struggled, his words quiet, and obscured by the growing swell of his bloodied lips. He slowly, awkwardly removed his hand from his ribs and pointed across the room.

"Don't let them find it. Neil… Neil will know,"

"Try not to talk Frank, it'll be okay" Anna lied as the tears began to well up.

"No, no" The old man said, as he put his hand to the side of Anna's face. His blue eyes locked with hers, and Anna was taken aback by the fierce lucidity behind them. "Don't cry girl, this isn't the end, this is where it all begins, keep him

143

safe, keep the secret safe". He gestured weakly across the room one final time towards her bag, and the flaming fist patch that faced them.

"That boy saved us all..." Frank Wells wheezed. The lucidity dimmed, he smiled into the middle distance, and his final breath fell from his body. The man's gaze turned hollow, and his head slumped forward.

Anna, her face hot and wet with tears, gave his hand a squeeze, and began to sob. Turning her head away and wiping her cheeks with her sleeve, her head was a mess, filled to bursting with roiling, conflicting emotions, and Frank Well's final words. Sitting across the room, where the old army veteran had gestured lay Anna's rucksack. The Eternal Flame patch blurred with tears. Paramedics and orderlies burst in through the open doorway of the room, finally taking the door from its hinges. Shards of splintered wood arced gracefully from the door frame as the emergency workers scanned the devastation. Anna's focus remained on the bag, their voices were muffled to her, she felt numb to the hands guiding her to her feet, immune to their caring questions. Frank's final words echoed in her brain.

"Keep the secret safe... Neil will know..."

Pulling away from the gentle grip of two medics, Anna slumped back to her knees and scooped the bag up to her chest, squeezing it tight. The noise of the world came crashing back in, and this time the tears came unrestrained...

CHAPTER TWENTY FOUR: WELLS

A voice was speaking. It was telling Neil Wells something, but he could no longer make out what exactly was being said. Like the simplest of words repeated over and over again, the sound had become unrecognisable, almost alien to him. He was aware of a piece of solid plastic in his hand, pressed to his ear, but that was all he felt. The noise had created a numbness, a numbness that entered through his ear and spread all the way down to his toes, eating away at his emotions and senses along the way. The muffled, incomprehensible sounds became a monotonous background beat as his thoughts formed on a long past, childhood memory.

So many years ago in a simpler time, a young excitable boy climbed onto the lap of his heroic, mountainous father. He looked into the face of the man, saw the lines there that held a thousand stories, marvelled at the distant staring eyes that kept them guarded. He so wanted for his father to tell him a tale, to spin a great yarn about his secretive past or the romantic days of warfare. For what could be more exciting to one so young as something so revered by their elders? But before he could pluck up the courage, his mother would call him into the kitchen, chiding him with a warning to leave his world-weary father in peace. As the young boy, Wells headed towards rich smells, and the thick steamy air of the kitchen, casting a final glance back at his stoic father. But Wells the younger did not feel downhearted. As always, he would honour his mother's request. *After all, he knew that he could always ask for a story tomorrow…*

But fifty years worth of tomorrows had come to pass. With each, the potential promise of great life secrets revealed remained just that… potential.

Young Wells stood in a lush green field, a thick oak tree towering above him, the warm sun on his back. His mother and father's playful voices in-ear but out of sight. In his hands, a notebook. His fingers played over the worn, brown leather cover. A crack of lightning startled the boy. Jarred his senses. The roots of the tree began to twist and gnarl, the skies clouded, the voices shifted, deep and distorted. Wells screwed his eyes shut and clenched his teeth, the old notebook forgotten in his burst of terror, he clamped his hands to his ears.

The solid piece of plastic fell from the numbed grip of his fingers, away from his face, taking with it the muffled, maddening noise that permeated and corrupted his brainwaves. As it cascaded away to annihilation on the tiled floor beneath his feet, the sound cold and weightless.

Neil Wells' father was dead. With him a lifetime of stories and experience was lost to the ether.

The telephone receiver struck the floor, exploding into an infinitesimal shower of black plastic, green circuit board and the echo of words that he would take with him to the grave.

"I'm so sorry Mister Wells, someone will be in touch tomorrow to help make arrangements..." a distorted voice from the broken receiver spoke to no-one.

For Neil Wells and his Father there would be no more tomorrows...

CHAPTER TWENTY FIVE: BILL

"Who in the name of all bloody hell do you think you are, you egregious, muck-spouting oaf!?" Frederick Willerton-Smythe shouted, spitting out the question with righteous incredulity in Bill's direction. His face was barely a shade from bright purple such was the palpable rage spilling out from his normally pasty complexion.

Sitting back in a desk-side chair in the cramped infirmary office was Bill North; calm, composed, and faintly amused by the weaselish man's tirade. A slightly innocent look played across his rugged features, a deliberate response to his aggressor's demeanour, and one which only served to further exacerbate it.

"You come in here, with your, your," Smythe stabbed a finger down at Bill, "relaxed dress code, and, and non-regulation facial hair, and surly attitude and think you can denigrate MY role in THIS base!!"

Smythe began to pace the small room, which was scarcely a handful of steps between turns. The outraged man caught his foot on another chair, and stumbled slightly. Bill, using all his years of combat training, fought down the temptation to let out a laugh. Anticipating a reaction only furthered Smythe's cause, who swung out a boot and kicked the metal framed chair to one side. The clanging sound of metal on stone caused both men (and Bill knew, the two recruits listening on the other side of the door) to wince.

Willis' tirade had gone on long enough. As a soldier, Bill would've normally have ended it with a solid uppercut to the stomach, but in this instance a softer touch was required. Although not a man who *commonly* bowed to inter-company politics, Bill was aware that his position in the officer ranks required a softer touch.

"Wind yer neck in Willy."

Willerton-Smythe's eyebrows arched, and his nostrils flared.

"My name is…"

"I know what yer bloody name is son." Bill said, rising to his feet effortlessly to stand several inches taller than his counterpart. Smythe, anticipating physical confrontation, took a reflexive step back. Bill's demeanour however, remained calm. When he spoke, his tone was well measured; strong and direct without being loud. What he had to say was not for the suspected prying ears outside.

"Now, I want yer to listen to me very carefully, because I am only going to say this once…"

On the other side of the door, Privates Green and Welsh crouched below the eyeline of the frosted glass, straining to hear what would undoubtedly be the talk of the barracks that night. From across the room the bed bound Private Parkinson, sporting a fresh bandage on his damaged ankle, craned his neck to get an equally unrevealing vantage point.

"What are they saying?" he hissed.

Welsh's eyes widened in horror. He turned to his wounded comrade, jabbing a finger to his lips as his expression turned to a vague snarl.

"Shhh!"

Green shook his head jovially, far too amused by the situation unfolding to be scared of the consequences.

"The Captain is flipping his lid on Major North." he relayed in a hushed tone.

"What's he saying now?"

"He's saying I'm not surprised Green can't hear me, he's too busy talking to that soft lad Parky!"

Parkinson looked shocked, until he saw the wry smile on Green's face and finally registered the sarcasm. Green shook his head playfully and turned his attention back to the door. He pressed his ear up to it, and tried to tune back into the conversation within. His smile slipped to confusion, and then to panic.

"Christ!" he yelped and scrambled to his feet, motioning for Welsh to do the same.

The brass door handle turned and an enraged Captain Willerton-Smythe came storming out of the office. Green and Welsh reached their feet just in time and snapped to salute the balding man. The dutiful act was wasted on him, as he marched straight past them and out of the infirmary, muttering posh sounding obscenities as he did. The textured glass in the door rattled as he slammed it behind him.

Green and Welsh, who had turned their heads to follow, raised sceptical eyebrows.

"Well he was in a good mood wasn't he?" Green asked rhetorically. "And what do you think you're doing soft lad, playing hide and seek?" he asked Parkinson, who had pulled the bed sheet up over his head. The freckle faced young man sheepishly withdrew the thick green blanket, still cautious in case Willerton returned.

"Aren't you the big man?!" Green chided.

"Yeah, nice one Parky." Welsh added with a smirk.

Parkinson smiled weakly, an expression almost immediately transformed to fear. In a panic, he threw the blanket back over his head. Welsh looked over at Green with a puzzled expression. Green winced and hunched his broad shoulders. Comprehension dawned quickly on Welsh's freckled face as Bill North stepped between them.

"Second Lieutenants." he said coldly.

Welsh and Green snapped back to attention again.

"Sir!" they shouted in unison.

"Are we bored gentlemen?" Bill growled.

"No Sir!" they replied instantly without really considering the question.

"Really? Because it seems to me that young men such as yourselves who 'ave time to roll around on't floor listening to

149

conversations well above their rank, are young men who need more constructive ways to occupy themselves..." Bill continued gruffly.

Welsh, not one used to being dressed down, stood frozen, staring straight ahead. Green, whose cocky attitude had gotten him into more than his fair share of trouble grimaced, he knew what was coming.

"Which is an amazing coincidence because I've heard the shower room is in desperate need of some love and attention. Sounds perfect for two young men with some time t' kill ey lads?"

Green screwed his eyes together for a moment and fought down his instinct to argue back. Bill clearly sensed this. Despite his outwardly angry appearance, making Willerton lose his rag had actually put him in his best mood in weeks. He decided to test the young man's self control.

"Is there a problem with that Mister *Breen*?" Bill probed.

Having heard the earlier altercation between his commanding officers, Green knew exactly what his superior was trying to achieve by getting his name wrong. He knew that Major North was trying to goad him into reacting. He knew, but he reacted anyway.

"It's *Green* sir." he said through gritted teeth.

Still standing half a yard behind the pair, Bill was able to keep his smirk hidden from the recruits.

The fish has taken the bait.

"It's what?" Bill said flatly.

"Green, sir my name is G..." he said, trying to keep the irritation from his voice.

"Are you questioning me, recruit?" Bill pushed further.

Green opened his mouth to answer, but Bill continued over him, raising his voice to a loud growl.

"Don't you talk back t' me son, or I will put your bloody teeth down the back of yer throat, so help me god. Just for that, the pair of you can scrub the latrines first!"

Welsh's shoulders slumped and he let out a depressed sigh, which immediately drew Bill's wrath.

"Problem sunshine?" he growled into Welsh's ear. The dark featured man's posture returned instantly.

"N-no sir!"

"What about *you*?" Bill said, returning to Green.

The brief moment of distraction had allowed Green just enough time to get a grip on his emotions. He swallowed hard and squared himself back to attention.

"No Sir!" he replied.

"Sorry?" Bill asked, having one final push at Green's restraint.

"No SIR!"

"Job's a good 'un. Now you two love birds best get stuck in, the devil makes work fer idle hands."

"Yes Sir!" they responded.

"Good. Dismissed."

Without another word the pair hurried off. Bill shook his head and allowed himself another smirk. He'd laid the law down to both his pain in the backside second in command, and even the outspoken mister Green seemed to be coming around. Things were looking up.

"I'm sure the two musketeers could use a third, yev' a sore leg not a broken scrubbin' arm after all."

"Sorry sir." Parkinson whimpered from beneath his hastily pulled up bedsheet.

"You bloody will be…" Bill replied as he watched as the other two disappeared into the gloom of the basement corridor.

What 'ave you gotten yourself into this time William? Two months t' mould a bunch of kids, a moody superman, and a temper tantruming toff into something that won't get yer turned into Nazi dog food. Wonderful…

151

CHAPTER TWENTY SIX: ANNA and THE DETECTIVE

"He had on a grey trench coat and suit, and he had a bunch of Frank, I mean, Mister Wells' stuff under his arm. That's all I remember." Anna recounted.

"Are you sure that's everything? There are no other details you can recall? Because everything, no matter how inconsequential it may seem, can be important." Police Detective Sandford Kennedy said, his dark features matching his serious tone.

Anna squinted, trying against her better judgment to place herself back in the scene. She could see the cold, calculating look in the Grey man's eyes. The blood seeping from the corner of his mouth. "Wait, no, he was bleeding," Anna said, "He, he, spat some on the floor." She opened her eyes again.

"Are you sure?" The Detective asked quizzically as he flicked threw his pocket sized notepad. "Only, there's no mention of it in the report."

Anna played it out in her mind again. She was certain she'd seen him spit on the floor, but then again.

"Oh, well, I was sure I saw him, well…"

"It's okay Miss, it was an incredibly emotional incident, the mind has a way of playing tricks."

"Y-yeah." Anna stammered, deterred, but not entirely convinced.

I'm sure he did…

"No bother at all, you've been a big help. What you did was incredibly brave." The Detective continued, there was a light Northern Irish twang to his accent that he had clearly spent years trying to suppress. "Thank you for your time Miss Harrison, if we need anything else from you we'll be in touch." he added with a kindly smile.

Anna nodded and returned the smile weakly as the Officer got to his feet, brushing off the light creases in his dark blue suit as he did so. She sat with her feet tucked under her on the cheap, black leather sofa, in her mother's garishly furnished living room, the bric-brac graveyard. She hugged a faded pink fluffy cushion to her chest and stared blankly at the empty space vacated by the Detective on the matching sofa across the room. Out in the hallway, her father's muffled voice carried as he said goodbye to the officer and closed the front door.

Anna felt numb to everything but the touch of the soft, worn cushion clutched tightly in her arms. It had been hers since birth and despite her ever-maturing teenage outlook it remained an integral part of her bedroom to this day. It was the closest thing she had to a security blanket, but try as she might right now it brought her little comfort. In her time at Humberidge House Nursing Home she'd had the heartbreaking misfortune of seeing several of its residents pass on, but this was different. Frank hadn't *just passed away*, *he'd been murdered; Murdered by a man who had then run away right in front of me! Arrgh!*

Anna gripped the cushion in frustration. Despite her best intentions she replayed the incident in her head once more. The slender man, his menacing look, spitting a cob of blood on the floor. She was SURE he'd spat on the floor!

But they'd surely have found some evidence if he did…

Anna's mental playback was interrupted by her Dad entering the room. Tom Harrison was a middle aged man of average height and skinny build, with a world-worn face and kind eyes. He ran a hand over his thinning hair as he checked the watch on his other wrist. He winced as he took in the information, and Anna knew what he was going to say before the words began to form.

"I'm really sorry 'Belle, but I've got to go to work" he said, his face showing just how genuinely heartbroken he was to be leaving his daughter at such an inopportune time. "Your mum should be back in an hour or so, will you be okay 'til then?"

Her Dad had worked at the hospital all of her life, long enough for her to know that no amount of pleading, or tantruming had ever kept him from his shift. So she put on a brave face and nodded. She always found it tough, but had a profound respect for his commitment to his patients. Her father smiled, desperately proud of his beautiful daughter's resilience. He leaned down and kissed Anna on the top of her head, and for the briefest of moments she felt comforted.

"Are you still coming over to the flat next weekend?" he asked tentatively.

She nodded again.

"Great, we'll rent one of those horror films if you want, the ones your mother really hates" he said cheerily. Anna nodded again.

"Cool, well if you need me for anything just ring the hospital. Love you 'Belle, see you soon. Be cool."

"Cheers Dad, love you. You be cool too…" Anna said, the childhood nickname doing a slightly better job of consoling her than the cushion.

Tom Harrison's smile failed to hide the worry in his face as he closed the door behind him. Whilst his divorce from Anna's mother had only recently been finalised, the couple had separated for a couple of years. Anna's elder brother had taken it badly, so much so that they hadn't spoken in that entire time. The situation had left Thomas with the gnawing fear that his relationship with Anna might go the same way. She *seemed* to be coping well enough, he knew his daughter was made of sterner stuff. But as a hospital nurse of twenty years, he had seen the full gamut of human emotion, enough to know that often it was the ones who complained the least that were those in the most pain.

From the driver's seat of the luxury black Mercedes, Detective Kennedy watched as Mr Harrison unchained his pushbike from a lamppost outside the house and cycled away.

From the back seat, a croaky voice spoke over the gentle hiss of an oxygen tank.

"What... did the girl... see?" The Grand Leader asked, before putting the transparent mask back to his face with a gaunt, shaking hand.

The Detective adjusted his rear view mirror. The Leader was seated beside a slender man in his early twenties, with cold dark eyes, and a cut on his lip. Nathaniel Greymalkin.

"Nothing that can incriminate our hot headed friend here"

Greymalkin reacted with a cocky grin. "You *see*, I told you I was careful. It was a complete *waste* of my time anyway, killing some geriatric for what? Nothing. Two stitches for a bunch of tat that the plebs at a car boot sale wouldn't touch." He gently touched a finger to his lip.

"You weren't careful, you got lucky." Kennedy snapped back. "Your brash, arrogant, and downright stupid approach could well have drawn the full attention of the Police down upon our organisation!" he continued, keeping his voice low and tone measured in spite of his clear displeasure at the younger man's attitude. "You're just lucky that I caught the case first."

"Just because you think you're too good to get your hands dirty, don't give me your sanctimonious claptrap, there's nothing wrong with my methods, the old man just caught me by surprise!" Greymalkin retorted, a sharp edge to his Eton-schooled pronunciation.

"You left a DNA sample at the scene of the crime. If I hadn't gotten rid of it before forensics arrived you'd be bang to rights you snot nosed..."

"Quiet, the both of you!" The Leader snapped, belying his physical frailty, and shocking both Kennedy and Greymalkin into silence. "That you... were fortunate not to be

155

identified... is not in question... Master Nathaniel. What *is* in question... however is whether or not this girl... holds any other pertinent information... with regards to our quest... for the 'Guardian of the Flame.'

Nathaniel Greymalkin crossed his arms, and slid lower in his black leather seat, but said nothing more.

"And you," The Leader addressed Kennedy with a low hiss. "Do not get ideas... above your station *Detective*... Such skills of deception... are part of why The Order helped you... attain your station... and you'd do well... to remember that. You have been a faithful servant... but you are not blood."

The Detective took a deep breath. "Yes sir."

"Good," The Leader said through his mask, taking a pained, shallow breath. "Now... continue your report."

Detective Kennedy nodded taciturnly, "The girl is in shock, more than likely a result of seeing an old man beaten to death," Detective paused to look at Greymalkin, who stared intently at the floor.

"But you suspect more?" The Leader asked.

"It is my belief that she may have held a deeper connection to the deceased, one that warrants further investigation." Kennedy finished.

"Good, good." The Leader replied, "And what... of the other link... the son... the teacher?"

"Clearly our strongest lead. Although preliminary investigations tell me that this teacher and his father were not close. An orderly at the home told me that his visits had been sporadic at best."

"What orderly?" Greymalkin asked incredulously.

"The one I spoke to on the telephone earlier. Not all information needs to be beaten out of people." he said, obviously baiting his younger counterpart. Greymalkin opened his mouth to reply, but was stopped by the bony, raised hand of The Grand Leader.

"Excellent work… Mister Kennedy. Now… the hour is late… I feel… It is time for me to retire. I want you both… to focus your surveillance… on the teacher… I have a feeling he… will lead us to our goals."

"As you wish, my Leader." Kennedy and Greymalkin said in unison.

Kennedy readjusted the rear view mirror and with a turn of the key, the car's engine purred to life. As he pulled the vehicle smoothly away from the curb, he thought back over the day's events. Following the teacher certainly made sense, but he was sure the girl still had an important role to play somehow. More worryingly though was the attitude of Greymalkin. Sanford Kennedy had been in The Grand Leader's employ now for over thirty years, a loyal servant to the man, and a fervent devotee to the Order of The Flame. He'd worked hard for the cause, a loyal and diligent soldier, but he was not born to the role. The Kid was. Nathaniel Greymalin was part of a bloodline, a heritage, a privilege. If Kennedy was a trapeze artist who had grown up without a net, Greymalkin was one who'd grown up being told that there would *always* be one. That made him dangerous. Sandford Kennedy would watch the teacher AND the girl, but he'd also have to make sure he kept one eye on his blue blooded protege too. He'd come too far to let it blow up on him now…

CHAPTER TWENTY SEVEN: RICHIE

"Change, change, change, *change.*" Richie repeated. Standing topless and sockless before his bedroom mirror he clenched and unclenched his bony hands into fists. As the sinews in his skinny forearms tensed, frustration crept into his tone. He had been at it for the best part of twenty minutes, and thus far all he had achieved was annoyance and dry mouth.

"*Change,* CHANGE, CHANGE! *CHAAAAAANNNNGE! Oh SOD IT!!!*"

he shouted and lashed out his left foot in anger, accidentally smashing it against the wall in front of him. The mirror wobbled, and Richie collapsed to the thinning carpet in agony, clutching his mangled big toe.

Stupid! Stupid! STUPID!

Richie groaned as waves of nauseating pain shot up his leg. His blood began to boil as the realisation, not only of the pain he had caused himself, but of the helplessness of his situation collapsed in on him.

What the hell is happening to me? Why can't I control it? Why am I so STUPID!!!"

His face felt hot, he ground his teeth and screwed his eyes closed.

"Well that fight was only ever gonna end badly." a familiar voice chided him. Through the pain, and one eye, Richie looked up to its source. With a beaming smile of white teeth his sister peered around the door.

"You're s'posed ta kick balls, not *walls* silly." Kathy said in the sugary sweet American cheerleader voice she reserved for such mickey taking situations. She gave one of her infectiously wicked laughs, and in spite of his damage, Richie managed a pained chuckle too. His sister stepped into the room, and sat down on the edge of the unmade bed, in one hand she held a paperback book, and in the other was a package. She set them both down beside her, and tucked a stray strand of freshly dyed, bright red hair behind her ear. The plethora of bracelets on her pale wrist slipped down her wrist and she reflexively readjusted them before Richie could see what was beneath. Smiling again, even more broadly than before, she shook her head at the crumpled heap of brother at her feet.

Richie gingerly let go of his wounded appendage, and taking deep breaths, stretched out his long, gangly frame to lie flat on the floor. Once he was sufficiently composed he turned his head towards his sister, who judging by the grin on her face was finding his discomfort highly amusing.

"What are you smirking at?"

"What? Me?" she said with mock innocence.

"Yes you, grinny. I'm lying here wounded, and you laugh!"

Kathy bit her lip, trying to contain the urge to laugh again.

"I mean, I'm gonna have to have my bloody toe amputated and you're just…

Laughter bubbled up, and burst out of Kathy's mouth uncontrollably. "Ha Ha Ha HA!!"

"Oh yeah you just laugh it up chuckles! I'm gonna lose my foot, and all you can do is…"

Kathy began to ROAR with laughter. Tears streamed down her face. "HAA HAA HAAAA!!!"

"Oh, I'm *deliiiighted* that my life threatening pain is so amusing to you…"

Kathy clamped both hands to her mouth, trying to contain herself. Tears still ran down her cheeks and over the black nail varnish on her fingers, her shoulders began to shake.

Kathy's taste in fashion, music and men might've been in a state of flux in recent years, but Richie knew that some things never changed. Kathy was the single worst person on earth to have around when you hurt yourself. It wasn't that she didn't care, far from it, she was just a sucker for physical comedy. She knew it, her friends knew it, and Richie knew it.

The time Richie fell out of the tree and fractured his wrist; the time Richie got hit in the face with a cricket ball; the time he had slipped on a roller skate and banged his head on the coffee table. Yes it *had* been Kathy who'd been there and helped him- but only after she'd "*gotten the laughter out of her system*".

He knew it was her weakness, and that no matter how much pain he was in, and whatever else was going on in her life, she would find it hilarious. As a kid it annoyed him, but now he played up to it. The flipside was that if someone else had inflicted the pain upon him, she'd be the first to stand by his side. Richie enjoyed making Kathy laugh either way and with the household turmoil of the last few months he knew it best to take the opportunities when they presented themselves. No matter how painful.

He shook his head and smiled as he watched her composure begin to return. Kathy was taking deep breaths and fanning her eyes with one hand. The bracelets slipped down her forearm again, revealing a tattoo of a flaming skull, and a white bandage wrapped around her wrist. Richie bristled at the sight, knowing all too well what it was there to cover up. It reminded him that he wasn't the only one struggling to cope with their domestic "situation". With only a few years between them, Richie and Kathy had been at each other's throats since childhood, but the parental issues over the last year had served to really bring them together. "A unified front against the parental units" Kathy had called it. His big sister had a funny way with words that Richie really admired, not that he'd tell her that, regardless of how close they'd become. So he kept laughing, better to stay in the moment.

Suitably composed Kathy wiped her face dry with the bottom of the black vest top she wore, revealing her glinting belly button ring.

"So what are you up to, you know, aside from getting kicks from a dying man?" Richie asked with a wry smile.

Kathy chuckled again. "Oh not much." she replied. "Dad's gone out- the pub probably, and the Ice Queen has hit the glad rag trail once more with her plastic friend."

The Ice Queen was one of Kathy's many barbed names for their mother, and a clear indicator of who she backed in the ongoing marital battle. It was an opinion that she often broadcast to anyone liable to offer an ear. For his part, Richie didn't see it as that cut and dry. He loved both of his parents, and despite his sister's attempts to coerce his thoughts on the matter, Richie was at heart a blue sky thinker. No matter how bleak the situation seemed, he still held out hope for their reconciliation.

"...And I just thought" she continued, "I'd check in, see how my not so little bro was holding up." she gestured towards the flat out Richie. "But *clearly* everything is just peachy! I mean presuming your wall kicking came about through a mistimed step in your 'happy dance'?" She continued sarcastically.

Richie pulled a tongue at her. "Yeah, I'm okay, just got some stuff going on at the mo."

"Hmm, tell me about it." Kathy replied, unconsciously rubbing the bandage on her wrist.

Not wishing to discuss his stresses further, Richie pounced on the opportunity to change the subject. "How about you? What's uni like?"

"Hell." she said instantly. "Well, not hell exactly, but let's put it this way, what was the last book you read?"

"Err... I can't remember" Richie lied, not wanting to admit to his sister that it was a Star Trek book written by William Shatner to his Literature-student sister.

"Well either way I bet you read it a) Because you wanted to and b) You read it at your leisure, for sheer enjoyment of the thing."

"Yeah." Richie nodded.

Captain Kirk versus the Borg was pretty sweet to be fair.

"Well when you do 'Lit' at Uni you do the exact opposite. You get given these godawful, ancient English tomes that stopped being relevant when god invented the computer, ram them down your throat and make you write "War and Peace"-length essays deconstructing their 'deeper meanings' and 'social significance'"

Kathy let out a sigh. "I swear, if I had a time machine I would use it for the sole purpose of going back in time and strangling the Bronte sisters... Speaking of which..."

Kathy got reluctantly to her feet, picking up the book beside her. She waved it ruefully. "I've got about, oooh..." She mimed looking at the time, "twelve hours to read Jane Eyre AND write a two thousand word essay extolling its virtues. *Fun*!!!" she said, crossing her eyes and hugging the book to her chest for emphasis.

"What's it about?"

"Huh? Oh, some bang average girl who has to face loads of mad challenges in life."

"Sounds familiar."

"Don't I know it."

"Well, if you use that line, you've only got..." Richie bit his lip as he did the mental calculations, "one thousand, nine hundred and eighty six more words to go."

"Ever the optimist." she said with a tired smile. "Anyway, smell ya later." Kathy said playfully as she walked back to the door. "Oh, I nearly forgot, that package came for you before..." She gestured towards the bed where it lay. "It looks wrecked though, I thought I told you to stop buying things from people with bad feedback on Ebay?"

Richie shrugged, "but they're soooooo cheap!" replied with a knowing smile.

Kathy shook her head playfully.

"Hey Kath."

"Yeah?" She stopped in the doorway.

"If you could travel back in time, what would you do?"

"Apart from eviscerating the Bronte's?" she laughed. "Probably just find myself a nice quiet place, away from everyone and just… live. No parents, no immature guys, no pointless literature. Yeah, that would be nice."

"Would you tell anyone?"

"Not a soul. Well…" She winked. "Maybe I'd find a little space for my wall-Karate loving little bro."

"Cheers Kath, enjoy the book."

Kathy crossed her eyes, smacked the book on her head and laughed as she closed the door behind her.

Richie smiled at the door for a few moments, digesting what she'd said before remembering the package. From his floor bound position, Richie looked up at the bed that was across the room. A yellowing paper corner overhanging the mattress was all that was visible.

Don't actually remember ordering anything off ebay…

Gingerly, he sat up, bringing the mystery package, and his messy bed into clearer view. Richie's mind ran over the possibilities as he got to his feet, and hobbled over. He sat down beside the package and carefully picked it up.

It was thick, yellow paper of about ten by seven inches, with whatever it contained making it a few inches thick. The paper was old, damaged and slightly dusty. The four corners were dog eared and worn. Written in smudged black ink was his name and address, and in the top right corner were several strange postage stamps. They were blue, with white trim, and bore the words "Postage Revenue" either side of a man's face. Never having seen a stamp without the Queen's head Richie knew he had no idea what country they came from.

Somewhere that speaks English though…

He dismissed the riddle as unsolvable and gently turned the package over, with all the careful precision of a master Christmas present hunter. Richie's eyes widened in surprise.

163

On the flipside, across the fold, was a blob of red wax, no more than an inch in diameter. Pressed into its centre though was the imprint of an insignia- a circle containing a flaming fist. Richie nearly dropped it.

"Holy Hell!" He exclaimed out loud.

He gulped and stared down, mystified at the package in his pale, bony hands. His softly, softly approach abandoned, he tore quickly through the tatty packaging to reveal its contents. Discarding the shredded paper to the floor, Richie held a simple wooden box in his hands.

The box in itself was unremarkable. It was made of rough, untreated pine, and had a number of superficial dents and dings to its surfaces. It bore no obvious markings, but it reminded him of a dominoes box, albeit about twice as wide. On the top surface was a thinner piece of wood, several millimetres thick, with a slight groove cut into it at one end presumably for grip. As he manoeuvred to slide the lid open, Richie found that his hands were shaking.

Christ...

He held one of the trembling appendages up to eye level. He made a fist, opened it and then shook it. The incredibly scientific approach seemed to do the trick, the shaking faded and he slid the box open.

Inside was an envelope, several shades lighter than the exterior packaging, but yellowing with age none-the-less. He placed the box back down beside him, and withdrew the envelope. It was, for all intents and purposes, like any other envelope he'd encountered in his fifteen years. "RICHARD" was inscribed on it in faded blue inked capitals. Richie's head swam, and his mouth was dry. It was then that he realised he'd been holding his breath. He let the breath out, took in another and couldn't help but chuckle at himself. It helped to ease his nerves. He flipped the envelope over nimbly in his slender fingers. It too was sealed with the Eternal Flame insignia in red wax. Not wishing to ruin this one as he had the previous, Richie opted to tear the side open. He cringed as his clumsy attempts tore too far into the paper, damaging the contents. A sufficient hole made, Richie slid his fingers inside, clamping the letter. He felt a rush of adrenaline at its touch.

Oh my god, this is it, answers at last!

He withdrew the folded sheet and paused a moment, savouring the last moments of ignorance. He licked his lips, brushed his fringe away from his eyes and carefully unfolded the letter. In the middle of the sheet, in the same blue ink as the envelope was a solitary paragraph.

RICHARD, I KNOW YOU ARE LOOKING FOR ANSWERS, BUT I'M AFRAID I CANNOT GIVE THEM TO YOU.
DESTINY IS ITS OWN MASTER, AND WE ARE BUT SLAVES TO IT. WE ARE THE ETERNAL FLAME, AND YOU SHOULD ACT ACCORDINGLY. WELLS HAS THE PATCHES. THE KEY TO THE LAST OF THE POWER IN THIS TIME.

FIND HIM.

Yours Faithfully,
TT.

He flipped the page over, it was blank. He held it out in front of him, to the light from his window. Nothing.

The page slipped from Richie's fingers. His nostrils flared and a scowl formed on his pasty features.

THAT's IT!!!???

"THAT'S BLOODY IT!!!!!???" he cursed, a fury building inside him.

"URRGH!!!" Richie threw the wooden box across the room. It struck the radiator beneath the windows with a loud

CLANG! He jumped to his feet to deliver a follow up beating, but in doing so, excruciatingly stubbed his bruised toe on the floor. Like a felled sapling Richie fell forwards. As the worn red carpet came rushing up to greet him, he clamped his eyes shut and waited for his face to stop his inexorable descent. It never came. He felt his equilibrium loop-de-loop, his stomach churn, and then a gentle breeze. That was it, no skull versus floorboard slams, not even so much as a carpet burn, just a gentle breeze, and the pleasant aroma of nature. He tentatively teased open an eye. The sight caused him to instantly open the other.

"Whoa..." he exclaimed in the deep, manly voice of The Eternal Flame.

He was standing in a lush, green field beneath a clear blue sky. Atop the long grass was the faintest hint of frost. Some two hundred yards ahead across the clearing was a dense wooded area, thirty yards behind him, the same. He took in a lungful of clean, countryside air and then let it out slowly. The slight cloud of condensation it made, coupled with the frost told him that it was cold, though he couldn't actually feel it.

Must be this heavy uniform... He supposed, though again it *looked* but didn't *feel* heavy.

He took a few more breaths and felt his troubles melt away. A city boy born and bred Richie had never been in such a calming, peaceful environment. The closest he had back home was the park, but that was usually frequented by Sleight and his cronies, not factors one would look for in a calming place. *So* relaxed had Richie become that he hadn't even begun to question exactly where he was, or why he was there. And in truth he didn't care, all he wanted was to...

"Oi! Flame, what yer doin son?" came a shout from behind, disturbing her reverie.

Richie craned his muscular neck around, feeling the mask covering the upper part of his face shift slightly as he did.

"Eh?" he replied eloquently, before he recognised who the voice belonged to.

"*Will?* Is that you?!" Richie shouted back.

"Keep yer bloody voice down will yer?" Will responded in a loud, yet purposely hushed tone. "Christ!"

There was a rustling in the undergrowth, and Will's head came into view. He was wearing his now familiar uniform, this time with added camouflage in the form of face paint and bits of fresh, green foliage. He muttered something under his breath that would make a bin man blush and quickly made his way over to Richie. The wiry man kept himself low and alert as he did so, with his rifle in both hands, trained on the tree line ahead.

"That you Richie lad?" he asked without taking his eyes from the horizon.

"Y-Yes sir, it's me, what's going on sir?" Richie asked, trying not to let his fear show. Seeing someone as deadly as Will in such a serious mood had ended any notions of peace. A knot had formed in the pit of his stomach, and it was tightening by the second.

"Long story short: through that clearing is a Jerry strong hold and inside it is something I want. Now, the plan had been to send the Flame into those woods first to take out any traps or hidden sentries. So that's what we're going to do right?"

"But I, I don't know how to do… I don't understand… I can't I'm…" Richie blustered, his panic rising.

"Now, now lad, don't worry, it'll be 'raight'. I'll go with yer, all you need to do is listen to what I say, and…"

A GUN SHOT RANG OUT from the trees, the bullet kicked up a tuft of sod an inch in front of Richie's foot. A flock of birds scattered up into the sky.

"AHHH!" Richie screamed, pulling his foot away in a squeamish reflex.

167

"Bastard!" Will swore as he aimed his rifle at the origin of the shot and squeezed the trig…

ANOTHER SHOT RANG OUT! It struck Will in the chest with a splatter of blood, and knocked him onto his back.

"WILL!!!" Richie exclaimed in horror, as several German troops came storming into the clearing with a blood curdling war cry!

"ATTACK!!!" came a shout from the other side, as four British soldiers burst out from their hiding places, rifles cracking off a flurry of shots.

"Oh my god, oh godohgodohgod! Will! What's happening!? Will? WILL!!!" Richie shouted amid the deafening gunfire. "What do I do!? What do I do!???"

Like in so many situations he'd faced in his short life, Richie Spink was out of his depth, and as his pleas for help were drowned out by the sound of gunfire he thought back to the letter.

What would the Eternal Flame do?

CHAPTER TWENTY EIGHT: THE ETERNAL FLAME

The Eternal Flame opened his eyes to searing pain. Everything hurt. Red spots swam across his vision. He tried to focus on the pain, to locate it, to block it out. The Flame was no stranger to pain, but it had been more than a decade since he had felt it for anything as mundane as a stubbed toe. He gritted his teeth and ran through the mantra that had helped drag him through the dark days of boot camp and beyond.

Get up, get in it, get on it, get through it...

He repeated this until the pain began to subside, and his vision cleared. Another change had clearly happened- it didn't take a genius to figure that out. Although The Flame had a rudimentary idea of when and where they were going to occur, years of training had taught him to obsess over fine points: Mere moments earlier he had been in a field near the French-Belgian border, now he was face down on a warm, thinning, red, and all too familiar carpeted floor. With some effort he peeled his grazed cheek off of the polyester fibres, and manoeuvred his frail form into a seated position. He was in the bedroom.

My bedroom... he mentally corrected himself.

Although the change had once again left him hazy, he knew well enough that failing to prepare was preparing to fail. The army had taught him to adapt to all circumstances, but his rather disastrous early forays into this world had taught him that he needed to be better, adapt quicker. For all intents and purposes he was awkward teenager Richie Spink again, and it would not do for anyone to suspect otherwise.

At least not yet...

The Flame propped himself up against the bed, and assessed his physical condition. Superficially there was the faintly moist graze on his right cheek, a similar one on his bare right shoulder, and a mild headache. He stretched his

169

gangly legs out, keeping his feet together. This allowed him to thoroughly verify what his pain receptors had told him already. The big toe on his left foot was badly bruised, and given how raw the pain felt, coupled with the situation he had "arrived" in, he knew it had happened recently. He allowed himself a thoughtful smile. His memories in this time were a blur; a broken collection of ill-fitting jigsaw pieces. But as he looked around the room, at the shelves of dusty toys, creased posters on the walls, and at the sticker-covered furniture, the brief flashes of recognition gave him an overriding sense of comfort. It was a simpler life, and one he wished to explore more. He tried to lean into his own memories, to piece them together, but the harder he tried to gather his thoughts, the further apart they fell. The familiar walls around him crumbled and smashed, above him the dark sky filled with streaks of light, and explosions and screams.

The Eternal Flame shook his head, annoyed by his break in focus. The mission needed his full attention. He returned his gaze away from the nostalgia and back to his right foot. Under and around the nail was already a deep purple, and from his field medicine training he knew that to be a good indication of a break or ligament damage, but with a scientific wiggle of the wounded appendage he assessed himself as fit to resume his duties. He jumped to his feet. The pain shot up his leg and The Flame winced in surprise. Again, he forced a smile through the wince. Chronologically speaking it hadn't actually been that long since he'd been just an ordinary man, but it was still a shock to his re-settling senses.

To his relief the toe began to move. With several more attempts it began to move more freely, and with less discomfort.

Just bruised. Good.

With the risk of permanent damage minimal and the pain manageable, The Flame paced on the spot. A rustling noise drew his attention to the torn, brown paper beneath his bare feet. He stepped off it, noticing a folded sheet of off-white paper that had been slightly behind him, atop the shreds. Putting his weight onto his right foot, he bent to retrieve it. Limping slightly he made his way over to the bay windows to look out over the unkempt garden below. The grass was overgrown into the surrounding borders, which themselves contained a variety of untended plants and dead shrubs. A faint smile crept in at the corners of the Flame's mouth. It lasted barely a moment, to be replaced by wide eyed shock as he unfolded the piece of aged paper and read.

"What in the name of hell?!" The Flame said, his teenage voice wavering on the word "name".

The words written there were impossibly familiar. Familiar because the writing was unmistakably his own.

But that's... that's impossible.

He held the paper at arms length, as though a shift in perspective would give him some sort of greater understanding.

I've never written this! Unless...

Forgetting the pain in his toe he rushed two steps across the room and dropped to his knees before the discarded brown paper. The Flame frantically turfed through the shreds, searching for a tell tale sign.

It doesn't make any sense! It doesn't make...

And there it was. A blue stamp, with its unmistakable profile picture of King George VI, but even more telling was the hand stamp over and around it. The red ink had smudged making the date and postal office unreadable, but not the year. Even without the benefit of his enhanced sight, that was as clear as day.

"Nineteen Forty...Five?!" he exclaimed. "But it's not possible, that's... the future..."

His eyes narrowed as he contemplated that revelation.

He examined the envelope further and, gathering several pieces, put together the hand-written address. This writing

171

was also familiar, he couldn't place how, but this time it was definitely not his own.

Curious… So I wrote the letter, WILL WRITE the letter, but it won't be me who posts it… hmmm.

Suddenly, a bolt of clarity hit him, like a nagging intuition turned fact. He turned his head back towards the windows, to the radiator beneath them, to the small wooden box on the floor beside it. On hands and knees he crawled over to it, and picked it up with both unblemished hands. He turned it over and looked inside. The wooden bottom to it was askew, but this did not correlate to its exterior shape. He tilted the box, and felt a loose object slide down its length.

A false bottom?

With thumb and forefinger he gripped the rough edge of the wood and yanked it out. Another letter, in a pristine, but again, yellowed envelope. Above the vaguely familiar address was a name, black inked in his own familiar scrawl.

"Mister Neil Wells" The Flame sounded out as he read. He withdrew it from the box, the rich, musty scent filling his nostrils. Beneath the envelope was a small metal object, a crescent shape. One end was thinner and jagged, and The Flame pricked his finger as he withdrew it for closer inspection. It was a silver signet ring, or it had been. Now it was roughly cut in half, as though the sheers or cutters used hadn't been quite sharp enough for the job. On the inside of the ring the words "SED OMNIBUS" were inscribed, on the circular signet, though warped by the cut, the Flame recognised his own insignia.

Fascinating…

The Eternal Flame got to his feet again and strolled awkwardly over to the bedroom mirror, a puzzled look replaced by one of quiet confidence settled on Richie's face, *his face.* A mystery wrapped in another mystery. His toe hurt and his memory was a bag of broken glass but his next step had become crystal clear.

There's only one man who can help me now...

CHAPTER TWENTY NINE: WELLS

Wells the younger cowered in the darkened space beneath the stairs. The musty smell of boot polish and muddy wellington boots filled his sensitive nostrils. He pushed himself deeper into the darkness, away from the thunderous noises in the kitchen next door. The booming bassy bellow of his fathers voice. The screeching tearful replies of his dear mother. A shatter of glass. The door opens and light spills in, blinding the boy in his darkened cocoon. The hulking figure of his father, a tin box in hand, wrenching open the back door and storming out into the cold night air. The comforting yet tear streaked face of his dearest mother, her warm eyes fixed upon him, reaching for the small, frightened and confused boy beneath the stairs. "Shhh, my darling, don't cry. They can't hurt us any more…"

The piercing, rattling bell of Wells' antique bedside alarm clock startled him awake. In his haze he reached out, with a shaky left hand, and turned it off. As he pulled it back towards the covers, its grasp fell upon a small open whiskey bottle. He pulled it in, and within the warm embrace of his bed, took an extended swig, replaced it on the table, and drifted back off to sleep.

His fitful dreams spat back horror filled surrealities, his father's life in corrupted black and white film, his mothers screams, bloodied knuckles, blue flame, and the sounds of digging…

CHAPTER THIRTY: THE ETERNAL FLAME

With the letter to Neil Wells set aside, The Flame finished reading through the open letter to/from himself, absorbing the cryptic message contained within.

"Are you okay?" a muffled female voice came through the door. The voice jolted his muffled brain like a bolt of lightning.

"Err, yes, I'm fine. I just… fell."

There was a momentary pause, and the Flame felt his heart race. He hoped his answer was sufficient, he had not mentally prepared himself for any social interaction.

"You divvy!" came the laughing reply. "Well anyway, I'm going out for a bit, try not to kill yourself while I'm gone!"

"Okay. Thank you." was The Flame's stilted response.

He waited for a few moments, listening to the footsteps descending the stairs followed by the front door opening and closing. He allowed himself to relax. The Flame had faced down German tanks, but a simple near run in with Richie's sister had left his nerves in shreds. He let out a deep sigh, and composed himself. He hadn't become the man he was by sitting around feeling sorry for himself. Careful not to put too much weight on the injured toe, The Flame got tentatively to his feet. He walked gingerly over to the bedroom mirror and inspected himself. He couldn't say with any certainty how long this change would last, but he knew that as a trend they seemed to be getting longer. His early forays in this time had been somewhat hazy and unplanned. This time his head felt clearer, it was time to take positive action.

It took him the better part of twenty minutes, but The Eternal Flame managed to locate some respectable clothing amid the drawers of tatty t-shirts and ill-fitting jeans, although his attempts to find a pair of matching socks had proved frustratingly fruitless. He reappraised his appearance. From the fitted, round necked black jumper, to the navy blue jeans and right down to the black Doc Marten shoes- all new and unworn at the back of the wardrobe. The Flame instantly felt far happier with what he saw. Though was slowly re-acclimating to the role of teenager, he saw no reason not to utilise some of the discipline garnered during his adult years. Something was still amiss however, and his focus was drawn to Richie's messy mop of hair. He sighed a blew it out of his eyes.

This will never do.

Having searched every drawer, and knowing what he did about his host, The Flame knew better than to waste time looking for a hairbrush in his current location. Unsure as to who else might be in the house, and unwilling to risk any other unplanned interactions, he crept across the landing to Kathy's bedroom. The first thing he noticed was the smell- an overpowering mix of hairspray, perfume and nicotine, all poorly masked by the incense that smouldered away in its wooden cradle on the window sill. If Richie's room was an affront to the Flame's military cleanliness, then Kathy's was an abomination. The room was about two thirds the size of Richie's, with the floor space dominated by an unmade double bed. Being on the opposite side of the house the windows overlooked the empty driveway and street beyond, a sight visible only through a six inch gap between the heavy, black curtains. In the gloom, The Flame could make out piles of clothes strewn across the bed, and the majority of the remaining floor space. Being in the room made him feel uncomfortable, so when he spotted the tell-tale glint of her diamanté encrusted hair brush atop the dressing table and a golden metallic bottle of hairspray, his relief was palpable. Picking them up from amidst a sea of used makeup items, The Flame paused briefly, looking around the room once more, before retreating back across the landing.

With his gathered resources in hand, he crossed the landing again, this time towards the bathroom. Once inside, he methodically checked the corners and behind the green floral shower curtain, before sliding the brass lock across to secure the space. He checked himself again in the mirror fronted bathroom cabinet and began, painfully at first, brushing his mop of hair into some semblance of order. Working the knots out, he put in a side parting and then swept it backwards out of his eyes. Then, with a wet sounding hiss, fixed it in place as best he could with the can of hairspray. He then found the catch beneath the mirror and pulled the door open, scanned quickly inside and withdrew a packet of paracetamol. He popped two from the metal foil blister pack, put them in his mouth and leant over the sink to take a gulp of water from the tap.

The Flame closed the cabinet and checked Richie's appearance in the mirror one final time.

Acceptable.

With his head clearing and the pain in his toe receding, The Flame headed down the stairs and grabbed Richie's Navy blue parka coat from the bottom of the bannister. He looked around the hallway, and took a deep intake of breath in through his nose and out through his mouth, allowing himself a moment to smile. It had been four years since he'd been bestowed with the power of The Eternal Flame but his war had begun long before that. As he stood in the hallway of a normal life he embraced a peaceful moment of inaction. He couldn't be certain what was to come, but he had an innate sense that this might be his last chance to do so. He closed his eyes and counted to ten, and allowed a deep sense of calm to flood through him. At the end of the count he nodded.

That's enough.

He took a final deep breath and stepped towards a pinewood side table opposite the front door, opening the left drawer and pulling out a set of keys. The keys in question had

177

a Nintendo Gameboy style acrylic keyring and another with the initials RTS engraved on the back. The Flame allowed himself another smile and a disbelieving shake of the head.

"Incredible" he muttered, turning the keys over in his slender fingers. He pocketed them and with his clear focussed intent returning, he headed out of the front door, closing it firmly behind him.

He strode purposefully down the path, swung the squeaky garden gate closed behind him, and headed off on his mission. He put his hand into his trouser pocket, playing the rough edges of the sliced silver ring around with his fingertips. Mr. Neil Wells, the history teacher, was his target and he only hoped that he would reach him in time.

Peering from behind the curtain, Kathy Spink looked out on her brother, with his uncharacteristically groomed appearance, and straight backed posture. As Richie left her line of sight, she again turned her attention to the yellowed letter in her hand and allowed herself a warm smile.

CHAPTER THIRTY ONE: BILL and GREEN

"So far so good Gentlemen." Bill said, and though his words were encouraging, the tone they were delivered with was not.

Once again he and the troops were out on the training field. This time however they were all kitted out for combat, even Willerton-Smythe alongside him, who uncomfortably shifted the heavy pouches strapped around his middle. Some one hundred yards in the distance, General Sutherland, his personal secretary Ms. Summers and a clutch of scientists watched on. A sense of eager anticipation buzzed between them as they stepped behind a protective screen.

Can't have the top brass caught in accidental friendly fire, heaven forbid.

In truth, over the past few weeks, the recruits had been shaping up nicely, but now was the time to take things up a gear. Bill's attention returned to his charges.

"In my book though, good is one bad day from bang average. In this squad it's greatness or nothing. Peak performance or death." Bill walked along the line, making eye contact with each man in turn. "And as such, today's assessment will be a live fire exercise."

Several of the now twelve man squad muttered anxiously amongst themselves. Green, Welsh and even the freshly fit again Parkinson, Bill was delighted to note, didn't even flinch.

Progress.

"But sir," One of the muttering men piped up. "How can it be "live fire" if we don't have our weapons?" he said, half panicked/half matter of factly gesturing down the line at the empty holsters on each of the men's hips. In a true live fire exercise all ten of them would have a sidearm pistol and a rifle. Right now the only offensive weapons they carried were

179

a small bayonet knife and bad breath. A wicked smile grew on Bill's lips.

"I never said it was you lot that'd 'ave the live ammo nar did I?" He said, looking across their faces. All showed some degree of shock, surprise or panic, apart from Green and Welsh.

We'll see how long that lasts.

Bill looked up into the sky, squinting against the sun. When he found what he was looking for, his smile grew wider.

"There is however, one more surprise, and one more substantial asset in your corner. Gentlemen, let me introduce you to the final member of your squad, and also your objective for the day."

The squad all raised their heads to follow Bill's eye line. Above them and several hundred yards in the distance, three parachutes opened, their dark green colour in stark contrast to the blue sky above. As his vision began to focus, Green's eyes widened in surprise. Two of the chutes carried large wooden weapons crates. The central chute however was not a crate at all.

"Is that a… man?" he said out loud, his jaw slackening as he prodded the equally dumbstruck Welsh in the ribs.

Got 'em.

"TAKE AIIIMMMM!!!!" Bill suddenly roared at the top of his lungs, and the troops turned to him in shock. From behind Bill, concealed by a dip in the land, five men in white lab coats appeared, two of whom had an RPG resting on their shoulders, whilst the other three manned M2 mortars. A sixth walked over to Bill and handed him an RPG. He nodded in approval, and slung it onto his shoulder.

"TAKE 'EM DOWN!!!" he shouted, and on command, with an eardrum rattling blast of noise and heat the first two RPG toting scientists sent their rockets spiralling off towards the targets. Green watched on in aghast amazement as one collided directly with the right hand munitions crate, sending a hail of wooden fragments and what looked to be a variety of weaponry scattering into the forest below. The 2nd rocket looked to be heading directly for the falling man, but at the last moment he pulled up his legs, and it sped away beyond him. Bill grimaced, and rolling his shoulders took aim. Down his sights he could clearly see the bulky figure of The Eternal Flame, who pulled hard on the hanging cord to his left, arcing his flight path deeper towards the treeline. Bill tracked him the whole way, keeping the centre mass of his body dead centre in the crosshairs. He took a big, deliberate intake of breath and as he slowly let it out squeezed the trigger, sending his rocket shooting off towards the target with a force that knocked him back a step.

The Flame tried to change his angle of descent again, to move his body out of the way, but Bill wasn't aiming directly at him.

Dodge that you big bloody menace...

The rocket instead skewed high, and tore straight through the fabric of The Flame's parachute, igniting it as it went. His flight path began to wobble wildly, but as he fought to right himself, the rocket exploded in midair. Super heated metal fragments tore through more of the chute, and his uniform, but even more deadly, the concussive force of the blast pushed his chute nearly inside out, like an umbrella in a hurricane. The Eternal Flame suddenly dropped like a stone, tearing through the thick branch and leaf canopy of the forest and out of sight of the assembled squad.

In unison they turned to face Bill. Shock, horror, anger and confusion sprang from the faces. Parkinson had his hands clamped over his eyes.

"'Raight gentlemen, today's the day. It's time to meet the final member of the squad. Every man fer himself. First one t'bring the target back alive gets an extra day's leave. I'll even buy the first round me'self. But be warned, if yer think that

181

fall will've stopped him, yer in fer the surprise of yer bloody lives. Get in there, gear up. Take 'im down."

Green was the first to recover his composure. He watched as the second crate gently floated, untouched, beyond the treeline, roughly half a mile west of the point at which their target had entered. He grabbed Welsh and Parkinson by their lapels. "With me lads."

Parkinson, whose attention was still very much on the easterly spot that their mysterious final squadmate had landed, half turned to look at him sceptically. "Come on mate, you saw that fall. The only way anyone is getting him back alive is getting to him first before he's dead." He scratched his short cropped hair absentmindedly. "Probably dead already to be fair."

"Maybe, but look at what the Major just did! Did you listen to how he spoke about him? Why shoot down your own man? Why even bother sending the weapon crates? Use your head." he said, wrapping his knuckles atop Parkinson's crew cut skull.

"Hey!" the smaller man replied, swatting Green's hand away in annoyance.

"Nothing about this makes any sense, and if you think I'm running head first into a situation that makes no sense armed with nothing but a knife and a winning personality, you've got another thing coming my son."

The other nine men in the squad, finally free from the initial shock of the scenario, began sprinting off in the direction of the felled soldier, shouting and whooping as they went. Green gritted his teeth and pressed on.

"And besides, I don't know about you boys, but after all the toilets he's had us scrub, I can't think of anything that'll taste sweeter than a pint off that miserable bastard. Now come on. I want that crate. We're getting that crate."

No question was asked, and so no answer was needed. Welsh and Parkinson, after one more look to the East and their squadmates heading into the brush, adjusted themselves and followed Green on a Westerly heading instead. The three broke into a steady jog into the unknown.

It took them a little under twenty minutes to find the downed crate, and when they did all three were delighted to see that, as expected, none of their squadmates had gotten there first. Although the contents was far from enough to win the whole war, Green knew he'd feel far more at ease with a rifle on his back, three grenades attached to his hip and a handgun gripped firmly in his right hand. When he opened the lid however, he could barely contain his irritation.

"What's all this junk?"

"Ey lads, check this out." Welsh exclaimed, opening up a smaller box and withdrawing a strange gun that appeared to be loaded with a giant webbed net, with several spherical weights attached to it.

"What's that for? Are we tryin' to catch a bear or something?" Parkinson responded innocently.

"I dunno, but you lads couldn't catch a cold at Christmas let alone a bear, best give it here ey?" Green said, wrenching it from his friend's grip and clipping it to his belt.

As they dug deeper, the trio unboxed three more non-lethal devices seemingly geared more towards capture than kill. The first bore a striking resemblance to a boomerang, painted in a dark green colour, with what appeared to be a short, self lighting fuse and a small brass cone attached in its centre. Puzzled as to its purpose, but unwilling to leave it behind, he handed it to Welsh. The stocky man's brow furrowed between his dark eyebrows as he held it tightly and swished it around in the air a few times. When he caught Green staring sternly at him, he sheepishly stopped and tucked it into his belt at the small of his back.

The second item was a bulky glove and wrist strap. On the outside of the forearm a three pronged hook was mounted, with a thin wire attaching it to a circular metal reel, similar to that of a fishing rod, but flatter. Green slid his left hand into the glove, fastened the buckles around his forearm and flexed his wrist. It was a tight fit and limited movement. He sharply rotated his wrist to the right, and with a whoosh of compressed air, the steel hook shot off, trailing the wire behind it and embedded itself with a thud and a tiny hail of splinters into the side of the weapon crate, barely a foot away from where Welsh stood, sending him leaping reflexively backwards.

"Jesus wept!" Welsh exclaimed.

Green tilted his head back in surprise and looked down at his wrist. He traced the path of the metal wire, glinting in the light that broke through the tree canopy, all the way from the spool to the crate.

"Well, that's something isn't it?"

"What the bloody hell was that?!" Welsh shouted, clutching his chest.

"Do it again!" Parkinson shouted happily.

Green shrugged, and snapped his wrist to the left this time, and with an almighty cracking sound, the side of the crate violently snapped off and came hurtling back towards Green at a tremendous speed.

"Christ on a bike!" he shouted, ducking quickly as the thick, metre wide panel flew inches over his head. Instinctively he snapped his wrist upwards. The hook disengaged and the panel smashed into the trunk of a nearby redwood, sending thick chunks of painted pine everywhere. A flock of birds that had been quietly minding their business in the branches took off in a panic up through the branches and out to the silent freedom of the afternoon sky.

Green blew out the deep breath he hadn't realised he was holding, and looked down again at his wrist as the hook recoiled into the spool and locked back into place. He nodded at it in appreciation.

Not bad at all.

The final item was, at first glance simply an military colour coded variation on a standard policeman's truncheon, indistinguishable in fact but for a bright red thumb switch embedded into the handle. Parkinson hefted it in his left then right hand. Noticing two small, raised metallic nubs at the tip lifted it closer to his face to examine them.

"Be careful with that, we don't know wh…" Green's warning was cut off sharply as Parkinson accidentally touched the red switch and a short white arc of electricity cracked loudly between the two nubs jumping to make contact with his freckled nose. Instantaneously the young man was thrown ten feet backwards, sliding limply across the scattered leaves and twigs of the forest floor.

"Parky!" Green and Welsh yelled in shock, and sprinted over to their fallen pal, sliding on their knees to either side of him. Green pressed his fingers to Parkinson's neck.

Don't be dead, don't be dead, stupid idiot, don't be dead!

Their immediate fears for their comrades' life were eased when they turned the diminutive lad's shaven head to one side and he let out a loud snore.

Welsh blurted out a reflexive snort of laughter.

"He's only gone and bloody knocked 'imself out cold 'asn't he?"

Green shook his head, stifling a laugh of his own.

Poor old Parky.

Shaking his head he removed his canteen from its pouch, unscrewed the metal cap and tipped the contents onto his unconscious friend's face. Parkinson's eyes snapped open and he sat bolt upright.

"No mum it was Francis who stole all the biscuits!" he blurted out.

Welsh snorted again.

Parkinson blinked twice and slowly looked around as though seeing the forest for the first time. He turned his head to look first at Welsh, then at Green. He blinked again, trying to clear the glassy look in his eyes, and failing.

"Probably best if you have the net one, and *I* have that one then yeah?" Green said softly.

Wide eyed, Parkinson nodded rapidly, and with a shaking hand passed the baton over. The other two helped him to his feet and dusted the loose leaves and earth from his uniform.

In the distance Bill North, laying in the underbrush, watched the trio through his binoculars as Green patted Parkinson playfully on the back and clipped the Net Launcher to his own belt.

"The Stun Baton works a rip roaring treat doesn't it?" Willerton-Smythe whispered jovially alongside him, scribbling in his small, black, flip covered notebook with a tiny, well chewed pencil. Bill grunted.

"Yeah, the perfect weapon for the man who wants to give his'self a quick nap."

Willerton shot him a sour look, which Bill joyfully ignored.

"Raight they're on t' move, let's crack on." Bill said, smoothly rising to his feet and silently adjusting the strap of the small bag he had slung over his right shoulder. He took a look at his second in command, who used the trunk of a nearby tree to aid his rise. Bill rolled his eyes as his weaselish companion awkwardly and noisily shuffled and adjusted every single strap, pouch and holster he had on his person.

This daft Toff is going to get someone killed if he ever makes it in' t'field. We'll all be lucky if it's just 'imself.

But then again, from what Bill had come to know of Captain Frederick Willerton-Smythe, and more importantly the social standing of his family, he'd probably get made General, or even Prime Minister before he got within fifty miles of a trench.

Born to rule. Lords and Ladies don't send their kids t'war. Not when they've got the rest of us.

186

Bill began to stalk after the three young soldiers. He had to admit, he was quietly impressed by Green's decision to take them to the cache. There was a chance that some of the others may have stumbled upon some of the scattered weaponry from the other crate on their charge west, but it was a gamble. A gamble to find it, and just as big a gamble that it was still functional from the explosion and fall.

The kid's got something. But will it be enough?

Another twenty minutes passed, and Parkinson seemed to have shaken off the worst effects of his little mishap and was back to his usual energetic self. Green checked his compass again. They were broadly heading East, but based on his own view of the fall, he'd also chosen to head fractionally North too, taking them deeper into the more densely packed forest and towards the boundary of the estate grounds. Once they reached the fence, they could head towards the landing zone safe in the knowledge that their backs would be clear.

Since they'd uncovered the cache, the only other signs of life had been several loose weapons they'd found scattered in the underbrush, all of them were the standard issue equipment they were accustomed to, a couple of rifles, a pistol and something that looked a little like a submachine gun. All infinitely more useful than the toys they were currently carrying, but all were damaged beyond use.

For the forty something minute hike so far, the only sounds other than the rustle of their own footsteps was the occasional birdsong, and a red squirrel that darted out from beneath a fallen branch before scurrying up the thick trunk of a nearby tree and into the dense green foliage overhead. Parkinson watched it go with a gleeful smile on his face.

"Beautiful that innit lads? See it's big thick bushy tail?"

"Yeah I know, we used to get them on my Dad's farm all the time" Welsh replied. "My big brother used to use them for target practice with his old spud gun, but I never saw the point really. Funny when you think about it, ey?"

"How's that?" Parkinson asked.

"Well, that I should end up having to shoot people for a living, when I never even wanted to shoot a bloody squirrel as a kid."

"Yeah that is pretty funny actually" Parkinson said, with a cheerful chuckle. "What about you Greeny?" he asked, "Ever go hunting or anything?"

Green, whose senses had been on high alert for any signs of their target, *or competitors*, kept his eyes fixed ahead. "Not really no, not really my thing either, but it seemed a damn sight better shooting Nazis than taking another belt off my old fella. Turns out that a childhood of dodging backhanders and getting chased by the local Bobby's for stealing is pretty good preparation for the army."

Parkinson nodded thoughtfully and the younger man was about to issue a follow up question when Green held up a clenched fist. They had reached the bordering fence, but something was amiss. The acres surrounding the Manor were so expansive that he'd come nowhere near close to exploring every nook and cranny, but what he did know was that the estate was ringed by 8 foot chain link fencing, topped by razorwire. Every twelve feet or so were incredibly forcefully worded signage warning away potential trespassers with threat of death and prosecution. Enough to deter most. But, as the trio drew close to the fence it became clear that most was not all.

Towards the bottom of a panel, part obscured by a small, waist high bush, was a hole, neatly clipped open by wire cutters, then forcefully pushed bigger around the edges.

"That's a bit mad innit?" Parkinson said, scratching the back of his neck. "What d'yer think boss? Reckon it's a bear or somethin'?" he continued, looking around nervously.

Green crouched down by the hole, examining the cuts more closely. Noticing a small dark scrap hanging from the

188

ragged edge of one of the pieces of wiring, he reached out to collect it.

"Not unless bears wear knitwear." he said looking at the snagged thread of dark wool between his thumb and forefinger.

"Local kids?" Welsh asked.

Green nodded tersely. He'd jumped many a fence, trespassed on many a property in his day, but this was different. Dangerous. He got back to his feet and turned to address the others.

"Maybe it's just an old hole, but keep your eyes peeled, hopefully the kids who made it are anywhere but here."

Both men nodded.

"Right there's nothing we can do about this now, let's get back to the job at hand. By my eye if we start to cut back 10 degrees South-East towards the Manor then we'll be to the landing spot in the next 10 minutes. Eyes up. Stay sharp. You see anyone or anything, you freeze and you tell me. Good?"

They both nodded again.

"Excellent. Let's move."

CHAPTER THIRTY TWO: RICHIE

The ear splitting cracks of gunfire, punctuated by strange, intermittent hissing sounds, like drops of water on a frying pan, filled the air as bullets whizzed past his head. Will lay at his feet, baring his gritted teeth, with his right hand pressed firmly to his upper left arm. With well practised precision, and despite the clear pain, he pulled a roll of gauze bandage from a pouch on his belt, and with another grimace, wrapped it around his arm, covering the torn patch, and pulled it tight. Blood immediately began to seep through, and Richie felt the bile rise in his stomach. Will though seemed to consider the matter dealt with, and recovered his pistol from the dew covered grass. Machine-like he quickly checked it over for damage. Richie, who had been known to cry over papercuts, was amazed.

"Are-are you okay?"

Will, now back up into a crouched position, leaned around Richie's khaki trousered legs, and quickly popped off two shots.

"Fine." he said curtly. "Now, Richie, I know you must be scared, but there's no time fer that nonsense. Right now, we're in an open field with zero cover, and ten…"

He leaned out again and fired two more shots. A hundred yards away, Richie heard a cry from the thick underbrush.

"…Nine opposing forces. Beyond them is a bunker. Inside that bunker is an agent who I very much would like t'talk to."

Tufts of turf kicked up even more rapidly at Richie's feet as the German forces dedicated yet more of their fire towards them. The strange, small hissing sounds became louder and more frequent.

"So, we're goin' t'take a deep breath, and then nice and steady, take a walk towards them. Okay?"

"Okay" Richie nodded automatically. "Wait. What??!" Richie felt the mask on his face rouche up as his eyes widened in horror.

"You 'eard me lad. Now about-face. We call this the Barricade manoeuvre. One foot in front of the other, nice and steady."

Richie gulped, took a deep breath and slowly rotated around to face the barrage of enemy fire. He closed his eyes firmly shut.

Ohmygodohmygodohmygodddd

The hissing sounds filled his ears.

"Right son, that's it. Now, time to move." Will said, barely audible above the hissing, sizzling sound.

Come on Richie, you can do this. One foot in front of the other. What the hell is that noise?

With monumental effort he wrenched open his eyelids. One hundred yards in the distance beyond the clearing, amid the waist-high, overgrown grass and brush and trees he could see the muzzle flares of the enemy guns. The bullets they fired seemed to gradually slow down, each coming into crystal clear focus before him. He followed one as it soared past his right ear. Another two gracefully arced towards him. With morbid fascination, Richie tracked their trajectory as they drew closer and closer to his body. He braced himself, but couldn't avert his gaze. Like a one-two punch, the bullets impacted him in the chest, and were immediately disintegrated in a flash of blue flame and a slight tickling, itchy feeling.

Huh.

He watched the process repeat several more times. Bang. Arc. Impact. Hiss. Tickle. Repeat. With each hit something inside him built. Bigger. Irrepressible. Uncontainable.

Richie let out a maniacal cackle.

An explosive, roaring cackle that quickly turned into an hysterical belly laugh! "HAHAHAHAHA!"

191

Sheltered behind the broad frame of the Eternal Flame, even Will allowed himself a smile at the childish enthusiasm, before the look of liquid focus slid back across his grizzled features and he went back to picking off carefully aimed shots.

Wisps of blue flame sparked across Richie's thick body and tufts of the earth kicked up around him as he steadily strode towards the treeline. One by one he watched as Will's shots found their target, the muzzle flashes began to thin and the volume of fire began to decrease. Still Richie's maniacal laughing continued. His head swam with the power and surreality of it all. As they reached the edge of the clearing, only two enemies remained, one twenty yards off to the right, positioned behind a thick, bullet riddled tree trunk, and the other dead ahead. The young German soldier continued to fire at him, a look of wide eyed terror on his mud and sweat streaked face. The man, who couldn't have been much older than eighteen, shouted a wide array of what Richie vaguely knew to be Germanic swear words, emptied the clip of his rifle, switched to his handgun, and emptied that too. If that fact registered it didn't show, as the terrified young man continued to press the trigger another dozen times. Will rolled past Richie and vaulted the underbrush, delivering a meaty, full weight kick to the soldier's chest. He pounced on him, landing a knockout right hook, and quickly front rolled over his unconscious body to land behind a tree as three bullets embedded themselves into the trunk. Richie was showered in a hail of splinters and sharp chunks of bark- most of which sizzled away like the bullets had. Further down the way, the last soldier had clearly weighed up his chances of success and used the cover of that final barrage to beat a retreat. He turned and ran at full tilt into the woods.

In a half dreamlike state Richie watched him go, hurdling a fallen tree branch, sweat pouring, arms and legs pumping; best possible speed, as far away as possible. With the shootout at an end, a peaceful silence fell upon them, but still it took a moment for him to register the new noise trying to grab his attention.

"Richie!" Will roared.

"Huh?" Richie replied dimly, turning from the runner, back to his grizzled mentor, who was reloading his gun, back pressed to the tree trunk.

"Your man. Go!" He pointed firmly.

"My... what?"

"Your man, get after him, stop him reaching base. Any means necessary."

Will's tone left no room for negotiation.

"Oh, right, erm.. Okay." he replied, pointing a hitchhiker's thumb in the direction of his target.

"Get that man there yeah?"

"Yeah. Now. Run. We'll be right behind you."

"Okay, okay." Richie said, moving away. Five more men wearing the same British army uniform, each with the same flaming fist patch on the left shoulder reached them. One of them, a tall handsome man with blonde hair, gave Richie a playful smile. As he turned to give chase, the sounds of Will's barked orders drifted away behind him. "Gather resources and get after The Flame!"

Richie's mind drifted back to his cross country lessons, to the countless lung burning, feckless attempts to keep pace with the sporty kids in his class. As he started to pump his legs, a cold shudder ran down his back as he recalled all those early starts, those times when he truly gave his all; those first few dozen yards when everything felt good, felt possible, and how they very quickly tailed off to discomfort, breathlessness and pain. The first dozen yards passed, then another, then another. They became a hundred yards, then two, then five. Faster and faster he began to eat up the ground, his boots securely finding ground, and propelling him forward powerfully, but almost effortlessly, within seconds, the back of the fleeing soldier drew closer in his eye line.

Whoa! This is... easy...

His right foot immediately kicked the back of his left, and Richie Spink in the hulking form of the Eternal Flame, stumbled and face planted with a mucky thud into the overgrown grass and dirt. His incredible momentum carried him forward; face, chest and knees sliding through several yards of grass, twigs and mulch.

Richie lay there for a moment, feeling the cool wetness of the earth seeping into his mask.

Perfect form Rich. Absolutely perfect. You're so good at this. Idiot.

Will's order's replayed at the back of his mind, and despite his normally overpowering desire to wallow in his gangly legged shame, Richie Spink pushed himself up to his knees, brushed off his face and chest and rose to his feet again.

Come on Richie, for Godsake. You've survived being shot like, a MILLION TIMES, this is just running. People do it everyday. It's like walking, but faster. Come on.

He looked into the distance, and caught a fleeting glimpse of his quarry. Richie took a deep, centering breath and set off again.

Quickly, quicker this time, he reached top speed. He kept his breathing clear and even and his attention on the terrain just in front of him, ducking and jumping under and over obstacles and flat out sprinting when needed. After less than a minute, he was right on the soldier's tail.

"Oi!" Richie shouted.

Smooth Rich. "Oi", the lesser known German translation of "excuse me sir could you stop running away from me so I can tackle you?"

The soldier looked back over his shoulder, the sweat absolutely gushing down his exertion reddened face. Again Richie saw the look of abject terror in his eyes. The look back was ill advised, and the young German soldier ran face first into a shoulder width tree trunk with a sickening thud, and slid, unconscious into the undergrowth at its foot.

Richie, taking a leaf from his sister's book of empathy let out a snort of laughter as he decelerated and stopped over him. With an exaggerated point at his fallen prey Richie doubled over laughing.

"Alright George of the Jungle, watch out for that tree yeah?" he said, trying to wipe away the tears of laughter that had escaped the bottom of his mask. In the distance he heard the sounds of approaching footsteps. His laughing fit immediately replaced by fear, he spun around on his heels to face the direction he'd just come from. Out of the gloom and into the small clearing, moving with grace, focus and precision, came Will and the rest of the unit. They fanned out, moving their rifles from tight to their chests to aim out ahead of them.

"All clear sir." said the guy with blonde hair. His playful look was gone, his pale blue eyes held an intense, vigilant demeanour as he scanned their location for danger.

"Good man Mister Green. Keep yer eyes peeled. We're not more than half a mile from the bunker. Unless they've got Vera Lynn full blast ont' wireless there's a fair chance they've got wind of us. Send one of the lads on ahead, get the lay of the land."

"Yes sir." Green said dutifully and turned towards the rest of the troops.

"Welshy, you're on reconnaissance. Go get your eyes on the target. The rest of you, on pins."

Richie watched as one of the men, shorter and stockier than Green, with dark hair and eyebrows nodded and disappeared in the thicker woods ahead. The other three all saluted and spread out to the edges of the clearing, rifles still drawn and ready.

"Good work Richard." Will said.

"Err… Yep, no problem sir." Richie said, shuffling awkwardly and trying to puff his chest out.

"Next time though ye'll need to be a bit more switched on, that's a big old truck you're drivin' there. Lots of horsepower, great in straight lines, but if yer putting it round a track, ye'll need to learn to drive it like a pro. Or…" He looked down at the caked mud on the knees of Richie's trousers. "You'll be spending more than a few seconds face down int' mud."

"Ahh.." Richie said. "Yes, well, it was all part of my, err… cunning plan of course." Richie coughed trying to cover his embarrassment with mock bravado. "Had to make sure I blended in more effectively with the, erm… situational, environmental, biome."

Biome? Biome??? What are you saaaayingggg??? Urgh, you might as well just keep going.

"… The added camouflage actually gave me a tactical advantage, not just in terms of blending in with the locale, but also in that it helped to cool my core… err, temperature allowing me to reach and maintain maximum velocity with greater ease." Richie finished his verbal diarrhoea, and planted his hands to his hips, turning to look heroically off into the middle distance. A moment passed, then another. Richie had that itchy feeling that always came with socially awkward moments. He watched Will, just barely visible out of the corner of his eye, standing right there, uncomfortably close, saying nothing. Just as Richie was about to internally combust from cringing at himself, Will spoke.

"Yeah, it was raight cunning of yer to have that tree planted there fifty years ago and grow up to smash in ter 'is face." he said flatly, and walked away.

Richie's soul sank to his toes.

All part of my plan. Urgh… What a divvy.

Before he could formulate a plan for making the lush earth beneath his booted feet swallow him whole, Will gathered the squad.

"Raight gents, we'll be losing light soon. While we wait for Welsh's recon report, let's bed in here for t' night. Flame, you secure the prisoner. Skinner, overwatch."

Skinner, a wiry man with close cropped hair nodded. Richie's eyes widened. They widened further when he watched Skinner raise his left arm, and, with a quick twist of his wrist, fire off a bolt into the canopy of the tallest tree. A metal wire unspooled behind it, there was a small, distant thud of impact, and then with another wrist twist, it recoiled, hoisting him rapidly upwards, into the branches and out of sight.

"Whoa…" Richie mumbled in amazement, his eyes locked on the rustling tree canopy. As Will approached, he made a conscious effort to pick his jaw up off the floor. The squad leader, 5ft 10ins of sinew and stubble strode across the clearing with a purpose and confidence unlike any Richie had seen before. Here was a man. A real man. Richie knew that if he was to get through this situation, this was the guy to impress.

"God, he's like Batman isn't he?" Richie said chirpily pointing to the spot where Green had departed.

"Who?"

"What?" Richie covered quickly. "Nothing. Err… what was it you wanted me to do?"

Will chuckled softly. "Secure the prisoner. There's a coil of rope in the pouch behind your right hip. Yer do know how to tie a knot don't yer?"

"Ooh, yes." Richie replied, genuinely pleased to possess an actual, honest to goodness, useful skill.

God bless you those five times I went to Scouts.

"Good. Sit him up, tie him t' that tree. When he wakes up we'll see what he knows. Make sure it's nice an' tight. If he gets away in the night and gives away our position, we'll all be eating Nazi bullets for breakfast. Understood?"

A chill ran down Richie's spine and he nodded rapidly.

"Good. It looks like we'll be setting up camp 'ere. The plan is t' move at first light." Will finished, his attention already turning to his next task.

"Will?" Richie asked.

"Yes lad?"

A million questions ran through his brain, like a flock of spooked pigeons. Will clearly had other things to attend to so Richie knew he'd have to keep his questioning brief. A good, short, insightful question. He let out a deep breath.

"What the hell is going on?"

Will turned back to look up at Richie and smiled warmly.

"That, Mister Spink, is an absolute belter of a question." He chuckled and firmly patted Richie on his broad shoulder. "An absolute belter." he said, turning back to the rest of the troops and leaving Richie to the task at hand. "Secure the prisoner. We'll set up camp, and then let's see what we can figure out."

Richie allowed himself a fractional sigh of relief, and looked down at the German soldier, lying prone on the floor.

"Could be worse ey mate. I could be you."

Later, the squad, minus the yet to return Welsh, and the presumably still tree bound Skinner, sat around the small campfire. The air was filled with the crackle of burning wood and the low bassy tone of conversation. Richie studied each of the men, trying to soak up as much detail as possible. He watched their mannerisms, the way they spoke, the way they listened, the back and forth of their testosterone fueled banter, everything even down to how they sat and how they ate. The thick powerful body in which he sat was beginning to feel comfortable, more familiar somehow. He thought back to his Dad teaching him to play football in the back garden.

Practice doesn't make perfect, practice makes better.

After mis-controlling the ball for the hundredth time and falling on his backside in the mud, Richie had grabbed it, angrily kicked it over the back fence, and stormed off in

198

floods of tears. It was the last time they'd played football together, so whilst the advice certainly sounded good, it wasn't something he'd yet proven to be true. This wasn't some daft sport though, this was, against all logic and reason, real life.

Real life AND death.

He should've felt utterly terrified, but bizarrely there was something about the situation that he actually found… kind of thrilling.

Damn sight better than revising, listening to Marc preen over himself, dramatically failing to speak to Anna Harrison or getting the snot beaten out of me by Jackson Sleight.

He looked around the clearing again, and saw their German captive, seated and safely secured at the base of the tree.

God, what does it say about my life, if THIS is better?

He let out a chuckle. Beside him, just finishing off the last scraps of food from the small tin in his left hand, Will stirred.

"Summat tickle y'there son?"

"Oh, err… Just all of this Will. It's madness. I've tried pinching myself, punching myself, wishing it away. Nothing. Here I am. Sometime, somewhere in the past, wearing someone else's skin. I feel like if I don't laugh at it, my head might pop."

"France. 1942." Will said.

"What?"

"France, 1942. Just outside of Petite-Foret in fact." He pulled a map from his pocket and unfolded it. Between the flicking orange of the campfire, and the clear white glow of the moonlight, it was just about visible. "Here." He pointed with his calloused index finger. "And up ahead.." He traced his finger in a line. "…is our target." It all looked like map to Richie, but at least knowing that he was definitely, actually *somewhere on a map* provided a crumb of comfort. They fell silent again, and Richie's gaze fell upon the fire, its dancing orange flames punctuated by the occasional pop and crackle of the amber glowing wooden twigs and branches at its heart. Richie held up his left fist, turned it around, wiggled his fingers then firmly clenched it. He made the Spider-man web shooter fingers. Nothing, If there was some sort of blue energy inside him, it wasn't there now.

"How does it work?" he said, half to himself.

Will watched Richie flexing his hand as he finished the final bites of food, wiped out the small tin with a small cloth, and placed it back into his backpack. Richie watched the older man's clockwork-like movements, almost as impressed with his fastidious economy of motion as he had been his skills in battle.

"That my young friend, is the big question." he said with a faint smile. Will shifted his position, and withdrew another small, sealed tin from a pouch on his chest. As he opened it, the rich smell of tobacco filled the air. A smell unpleasant to most, but one that immediately reminded Richie of Sunday afternoon at his Grandmother's house, and the rich smell of his Grandad's traditional post-dinner pipe. Will carefully, slid a thin, white paper from a crumpled pile pressed along the inside of the tin, sprinkled in a pinch of the pungent brown strands, quickly and efficiently rolled it all into a cigarette and licked along a seam to seal it shut. From the right pocket of his trousers, he produced a burnished steel lighter. He put the cigarette to his lips, clicked his fingers above the bezel, and with a spark of flint, it ignited with a thick orange flame. He took a deep inhale and blew out a plume of smoke into the night sky. Richie looked at the lighter; just like the patches on the upper arms of each squad member, there was a flaming fist in the centre of a circle, this time engraved into the metal. Will clocked Richie's gaze.

"Cute, raight?" he chuckled and with a snap of the wrist, the lid flipped shut and he pocketed it again. "Standard issue for everyone in the Eternal Flame Squad. Even those who don't deserve it." His voice tailed off, and Richie made a mental note to pull on that thread at a future date.

"Anyway, yes, you. Richard Thomas Spink. Have y'had yer 16th birthday yet?"

Richie's eyes widened again, "No sir, just turned fifteen."

Will nodded as though squaring that information against some invisible file in his head.

"So, yeah the power?"

Richie nodded, suddenly aware of how dry his throat felt.

"Now, I can't claim to be an expert here." Will continued, blowing another plume up into the air. "When I first heard it, it sounded like nonsense. In fact, even the experts back at base have spent the last year or so scratching their heads. But fer what it's worth, here's the kiddies bedtime story version. You…" He nodded up and down Richie's broad figure. "… are The Eternal Flame of British Resistance. Stronger, faster, more resistant to injury than any soldier in history."

Like Captain America!

Richie's brain buzzed with the notion, but Will still hadn't answered his question.

"But, what about..?" He held up his fist, gestured to the places on his body where the bullets had struck him earlier, pointed to the patch on Will's shoulder, the intricate stitch work of the blue flaming fist half obscured by his blood crusted bandage.

"Yeah. That. That's where the bedtime story gets more like Alice In't Wonderland. So…" He took a deep breath, and shifted uncomfortably. "From what we can figure out, the power, the strength, those… flames. They come from three things. The most important of these is…" He took another drag on charred and brown stained cigarette stub, and tossed it into the fire. "At their core, they come from your own innate skill and willpower." He poked a calloused finger into Richie's chest. "You have the power inside you so you can be strong and resilient, simply because you WANT to be strong

201

and resilient. Above that," He made a stepping up gesture. "those powers are boosted by the strength and willpower of those who you surround yourself with. The more they, we… " He nodded to the rest of the squad, "believe, the deeper the power becomes. And above that, well…" he coughed, letting out the last whisps of smoke from his lungs. "The Eternal Flame is nothing less than the collective spirit of the British people's resistant spirit, their will to survive, and with Nazi boots beating their way across Europe, with their bombs dropping flattening our cities, let me tell you, that spirit has never burned more brightly."

"Whoa…" Richie whispered, looking at his outstretched fist against the backdrop of the roaring campfire. "You're right, that does sound like nonsense." He smirked and gave Will a side eye glance. Both broke out into laughter, and Richie felt the tension in his brain finally fizzle away.

When they finally regained their composure, Will shifted on the ground and placed a hand on Richie's shoulder.

"I have fought in wars around the world, I have seen things that no normal man ever has, could or would ever choose to, and I can tell you that The Eternal Flame is a power above and beyond all else. But. And this is important. That Spirit of Britain thing is real, and it is mighty, but it is not you. This power you have, the most important part of it comes from in here." He pointed his nicotine stained finger again at Richie's chest. "Same as all these lads." He opened his palm to encompass the others around the fire. "A man who is prepared to dig deeper, fight harder and hurt more than his enemy and can *still* find a way to keep going? That man can overcome any obstacle. Any. Understand?"

Whoa.

Richie felt the hairs on the back of his neck stand up.

In truth, he didn't really have a clue what Will was talking about. In his fifteen years he couldn't think of many situations where he'd had to dig that deep, and certainly couldn't think of any where he'd done it and succeeded. Richie was the "shows promise, but needs to apply himself more" type of kid, and had a drawer full of school reports to back it up. But, there was something in this man's words and his nature that made Richie feel like he might be able to learn.

"Yes sir."

"Good lad. 'Raight. Try and get some shut eye. We move at dawn."

Richie nodded, but before he could get up from his position at the fire. Welsh, the stocky scout from earlier, burst into the clearing. The dark featured man was breathing heavily. Will and Green both shot to their feet to meet him.

"Welshy?" Green asked.

Welsh clawed in a couple of deep lungfuls of air and wiped his sweat coated brow with his forearm.

"Trouble gaffer."

CHAPTER THIRTY THREE: ANNA

It was Saturday. Anna lay on her bed, under the watchful gaze of Bob Dylan, Marilyn Manson and The Powerpuff Girls. In poster form at least. It was nearly 8am, but she'd been awake since a little after five. Just Anna, the ceiling and her terrifying thoughts of death.

Only I could experience a life changing trauma and not even get to miss any school...

Her phone bleeped and vibrated on the bedside table next to her head. She reached out to launch the battered Nokia across the room, but thought better of it, instead looking at the green glow of the screen. A text from Marc. 8:01am.

Blimey, he's keen.

'STILL ON FOR L8R?' it read, and Anna felt her internal organs folding in on themselves with cringe at his use of text speak. From what she knew of Marc, there was every chance he'd typed it out correctly then gone back and changed it just to make himself look cooler. Marc Townsend was an open book. An expensively dressed, well groomed, but totally open, book. As insufferable as his vanity was, on three hours of grim pre-dawn reflection, it was better than a Saturday spent on her own, endlessly replaying last night in her mind's eye.

Anna mentally counted to three, took a deep breath and threw the covers back. Still in her pyjamas of thick grey socks, shorts, and her, 100% ironically worn, Britney Spears t-shirt, she got out of bed and went through her usual morning stretch routine. The passion for late night/early morning curricular activities (and scraping her hair into a bun every day) had faded in recent years, but the mental conditioning of countless childhood gymnastics and ballet lessons remained. The natural competitive spirit that had helped fill the shelf above her TV with dozens of medals and trophies still burned. Nowadays that spirit was focussed on getting through GCSEs, and (as she pushed through her regimented course of a hundred sit ups) into her morning fitness routine.

Once she was done, she grabbed a quick shower and returned to her room to dress. Her usual weekend attire consisted of her Docs, black hoodie, the super cute black and white tartan skirt she'd picked up from the "Goth Shop" in town, and some form of fishnet tights. Today though the skirt was out, and her baggy black jeans were in. Last night had left her feeling on edge. Despite the lunacy of it, it had taken all her willpower not to chase after the Man in Grey. There was the initial shock of course. Humberidge House was a place rarely lacking in drama, but that drama never tended to occur above a gentle walking pace. Seeing Frank Wells hurt had taken priority, but on the morning's reflection Anna felt more annoyed at not having done more, than any lingering feelings of fear. It was a small thing, but if the Man in Grey showed up again, she knew she'd feel a damn sight more prepared to fight her corner if she wasn't having to protect her modesty at the same time.

Get back here Grey man or I'll flash so much undercarriage at you!

Testing her range of motion, she kicked her right foot straight up above her head height, and brought it back down smoothly, keeping balance on the ball of her left foot. The jeans were baggy enough to allow the full range of motion, and she nodded in satisfaction. Anna tied her hair up into a high ponytail, threw on a touch of mascara and dark red lipstick and checked out her completed look in her full length mirror. She clenched her fists, stood in a fighting pose and bared her teeth. If Tim Burton made an arthouse movie about Sporty Spice she'd be nailed on for the role. Slinging the mascara, lipstick and her school notebook into her backpack, she picked up her phone and with a lightning right thumb text Marc back: 'ON MY WAY'

She was about to slide it into her pocket when it buzzed again: GR8 C U SOON.

Eurgh.

She shuddered, slung the graffiti mottled backpack onto her shoulders and headed out.

Twelve minutes had passed since she'd arrived at Marc's. Eleven since she'd been invited up to his bedroom. The longest eleven minutes of her fifteen years to date. Longer than the parents evening when her mum had spent the whole time flirting with Mr Rainford, her Chemistry teacher. Her very openly gay Chemistry teacher. Longer even than the time when she'd had to work late and give old Mrs. Sloughbury a sponge bath.

Soooo many wrinkles…

She shuddered at the thought and tuned back into Marc's near continual self-congratulatory prattle.

"And then he said, 'why don't you make like a tree, and get out of here!' Which is stupid because that's not even the saying!"

She was perched on a leather clad swivel chair. Marc was stood in the middle of the room, confidently holding court in his pristine black Converse, designer ripped pale blue jeans, and what looked like a genuine US Air Force brown leather jacket, replete with sheepskin lining around the collar. His hair was immaculate and his perfectly straight white teeth veritably glowed in the morning sunlight streaming through his large bedroom windows. She looked around his room. Above his single bed, much like her own, were a number of large posters, Incubus, Foo Fighters, Top Gun…

No shock there…

On the wall opposite her was a floor to ceiling bookcase packed with CD's, DVD's, Books and VHS, she tilted her head to see past Marc, trying to identify as many as she could from their spines, and was again pretty impressed. Ferris Bueller's Day Off, Breakfast Club, Buffalo 66…

Damn, Marc's got taste…

She had to admit, on the surface, Marc had a lot going for him. Good taste in music and movies, his room was tidy, very atypical for boys their age, and he was objectively, a good looking boy. But my god he was a bore.

Thirteen minutes.

Marc blithely continued to talk at her. "And then he says 'THOSE BOARDS DON'T WORK ON WATER, UNLESS YOU'VE GOT POWEEERRR!" He chortled again, more than a person should, given the material.

Anna had reached her limit. "SO, is that the jacket Richie didn't like?"

"Huh, oh, this?" Marc looked down, thrown from his freight train of thought and all of a sudden a little self-conscious. Anna had made a gap in their one sided conversation, and she decided to push into it.

"Didn't you say he was coming over too? Did he say when?"

Marc had shuffled further across the room to examine himself in the floor standing mirror. "Rich? Yeah, yeah, he's normally here pretty much dawn til dusk over the weekend. His Mum and Dad are going through a split, messy stuff." He flicked the collar up on his jacket, it seemed to calm his insecurity.

Anna knew her window of opportunity would close again soon, she needed to move quickly. "Ahh, so is he normally this late?"

"Hmm?" Marc responded, and Anna could feel his focus drifting again. "Oh, yeah no, we've normally completed the Brotherhood of Nod missions on C&C by now."

"The Brotherhood of what?"

Marc's expression froze for just a moment as he realised his "Cool Geek" persona mask had slipped and the 'computer game nerd' face underneath had peered out. "What? Ohhh, nothing." he blustered. "So, Richie ey? Yeah…" He looked up at the clock on his wall, it was nearly half past eleven. "Oh wow, yeah he is late. That's not like him at all. I hope Sleight and his gang of pituitary morons haven't gotten hold of him." he said, trying to push past his mistake, but also knowing there was more than a grain of possibility to his fear.

"Oh God those idiots."

"I thought 'those idiots' were your friends." Marc said half-playfully.

"*Katie's* friends. Not mine." Anna replied flatly, ending Marc's growing accusation. "Do you think we should go and look for him just in case?"

"Yeah, yeah, we should." Marc said, his fear for his best friend's safety fractionally superseded by the idea that Anna wanted to go outside in public with him.

"Cool." Anna said, standing up and shrugging her backpack onto her shoulders. She looked Marc up and down. "Shall we go, oh, you're not going out in that jacket are you?"

Marc's eyes widened just fractionally. "Ha Ha Ha!" he laughed, much too dramatically, and slipped out of the bomber jacket. "Nah, this, no chance ha ha ha, just a bit of fun, I wasn't even me that bought it…" He threw the jacket casually, or at least mock-casually, at the waste paper basket. The leather slapped the wall and fell in a crumpled heap. Marc winced, secretly hoping that no damage had been caused, but snapped back to his usual, confident, beaming smile. He picked up a black leather coat hanging on the handle of his wardrobe and folded it over his arm, gesturing gallantly towards the door. "Shall we?"

Anna who had thoroughly enjoyed watching Marc squirm couldn't resist a final poke.

"Sure thing Goose" she said, nodding to the Top Gun poster over his shoulder.

Marc winced again, before recognising the jibe. "Hey! I'm Maverick not Goose!"

Of course you are…

208

It took the pair around thirty minutes to walk to Richie's house. A long half hour spent trying to engage Marc as he fell down more of his pop culture conversational vanity holes.

God lord, why am I doing this for a random boy I've barely said two words to in four years?

"And it was actually Eric Stoltz who played Mart... Oh, this is his street now..." Marc said mid sentence and Anna fought back to the urge to throw up her arms in celebration.

As they rounded the corner, Anna looked down the long street, lined on both sides by mid-sized semi-detached houses, each with a small driveway and myriad variations in their small front gardens. The houses were neat and clean, most of the driveways had cars on them, most of the patches of grass out front were well kept. Compared to the near-mansions of Marc's road it was nothing special, but compared to the tiny, packed terraces of her Mum's street, it was... lovely.

"Hey, there he is!" Marc said, breaking Anna from her reverie. "Rich! Hey Richie!"

Anna looked up, and there he was, a good couple of hundred metres down the road was the lanky figure of Richie Spink. At least she thought it was. There was the distance factor to be sure, but even at that range she could tell there was something different about him.

"Has he... brushed his hair?" Marc said with a confused tone. "Where did he get those clothes from? He looks, he looks..."

"He looks good." Anna said.

"Yeah... Hey!" Marc blurted out. "Oh my God. He came to a sudden stop, and Anna took another few steps before realising. "You're not here for me are you? You're here for *him.*"

"What? NO!" Anna said, just a bit too quickly, loudly and defensively.

Oh God, here we go Anna, smooth as always.

"Hahahaha! You are too!"

"Am not." Anna retorted

Oh yeah brilliant Anna. You read three books a week, get straight A's in English and the best you can do is "am not". Give it up.

"Are t…"

"ALRIGHT!" she snapped. "Yes. I am."

"Yeah you are, wait what? Seriously?"

"Yes Marc." she sighed.

They stood there in silence for a moment. Anna felt the tension tighten between her shoulder blades. If she'd been a turtle she felt for sure her head would've retracted into her shell. Marc turned the reality over in his head, his bottom lip turning out in a face resembling grudging acceptance, but only for a moment.

"Wait. Why?" he asked sceptically, wrinkling his nose and screwing one eye shut.

It's a bloody great question.

Anna was about to break it all down, but as she watched Richie stride confidently away towards the horizon, the hulking figure of Jackson Sleight appeared from across the street.

"Hey! That's Sleight! He must've been waiting there for him.

"Ahh crap." Marc said. "That stupid idiot will probably pound Richie's face in again. We should tell someone."

"Tell someone?" Anna snorted. "What are you going to do? Call his mum? Come on you! Let's get after them!" she said, and began fast walking down the street.

"Us? I'd rather call his Mum than the mortician! Anna. Anna?"

Anna had stopped listening, and Marc after a moment of agonisingly weighing up the options of getting beaten up versus looking like a total coward, fell down on the side of the beating. But only just. He broke into a jog to get back into step with Anna.

Although Richie, and now Jackson, had a significant headstart Anna, opted instead to hang back. She feared losing sight of them, but was more fearful of how psychotic she'd look if she broke into a sprint only to find out they were both popping to the shop for a pint of milk. As Richie's street turned onto the main road, and in turn onto a series of smaller twisting and turning side roads, she began to regret the decision. Each time she turned a corner she did so just in time to see one or both rounding another. Ten minutes passed, and as she mentally made the call to go up a gear, Anna all of a sudden realised that she'd lost sight of her prey. And her prey's hunter too. She stopped to get her bearings and the laboured panting of Marc Townsend, sweating buckets in his leather Matrix-style trench coat shambled up alongside her.

"You okay there Neo?"

"It's... not... a... Matrix... coat... it's... more... an... homage... to Wesley... Snipes... In... Blade..." he said whilst his burning lungs wrestled with the concept of oxygen.

"Cool." she said bluntly. "Did your awesome vampire vision happen to see where they went?"

"Ohhh god." Marc said, doubling over and putting his sweaty palms on his knees for support. "I think I'm going to be sick."

"Keeeep breathing there, Daywalker." she said, patting him lightly on the back as she scoped out her surroundings for any indication of direction. A small movement caught her eye about one hundred metres down the way, the fleeting bob of the top of a head above one of the green, well pruned bushes that ran around the front gardens of the houses. "There!" she said, ready to continue the chase. "You okay?" She asked Marc, who had managed to get himself upright again and had regained enough oxygen in his bloodstream to give her a weak smile and a thumbs up.

"Where... Are we?" he asked.

211

"Not sure, it kind of looks familiar though." she said, studying the houses as they both began walking, at a much slower pace this time. Tall Sycamore trees ran the length of the road, placed opposite each other every ten metres or so. Each house they passed had its own small quirk, different coloured window frames, or a variation on the wrought iron gates, but there was by and large, a uniformity to them all. White paint crossed by Tudor style black wooden beams, and the aforementioned, beautifully trimmed evergreen bushes. Neat as a pin. Each and every one. Well, all but one, and when they reached it Anna's feeling of deja-vu began to scratch even louder at the back of her brain. The house in question stuck out like a Nirvana t-shirt at an S-Club concert. Though it was in principle the same as the other houses, neat as a pin it was not. The paint work on the window frames was brown, cracked and peeling. The front gate, seemingly attached to the frame only by the mass of spiderwebs at each joint, was flaky and rusted. The bushes grew out in wild spikes and plumes, like shrubbery bed-head. Still Anna couldn't place it.

"It's Mister Well's house!" Marc shouted, and the recognition came flooding back.

"Oh god, yeah of course it is."

"I'd know that car anywhere." he continued.

"Eh? What car?"

"Are you kidding? *What car*??? THE Car!" he said, pointing to Mister Well's garish, lime green mid-life crisis mobile.

"Oh, is that his, is it?"

"Yeah, of course! Are you mad??? That car is probably the most interesting thing about our entire bloody school! Hey, wait. If it wasn't the car, how did you know it was his house too?"

Anna thought back to a few Halloweens ago, and how, in tow with Sleight's cronies, she and Katie had decided to egg and flour all of the houses on this street. All good, harmless, brainless fun of course until one of the home owners emerged in his bathrobe and chased after them. Mister Wells no less. He'd actually jumped onto his push bike, and peddled furiously after them for a full three blocks, waving his fist and screaming posh obscenities with his robe billowing behind him, before finally running out of steam and giving up. It was, at the time, for her bubblegum and cola addled 'tween' brain, the funniest thing that had ever happened in her whole entire life. The gang spent the rest of the night fooling around in the nearby playpark, re-enacting every moment until their sides hurt. Re-inhabiting that younger version of herself, with her bright white and pink tracksuit, and awful attempt at eye make up made a shiver run up her spine.

"Oh, err… A friend of mine told me. Anyway, shush! This is the house, I know it is. Richie went in here, I know it."

Marc, still quietly pleased that he was still somehow in her company, decided not to press the issue further. "No sign of Sleight either. And it's not like you could miss that giant tub of…

"Tub of what?" a gruff voice said from behind them. Marc's entire body stiffened in fright.

"Oh God…" Marc whimpered.

Jackson Sleight had found them.

CHAPTER THIRTY FOUR: WELLS

Sleep came readily but fitfully. With heavy drapes drawn, alarm clock smashed, phone battery exhausted and all on-hand bottles of alcohol drained, Neil Wells was faced with two choices: Wake up and face his life, or continue to drift back into his vivid yet barely coherent dreams of childhood. He chose the latter...

His concept of time became a blur. Raindrops on fresh ink, legible only to the original author. Waking and sleeping thoughts intertwined, and from the impossible jumble of nonsense, he kept returning to that night. At the bottom of his bed, a voice rose up. When he looked to find its origin, he found himself in the hallway. Then. Small. Young. Embarrassed. Frightened.

"THIS WAS NOT YOURS TO TAKE!" his towering father roared, with rage he'd never before known. Blood seeping from a cut on his lip, another just below his right eye. In his clenched fist a small, purple tin. He raised it menacingly above his head, his teeth clenched. Young Wells cowered and simpered, and cried, and begged for forgiveness. Swinging down to strike, a piercing scream, his father's powerful arm caught in both hands by his mother. Wells scampered back, fleeing for darkness, for safety.

"LEAVE HIM BE, HE'S JUST A BOY, HE DOESN'T KNOW," she screeched, her voice cracking, on the verge of hysteria,"HE CAN'T KNOW, HOW COULD HE?!"

His father, veins bulging in his forearms, rain matting his hair to his skull, a flash of blue in his eyes as he slammed open the back door with an ear splitting crash! His mother, her face wet with tears, but with a kindly smile that soothed his soul, had taken his hand, led him gently back up the stairs, the warmth of her touch, and softness of her tone grounded the boy. Safe, warm, nothing to fear. But now as he lay in his room, the walls seemed close, too close, the wild noises outside threatened to break into his world, to shatter Mother's calming words. Thunder shook the glass of his bedroom windows, the young Wells tucked his knees to his chest, and pulled his covers up to his face. A flash of lightning lit up the room, filling it with menacing shadows. Thunder. Rattle. Flash. Thunder. Rattle. Flash. Thunder. Rattle. Flash. SHUNK. Thunder. Rattle. Flash. SHUNK. Thunder. Rattle. Flash. SHUNK. Wells felt a cold sweat run down his back, he knew better than to look, but felt his young body drifting away from the warm comfort and safety and edging closer to the window. Closer to the sound. FLASH. Thunder. Rattle. SHUNK. FLASH. Thunder. Rattle. SHUNK. He reached the drapes, his pale white fingers trembling, pulling them back an inch. One eye to the gap. Flash. Thunder. Rattle. SHUNK. Straining to see in the darkness and the beating rain. FLASH. A figure. A hulking, hunchbacked figure, a monster in the darkness. THUNDER. RATTLE. It turned to face him. Growled in anger, its eyes like blue flames against a sodden wet mountain of muscle and rage.

Wells awoke with a start. Sweat poured from his brow, the sound of his own heartbeat filled his senses. He sat up, desperately trying to find his bearings, as his eyes fought against the gloom. Instinctively he reached for the bottle at his bedside, pulled it to his lips, but found it empty. He tossed it to one side, the impact further smashing the plastic casing and circuit board that had once been his alarm clock. He sighed and slumped back down into the covers. He turned the dream fragments over in his head.

Did that actually happen or am I just cracking up?

Something about this felt significant, amid the jumble and the sleepy haze, there was a truth, no, *a secret* there. Somewhere. He could feel it, tantalisingly close but too intangible to grasp, gossamer, breaking apart like spider webs at his grasp, but each contact leaving more residue behind. The tin in his father's hand, the thought of it thrilled and

215

terrified him, but he couldn't place why. His father. Gone. A wave of sorrow crested over him. Neil Wells lay in his bed and stared into the near blackness of the ceiling, turning over his fleeting memories, turning them over and rubbing them between the thumb and forefinger of his mind's eye until sleep took him again...

CHAPTER THIRTY FIVE: THE ETERNAL FLAME

As he made his way down the street, The Flame felt the biting cold wind on his cheek and smiled. He pulled the zip of his coat up a little higher, and allowed himself a moment to soak in the wondrously, beautifully unremarkable nature of his surroundings. The pavements beneath his feet, the pebble dashed rendering of the houses, the cars of every shape and colour imaginable lining the streets, and occasionally passing by apace, presumably off on their equally magically mundane trips to visit relatives, go to work, or do the weekly shopping. It had been four years since the fateful night that had granted him his powers, with them had come access to an incredible new depth of sense and power, but they had also come with a trade off. A higher calling and all the responsibility that came with it. All of the distance. Between himself and feeling, between himself and those around him. *When you can fight off a troop of soldiers without breaking a sweat, you tend to stop noticing the little things.*

At the peak of both the conflicts he'd fronted, the unbridled willpower of an entire nation had coursed through his body. It had given him an elevated sense of humanity, and a deep respect for the strength of the individual; seeing and feeling first-hand what the willpower of even one deeply passionate person could produce. He'd travelled the world, fought with and against do or die zealots, and witnessed sights his once young eyes could not have imagined in his wildest dreams. He'd spent his post school years and the early years of adulthood waiting to find his calling, searching for deeper meaning and a place to fit in. In the army he'd found it, and from there the calling had found him.

As he felt the cool air tousling his hair, his mind drifted back to that night. The cold, dark, scream filled night. The electro-static charge of the enemy weapons that seemed to make the metallic fillings in his back teeth vibrate. The cave. The dank. The smell of moss and death in the air. The Blue Flame. His future and his past laid out before him…

At the last moment, he quickly sidestepped a pile of half-dried dog muck on the ground, shaking his attention back to the world around him. The Eternal Flame shook his head, and smoothed back his freshly combed hair with his left hand.

Life moves pretty fast, if you don't stop and look around once in a while, you might miss it.

He chuckled at the thought, a fitting quote, the origins long lost to him, like so much of his memory since the Battle. He fought the urge to break out into a full blown laugh at the absurdity of his situation. Last week he'd kicked a grenade the length of a football field, now look at him. He examined his slender hands, tensed the muscles of his puny arms beneath his bulky coat. The cold sting on his cheek, the goosebumps on his neck, and even the dull throbbing pain from his wounded toe felt marvellous. For the first time in the longest time he chose to embrace those small things. He took a deep inhale through his nose, feeling the cool air stinging his sinuses, and let it out slowly through his mouth. Somehow he knew his destination, knew the potentially perilous path that lay ahead, but pressed ahead anyway. With or without the power of the Flame, he was duty bound to see it through, and Neil Wells held the answers he needed.

CHAPTER THIRTY SIX: BILL and GREEN

"Children on the grounds?" Willerton-Smythe said with a distasteful sneer to this voice. "Out here as well! I would expect such loutish behaviour in the city, but it seems the war has spread the urchin rabble far and wide." He tutted in disapproval.

Bill fought the urge not to thump him in the side of the head, instead, he gritted his teeth as he examined the hole in the perimeter fence.

Willerton jotted a quick note of the location in his notebook, and primly replaced it in his top pocket. "Savages." He muttered under his breath.

"Kids'll be kids Willy, didn't you ever break in somewhere you weren't meant to be?

Apart from the army.

"Heavens forbid no. What do you take me for some sort of common plebeian wastrel? Of course there was one time, when Nanny called us in for supper and we chose to hide in the lower gardens as a jape, but…"

"Nevermind." Bill growled, moving away from the fence. His eyes scoured the landscape for any further signs of intrusion. "Keep yer eyes peeled" he said firmly. Unlikely as it was that his 2nd in command would spot anything that he hadn't, it always paid to be thorough.

Green felt the hairs on the back of his neck begin to stand on end. For the first dozen or so minutes since heading deeper into the forest there had been no sign of either their target, their fellow troops, or any young intruders. But now as he stood at the foot of another thick-trunked sycamore, looking up at what appeared to be a rudimentarily constructed treehouse, he swore under his breath. On high alert, he purposefully took a 360 degree look around their surroundings, seeking with eagle eye any signs that someone, or ones, were close by. Without speaking he nodded to Welsh and gestured upwards. His squadmate nodded in return, and began quickly climbing the wooden rungs that had been nailed into the tree. Once at the top he quickly surveyed the situation. Roughly twenty five feet in the air a flat floor had been put in place, scattered around it was sufficient evidence of its recent use. A couple of tatty copies of The Beano and the Hotspurs along with four well worn cushions, two cups, and a flask. Welsh picked up one of the cups, a ring of brown, damp residue ran below the lip. He picked up the flask and tipped it sideways with a faint sloshing sound. With a slight clenching of his jaw, he unscrewed the cap, and wisps of steam rose from within. He replaced the lid, and leant over the side of the structure.

"Heads up lads," he said, and tossed the bottle down. Parkinson grabbed for it, but fumbled, knocking it into a pile of leaves at Green's feet. He looked up sheepishly, "sorry mate, butter fingers innit?".

Green shook his head and retrieved it from the dry ground. He opened the lid and raised it to his nose, a rich, sweet aroma filling his senses. "Hot chocolate." He muttered.

"Ohh magic, hot chocolate, really? Ey are, can I have some?" Parkinson perked up. Green handed him the bottle, and he took a satisfied swig. "Fantastic. Just like granny used to make."

Green ignored him, and craned his neck to look up at Welsh. "Any sign of the kids?"

"No mate, maybe they legged it when they heard the explosion?"

"Maybe. But then these are kids who've cut open a fence, built a treehouse, and are using it on a school day. If that was you and you heard that noise would you run away?"

"No," he laughed. "I'd be running towards it I reckon."

220

"Yeah, same." He took a deep breath. "Okay, what's the view like, anything else to report?"

Welsh stood tall again, looking off into the distance that was partially obscured by the cross hatching of tree branches and leaves. "No, nothing… Oh hang about." He opened a pouch on his back and pulled out a compact set of binoculars. "Yeah, yeah, there, 11 o'clock."

Green strained his eyes in that direction but saw nothing. He flicked open his compass and nodded. "Right, okay, that's on our heading anyway, let's go and check it out."

Welsh nodded and began to climb down. Green looked to Parkinson who was trying to lick the final drops from the upturned flask. Green shook his head again and slapped it from his hand, sending it skittering away into a pile of dry leaves. "Focus." he said sternly. Parkinson momentarily considered protesting, but thought better of it.

"Sorry gaffer."

With Welsh once again alongside them, the trio began to move again. "Ay, missed a bit there lad." Welsh said to Parkinson, nodding towards the clown-like smile of chocolate residue on the smaller man's freckled face. His eyes widened in embarrassment and he quickly scrubbed it away with the back of his sleeve. And then, looking at the mess it left of his sleeve, in turn wiped that quickly on the leg of his khaki trousers. Welsh laughed softly, and gave him a playful prod in the ribs.

"Eyes up you two." Green snapped, in a strong but quiet tone. The picture of focus.

They pressed on and within seconds Green laid eyes on a glimpse of an all too familiar khaki green uniform, partially obscured by another of the myriad tall trees and underbrush. Green silently pointed towards it and then gestured right to Welsh, and left to Parkinson, both nodded taciturnly and spread out to either side, flanking the target.

Drawing closer, Green slowed his pace as he became increasingly aware of the rustling sound each step made. His blood seemed to thunder through his veins, his vision myopically focussed on what was clearly a hunched figure just beyond the next treeline. Slowly, deliberately he unhooked the net gun slung on his back, gripping the cool metal of its barrel in his right hand, centring himself, controlling his breathing, fighting back the cold rush of adrenaline coursing down his spine. Twenty yards became ten, became five, became touching distance. Something wasn't right. As he came up behind he heard a rustling in the distance, and Parkinson stepped out with a puzzled look on his young face. Green was about to shout out a reprimand, when Welsh appeared too; equally confused, but with a hint of panic. He followed their eye lines. At his feet was the person they'd been tracking, slumped against the trunk. Green reached down and checked the man's pulse.

Unconscious. What the hell?

He looked up at the other two hoping for some explanation. Instead he found them even more perplexed; the faint hint of worry spreading into a more broad unease, as Parkinson discovered another comatose member of their squad. Welsh found another, then another. In total five of their fellow squad mates lay spread out around the area. All out cold, but alive.

The trio made sure to move each into the recovery position, before stepping away to survey the situation.

"Five of 'em boss. Five." Welsh said, shaking his head.

"Think they knocked themselves out fighting each other?" Parkinson chipped in, scratching his head.

"Not likely, for a start, look who it is." He nodded down to the prone bodies.

They recognised them all of course. The five in question, Adams, Gwilliam, Redfearn, Turpin and Skinner, were another fairly tight knit group within the wider unit.

Tough bastards too.

"Maybe another gang of the lads jumped them?" Welsh offered.

"Yeah, maybe…" Green replied, unconvinced. The numbers didn't add up. Of the other squad members he struggled to think of another group that had either the numbers, or more importantly the skill to do such a thorough job. It was possible that a couple of lads together could get the drop on them, sneak up on one or two. He could see that. But all five? Without losing a man themselves? No chance.

"Look at them though. If they'd been in a big fight, they'd have cuts and bruises." He lifted up the limp arm of the nearest, Skinner. The knuckles were generally calloused, but nothing fresh. "Have you ever knocked someone out?"

Welsh and Parkinson looked at each other and shrugged. "No." they replied in unison.

"Well let me tell you, it's not easy. If it was, Boxers wouldn't need a dozen rounds, i'll tell you that for nothing. These lads were either choked out, or knocked out with one straight punch each."

"So yeah, they must've been choked out then? That makes sense right?" Parkinson said, brightening at the explanation.

Green shook his head. "Look at how they were all spread out." He gestured around them in a circle. "They were all facing this spot. It's like they all closed in on something, and were sent flying away in turn." He continued, turning around the circle and pointing to the spot where each man landed as he did. The bodies fanned out from his central point, like petals on a flower.

"Okay yeah, that makes sense, but what kind of thing would cause them all to attack at once?" Welsh asked.

"And what kind of thing takes on five men…" Parkinson continued.

"… and then knocks them all out with one punch each?" Green finished. "I've got no idea. But if it's the same guy

223

who survived being shot out of the sky then we might be in trouble here."

A cold feeling filtered into the pit of Green's stomach. He gripped the net gun tighter, the knuckles of his hand turning white with the pressure.

All of a sudden a loud rustling from the bushes broke the silence, and they snapped their attention towards it. A figure broke from cover, sprinting away at top speed. "Go!" Green barked at Welsh, who set off after them. Green and Parkinson followed behind as fast as they could.

With his net gun held out in front of him, muzzle face down, Green, with Parkinson a step behind, tried his best not to lose ground to his admittedly much faster teammate and his quarry. Dodging between the trees, jumping over a fallen tree trunk, and trying not to turn his ankle on the thick black spider-web of gnarled roots, he kept one eye on them in the distance for maybe a minute before they accelerated out of sight. Still he pressed on, trusting that the fleeing person, with Welsh hot on his heels, would be too frightened to deviate from their path.

Three more minutes passed, with their lungs burning, Green and Parkinson burst into a smallish clearing, the daytime sunlight coming down in thin spotlights through the overhead canopy of leaves and branches. Green pulled up sharply, and Parkinson, fighting for breath, stumbled as he tried not to slam straight into the taller man's back. Green spun around on his heel, net gun held up at chest height, looking for any signs of Welsh or the target.

"Hey gaff…" Parkinson said, between huge gulps of air. "'ave you seen this?"

Green looked across to see what had distracted him this time. Parkinson was down on his knees sifting through the remains of a green painted wooden crate, much like the one they had discovered earlier. Parkinson picked up an Enfield Mk1 Revolver, or at least what remained of one. "Ay, it's a proper gun! Well…" he said, as the cylindrical barrel fell to the floor. "It *was* anyway. Ey, there's all kinds here." he continued, greedily scrabbling through the distinctly exploded remains of the weapons crate.

"Anything salvageable?"

"Not much, oh, 'ang on a sec!" Parkinson said perkily, holding up a dented, charred, but intact metal tin. With some effort he prised off its misshapen lid. Inside, nestled in a bed of straw, were three pristine looking grenades. "Reckon this'll do you?" He said with a broad, cheeky smile.

"Yeah, they'll do nicely," he said, taking the box, handing one to Parkinson and clipping the other two to his belt.

"I wonder why this one had all the proper gear in when ours was just funny stuff." Parkinson said more to himself than conversationally.

Green scanned the debris one last time

Another mystery, this whole exercise just keeps getting more and more peculiar.

Before he could express this to the other, the rattling sound of gunfire filled the air, snapping their attention back to the task at hand. Through an overhead gap in the trees he saw a flock of birds frantically take flight back past them. Without a word both men began sprinting towards the sounds.

Once again the rich greens and browns of the forest whipped by as the sounds of combat grew closer and closer, and then all of a sudden they were clear, and what lay before them caused Green to stop dead in his tracks. This time Parkinson, unable to adjust, ran straight into his back, sending both men tumbling to the ground.

Slowly looking up and wiping loose earth from his face, Green tried to process the scene unfolding before him. The deafening, repetitive bangs of gunfire drowned his brain. Straight ahead, and half obscuring his view was Welsh, his left hand firmly gripped to the collar of a young boy no older than nine or ten years old. The child, whose shirt was

225

untucked and the sleeveless jumper over it ruched up, had clearly been fighting to free himself, but no more. Both stood frozen. To the left and right of the small field before them the final four members of the squad, two on either side, unloaded shots from rifles and handguns. Green studied their anguished faces, Andreo and Marsh, Ainsworth and Hicks, the unmistakable tableau of fear and panic etched deep into faces and body language. Green crawled forward, inch by inch, the damp moisture of the soil and leaves beneath him seeping into his uniform, until, in the gap between Welsh's legs he could finally see the object of their fears.

There he was, a giant in British army combat fatigues. The upper part of his face obscured by a pale blue bandana. His arms up and crossed in a defensive posture, blue flames licking from his hands and torso as the hail of bullets struck him. Marsh was the first to run out of ammunition, although it took several extra presses of his pistol trigger for that fact to register. When it did, he looked at the useless object in his hand, tossed it into the ankle high grass and with a blood curdling war cry, charged at the masked figure. He covered the ten yard distance quickly, and locking his hands together, raised them over his head to strike. His opponent moved with lightning reflexes, pivoting on his left foot to face Marsh, and throwing out a left handed jab which connected square with his chest. The punch immediately halted and reversed his attackers momentum, lifting his feet off the ground, folding his body in two, and sending him flying back the way he came, to land unconscious at the feet of Andreo. The ruddy cheeked auburn haired young man stopped firing, and looked down aghast at the crumpled teammate at his feet.

Green dragged himself to his knees and watched as Ainsworth and Hicks followed suit, each to similar, disastrous ends.

What the hellfire?! What is that thing???

Green dragged Parkinson up with him to standing, and stepped forward to Welsh, placing a hand on his shoulder. The man flinched and swung a punch, which Green managed to catch with a firm SMACK, in the palm of his hand.

"Easy lad." he said, pushing his fist down, seeing the shocked, wide eyed expression on his face for the first time. The last of the four, Andreo, a manic look of utter desperation on his face, looked up at the monster, then down at himself. He unclipped his belt, which had three grenades attached to it, quickly pulled their pins and, whirling it around his head to gather momentum, hurled them across the field. At that very moment, the young man in Welsh's grip broke free, breaking away into a sprint across the field. Green, Welsh and Parkinson watched on in horror as the grenade arc'd through the sky, and the boy got closer and closer.

"NOOOO!!!" Green shouted, and began to give chase, only to find Welsh and Parkinson holding him back, dragging him to the floor, dooming the boy but protecting their friend from a grisly death. "Noooo. Let. Me. Go!" he heard himself roar as he fought against their hold. It was too late though and he knew it, the distance, the power of the explosion, it was certain death.

CHAPTER THIRTY SEVEN: RICHIE

Welsh, Green and Will had spent a short time in quite serious conversation before the older man ordered the rest of the squad to bed in for the night. At some point Richie had drifted off to sleep, but it was short and fitful. He dreamt about doing his impending GCSE's naked, he'd dreamt about a twelve foot Marc in his awful Top Gun jacket stomping Godzilla-like over a city, and of course he'd dreamt about Anna Harrison, her raven black hair, and her wicked smile. He'd never camped outdoors in his life, the sole exception being that time he, Kathy, his Mum and Dad (pre-troubles) had set up a tent in the back garden. They had roasted marshmallows on his Dad's portable barbeque and told stupid ghost stories and then, half frozen to death, abandoned everything at about 2am for the infinitely warmer refuge of their central heated house and duvet laden beds. To a city boy like Richie, sleeping outdoors was as alien to him as a Playstation and flat screen telly would be to Will. His disquiet though, was far more the result of his overactive mind than his surroundings. Despite the rough environment, he actually found the camp surprisingly comforting. He thought back to Will's explanation of his powers and wondered whether that feeling stemmed from the men around him.

The more I find out, the less I seem to know.

The changes he'd been undergoing, he figured, must conform to some of the established tropes, and so as the rest of the squad settled in for the night, and the fire began to burn low, Richie made a mental list of any similar situations from tv, film and comics that he could recall.

Character	Instigating Factor	Yes No Maybe?	Notes
Billy Batson/Captain Marvel or Mike Moran/ Marvelman	Magic Word: Shazam/ Kimota	No	Unless it's a mad accidental boring word, it's a no.
Gary Sparrow/ Goodnight Sweetheart	Time Portal	Definite No	Changes occurred in different places. Also, different body.
Sam Becket/Quant um Leap	Weird sci-fi device. Leaps within his own lifetime.	No/ Maybe.	Not within my own lifetime. Also, no hologram companion (sadly)
Bruce Banner/ Hulk	Stress induced	YES!	All changes during stress/ended during calm!!!
Marty McFly	Delorean	No	Too young to drive, lack of awesome, flying, time travel car

Richie replayed the memories of each of his changes, and at the heart of them was the overwhelming feeling of stress, physical or mental. Despite the lack of a time travel element, 'The Banner Theory' felt as close to correct as anything else he'd come up with. Feeling a slight sense of peace from this miniature revelation, he allowed himself to relax and drift off to sleep, safe in the knowledge that this particular change had at least given him a deeper understanding of his situation.

We're making progress at least. Next time I'm here, I'll make sure I find out even more…

When he awoke from his disjointed dreams, it took Richie a few moments to place himself. A few blissful moments until he realised that the warmth he felt was not from the duvet of his bed or the central heating, but instead from the dying embers of the campfire.

He was still in 1942.

There were the other three soldiers asleep on the ground. There was the tree/face-planting German prisoner tied up and there was Will, effortlessly doing pushups in the faint orange light of the fire. The thing more strange than all of that though, was that as much as he'd expected to see his Ferris Bueller (Marc's influence), Incubus (Kathy's influence) and C&C (all him) posters, he found himself feeling strangely relieved. He again attributed that feeling to the power of The Eternal Flame, but had to admit that waking up in a forest might actually be preferable to waking up in the middle of another parental divorce skirmish. Judging by the fire, and by how soundly asleep the other members of the squad were, Richie knew he hadn't slept long, but was surprised to feel no sense of fatigue. He stood up and stretched out his powerful legs, and flexed his arms and couldn't help but be amazed at how good he felt. Across the way, Will finished his workout and let out a low whistle, gesturing him over.

"Mornin' lad. Sleep alright?"

"I didn't think I did, but I feel pretty great."

"Well you look like boiled crap. Make sure you grab a shave before we head out."

"A shave?"

"Ye'. Self discipline above all else. A good soldier follows orders, but a great one keeps himself in check." he said, and handed him a small, shiny leather case.

"Oh, okay. Erm…" Richie said as he opened it to reveal a comb, a steel razor and a number of other alien looking implements.

Will chuckled. "Let me guess, first time?"

"Oh, err, no sir. I had this annoying little bumfluff moustache thing going on and got skitted in school for it. I borrowed my Dad's Mach Three, erm, I mean my Dad's razor. Cut my top lip to bits." He smiled weakly.

"No worries lad. 'Ere let me show you."

"Are, you going to do it?" he asked sceptically.

"Me? Don't be daft. If I do it, how does that help you learn to do it next time?"

"Fair enough."

"Right, go an' get some hot water from t' fire and we'll crack on."

An hour later, freshly shaved and feeling even more at ease in his own skin, Richie and the rest of the squad stood to attention in front of Will. His playful tone from earlier once again replaced by stern focus. The first light of dawn was breaking, and a faint mist hovered over the forest floor, giving the forest an eerie, supernatural feeling.

"As you all know, the Panzerkampfwagen, or Panzer tanks to you and me, have been at the forefront of the enemy's advance across Europe. Last year our intel boys stumbled upon a secret order from the Fuhrer himself. A birthday pressie to himself. He challenged the country's best engineers to build the next generation model, a Sherman killer, a tank

231

more powerful and indestructible than anything else on the battlefield."

Richie looked across at the others, and tried to mirror their upright postures and impassive faces.

"The final plans for what we believe will be the Panzerkampfwagen VI, are bein' developed in the bunker up ahead. Inside that bunker is Agent Tempest, our man on the inside. Originally the plan had been to sneak in undetected, rendezvous with Tempest, take the plans, destroy the backups and get off back home in time for tea. 2nd Lieutenant Welsh though," he nodded towards the stocky man. "reports that although the base seems not to 'ave been alerted to our presence, there is a full infantry platoon stationed in Petite-Foret, blocking our path to the extraction point. That means we need to play this extra smart, and extra quiet. That is, of course, provided you all prefer to reach a ripe old age being fanned in the sunshine by yer big bosomed wives, and not turned into human watering cans instead.

The men around him laughed, startling Richie, who was lost in his visualisation of the swarm of German soldiers, Will was describing. He had no idea how many men were in a platoon, but it stood to reason that it was more than the six that totaled the entire Flame Squad. A little taken aback by their aloof reaction, he looked at the faces of the group. He'd expected to see fear, but instead he saw... relish? Most of them had variations of calm, bordering on excited looks on their faces. The tall guy called Green grinned and cracked his knuckles. Welsh, the broad fella who had run off on the scouting mission nodded confidently. The rest, whilst still maintaining total focus on the words of their leader, managed to also portray a cool confidence.

These guys are friggin' crazy!

The group all smiled, smirked, grinned and/or nodded. Richie, who very much thought they were all batshit crazy, but was too socially awkward to say so, nodded along with them.

"Raight. Twenty minutes. Pack up. Make sure yer've all eaten summat and then we head out. Ainsworth, you're in charge of Hans Sonny-Jim o'er there." he said pointing a thumb behind him to the tree trunk with the bundle of loose rope at its foot. The collective gasp from the assembled troops alerted him to the problem. In his fifteen years, Richie Spink, between school, late night TV, video games, an older sister and two divorce-bound parents, had heard his fair share of swear words. He was partial to the occasional one himself too. The words that shot from Will's mouth like molten lead however caused even the battle hardened men alongside him to clench their jaws. The prisoner was gone. The prisoner whose job it has been for Richie to secure. As Will's fury hosed them all down, Richie felt the icy cold feeling of fear and panic run from the pit of his stomach, spreading out and coursing through his veins.

"Two minutes. Grab what yer can and let's get a move on. Go. Now!" Will barked and the men busily gathered their things. He walked around the fire, with a demeanour of menace, and Richie began to tamely babble an apology.

"W-Will, I'm sorry, I thought I'd done it tight, it's just I'I've never done that before an…"

Will pushed past him, picked up his rations bag and shaving kit from the floor and put them back into the respective places on his belt.

"And… Well I didn't want to look stupid by asking for help beca…" Richie continued.

Above his tightly shaved pencil moustache, Will's nostrils flared. Turning instantly he marched the handful of steps between them until they were stood toe to toe. The older man was five or so inches shorter, but to Richie it certainly didn't feel that way. He felt every inch the young boy he was inside. He could feel the anger of the man coming off him in waves, feel the rage in his breath, see the vein bulging in his temple up close and personal.

"The only truly stupid person is someone who would rather pretend to know something than learn how to actually do it."

He looked Richie straight in the eyes and held his gaze.

"Brave men are going to die today because you didn't even have the courage to ask how to tie a bloody knot."

"Will I'm so…"

"Don't be sorry. Be better." he interrupted, still refusing to break gaze, his rage receding, but with a cold aggression remaining in his tone.

"Look at them." he said, his eyes still fixed on Richie, but tilting his head towards the flurry of activity around them. "Each and every one of those lads has dedicated themselves to this squad, they've each reached a benchmark that few on this earth could even dream of, let alone achieve. We are fighting for King and Country, yes, but first and foremost we fight for each other."

Richie looked around the camp, the cocksure looks from earlier had been replaced by those of pure focus. These guys had their orders, and were about to run off into God knows what, and do so willingly. Richie felt his lip twitch, and a hot feeling built behind his eyes. He bit hard into his lip to stop the tremble, to keep the tears at bay.

"Now grab yer stuff. We've got a mission." Will said.

"Yes sir." Richie nodded, and as Will spun away to lead the troops he felt the tension drain from the muscles in his necks, arms and back he hadn't realised he was clenching. He wiped his eyes with his sleeve, readjusted his mask and grabbed his backpack from the floor. He took a deep breath and stepped into line as Will led the troops out of camp and into the unknown.

Twenty minutes later, the Eternal Flame Squad reached the edge of the forest, and Will gathered them around. Despite the pace of the jog, not to mention the terrain and weight of equipment. Richie couldn't fail to be impressed that none of them seemed even remotely out of breath. He'd never even completed a Cross Country lesson without getting a stitch.

"The bunker is up ahead. Our target is inside. Agent Tempest has been in deep cover for the past two years so you won't be able to differentiate between them and the others in there. We'll need him to initiate contact, so when we go in, it's non-lethal's only. Understood?" Will asked and the group nodded confirmation. "Raight then. Me, Flame and Green will be going 'int back door. Skinner, Ainsworth, Welsh, go on ahead and secure the extraction point. Steer clear of that town. If we're not there within the hour we've failed. You're to return and set charges on the bunker. Blow it to hell."

"If we run inta trouble, we using lethals or non, sir?" Skinner asked in a heavy cockney drawl.

"At your discretion son." Will replied to a satisfied nod and smirk from Skinner.

Richie stood at the back of the group listening intently and mentally tallying names to faces. The deep rooted shame of his mistake earlier threatened to bubble up and overwhelm him, so having a simple task to follow gave him blessed distraction.

"Their man will be home and dry by now, so keep yer wits about yer, all of yer. Now, off you go." he said firmly. The advance party ran off, leaving just Richie, Green and Will. With the squad leader setting the pace they headed off to the south, sticking to the cover of the forest.

"Raight gents. We get the fun job." he chuckled, lightening Richie's tension fractionally. "Tempest's last message gave us the layout of the facility. Ground level is the maintenance hangar, and the control room. Five soldiers, in rotation. In the sub level, twenty storeys below ground is a laboratory. It's accessed from an exposed staircase outside the control room that runs down the open shaft to the bottom.

235

Guarding the lab are three more sentries. Our target will be on that level. There is, though, another way in, a supply tunnel used during construction. It'll take us straight to the sub level. There's less cover if we're caught, but it's quicker and according to Tempest unguarded.

"Unguarded sir?" Green asked.

"Tempest says it's been unused since the facility came into service. It's not on the official plans, and they never bothered to install surveillance."

"Sounds a bit fishy to me boss."

"Yer might be right, but right now it's the best plan we've got. Tempest is one of the best. I trust 'em with my life, but we should still keep our wits about us."

Green nodded, his scepticism had been noted, and now was the time to press on.

Richie fought to maintain an equilibrium between the calmness and surety that Will was projecting, with the blind trouser soiling panic that threatened to burst out of him. He thought about that stupid Yoga class his mum had dragged him to that one time, or 'Middle aged women, breathing and gossip' as Kathy had dubbed it. The most boring hour of his life, but as Will's words began to blur before him, he focussed on his own breath, gently in through the nose and out through the mouth, and after a few seconds things started to shift back into shape.

"Flame…"

Richie's attention returned just in time.

"You bring up the rear, keep your eyes peeled for anything unusual. If anyone gets past us, it's your job to bring them down. Got it?"

"Yes sir."

Simple. But still terrifying.

Will stopped his jog and consulted a crumpled piece of paper in his hand. He took three deliberate steps forward and two to the right. He swiped his boot sideways, shifting loose soil and vegetation, to reveal a hint of a metal hatch beneath.

"Whoa, just like Lost!" Richie murmured.

"What was that lad?"

"Oh, nothing sir." Richie smiled weakly.

Minutes later, the ground was cleared, and the hatch exposed. With a little exertion, Will turned the rusted metallic handle, and wrenched it open as smoothly as possible. The three men leaned over the open hole, the rungs of a ladder, embedded into the concrete wall led down into the thick black soupy darkness below.

"Nothing to it but to do it." Richie said, knowing full well that it was a line from a dreadful action film Marc had exposed him to last year. Will and Green seemed to like it, both nodding in thoughtful agreement

Will was the first down the hole, and Richie watched as he vanished into the gloom. Green was next, but before he descended he turned to face him.

"Don't worry Richie lad. Stick with me. We'll get through this." he said, and Richie, a little taken aback to discover that another of the men knew his secret, managed a gulp and an eager nod in return.

"Just make sure I don't do anything stupid okay?"

Green let out a small laugh, before stifling it.

"Sure thing."

And then he was gone too, and Richie stood there. His future was a potentially bottomless pit of darkness, fear and pain. He shrugged.

Still better than being at home...

He began the descent into darkness.

CHAPTER THIRTY EIGHT: ANNA

Anna sighed in annoyance. Beside her, Marc stood frozen but for his eyes, which gave her a pleading look.

"He's behind us isn't he?" Marc said with a fearful tremor in his voice.

"Hello Jackson." Anna said, barely able to contain the disdain in her voice as she turned around.

And there he was. All 6ft plus, broad shoulders, freckles and acne. Scourge of the school and all those unfortunate enough to be less sporty, have a different dress code or be moderately intelligent within it. Jackson Sleight. Bully. Idiot.

Marc, his shoulders hunched in fearful tension, one eye screwed shut, slowly turned around too. Sleight's cold beady eyes bore deep into Marc's, his demeanour negatively dripping with malice. Marc seemed to whither back into his long leather coat beneath the gaze.

"You weren't talking about me was yer?" he said in his typically bassy, semi-literate way.

"Us, me? What? No, Ha! Of course not. I was talking about Anna here, yeah, yeah, you, you big tub of lard you!" Flustered he reached to rub her belly, and had his hand instantly slapped away. "Ha!" he shouted in shock, before somehow continuing his frantic back pedalling, "You, you want to, to watch out! Yeah, watch out, that metabolism won't save you forever, same thing happened to my cousin Janice, y'know? Yoghurts and microwaveable burgers every day of her life, skinny as a rake, then she hit twenty five, and, err… well, y'know?" He looked at both Sleight and Anna and then puffed out his cheeks and stuck out his belly. "Human balloon." he said, his voice distorted by his air filled face.

For what felt like four painful lifetimes lived on top of one another, Anna and Jackson Sleight stared at him dumb founded. She rolled her eyes.

I'm surrounded by morons.

"So you're saying Annie is a fatty then yeah?"

"Err…" Marc deflated his cheeks. "Yeah?" He turned to Anna, winced and shrugged.

"Oh right. Want me to pound his face in for yer Annie?"

"It wouldn't be worse than the worst idea I'VE had today." she said, her voice dripping with sarcasm.

Jackson looked puzzled for a moment, before realising that it was a good idea with or without her approval and grabbed a ham-sized fistful of Marc's leather.

"Hey! Anna! I'm sorry, I…"

Anna sighed again, even more deeply this time as she quickly digested the car crash her life had become.

"No! Wait!" she said, with the palm of her right hand held out towards the boys, and the other pressed to her temple. "Let him go, it's fine."

Sleight thought about the request, weighing up the choice like a butcher slapping slabs of meat onto a scale.

Good Lord, are all boys this dim?

For her own sake, given the driving force behind this wholly moronic expedition, she hoped not.

Eventually, grudgingly, he released Marc, who quickly stepped to the side, and half behind Anna and began to pout over the wrinkled leather of his coat.

"What are you doing here Jackson?" she asked directly.

"Me, I err…"

Anna watched as the boy tried to come up with an excuse, and swore that she could actually hear the sound of rusty cogs turning in his head.

"Come on Jackson, I haven't got all day. Why were you following Richie Spink?"

The burly boy's eyes widened as though Anna had just used a form of witchcraft to read his mind. "How did you?"

"Telepathy is one of the core powers you receive when you become a goth. You get the "Beautiful People" LP, a pair

239

of fishnets, telepathy and a copy of The Nightmare Before Christmas on VHS when you sign up."

"Eh?" he said, wrinkling his wide freckled nose.

Why do I even bother?

"Nevermind. We saw you following Richie. Why?"

"Oh, just wanted to speak to him about sumfin'.."

"Wanted to flatten him more like" Marc muttered.

Jackson grunted in retort, and Marc took another fractional step behind Anna.

"Now, now, boys. Settle down, you can both go and have a wee on that lamp post when we're done, mark your territory and see if that makes you calm down a bit. He's right though Jackson, from what I've seen, that does seem more your style."

"Yeah, well, maybe it is," Sleight said, suddenly adopting a more defensive tone and posture. "But this time I just wanted to talk to him about sumfin'... sumfin' personal innit?" he said, crossing his arms. "But he went an' knocked on Mister Wells' door and then went in. I see enuff teachers during the week, no chance I'm seein' one on the weekend too."

The answer made sense, in a typically Sleightish kind of way. Of course she had seen Jackson both deliver a slap to Richie AND still have some form of conversation with him that Friday by the shops, so it wasn't outside the realms of possibility. But for a boy who normally communicated in grunts, smells and mono-syllables she still found it hard to believe that Sleight had ever sought someone out for the sole-purpose of conversation in his entire life. It warranted further investigation.

As she was about to press further, a black sedan cruised towards them, catching her eye line. In the passenger seat was a figure that made her blood run cold.

The Man in Grey!

240

It was a fractional moment, but it passed in a lifetime. The car slowed outside Mr Wells' house, and the passengers all turned to look down the pathway. Instinctively Anna spun and ducked down behind the nearest parked car. The vehicle drove another couple of car lengths down the road and pulled to a stop.

"Get down you idiots!" Anna hissed, and both boys crouched down in front of her without question, their earlier spat forgotten. "That's the guy who killed Mr Wells' father! He must be after *him* as well!" Keeping her back pressed to the maroon coloured estate car, she edged towards the rear and peered around the corner. The Man in Grey exited on the far side, smoothed down his suit jacket and adjusted his sunglasses. From the nearside back seat, another young, far less stylish, rather plump young man with thick glasses and ratty t-shirt struggled to get out. As he did, he tripped on his untied laces and stumbled out into the road, bumping into the opposite car that was Anna's cover. She gasped, and rolled back out of sight. Anna could feel her heart pounding ceaselessly in her chest. Swallowing hard, she rediscovered her resolve and slowly risked another peek out.

The Man in Grey had come around the car now and grabbed the pudgy man by the scruff of his jacket, hauling him back towards Mr Wells' house.

"Go and knock on the door, we're going to have a word with your old friend." The Man in Grey said, his voice smooth as cut glass.

"He's not my fr.." The man protested, but was cut short by a firm push to the back.

The Man in Grey slammed the rear door shut, and the car eased away.

Anna crouch-walked the length of her cover-car, and lifted her head to watch as the man grudgingly made his way to Wells' front gate, opened it with a jarring squeak, and walked in. The overgrown hedges blocked any further view as they made their way up the garden path.

Anna took a deep breath, and leaned her weight against the cool metal of the car door. Only then did she remember that Marc and Sleight were there, a look of sarcastic puzzlement and utterly blank confusion on their faces respectively. Marc was the first to speak.

"Anna." He reached out and placed a caring hand on her shoulder. "Are you on drugs?"

"Yeah, can I have some if you are?" Jackson Sleight asked with his usual level of slab headed tact.

"What?! No, I'm not on drugs!" she snapped, slipping her shoulder free of Marc's hand. "That man there, the skinny one in the grey suit? He broke into the nursing home I work at the other night, killed Mister Wells' father and ran off before he could be caught. Before he died though, he gave me this." she said, and slipped her backpack from her shoulders, turned it round and pointed to the flaming fist patch she'd sewn into its centre.

The boys leant in for a closer look. The blue flames around the fist seemed to glimmer in the sunlight.

"Eternal Flame Squad" they mouthed in unison, before Sleight squinted at the smaller text beneath.

"Non Sibi Sed Omnibus" Marc said without missing a beat.

"Haha, they can't even write proper words." Sleight snorted.

Anna rolled her eyes, and even Marc sighed.

"It's Latin. It means 'Not for oneself, but for all." he explained.

Sleight grabbed the bag for a closer look. "Not for oneself but fer all?" he said, making exaggerated shapes with his mouth as he did, like his speech was being badly dubbed. When he was finished, he winced slightly, as though speaking

242

the words had really been an effort. "Sounds like garbage words to me."

"Nope, definitely Latin, trust me." Marc said irritably.

Anna and Sleight both looked at him.

"What? You plebs drink cider in the park, I know Latin. Who's the real loser here?"

Anna raised an eyebrow.

"Okay, well yeah it's me isn't it? But still. Latin for the win right? Right?" He gave them both a thumbs up.

"Huh, huh, huh, wet wipe." Sleight chuckled.

"Foetorem extremae latrinae" Marc retorted.

"Ey? What did you say to me?" an incensed Sleight said and grabbed Marc's arm.

"Hey! Hands off what you can't afford you… you… malus nequamque!"

Sleight growled and bared his stubby, yellow teeth.

"Children!!" Anna snapped, and smacked Sleight's wrist. The brute withdrew it and rubbed it with a sulky face, Marc looked forlornly at the crumpled leather of his jacket arm. "This is serious!" she continued unwilling to give either the attention they were so clearly used to.

Big babies!

"That is our teacher's house. Yes?" She looked sternly at Sleight.

"Yeah."

"And you saw Richie Spink go in there?"

"Yeah."

"And I just watched a man who LITERALLY MURDERED SOMEONE THIS WEEK, go to that very same house."

"Yeah so?"

Jesus wept, the king of bloody conversation!

"So??? So we need a plan. If you've got any ideas boys, now would be the perfect time to share them."

243

Both of the boys fell silent, looking off into the middle distance, running through tactics, options and strategies, or at least she hoped so. Jackson was captain of the football team, Marc, well, he appeared to be some sort of wargames nerd and possessor of a surprisingly plentiful supply of brain cells. Marc perked up first, a borderline "Eureka!" look on his well groomed features.

"I've got it!"

Thank heavens!

"Why don't we..." He opened his hands out in an inclusive gesture, and looked at both of them in turn. "Go away from here, away from our teacher's creepy old house, away from the dangerous, well dressed murderer and back to our respective houses faster than we've ever done anything ever?" He looked back and forth between them nodding.

Anna's eyes nearly dislocated from rolling so far back in their sockets.

"Are you kidding me?"

"What? Err... yes? Well, no. Well, everything seems perfect apart from the 'fast all the way home' bit. It's quite far, I'd say if we run out of this road, we can probably walk the rest."

"THAT'S YOUR BEST FRIEND IN THERE!" Anna fumed, unable to fathom the sheer level of cowardice on display.

"Yeah, true, but I'll be honest with you Anna. If it was just Mister Wells in there, a man for whom I currently have two pieces of late homework with, I'd be giving it a miss. Now let's just say for the sake of argument that you aren't hopped up on some mad, Woodstock level hippy drugs right now, and there is IN FACT an actual murdering person in there... then WHY IN THE NAME OF ALL AND HOLY HELL, HEAVEN AND EARTH WOULD I, ME, MARC TOWNSEND, THROWER OF EXACTLY ONE PUNCH IN MY ENTIRE LIFE, NOT TO MENTION WEARER OF A

QUITE FRANKLY, INAPPROPRIATELY-EXPENSIVE-FOR-A-FIFTEEN-YEAR-OLD LEATHER JACKET, WHY WOULD I BE THE MAN FOR THIS JOB???" Marc began to hyperventilate, and he put his head between his legs, taking in fast breaths that made him sound like an asthmatic baby cow on a treadmill. "Oh god, I feel sick."

Anna's eyes widened at the scene. Grudgingly, she reached a hand out and patted him gently on his hunched back. He was right of course. They were teenagers. They had no right to be mixed up in something this awful, and if they left now maybe they wouldn't have to be. But no sooner had she thought it, the sound of a car engine drew her attention. The black car that had dropped the two men off, came back down the road again. Anna turned and peered through the windows of the car, and as it passed again, a shiver ran the length of her spine. The driver. His face instantly familiar. It belonged to the Policeman who'd come to interview her at home.

Oh no, oh God…

They knew who she was, they knew where she worked, they knew where she lived. Anna turned back towards the boys, her legs gave way beneath her, and she slumped down to the cold stone kerb. She put her head into her hands, and rubbed her eyes in frustration. One way or another, she was already mixed up in this. When she opened her eyes, she was surprised to see Jackson Sleight with a look on his face bordering on kindly.

"Want me to go an' kick their faces in Annie?"

Anna let out a reflexive chuckle. It was certainly more dynamic than Marc's plan anyway.

"Thanks Jackson, maybe in a bit. I think we need to be a touch cannier here though." she said looking down at her hands, eternally grateful that she'd used her good mascara that morning, and not the cheap stuff that normally rubbed off with a light breeze.

Jackson Sleight nodded, happy to be given feedback, though still clearly puzzled as to what other type of solutions there could possibly be.

"The guy in the driver's seat? He was at my house the other night. He's police."

Sleight's lip twitched and he turned to look at the car again.

"Yeah, that's an undercover police car. If you look hard enough yer can see the blue light in the back window." he snarled like a dog looking at a postman's leg.

Anna bit her lower lip and pondered the situation. Her resolve returning somewhat, she checked for the black car again and noticed that it had come to park twenty yards or so down the road on the opposite side. It was clearly visible amongst the row of other parked cars, as the driver had opted to pull in rather than go for a full parallel park.

Probably wants to be able to get away quickly.

Her eyebrows shot up. That was it!

"Marc? Marrrrc?" she asked sweetly.

Marc Townsend remained in the closest shape a crouched person could get to the foetal position, rocking lightly back and forth on his heels, his head nearly wedged between his knees. He looked like black leather armadillo.

"Marc!" she hissed, her slim pickings of patience already worn too thin.

"Yes?" he said, voice muffled by knees/coat.

"What's your 80's action film knowledge like?"

Marc sniffed, his rocking stopped.

"Imperious. Why?"

"What's the film where the guy, is it Wesley Snipes, puts the bananas in the petrol tank to stop the baddies from following him?"

Marc lifted his head above his knee line.

246

"It's Eddie Murphy. Axel Foley. He puts bananas in the tailpipe of the car of the police who are tailing him. Beverly Hills Cop."

"Oh yeah, I love that film!" Sleight said. "That's the one where he goes to the theme park right? Classic."

Marc let out a deep annoyed sign and unfolded himself from his cocoon. "No, that's Beverley Hills Cop THREE, and it's an absolute abomination of a movie, you stu-" Marc saw the rising anger in Sleight's face and cut himself off. "*Cough* stu... studious lover of cinema. So yeah..." he turned back to Anna quickly. "Why do you ask?"

"So, we can't go kicking down the front door,"

Sleight perked up for the briefest of moments before his brain processed the "can't" part of Anna's statement, and he went back to furrowing his thick, caveman-like brow. He clenched and unclenched his fists restlessly.

"But we can't just do nothing." Anna continued. Marc lifted a hand to protest, she shot him a venomous look, and he withdrew his interjection.

"But we can be smart."
Probably.

"The car they came in is just a little way down the street, we could sneak up, do something to it, like the banana in the exhaust thing, or..."

"Stick a micro sized GPS tracker on to the bumper, like a Spider-tracer? That way if it goes south, we can follow them back to their lair or whatever." Marc offered, a touch of excitement entering his voice.

"Oh yeah, sounds good, any chance you have something like that to hand?" Anna asked, half seriously.

"Errr..." Marc patted himself down. "No."

"Cool. Anything else?"

"We could smash the windows with a brick!" Sleight blurted out. He seemed to be sweating, and struggling to keep still.

247

"Yeah, okay, interesting. Remember though, that guy there in the driver's seat is a copper. If he catches us, even the best case scenario is jail."

"It's alright, 'aven't got a brick anyway."

Anna strained every nerve in her body not to slap her palm to her face, instead managing to keep her cool. Just.

"It's okay, it's okay." She sighed. "We can do this. Right empty your pockets. Let's see what we've got."

Without much in the way of resistance the boys rummaged around and started to lay their discoveries out on the pavement slab between them. By the time Marc had produced his third comb, and Sleight his fifth used tissue, Anna was already beginning to plan for the worst. When they were finished she surveyed their shared wares.

3 x plastic combs (black, red, aqua blue)
1 x foldable travel toothbrush
1 x mini can of aerosol deodorant
 1 x travel toothpaste
1 x iPhone *(Marc very proudly contributes)*
6 x used tissues (urrrrrgh!)
7 x pebbles (various sizes)
1 x packet of chewing gum (half empty)
1 x cigarette lighter
1 x Slingshot *(my God, is this lad Dennis the Menace??)*
1 x Packet of popping candy

Anna, for what it was worth, was hardly laden with a bagful of spy-tech.

4 x bobbles (black)
2 x tampons *(seeing the boys squirm at the sight of them totally made it worth the effort of getting them out)*
1 x nail varnish (black)
1 x lipstick (scarlet)

1 x nail clippers
1 x Mini Disc player/recorder and in-ear headphones.
2 x Mini Discs. Incubus: S.C.I.E.N.C.E, and one 60's Mix
1 x Battered Nokia 3310 *(old Snakey faithful)*

It was not the inspiring sight she'd hoped it would be. Mentally she tried to put complimentary items together, but short of lighting Jackson Sleight's snotty tissues on fire, or firing his fine selection of pebbles at the car windows, she was drawing a blank. Idealess, she scooped up the packet of popping candy, tore off the top and tipped the contents into her mouth.

"Ey!" Sleight protested, and was summarily ignored.

As the sweets bubbled, fizzed and jumped around in her mouth Anna ground her back teeth together, her go-to action whenever stressed.

"Screw it." she said firmly. "Right here's the plan. Jackson, you go and distract the driver."

"Okay." He nodded, frantically, clearly ready to do anything but sit still. "How?"

"Use your imagination. It won't be the first time you've wound someone up."

Sleight nodded again. Again the cogs seemed to creek around in his brain. Anna left him to it.

"Marc. Does your phone do anything clever?"

"Yeah of course, it's an iPhone?" he replied like a kid explaining a Playstation controller to their Nan. "It's got a bunch of cool apps like a spirit level and a tape measure, a top of the range camera and there's this funny app where you can pretend to drink a beer…"

"Oooh yeah, perfect. The camera thing. Okay, I want you to go and get a photo of the licence plate. If we need to track it down later, that should help. Cool?"

Marc looked a little relieved at being given a job that was within his skill set and bravery limit, whilst also giving him an excuse to show off his new phone.

"What about you?"

"Me, well." She took a deep breath. "When the driver is distracted I'm going to put my Mini-disc player on to record mode and try to sneak it into the car somewhere. Hopefully it picks them up saying something incriminating that we can take to the police later." she said firmly, confident in the strength of her makeshift scheme.

"How're you getting it back though?" Sleight asked, and Anna nearly collapsed to the floor as the simple question cut straight through her plan.

Before she could answer though, all hell broke loose.

From the front of Mister Well's house came an almighty crash, the ear splitting sound of shattering glass and splintered wood. A sound that could only come from a large object being thrown through a window.

Oh god, here we go!

She spun to face Sleight.

"Go. Now!"

The boy, antsy to get moving, nodded dutifully, rose up to his full height, cut between a gap in the parked cars and began fast-walking towards the black sedan.

"Make sure you get a good clean picture okay?" She said, giving Marc's arm a reassuring squeeze.

"Cool." he said, his voice cracking as he did so. He quickly cleared his throat, and said it again, in a deep tone this time. "AHEM. Cool." He smiled weakly, and Anna gave him a lopsided grin in return

And then she was on the move, crouch-walking along the pavement, her delicate fingers moving expertly across the buttons on the silver, square device in her hands. When she was opposite the car, she poked her head up to watch for her moment.

Jackson Sleight slowed his walk to a stalk as he approached the vehicle. Then in a burst of noise, violence and speed, he roared at the top of his voice, "ARRRRRRRHGGGGGGGGHHHH!!!!" He kicked the drivers side wing mirror, obliterating it in hail of glass and plastic; ran to the front of the car, held up the middle fingers of both hands, stuck out his tongue, and then as the red faced, raging Police Detective began to step out, Sleight began sprinting away down the road, smacking his backside as he went. The driver, lost in his anger, left the car door open and began giving chase, flustering in his tan trench coat.

"Oi, you little toe rag, Police! Stop right there!!!"

Anna paused for a moment, wide eyed and totally stunned. *Okay, yep, that'll do it.*

Just about remembering the task at hand, she quickly made her way across the road, and around to the far side of the car. She was about to head for the rear door when all of a sudden the front passenger door opened. Anna's heart leapt into her mouth, and she quickly ducked down behind the bumper. She heard the shuffle of leather soles on pavement as the person got out and ambled away a few yards down the street, clearly trying to get eyes on the driver's pursuit. Anna, who was having the closest thing possible to a cardiac arrest without actually dropping instantly dead, held her breath, and clenched every muscle in her body. The sounds of violence from the Wells residence continued, the sound of the driver's threats echoed in the opposite direction. Her forehead pressed against the cool black metal of the cars' boot, her chin rubbed off grime from the yellow licence plate. Right there, a silver button protruded, a slit in the middle for a key. Behind her, the sounds from Well's house grew louder, ahead the driver shouted one last breathless, expletive-laden barrage after Sleight. Her window was closing.

She depressed the silver button. It slid smoothly inwards, and as it drew flush with its surroundings, elicited a dull mechanical thud. The boot lid opened. Anna gripped it tightly to keep it from flipping open. She peered in through the three inch gap. A small light on the left side plus the beam of sunlight allowed her to see inside. It was deep, surprisingly so, and pretty sparse, just a thick, dark coloured, crumpled blanket and a large bottle of antifreeze. Something caught her eye in her peripheral vision, and she snapped her head to the right in a panic, only to see Marc, wedged and cowering between two parked cars across the road. He hugged Anna's rucksack to his chest with one arm and held his phone out, aimed in her general direction with the other, still diligently waiting for his photo opportunity. He shot her a "what the hell are you doing?" look, and Anna half shrugged in return. Suddenly Marc's eyes fixed on something behind her towards Well's house. The colour drained from his face. He looked back at her and mouthed "Run."

It was then that Anna Harrison did easily the bravest and most stupid thing of her entire life. She put the mini disc player back into her jacket pocket, lifted the lid of the boot further, and slid herself inside.

Ohgodohgodohgodohgodohgod!

She carefully pulled it closed behind her, blocking out the outside light and disabling the bulb on the interior, leaving her in pitch black. Feeling around she found the thick, slightly dusty sheet, pulled it over herself, and shuffled as far back as she could until her back was against the backside of the rear seats. As she did, she felt the bump as the passenger got back inside. She pulled out the minidisc player and thumbed it on to record. Over the thumping sound of her own pulse, and the sound of her inner monologue screaming insults, she strained to listen to the world outside.

Idiotidiotidiotidiotidiotidiot!

She heard the muffled approach of voices and she stiffened in place. The voices died down for a moment and then her heart lurched again as the boot popped wide open. The sunlight lightly permeated the thick blanket that concealed her.

"Just dump them in there." came a well spoken voice, and moments later, two large objects were dumped into the boot with her one after the other. Something firm dug into her ribs and Anna bit down on her lip so as not to scream in pain. She felt involuntary tears form in the corner of her eyes, but she kept still. She kept quiet. The boot was slammed shut. The voices again became muffled. A person dropped into the other rear passenger seat. She heard the car doors slam shut. She heard the engine roar to life. She heard the crunch of tires on loose shale. She felt the car pull away.

Anna Harrison had been kidnapped, and it was all her own fault.

PART THREE

CHAPTER THIRTY NINE: WELLS

Young Wells opened the purple painted tin, the delighted gasps of his friends filled his ears. A warm feeling growing from the inside, replacing his nervous trepidations. He'd known not to touch his father's things, knew his warnings off by heart, but such rules only intrigued his young mind further. He held the tin close to his chest, a musty smell filled his nostrils. It reminded him of his grandfather's allotment. Soil. Sweet. Rich. He ran his pale fingers over the magical contents. Five circular sewn patches. Four of them,neat as pins. The other though, he felt his heart flutter at its sight. Torn through the middle, edged with a dark brown stain, like the varnish of mother's tea cabinet. The stitching around it frayed and crusted. His heart raced. His mind followed.

THUMP!

The school day ends, and the boy opens up his satchel, removes the tin again, one last look before heading home, one last intoxicating inhale before returning it to its hiding place. His father's stern chidings dim behind the rush of excitement. The scent though is weaker. The patches are gone. A cold, gaping hole maws in his stomach.

Young Wells runs home, the cold wind stings his tear soaked eyes. Light drops of rain begin to fall from a darkening sky. Through the front door, down the hallway, flying into his mother's arms. Warm. Safe. His tears mix with the light dusting of flour on her floral-patterned pinafore. Until she sees what is clutched to his chest. A coldness overcomes her. A separation. A fear. A distant look of dread in her once kindly eyes.

THUMP!

His father's fury is all that he can see. The patches and their tattered khaki cloth bunched tightly in one bloodied fist.

THUMP! THUMP!

255

Rain pounds down into the garden. The feel of voile curtains on his wet cheek. The SHICK-CRUNCH of digging permeates the water streaked pane. Lightning edged spider-webs flash across the sky, illuminating the blue-eyed monster's all too familiar face.

THUMP! THUMP! THUMP!

The rage-filled stomp of his father's boots climbing the stairs.

THUMP! THUMP! THUMP! THUMP!

The pounding of his heart. The pounding of boots. Cold, wet cheeks. The musty scent of old sweat, gunpowder and earth filling his senses. His bedsheets pulled up tight. His bedroom door slammed open. A spark of blue lightning. The menacing face of his father.

THUMP! THUMP! THUMP! THUMP! THUMP! THUMP! THUMP! THUMP! THUMP!

Neil Wells awoke with a start.

He sat bolt upright.

His face was wet with tears.

The faint breeze on the cool air played across his face.

Wells put a hand to his cheek. The scent of moist soil filling his nostrils.

He held the hand up to his eyeline. His sleepy vision clearing, his fingers stained black brown. Small clumps of loose soil fell from between his fingers.

Wait, a... breeze?

Resisting the urge to rub his eyes, he blinked purposefully.

Neil Wells, loose cotton pyjamas and all, a chill breeze on his bare, muddy feet, was laying in his back garden. With some strain on his cold joints, he sat up.

For a few moments more he stayed there blinking, certain that despite clear activation of his senses, this had to be another twist in his whiskey and grief-addled dreamscape.

THUMP! THUMP!

The strange distant noise persisted, as did the cold ache of his joints. Birds chirped. His overgrown garden grass swayed lightly in the breeze. Looking down he saw an object that nearly made his heart leap from his chest. Flattening the grass in a small patch between his knees was a dented and rusted, purple metal tin. Between blinks he reached his grubby hands towards it. It was cool to the touch, a touch which instantly conjured long buried memories of childhood, the same ones that had plagued his fitful slumber. He picked it up, tilted it towards him, felt the weight on the objects inside shift as he did so. Holding the tin on the palm of one hand, he carefully reached to prise open the lid. Inside were four sewn patches, each attached to a scrap of fabric, some torn, some neatly trimmed. He reached a trembling hand in slowly to touch them, his mouth dry with anticipation.

THUMP! THUMP!

"JESUS MARY AND JOSEPH! WHAT THE FLAMING BLUE HELL IS THAT NOISE??" He exclaimed to the sky. He put the tin under one arm, and with all the grace of an un-oiled tin man, rose awkwardly, wincingly to his feet. "CAN'T A MAN HAVE A NERVOUS BREAKDOWN IN HIS GARDEN IN PEACE???!!!"

He stomped in through the open back door, paused momentarily to painfully scrape the soles of his bare feet on the brown bristles of the floor mat, and then continued to stomp onwards towards the front door.

THUMP! THUMP! THUMP!

"Alright! Alright! Keep your shirt on, you impatient little twerp. Bloody postmen! Can't you just leave it with Mrs. Rowling next door, the stupid conspiracy lunatic spinster's got nothing better to do than…" Wells flung open the front door. On the doorstep was a vaguely familiar, confident looking, well groomed young man.

The boy smiled and opened his mouth to speak.

257

"I'm quite happy with my gas and electric supplier young man, now sod off!" Wells growled and slammed the door in his face.

Stomping off back down the hallway into the kitchen, he deposited the tin onto the table, and began washing his hands in the large stainless steel sink.

KNOCK, KNOCK, KNOCK, came a more civilised attempt on the door, and Wells sighed. He dried his now more or less clean hands on a tea towel. He splashed a double cupped handful of water on his face, and dried that too. Feeling marginally more human, he made his way back to the front door. He reached it. He looked down at his pyjamas and dirty feet, shook his head, took a deep breath and opened it again.

"Mister Wells, it's Tom... err... Richie Spink sir. I need your help."

Wells looked at the boy sceptically, recognition finally dawning on him.

"It's Saturday Mister Spink. At least I think it is." He blinked a couple of times and shook his head again. "Anyway, whatever day it is, it is certainly not the time or the place, and I am not, in any form or shape, the man to be providing anything resembling help right now." He gestured theatrically down at his soil stained PJ's. "So if you don't mind, perhaps someone from the English department might be able to provide some assistance. They're all young and probably fresh as bloody daisies." He said and with a half bow, began to close the door.

"Have you found the patches yet?" Richie asked.

Neil Wells froze. He held the door open a couple of inches, the boy's earnest face was still visible through the crack. "What did you say?"

"The patches sir? The Eternal Flame Squad?" the boy said, with a hint of uncertainty in his voice.

Wells flung the door open, grabbed the boy by the front of his coat, dragged him across the threshold, and slammed him back against the door, slamming it shut, rattling the wooden frame. He was a couple of inches shorter than the boy, but easily several stones heavier.

"Who put you up to this? Was it that awful neanderthalic Sleight boy and his gang of Halloween egg chuckers?"

"No sir."

"Was it the P.E department? I bet it was, those stupid sexy morons, always out for a laugh at my expense!"

"No sir."

"Was it Terrance and his merry band of unwashed cult oddballs?"

"No sir. It's just me." The boy said calmly. "There's trouble coming and I need your help. The patches. Do you know what I'm talking about?"

Wells released his grip, and carefully took a step back.

"How do you know about that?"

"It's hard to explain."

"Well try hard and try quickly Mister Spink, because this joke is perilously close to running out of funny."

"Here." Richie dug a hand into his pocket and pulled out the yellowing letter. He held it out, and Wells snatched it from him. His eyes scanned back and forth, and occasionally over the top back at the boy as he read the hand written text.

"Anyone can write a letter. Well, most anyone."

"There's also this." The boy reached into his pocket and produced the silver ring.

Wells' look of intense scepticism was swept away. Without a further word, he spun on his muddied heel and retreated to the kitchen. After a moment, with no further instruction, and Wells' menace seemingly at an end, the boy followed.

A short time later, with two mugs of steaming hot tea flanking the tins' contents, Wells and the boy sat and tried to process their discovery. Spread out across the kitchen table top were four of the glimmering Flaming Fist, "Eternal Flame Squad" patches, each attached to its own uniquely torn, frayed or cut scrap of khaki fabric. Additionally there was a battered, rusted cigarette lighter, a tarnished and cracked compass, a dog-eared photograph and the letter the boy had given him. In Wells' slightly trembling hands he held the ring that Richie had given him, and in the other hand its pair. He pushed them together to complete the image on the signet of a Flaming Fist. Wells recognised it, but couldn't quite remember how.

"Remarkable" he said, placing the pieces down. He

Ran his hands over the collection of artefacts and picked up another yellowed paper letter. He read it aloud.

"Margaret,

My love, my world, I hope nay pray that this package finds you in good health and in a timely fashion. Its contents are perhaps the most sensitive and important materials this world (or any other) has seen. Take them, and hide them well, for dark forces abound who seek to use them for means beyond even our wildest nightmares, both at home and abroad. Part of me thinks we should destroy them, but the trust I have in both the man and the boy alongside me runs as deep as even my love for you. I believe in the Eternal Flame, I only hope that faith will be enough for what comes next. We can win this war, we must, but I have been forewarned that there are yet bigger battles to come, and though it defies all reason, we must also prepare for a future war, one that we may not live to see.

If our will remains strong, our senses keen, and if God abides, I will return to you soon. One last push.

Thank you, my darling, for everything.

Yours eternally,

260

Sebastian.

P.S,
NW, RS, AH, JS, MT, TT, if insurmountable danger arises
hold the insignia in hand, and trust...
"Non Sibi, Sed Omnibus"

Beneath that last sentence were two individual signatures, one he recognised as his Father's, the other was the same as on the boy's letter. The information was overwhelming. His father's warm, yet foreboding tone. Wells let the letter fall from his hand to land atop the other. He sat back in the wooden chair, let out a deep breath and ran his hands up his face and through his hair. The boy picked up the letter and read it himself.

"I'm sorry Sir, I know this is a lot, but I'm afraid there's a heck of a lot more to it than even this."

"Spink," he said at last, his hands still locked inside his thinning grey hair, his eyes still screwed shut, "Let's get this straight. You are, by my reckoning, at best a C grade student. Now admittedly there's a chance that you are a bit lazy, or perhaps a little unfocused, and that could go some way to confuscating your true potential. It is conceivable that you are a germinating larva of potential, about to metamorphose into a cosmically intelligent butterfly. But even if that were true, I cannot fathom how in the name of all hell you could possibly devise something this deep, this conniving." He opened his eyes and sat forward, mustering his three-decades-practised withering glance. He looked the boy squarely in the eyes. "So tell me, what is this really all about? How do you know about that symbol? And moreover how on Earth could you possibly know about this stuff, when I've only just dug it back up?"

"What does your letter say? The one I gave you?"
Wells handed it to him. "See for yourself."

261

"Neil, trust in the boy, trust in The Eternal Flame." he read aloud.

"There you go then. Exactly."

"Exactly? Exactly what young man?"

"Well, this letter, which was sent to us from 1945 is telling you to trust me."

"You?"

"Yes, me."

"Oh really, which one are you? The boy or The Flame?

"Both."

"Oh really?" Wells retorted. "Poppycock. You are a silly young man with an overactive imagination."

"What about the ring?"

Wells looked down at the two pieces of that implacably familiar ring. He was wavering. The Flame knew he had to push on. He tried to recall something else of use, but so much of his memory was gone. Then it hit him.

Of course!

"Try it." the boy said calmly, the surety in his voice belying his youthful appearance, totally at odds with what little Wells knew of him from school.

"Try what?"

"The patch. Do as it says in the letter." A faint smile formed on his lips as he gestured towards them.

Wells looked down at the patches. Their pristine stitching, the faint blue shimmer to the embroidered flames. He picked up the top one, rubbing it between his thumb and forefinger.

Silly, stupid boy, just as bad as Terrance and his gaggle of unwashed morons. I should send him packing, I have a perfectly good hangover I could be wallowing in.

"Trust me." the boy said. There was something about the way he spoke, a command to his tone, an authority.

Oh well, here goes, let's get this nonsense out of the way.

Wells swallowed and cleared his throat. If he was going to give this story spinning swindler the satisfaction, he was

262

going to at least give him his most sarcastically theatric performance possible. He took a deep breath.

"Non sibi" he began in his best stage voice.

"No, no, translate it. That's just precaution."

Wells rolled his eyes and cleared his throat again. "Ahem. Not For Oneself..." he began, locking eyes with the boy, and totally missing the small crackle of blue energy that arced by his thumb. "But For..."

THUMP! THUMP THUMP!

Rapturous banging on the door rattled Wells' already frazzled brain. He dropped the patch to the table in frustration, his anger rising once again.

"Some of your friends ey? Come to help take the mick out of the gullible old teacher I bet! Right!" he said, banging his hands on the table, and standing up. His chair flew backwards on the linoleum floor and teetered for a moment on its back legs, before falling back to the floor. "I'll deal with you in a minute," he said, pointing sternly at the boy and stomped once again to the front door, flinging it open with righteous fury, ready to unleash both barrels of his rage onto...

"Terrance?" he said in bemusement. "What are you..."

"Sorry Sir." Terrance said, pushing his thick glasses back onto the bridge of his blackhead ridden nose.

All of a sudden, Terrance was shoved across the doorway, bumping into Wells, nearly knocking him out of his slippers in the process.

"Oi, you stupid oaf, you..." But Wells' protest was cut short when his eyes fell upon the man standing on the doorstep, and the brushed steel pistol in his right hand.

The slim man, lithe, menacing and dressed in an immaculate looking pale grey suit fixed his cold dark eyes on Wells as he stepped into the house. Without breaking eye contact, he reached behind himself and closed the door smoothly.

"Back through there, now" he said gesturing down the hallway to the kitchen, his measured tone carrying forceful intent.

"Now see here, you've no right to come barging into my home like this young man!" Wells barked back, hoping his righteous teacher voice would hold some sway.

The silver suited man raised the gun a little higher, and Wells quickly recognised that he was literally bringing harsh words to a gun fight. He and Terrance backed up awkwardly, the younger man treading on his toes with every other step.

"Who's your friend?" Wells whispered in his ear with a wince.

"Not my friend. I told you, you shouldn't have messed with the Order."

"Quiet. Move." the Grey Man ordered.

As they shuffled through the open doorway to the kitchen, Wells checked for the boy in his peripheral vision, and was too relieved not to see him to actually wonder where he'd gone.

The man waved the gun towards the table, and Wells and Terrance each took a seat. Still atop the table was the photograph, the lighter, the compass, and the two letters. Wells noticed however that the patches were gone. He felt a faint breeze on his ankles, and looked casually to his left to see that the back door was slightly ajar.

"Now sit there and keep your mouth shut."

Terrance, sat across the table with his back to the wall, raised a hand.

"Both of you." the Grey man said with visceral malice, and Terrance put his hand back onto his lap.

Wells found it oddly comforting that even smartly dressed gangster assassins were irritated by his spotty faced former pupil.

"Ohh, wow." Terrance said, and Wells winced, fearing the noise would tip their captor over the edge. But his young

264

charges' excitement at the artefacts on the table seemingly superseded the pant wetting terror of the loaded pistol. He picked up the worn, black and white photograph. "Is that? Oh my god it is!"

"Is what?" both Wells and the man in grey said in unified annoyance. The man pointed the gun again at Wells, and he raised his hands defensively and sat back.

"Is. What?" the man reiterated. His razor thin patience diminishing further.

"The Squad! The Eternal Flame Squad! All of them, together! Look!" he said excitedly, stabbing his greasy finger, "and there he is… The man himself, The Eternal Flame of British Resistance."

Wells squinted, damning his ageing eyesight as he did. Ten men in Uniform, the man in the middle, the tallest by an inch or two, wore a bandana that covered the top portion of his face and head. The superpowered man from the film clip Terrance's banal friends, "The Order" had shown him a few days earlier. Neil Wells pinched himself firmly on the leg. Too firmly. He grunted lightly in pain. This was not a dream, and there was now a reasonable chance he'd drawn blood on his own leg. He was not a man prone to flights of fancy, he was a historian dammit. Names, places, facts were his stock in trade. This outrageous yarn was far beyond his wheelhouse, and yet at the same time it was quite the opposite. The evidence, as mind bogglingly barmy as it sounded, was beginning to mount up.

"And oh, look…" Terrance continued, his voice taking on a hushed, reverential tone. "Is that the…"

The Man In Grey snatched the picture away. "Now, Mister Wells." he said, attempting warmth in his voice and failing. "This is all very nice, but you'll forgive me if I don't go as weak in the knees as our spotty friend here over a few trinkets. Where's the rest of it?" He tossed the picture back down and tilted the gun side to side menacingly.

Neil Wells, who scant minutes ago was prepared to turf young Mister Spink out on his ear, knew the smart move would be to cooperate with the man holding the pistol. Fanciful as it was though, the boy's story it seemed was absolutely true. As much as he'd spent many a long double period daydreaming about his students all spontaneously combusting, or being abducted by aliens he wasn't about to give one up to a gun toting gangster-type.

"I'm sure I have no idea what you are talking about, these artefacts belonged to my father, he passed away this week, I'm just sorting through his personal effects and stumbled on an old box of stuff. This is all there is."

The grey man let out a humourless chuckle. His eyes narrowed, and Wells saw a cold inhumanity behind them that made the skin on the back of his neck crawl.

"Oh I know all about your father." He chuckled again; an empty, joyless sound. "You see, you might be the one who's going to bury the box, but I'm the one who put him in it." he said with a razor thin smile.

Wells felt his stomach drop through the floorboards, a burning rage clenched his fists.

"You monster!" he said, leaping to his feet in front of the backdoor.

The grey man stepped to meet him, placing the pistol square into Wells' chest.

"Ah, ah, ahhh. Careful now." he chided playfully. "I've killed one Wells this week, easy as pie. Wouldn't be anything to make it two."

Inches from him now, Wells could see the man up close. The rich smell of his expensive cologne, his sneering lips, those soulless eyes. The slightly dark ring under his right eye. A yellowing of the cheek beneath that. A slight cut at the corner of his mouth. Wells flashed back to his dream. His hulking father stood in this very spot. Lip cut, fists bloodied. Wells smiled.

266

"The police told me that my father was attacked, and that his attacker fled the scene. My father was a near 90 year old man with later stage vascular dementia and a dodgy hip. So the question is son, how did it feel to have your arse kicked by a nonagenarian?"

A look of anger flashed across the young man's wounded face, he lowered the gun for a moment and as he did, a figure slammed through the ajar backdoor with a BANG, shattering the glass window in the process and sending the gun skittering across the floor into the hallway. The Man in Grey stumbled backwards, and fell to the floor whilst Wells was knocked back onto the table. Silhouetted by the light from the windowless door, Wells could see Richie Spink, the flaming fist patches clutched in his left hand. The boy quickly pressed one into Well's hand.

"Say the words. Trust me." he said firmly with strident confidence.

Wells nodded, as the Man in Grey leapt to his feet, grabbing Richie and hurling him across the Kitchen. He looked across the table. Terrance Whittaker was still sat there slack jawed, the photo in one hand. Both men looked down at the letter on the table, and then sprang for it. The younger man got there first.

"Ah ha!" he exclaimed.

Wells slapped his hand, and as the younger man yelped, he cuffed him around the head, sending his thick glasses off his greasy face and across the table to the floor. "Hey!" he retorted childishly.

"Stupid boy." Wells growled at him, and retrieved the letter.

Richie Spink was blocking a variety of punches and kicks from the grey-suited man, wincing in pain with every blow. Wells frantically opened up the folded paper and scanned down through the writing until his eyes fell upon the right passage. He shoved all the patches bar one into the pocket of

267

his trousers and gripped the last one tightly between thumb and forefingers. He looked up one final time at Spink, as the boy, struggling to hold his own, laid his hand on a decorative plate hung on the wall, and smashed it over his attackers' head.

"Quick Mister Wells do it!" he shouted, wiping a sweat soaked strand of hair from his forehead.

"That was a family heirloom!" Wells found himself reflexively shouting back.

The Grey Man recovered and grabbed Richie by the throat, hauling him back across the kitchen towards the table.

"Now!" Richie Spink spluttered against the man's grip.

Wells' mouth tightened in panic, and he quickly looked back down. He took a deep breath.

Stupid nonsense. At least the man might stop attacking and keel over from laughter.

In their wrestling embrace, the boy and the Man in Grey bumped heavily into the table, shoving it into Terrance's midriff, knocking the wind from him, and his glasses further from reach. The Man in Grey used the table as a pivot, and with the gathered momentum, threw the boy down the hallway. Richie's head hit the radiator on the way down and he fell limply to the floor against the skirting board.

Wells sighed. His options were limited and his remaining lifespan likely measured in seconds. He swallowed and cleared his throat.

"Not For Oneself But For All." he said forcefully. The muscles of his hands contracted tightly and his teeth ground together as an ice cold feeling shot up his arms, racing towards his heart before shooting away to his brain and down his legs. He grunted from the exertion, and fought to wrench his eyes open in time to see the letter ignite into blue flame in his hand and float away into ash. The patch in his other hand was still there, seemingly impervious. Tiny blue-white sparks arced from the stitching. Neil Wells looked around the room.

A bead of sweat ran down Terrance's aghast, spectacle-less face, his beady eyes widening in terror. The Man in Grey, his attention on the unconscious boy, tilted his head sideways, cracking his neck with a deep, drawn out crunch. The ashes of the letter, carried on the gentle breeze from the windowless back door faded away into their component atoms. Wells heard the thick crunch of broken glass beneath his slippered feet as he took deliberate, powerful steps towards their captor.

Neil Wells had never been a fighter, but he had at one time been a jolly good Rugby player. And so it came to be that as the aurora of the blue flames absorbed into his body, melting away decades of aches, pains and sprains the 57 year old history teacher with chronic sciatica charged, shoulder first into the back of a man half his age. He hit the man firmly and wrapped his arms around his waist; the force of the impact knocking the wind from the lungs of the younger man, lifting him off the ground. Wells drove on and with powerful strides, slammed the grey suited man face first into the front door with an explosive force that shattered it outwards in a hail of shattered glass and splintered wood. The pair barrelled straight through, and Wells lost his footing as he crossed the front step. Both went tumbling down the garden pathway amid a hail of broken door fragments. The Grey Man managed to shift his weight in time to take most of the impact on his shoulder, adapting it into a modified commando roll. The landing still hurt him badly, but somehow he remained conscious. Wells tripped, stumbled and fell to his knees with a painful thud. He couldn't bear to imagine how much more it should have hurt. In front of him the younger man spat out a cob of blood and hauled himself to his feet, dazed but enraged. With some clear difficulty he raised his fists into a fighting stance.

Oh dear lord, here we go.

Wells rose to his feet with greater ease. The blue flames on his hands were gone now, but he could still feel the power coursing inside him, like electric ice water in his veins.

"If you'd like a fight Sonny Jim, then let me tell you, you have come to the right house, at the right time, with the right ma…"

Wells felt a sharp and sudden pain at the base of his skull and the lights went out.

As his limp form slumped to the ground, Terrance Whittaker stood over him. The hilt of the pistol held like a club in one hand, he used the other to push his thick-lens glasses onto the bridge of his nose. A vaguely satisfied smirk crossed his usually gormless face.

The Man in Grey took a handkerchief from his top pocket and wiped the blood from the reopened cut on his lip.

"Get the kid."

Terrance opened his mouth to protest, and was met with a venomous look. It was not a request. With thumb and forefinger, he handed the gun back at arms length and shuffled off back into the house to gather the unconscious boy and the secrets of The Eternal Flame.

CHAPTER FORTY: BILL

Bill entered the clearing as all hell was breaking loose. Thirty yards away to his right, Green, Parkinson and Welsh with a young boy in his grip, watched on as four other men from the unit squared off against The Eternal Flame. The sounds of live fire rattled off the tree trunks, making it feel as though the shots were being fired from all angles.

Live rounds, what the hell?!

Desperately clawing for oxygen, a flush faced Willerton-Smythe shambled up behind him, limply placing a hand on Bill's shoulder to stop himself from doubling over. Bill shrugged it off angrily.

"Where in the bloody hell did they get them live rounds from, this was s'posed to be a field test of the non-lethals!"

Smythe, still radish red in the face, hadn't yet regained the ability to speak, and Bill shook his head, stepping aggressively into the clearing. As he did so, the sound of gunfire was replaced by the blood curdling battle cry of Andreo. Bill watched on in horror as the frantic soldier spun his belt of grenades around his head and launched them towards the Eternal Flame, just as the young boy broke free of Welsh's grip. Andreo's throw was wild, it span off to the right. The boy, too concentrated on his freedom to follow the action, was on a collision course with death.

"CIVILIAN ON THE RANGE!!!" Bill bellowed, but, too far removed, could only watch on as the dire scene unfolded.

Beneath his pale blue bandana mask, The Flame's eyes widened in shock. The pause was momentary though. With a speed that belied his bulk, he took two quick steps and leapt towards the boy, covering an inhuman distance and hauling him to the ground. As the bandolier's flight path brought it careening towards them, The Flame managed to use the momentum of their fall and the impact of the ground to his

271

advantage, rotating himself between the boy and the grenades as they thudded to the ground barely three feet away.

"GET DOWN!" he barked towards Green, Welsh and Parkinson.

Bill, though likely too far away to be in the blast radius, had no intention of taking the chance, and wrenched his second in command down to the ground with him.

"Well I…" he protested, before having his weasel-like face driven into the dirt.

The grenades exploded in a cataclysmic bang that rattled Bill's ear drums and sent razor sharp shards zipping outwards and a hail of dirt clods up into the air.

"… How dare you!" Smythe spluttered as the noise faded.

Bill ignored him, shot to his feet and broke straight into a sprint. Approaching apace, he scanned the thick smoke for signs of life. He'd seen the Flame stand up to rounds of gunfire, but an explosion from that range, all he expected to see was human broth.

Suddenly there was a sharp movement. Bill skidded to a halt still some twenty yards short of the visible crater on the ground. A dark shape pierced the haze. The boy, unharmed but terrified, ran out of the smoke like a scalded animal and disappeared back into the forest. Bill stopped still in stunned amazement. The smoke began to thin, and he could see further movement, much slower and more deliberate this time. He began to approach the epicentre again, and there he was. There he *still* was. The Eternal Flame. Not bloody chunks. Alive. Alive, but not unscathed. He was upright on both knees with his head drooped. Amid the smoke wisps Bill could see the damage, the centre of his broad back bore the most, a gaping hole in the fabric between his shoulder blades, charred around the edges, showed through to his muscular back, along with myriad rips and tears around the periphery. Bill's attention was drawn towards the hole. He could see

272

some signs of physical damage to his skin, but nothing like there should have been.

Incredible...

The Flame rose gingerly to his feet, and turned towards Bill, a slight grimace on his face. By all logic he and the boy should be dead. He did note however that it was, by his reckoning, the first time he'd seen him hurt, the first hint of vulnerability. He'd also gotten hurt whilst saving the boy.

Maybe he's human after all.

"You alright lad?" he asked, and The Flame gave him a wincing smile in return.

"Yes sir. 'Tis but a flesh wound."

Bill cocked an eyebrow, disarmed by the light hearted reaction.

The Flame twisted, and stretched slowly, a playful look matched by winces of discomfort. He laughed.

"That actually, hurt. It's been a whil..."

Suddenly, an ear splittingly shrill sound came from over their heads, The Flame clamped his palm to the sides of his head. The sound persisted, masking the soft click-SHUD-SHANK that came from behind him.

."Huh?" The Flame exclaimed, as he half turned towards it, hands still firmly locked over his ears.

Bill watched as the smoke whipped, and out of it came an expanding net. It wrapped around The Flame and locked into place.

"What's thi-"

A gentle rising hum was followed by a loud CRACK, and for the briefest moment electricity crackled around the netting. The Flame's body tensed, as every one of his muscles contracted at once. His legs buckled and he crumpled straight to the ground, unconscious.

The billowing smoke cleared, and there was Green, flanked by the distinctly stunned looking Welsh and Parkinson. Green held the discharged Net Gun up at eye level.

Parkinson, reached over his head, braced himself and caught a returning Sonic Boomerang. He exhaled loudly, his panic immediately replaced by a smug smile as he gripped it tightly to his chest.

Bill felt a grin wider than the Cheshire Cat's spreading across his face. This unit might just have a chance yet.

CHAPTER FORTY ONE: RICHIE

At the bottom of the shaft, a long concrete corridor, punctuated by low wattage bulbs every twenty yards, stretched away into the distance. The light coverage was insufficient to evenly light the full tunnel, with gloomy near black patches in the centre point between each bulb. It was enough that Richie could see Will and Green clearly but gave the walls, floor and ceiling of the corridor an almost snakeskin like appearance.

Richie had enough video gaming experience to know that stealth was the likely order of the day, and so pinned himself up tightly against the wall. He was therefore a little shocked when Will and Green jogged off loudly down the way, the various pieces of equipment and pouches bouncing around as they did.

We're running then, cool beans.

He caught them up at an intersection about two hundred yards later. As he reached them, Green put a finger to his lips and gestured to Richie to tuck in against the wall. Will held up a closed fist, and carefully peered around the corner. He gave a satisfied nod, and loosened the fist into a point. Green slipped past him. Richie watched the smooth unspoken operation play out in front of him.

"Will, why did we run then, but now we're being quiet?"

Will winced at Richie's too-loud-for-the-situation voice, but maintained his composure.

"You see that corridor behind us?"

"Yeah" Richie said, having a quick glance back.

"Now, look at this one."

Richie shuffled closer and leant out. This corridor was just as intermittently lit. It was shorter though, at the end was a blue metallic door, the big difference though were the alcoves carved into the walls. Maybe half a dozen on each side in the gaps equidistant between the light fixtures.

"The alcoves?"

"Cover." Will corrected. "All the stealth in the world won't save you from a machine gun."

"So it was worth being a bit noisier to get to a place with cover more quickly?"

"Exactly. Right, your turn."

Richie nodded and crept out into the corridor, all of a sudden painfully aware of just how big and cumbersome his muscle bound body was. As he crossed over the walkway, his hulking figure illuminated by the lights on either side, he heard the creaking of metal ahead, and his blood froze. At the end of the corridor, the door handle turned, and the blue metal door slowly opened, with a nerve jangling scrape on the concrete floor. Ahead and to the left, Green, wedged into one of the darkened hidey-holes, gritted his teeth and nodded firmly in the direction of the nearest safe space. Richie, battling his inner coward, somehow managed to wrench his leaden feet forward, and spun into the nearest alcove as the door was finally wrenched open. He pressed his back up against the cool concrete, praying that it was deep enough and dark enough to hide him. His mind swam with visions of that one kid who went behind curtains during hide and seek, only to leave their feet sticking out. The kid was him, he knew Kathy had found him by the sound of her deep, raucous laugh. If the enemy found him here, he couldn't imagine their reaction would be quite so light hearted. He felt a cold sweat pooling at the base of his spine, as the sound of approaching footsteps echoed off the walls around him. Closer and closer. Louder and louder. And then, the sounds of muffled violence then silence. Richie wrenched his fear-clenched eyes open. Back across the corridor, Green held the unconscious body of a German soldier tight to his body, one hand clamped around his mouth, the other around his waist, keeping his limp body upright. He nodded back towards the door.

Oh thank God...

Richie returned the nod, and like a man on a high rise ledge, edged his way around the corner and tip-toed his way forwards.

Be cool, be cool, be cool…

The door was hauled open again, and Richie let out what could only be described as a squeal of panic. This time though he was able to control his body enough to launch himself into the next alcove as another soldier emerged to the screeching chorus of metal on concrete. Again he tried to press himself into the corner, and again tried to suppress his breathing. The sound of boots approached, passing him this time, and were again cut off by controlled aggression.

He popped his head out again, this time it was Will who'd been the subduer, and it was his turn to encourage Richie onwards.

"Our target should be through there, in that room. Go and make the meet, we'll catch up." he said firmly but quietly. Richie gave him a weak thumbs up, and gulped loudly, once again stepping out of the shadows.

Just make the meet, yep, yessiree, no problemo, easy peasy, easy as pie, just walk blindly into a Nazi bunker and meet some mad secret agent. All in a day's work for Richie Spink, queasy super soldier. Eurgh. Why me??

He reached the door. At his feet he could see the arc that its swing carved into the floor. He reached out for the tarnished metal handle. Not wanting to make the same noise the two fallen soldiers had made, he tried to lift it as he pulled. The door snapped off its hinges and came away in his hand. Richie's eyes widened and he carefully placed it to one side. Risking a quick glance back over his shoulder he saw Green looking on in horror, and further away, Will rolled his eyes to the heavens.

"Sorry!" Richie whispered sheepishly.

Still, at least it was quieter than what them two fellas did!

277

Beyond lay another short corridor, this one was fully lit by overhead tube lights, their faint electrical hum was the only noticeable sound. To either side of the ceiling lights, myriad tubes and wires ran all the way to the far end, embedding into the wall above another blue metal door. As he approached, Richie noticed that, judging by the lack of floor markings, this door was a better fit than the outer one. It was also ajar by several inches.

He drew closer. From beyond he could hear a wider array of electric hums, crackles, clicks and whirs. As he reached the door, Richie angled himself to see through the gap, easing himself left and right to scan his narrow vertical strip vision of the room. Computer banks that looked like something out of an old science fiction movie filled the wall space. Each one a flickering multicolour tapestry of illuminated switches, buttons and diodes. As he panned to the centre of the room, his heart leapt into his mouth as his eyes fell upon the figure of a person in a lab coat. He stepped back in shock, but managed to freeze before making a giveaway sound.

Come on Rich, keep it together. It's not a soldier, it's just some scientist. You've literally been shot like a hundred times and lived. It's just a person.

Re-composed he leant forward again to get a better look. The scientist was hunched over a display on the far side of the room. Richie leaned as far left then as far right as possible until his viewing angle became too acute. There was no sign of any other soldiers, but still he wasn't stupid enough to just barge in. He placed his right hand around the lip of the door, and his left in the middle and gently eased it open. It felt almost weightless, like Balsa wood and it took a surprising amount of focus to keep from pushing too hard. Richie took slow, even breaths and as the gap widened he scanned his increased field of vision for signs of danger. All he saw were more beeping and whirring computer banks, and several

278

empty folding metal chairs, and still unaware of his arrival, the scientist.

He crept into the room, and could at last verify that it was just himself and the distracted other. On the far left was another door, green this time, which was closed. Richie felt a tingle of pride rise up above the pre-existing, pant wetting terror. He'd done it. This must be the target. Now all he had to do was initiate contact.

He reached a hand out. "Erm, excuse me, hi, err.."

The scientist stiffened, and in a lighting blur of white and amber spun, swinging a straight chop to his neck, a breathtaking knee to his stomach, and then, dropping down low, a spinning leg sweep that sent Richie tumbling to the ground. Before he could process the moves, the scientist pressed a high heeled shoe to his throat. He looked up as their long mane of dark red hair, haloed by the ceiling light above came to whip and rest just below her shoulders, her fists and jaw clenched in a fighting pose.

"What is the password?" she said with a thick German accent, pressing her foot more firmly down.

"Err… New England Clam Chowder?" Richie spluttered.

"What?" She replied, her stomp loosening slightly.

Just then, Green and Will burst into the room, their weapons drawn.

"Indigo, Delta, Excelsior." Will said with a debonair smile. "Hello Grace."

"Hello William, fancy seeing you here." she said, raising one of her dark eyebrows, all traces of Germanic lilt gone from her voice. "Shall we make tracks?"

"I reckon we should aye. Unless you've already got dinner plans?"

"Nothing that can't be rescheduled." she said, and lifted her foot from Richie's neck just as his vision was starting to spot.

She walked back to the workbench and from a drawer retrieved a brown paper file, a small camera and a film reel and handed them over to Will. "A few appetisers I've prepared. Shall I change for dinner?"

"Probably for't best." Will replied and nodded towards Green, who left the room and moments later returned dragging one of the unconscious German soldiers.

"Your evening wear my dear. Sorry it's not been freshly pressed."

Richie watched the flirty interchange from his position on the floor, with a puzzled look on his face. A puzzled look that eased when he saw the grin that had formed on Green's as he began stripping the uniform from the prone man.

Now he's bloody James Bond an' all.

Grace held out a hand and Will stepped forward for her to place it on his shoulder for balance as she reached down and slipped out of her high heels. Without this height boost, she was still roughly the same height as him, and as she slid out of the long white lab coat, Richie noticed the muscle tone of her arms. He rubbed his neck.

No wonder that hurt, she's ripped!

"So who's this then?" she said, nodding towards Richie. "Is this our famed secret weapon, or should I expect his horse to burst through the door any minute?"

"Ah ha Zorro!" Richie blurted out, and all three of the others turned towards him. "What? I… I understood that reference. Catherine Zeta Jones was well fi… Erm. Yes." Richie coughed to cease his babbling, and looked away, squinting as though trying to read a nearby computer. The others continued.

"It's a long story. Right now, we need t'get you out of 'ere before all hell comes down on our heads."

"Understood. Just give me a moment to slip into something more suitable and we can be on our way."

Will nodded, and walked over to help Richie to his feet as Green handed the Nazi uniform over to Grace.

"Did you just get your arse kicked by a girl?" Will whispered with a grin.

"Story of my life." Richie replied.

A few minutes later, Grace had changed out of her blouse and pencil skirt, and was dressed in the borrowed grey-green German infantry uniform. Her fire-red locks tied up into her cap, her face wiped clean of makeup, and her feet now in a pair of calf length black boots, Richie was struck firstly by how much more comfortable in her own skin she looked, and secondly by how naturally beautiful she was. He watched as she purposefully and confidently moved around the room, pressing buttons, pulling levers and removing tape reels. Bill and Green emptied out drawers and tore out cabling. By the time they were finished, the clicking and whirring of the computer banks had fallen silent.

"Are you going to blow it up?" Richie asked.

"Not unless we want the whole of Northern France to know we're here." Bill replied as he scooped the last of the files and tapes into a metal waste bin in the centre of the room.

"Not that he wouldn't love the challenge." Grace chipped in with a smirk.

"Not today. Today we get the files we came for, get you, get through the next town, and get the hell back home."

"Fair enough. Anyway, with the files we've taken, the damage we've done, it would take a minor miracle for the Germans to get this station back up and running again." She noted.

Richie nodded as Will flicked open his Zippo lighter again, set fire to a piece of paper and dropped it into the bin.

"Sometimes a subtle knife stroke can do more damage than a cannon." Grace added.

281

"Yeah. Sometimes." Will said, putting his lighter away in the top pocket of his jacket as the flames licked above the rim of the receptacle. "Raight, let's get out of 'ere."

"Follow me." Grace said, flashing her pearly white teeth, and in her right hand, a Green keycard. "You ready, new guy?"

she said in Richie's direction.

"Yeppity do." Richie blabbed, suddenly feeling as though his tongue and lips were as big as his pecs. Richie had developed the ability to stop bullets and run the 100m in under 9 seconds, but when it came to talking to girls he was still very much the same awkward gangly boy.

Oh god. The Banner theory is more right than I knew. I'm the Hulk. The thick, stupid Hulk. Quick, recover. You can do this.

"Yes. Good, I am. Good." he said unevenly.

Grace cocked an eyebrow, tilted her head to the side and gave his thick bicep a squeeze. "Hmmm. Pity." she said and immediately returned her attention to the task at hand.

"Okay lads, follow me. Try to keep up. This next bit could get a bit hairy." she said forthrightly before turning back to Richie. "Run fast, fight good, yes?" she said slowly in a 'me Tarzan, you Jane' vain to Richie, and opened the green door.

"Good work son." Will said playfully. "Seems we've found something you're even worse at than knot tying and running."

"Oh God. She thinks I'm a moron."

Will jogged past him "She always was a great judge of character." he said, patting him on the back with a smile.

Green passed him too. "Come on pal. Could be worse."

"Oh yeah?"

"Oh yeah of course. You could be a moron who has to escape a building and town filled with Nazi soldiers!"

Richie nodded, then paused as the others disappeared. "Hey! I am… Oh."

282

Oh Christ. I'm not even the Hulk, I'm... Rick Jones. Oh god, I'm going to die!

"Extraction point is beyond the next town." Will shouted as they ran up the metal staircase that ringed a large concrete shaft.

"There's a small guard house at the top of these stairs that we'll need to get past first." Grace added, without turning back. "The main door controls are inside."

As they reached the top, Grace gestured for the rest to fall in behind her. Richie made every effort to mirror the actions of Green and Will.

Now is not the time to be Richie Spink.

Grace smoothed down her uniform, and as she did so, her posture shifted from smooth and athletic, to tight, tall and authoritarian. She scanned her key card on a pad to the right of the green metallic door, and entered the room. Richie listened intently to the muffled sounds and half-heard syllables of German conversation. The voices quickly became louder and more fraught, and then the green door slammed open again as a body flew through it and rebounded hip-first off the guardrail to the stairs. A German soldier grimaced in pain and shook his head, looking up just in time to see the incoming clothes line from Will, which sent him tumbling over the side, and screaming downwards into the gloom. Richie watched in stunned horror. Will turned to him and Green, the muscles in his jaw clenched.

"In there now. Front foot. No one gets out but us."

Green nodded dutifully and bounded into the room. Richie's legs began to follow, and Will pushed him the final step into the control room.

At the centre of the square room, Grace, cap gone and red hair flowing loosely again was fending off two more soldiers, the air thick with coarse-sounding German language. Green and Will immediately engaged with another two, the younger man tackling his opponent into a bank of antique looking TV

283

screens, whilst Will adopted a boxing stance, and squared up to his. Richie watched on dumbfounded at the action as these highly trained soldiers engaged each other in mortal combat. The skirmish took place in a haze. Ducks and sidesteps, the dull meaty thuds of punches and kicks landing. Through the melee, Richie's eyes met those of another familiar face, sporting two black eyes.

The Prisoner!

Across the room their former captive stood frozen.

"Flame! Flame!" Will's voice echoed around Richie's brain, with only dull recognition. "RICHIE!" he shouted, shattering Richie's reverie like a stone on a frozen pond.

"Yes sir!"

"Your man. Take him down." he ordered, just before his opponent landed a cuffing blow to his wounded upper arm.

"Right." Richie nodded.

Okay Rich, you can do this. You are big, you are strong, he's probably more scared of you than you are of him. Like a small woodland animal. He has no idea that you've never thrown a punch in your life, and that most fights you've been in have ended in loss of pocket money, and/or public humiliation. It's cool. Cool, cool, cool.

Richie edged around the fighting, trying not to get caught by one of the many stray elbows, fists or knees. Across the room, the soldier began to creep away. Like two hands on the opposite side of a clock, with every step the othertook the distance between them stayed the same. The prisoner broke fearful eye contact, his attention suddenly else where.

What's he looking at? Oh crap!

The slowly fleeing soldier was edging towards a particularly ominous looking, large red button.

"NO! WAIT!" Richie, still half a room, and six bodies away, shouted in vain. But it was too late. With a shaking hand, the panic stricken soldier managed to find the clear plastic casing, open it and slammed his fist down on the button.

A SIREN BEGAN TO BLARE, and the room's lighting turned dimmer. Two red bulbs on opposite walls began strobing.

"What the bloody hell?" Will shouted, as he ducked a punch and landed one of his own.

The nervous soldier risked a glance at the smashed open door, then back at Richie.

"Don't do it mate!" Richie warned, trying to sound authoritative.

Whether it was a lack of English, the noise of the sirens, or that he just plain didn't want to listen, the soldier bolted for the doorway.

Dammit.

"DON'T WORRY, I'LL GET HIM!" Richie bellowed as he set off after him. It was his fault they were in this situation, and he knew it was on him to fix it.

Will dropped low, and with a sweeping kick knocked his opponent to the ground, hammering a fist across his jaw to end the fight.

"NO! WAIT!" he shouted, but Richie was already gone.

Richie skidded his hulking figure around the corner, hitting the barrier opposite the door. He teetered over the edge for a heartstopping moment before righting himself and setting off down the corridor at pace. Ahead, the terrified soldier slammed through a set of double doors. When Richie hit them, they splintered apart and skittered across the poured concrete floor of the giant open bay in front of him. The smell of oil and petrol filled his nostrils as he continued the chase. He could see the fleeing soldier, his body silhouetted by a tall, widening strip of daylight as the giant bunker doors slowly opened. The instant that the gap was wide enough, the man painfully pushed his slim body through, escaping to the other side just as Richie reached him.

"Dammit, get back here you idiot!" Richie growled as he plunged his left arm into the space, trying to grab hold of his uniform and missing. He took a step back and waited for the painfully slow opening, thick metal blast doors to open. He took a deep breath.

You can do this, it's just running. We've done it before. Run, tackle, punch his stupid face.

Richie pushed his thick frame through the gap, and out squinting into the daylight. "Right you little, idiot, you're mine now, you're making me do Cross Country. In real life! Again! Urgh!" He patted himself down, took another deep breath and set off after his prey.

The bunker itself had been built right on the edge of the forest, so within seconds, the wide dirt path he was sprinting down and the tree line surrounding it faded and Richie found himself approaching a small town. Ahead, the soldier crawled and wriggled through a tight gap in the ten foot high, chain link fence between two tall buildings, hurriedly tugging and ripping his uniform as it caught on a stray wire. Once cleared, and struggling for breath, he shambled down the alleyway.

Richie approached the fence at full speed.

There's no way I'm getting this body through that gap. Ahh well, here goes nothing...

He planted his foot, pushed off and leapt for all he was worth. He lifted his feet as he cleared the fence, and came down in perfect stride on the other side.

"Holy hell! Hahahaha!" he laughed maniacally, and kept running. Down the alley, the soldier looked back with eyes wide, and turned the corner out of sight.

"I've got you now mate!" he shouted, with a beaming smile on his face. "No one escapes the power of the Eternal... Crap."

Richie skidded to a halt on the dusty, rubble strewn cobbles. He was in an open square, surrounded on all sides by buildings in various states of damage and dilapidation.

Cracked wooden shutters hung from window frames, bullet holes riddled plaster and exposed brick. Richie was aware of all this, it was the kind of thing his history teacher Mister Wells had called "living history" once on a school trip. On any other day he'd have found it fascinating. Today however, his attention was more drawn by the thirty one German soldiers facing him with their weapons drawn.

Ahh, so THAT'S how many people there are in a platoon.

The escapee stood in front of them, hunched over and clawing for breath, he looked back at Richie and gave him a playful wink.

"Ooh, you little rat! I should have kicked your arse when I had the chance!"

The leader of the group, as best as Richie could figure based on his more formal (and cleaner) uniform. Barked an order, and the click-clacking sound of thirty one different guns being cocked echoed off the surrounding masonry.

"Oh, sh-"

The officer barked again, and the platoon began firing.

CHAPTER FORTY TWO: ANNA

The boot of the car was pitch black, hot, cramped, and for the next fifteen minutes, in motion. Anna spent that time buffeted, bumped, banged and occasionally squashed by the hefty unconscious bodies sharing the space. All of these things paled into insignificance compared to the scattergun, terrified ramblings of her inner monologue, which more than ever sounded like her mother.

Don't talk to strangers sweetie. Don't walk alone at night honey. Don't purposely climb into the boot of murderous gangsters my angel. Eurgh.

Anna's maternal monologue was interrupted at last with a crunch of gravel as the car came to a halt. She readjusted her dusty tarpaulin covering and held her breath, as the boot popped open and light flooded in.

"You pick up this one, and I'll get that one." said the well spoken male voice.

Be still. You are a stone. An invisible, frozen stone, stuck in amber. A fossil, unmoved, unmovable for…

"Ey, there's someone else in here too!" said a much less well spoken voice.

Oh shine a light.

The tarpaulin was whipped back, and as Anna's eyes adjusted to the sunshine, she made out the faces of two men standing over her. The Grey Man, his sharp features bearing fresh cuts, and the face of another young, though much more slovenly, bespectacled guy. Anna thought she recognised him, but now was not the time to play 'Guess Who?'

"Well, well, well, isn't this interesting. Boss?" The Grey Man said, and an older gentleman in a dark suit came around to peer over their shoulders. He chuckled when he saw her.

"Well, that's going to save us a job isn't it? Hello Miss Harrison, nice of you to join us." he said pleasantly. "Bring her inside with the others."

The Grey man nodded, and prodded the man in the thick glasses.

"Oh, but my back." he said in a whiney, pained voice.

The Grey Man held up a clenched fist, and the other quickly, though begrudgingly, lamented.

After being lifted out, she was then frog marched across a deserted, litter-strewn car park, repressing her instinct to break free and flee (whilst kicking the Grey Man in the balls if possible) the whole way. Glasses and the Man in Grey pushed her through a doorway, took her up a cold flight of stairs that stank of cheap bleach, and through another set of doors into what looked like a quite ornate, if somewhat run down, function room. There in the middle, tied up and still unconscious, were Mister Wells, and Richie Spink.

Well here you go Anna, you found him. Great, well done, now what?

Another metal legged chair was dragged across the scuffed wooden dance floor, and placed opposite the other two. The Grey Man shoved her down to it. Glasses man appeared with a length of rope, and tied her hands behind her back. She fought back her gag reflex at the scent of his foul breath.

Anna's mind raced, initially through all the horrible ways in which she was likely to die, but gradually she wrestled her thoughts back towards the situation at hand, and how best to act *and react* to it.

They clearly want us all for something, or they'd have chucked us in the river or something on the way. If they want something that means we've got power.

Anna pulled at her restraints, which held firm.

A small, teeny-tiny amount of power, but power nonetheless.

Having spent her week chasing answers, here she now was at the root of all the questions. Anna made two mental resolutions.

One: Ask them everything, and Two: tell them nothing.

289

"What do you think you're doing!?" she shrieked. "This is kidnapping, there's, there's laws against things like this."

Good start. Anna Harrison QC.

From her blindside, the Grey Man glided up alongside her.

"It's not really kidnapping when the supposed victim jumps into the boot on purpose now is it?" he said with a humourless chuckle.

"Yeah well, that's..." Anna began to protest. "Yeah, that's... That's a pretty good point actually."

Dammit.

The Grey Man shook his head, and with a gesture to Glasses, both left the room. Anna heard the sound of a heavy chain being slid across the door handles from the other side.

Ooookaaaay then.

Anna surveyed her surroundings again. The daylight from outside broke through the grime encrusted sash windows, breaking into shards of light that illuminated the well trodden dance floor beneath her feet. Somewhere from a side room she heard the hum and click of an industrial refrigerator, it fought with the blinking light of the emergency exit sign, and the bassy drone of Mister Wells snoring for the coveted prize of most irritating sound on earth.

At least he's breathing.

Finally her gaze fell upon Richie Spink. She tilted her head slightly to the right to get a better look at his face. His hair was slicked back, and even with his head drooped forward, she could see the cut above his right eye, bisecting his eyebrow. One loose strand of hair dangled down his face. His clothes, despite being somewhat roughed up by the situation looked, good. Smart. Smarter than she'd observed on him previously anyway.

"Are they gone?" he said.

Anna let out an involuntary "yelp!" and fought fiercely to keep it from blossoming into a full blown scream/panic attack.

"Christ on a bike!" she exclaimed and tried to pull a hand to her heart, but was held back by the ropes.

Richie's smile grew across his face. "Hey, Anna." he said quietly, opening his eyes, but keeping his head tilted forward. "Long time no see."

"Yeah, it's been like, wait, what?"

"Oh, haha, nothing, err... Head trauma." he said, looking up towards the cut and blowing the loose strand of hair off his face.

"So, have they gone?"

"They?" she asked. "Ohhh, hahaha, *theyyyyy*. *D'uh*." she said, rolling her eyes. "Yes, yep." Her brain and her voice box seemed to be operating in different time zones. Anna cleared her throat, as much for the moment to gather herself as for any practical purpose.

For Godsake Anna, get a grip. Listen. Have thoughts. Say words.

"Yes. The people are gone."

There you go! Coherent. Good start.

"Are you okay? Did they hurt you or anything?"

"Me? No, I'm good. I'm here by choice. Well, no..."

Oh God what are you saying now?

"I was following you and then the man that killed Mister Wells' Dad went into the house after you, and then there were explosions, and then there weren't, and then I basically jumped into the bad guy's car boot, and they put you and Sir in, and then they drove here. It was hot and stuffy and I got a bit squished, and then they stopped and found me and tied me to this chair and then left, and you, you said 'Are they gone'? And I started babbling total and utter wham and now I am going to stop and probably never talk again for the rest of my life." She cleared her throat again. "So... How are you?"

Marvellous stuff. If my hands weren't tied I would be slow clapping myself so hard right now.

Richie, who hadn't taken his big brown eyes off her the whole time, smiled again, and somehow Anna felt less like wanting the Earth to swallow her whole.

"I'll live." He lifted his head slowly and looked around the room. "Probably." He smiled again, radiating composure. "Did they use handcuffs or rope for you?"

Anna wriggled her wrists around. She already knew the answer, but for some reason felt the need to show that she was taking this all seriously. "Rope. You?"

Richie shook slightly so Anna could hear the light jangle of the handcuff chain. "Don't suppose you've got a bobby pin?"

"Don't suppose you've forgotten this isn't, like, the nineteen forties?

"Touché." he chuckled. "Hmmm… I guess we'll just have to get the keys then."

"That seems like a pretty prudent move." Anna replied, half-sarcastically.

"What can you tell me about the men who brought you in here?"

Anna, having regained enough of her natural composure not to spew out any further brain mush, caught him up with her side of the story in full, composed, human sentences. The Grey Man, Glasses, and the Police Detective. As she was finishing, Mister Wells began to stir from his slumber. The expression "Death Warmed Up", sprang immediately to mind.

Neil Wells squinted hard as the world began to seep in painfully through his eye sockets. There was of course his already monumental hangover, and the ever present weight of grief to contend with, but judging by the throbbing pain at the back of his head- probably a contusion and a mild concussion too.

He tried to reach up to inspect the wound, but found his movement blocked and felt the sharp pinch of metal handcuffs around his wrists.

"Is it Saturday already?" he muttered.

"Mister Wells, are you okay?" A female voice sang around his pickled brain.

He forced his leaden eyelids open, and as he did his vision coalesced into a vaguely familiar face.

"Sir, can you hear me? Do you think he's concussed or something?"

"Quite possibly. It looks like he's taken quite a whack." said another, slightly deeper, voice. This one was more recognisable. As a teacher, Wells had long since learned that you never remembered the mediocre students. The only kids whose names and faces ever stuck with you were the exceptionally bright ones, and the down right pain in the arse ones. Anna Harrison was the former, and as of this afternoon, Richard Spink had firmly graduated to the latter.

"Is there any chance that you two are a whiskey and sorrow-induced fever dream?" The question was rhetorical of course, and Wells was at least pleasantly encouraged that both seemed to get that. Looking away from his fellow captives, he tried to get his bearings, and was again met by a sense of vague recollection. This time, full recognition came quickly. The 1970's workman's public house rendition of opulence. The grime. He was back at the home of the Order of The Eternal Flame.

"Terrance." he said through firmly gritted teeth. "That intolerable little slug. I'll ring his neck when I get half a chance!"

"Who?" Anna asked.

"Glasses." Spink responded to a nod of comprehension. "How are you feeling, Mister Wells? Do you remember anything from earlier?" the boy probed.

293

"Yes, you were at my house. And then Terrance showed up with a man and a gun. There was a fight. No wait…"

"Did you use the power?"

"The… the power?" Wells said, screwing his eyes closed. Playing back his front yard scuffle. The sewn patch. The fire coursing through his veins. "My God, yes."

"Good, good. Anna, how long has it been since we left Mister Wells' house?"

"I'm not sure, maybe twenty minutes? Twenty five, tops."

"Hmmm. okay, it might be too late but it's worth a shot."

Wells continued to mutter obscenities, all largely centred around the gruesome torture of Terrance Whittaker.

"Mister Wells? Neil?"

As a career teacher, having one's first name uttered by a student was the equivalent of a ye olde duel challenger slapping a glove across one's face. He turned to look at the mysterious young boy.

"Do you still feel the power?" the boy asked.

"I'm… I'm not sure."

"Okay. Breathe. Focus. That anger you feel inside? I want you to push it down. Feel the heat running from your brain, to your heart, down your arms and into your hands. Can you do that?"

"Listen sonny, this new-age hippy dippy nonsense can take a long walk off a short pier."

"That's good Neil." the boy prodded. "Use that, feel that anger, push it out, tense your arms, tense your wrists, and PULL!"

Wells gritted his teeth, and visualised running Terrance over with his car. He felt the metal cuffs digging deeper into the flesh, the pain building, and his anger rising to meet it.

Stupid snot nosed, spot faced, four eyed toad, when I get out of here i'm going to…

All of a sudden the chain between the two handcuffs gave way and Wells' arms flew forward. He let out a gasp.

"Whoa…" Anna Harrison mouthed in slack jawed amazement.

Wells rubbed the abrasions on his wrists, wincing as he did. To his further amazement, his fuzzy head also seemed to have cleared.

"Better than a mug of black coffee right?" the boy said to him.

"I'll say."

"Think you've got another one in you?" he said gesturing behind his back.

Anna watched as her middle aged History teacher, dressed in his housecoat and slippers once again drew down his focus and snapped the handcuff chain binding Richie's wrists.

"There you go."

"How was it? More difficult this time?"

"Yes, I really had to force it."

Richie nodded sagely as he got to his feet. "The power burns brightly but shortly, even in the righteous."

Wells nodded in agreement. "I think that was probably the last of it. Still, at least my hangover has gone, and the back of my head feels, well, distinctly less punched in".

"Yes, we always tended to use it in one of two ways, either to strengthen or to heal. In your case it looks like a bit of both. Can't say it was ever used to fix a week long bender before though." he explained as he untied Anna.

Both men laughed.

Anna, found her proudly rediscovered grip on sanity slipping, and her nostrils flaring in anger.

"I'm sorry," she snapped, "but what in the name of all and holy bejesus are you two on about??? What is going on here? Why did those men kidnap you? Why isn't your head bleeding anymore? How did he break those cuffs? And… and… for GOD SAKE! WHERE ARE YOUR SHOES MAN???"

The two men looked down at Wells' feet. Wells took a moment to process it and then shrugged.

"My dear, when you reach my age and drink as much as I do, you tend to take the morning's after as they come."

"It could be worse, he could be barefoot." Richie offered.

Anna gave him a sarcastic smile, and stabbed a finger into his chest. "Don't think you're getting away with it that easily either matey-chops. I want answers. From what I've seen you've been acting weirdly for weeks, but this..." she gestured theatrically at the pair. "... this takes the absolute biscuit."

"You've been watching me for weeks have you?" he replied with a cheeky grin.

"What, no, I mean yes, but that's besides the point!" She wobbled before returning to a scowl. "Me, Marc and even Jackson Sleight, the crazy moron, have risked life and limb to save you here. I've seen guns, death, violence, my half dressed History teacher breaking the rules of physics AND had to put up with the mindless, endless flirting of two wholly irritating boys along the way. Answers. Now." she said, stomping her foot and crossing her arms.

Both men stood with frozen, wide eyed faces. Wells smiled and stepped around to her side. "I believe the stage is yours dear boy..."

"Okay. Right. Yeah, fair enough. So, I'm not Richie Spink, well... Look, that bit is complicated. To cut a long story short, I am the Eternal Flame of British Resistance, a "super-soldier" imbued with the spirit of the British people, a mystical tool for fighting oppression. For the last few weeks your friend and I have been trading places, well, trading bodies I guess. So while I'm here, Richie is somewhere on a battlefield with the rest of my squadmates.

"A battlefield?" she asked, wrinkling her nose sceptically.

"Yes. In France."

"Oh right."

296

"In 1942."

"Ahh."

"It's complex, I know, unprecedented actuall…"

"So basically like Freaky Friday, but World War 2?"

"Erm…"

"Cool."

"Cool?"

"Sure, why not? Everything else in my life has been bat-crap crazy, why wouldn't this be?"

"So what about the patches?" Wells chimed in.

"The patches?" Anna asked.

"Ahh, yes, well. In the early forties, not long after I joined up, we discovered that whilst my powers are boosted by the collective mental strength of those around me, in return I could imbue an aspect of my power into other people. But it needs direct contact, and as you've seen, the effects can be fleeting. Not much use in a combat situation if I'm not in touching distance. So an intermediary solution was created."

"The Eternal Flame Squad patches." Wells confirmed.

"Exactly. The boys in the lab discovered that a particular metallic element could hold the charge indefinitely, kind of like a battery. That element is woven into the patchwork. Before each mission I would charge them up and each member of the squad would have one added to their uniforms.

"Allowing them to 'power-up' at will, independent of your presence? Extraordinary." Wells said, running a hand through his hair.

"Wait a minute. Do these patches have a cool-looking blue flaming fist on them by any chance?" Anna asked.

"Yes, and the words 'Non Sibi Sed Omnibus'." The Flame added.

Anna looked confused, "And what does that mean again?"

"Not for Oneself, But For All." Wells and The Flame said in unison.

"Oh yeah, Latin of course. Seems all the cool kids are into dead languages these days." she said, rolling her eyes.

"You laugh, but it is a slight, if somewhat basic safeguard. Directly reading the text has no effect, but if the English translation is spoken aloud with enough focus and belief, the person holding it is enhanced by the power of the Eternal Flame."

"Pull the other one." Anna said, her suspension of disbelief currently hanging by a thread.

"He's telling the truth." Wells said. "Well, certainly about that last part. That was how I was able to break the chains, and, ahem, do a few other things as well."

"So you're telling me that your Father handed me a magical badge that gives people superpowers?" she asked.

"Yes. Wait, what?"

"Yes, your father was. *Is*," The Flame corrected himself, "a good friend and trusted ally. The members of the Eternal Flame Squad each took an oath, to protect this country, but also to keep the secrets of the Flame, lest they fall into the wrong hands."

Anna pinched the bridge of her nose and screwed her eyes shut, trying with all her might to keep her head from falling off. Richie Spink, the strange gangly boy she'd been crushing on for the last fortnight, a boy she'd hoped, given his taste (or lack thereof) in clothes, and messy hair might've at least shared her interest in 90's alt rock, had just stood right there in front of her and delivered a speech straight out of a bad History channel documentary. And weirder still, he'd used the word "lest', like some sort of bookish uni student. And weirder still, she kind of liked it.

Ahh well, it's a damn sight better than the farting contests and bus stop kicking of the other boys in our year...

"Okay. Because crazy pills are clearly the new paracetamol, let's just roll with it and say all of this is true. Two questions."

"Go ahead."

"What should we call you?"

"Call me... Rich, or Richard. It'll help you tell the difference in case Richie and I swap places again."

"Okay, simple enough, I guess. Second question. What the hell do we do now?"

"We need to get those patches back." Richard said clearly.

"How many of them still have power?" Wells asked.

"Unclear. The charge can usually be used a couple of times. But I have no idea what condition they were in when they went into storage, there's a chance a damaged one wouldn't work anymore, but we should assume the worst. By my count there are six. Five were with us at your house Mister Wells, and then there's the one you had Anna. Do you know where it is?"

"Yeah it's sewn onto my rucksack, but I left it back at Mister Wells' house with Marc." Anna responded.

"Damn. Okay. At least it's safe for now, but it does mean the enemy has the rest."

"Maybe, but maybe not." Wells said, his attention drifting purposefully to a side door, followed by his feet. "I've been here before you see, Terrance brought me here and introduced me to his gang of robe-wearing simpleton friends. They showed me some old footage of the Eternal Flame, well, you, in action, as well as one of those patches. It looked in pretty rough shape, but like you say, it might still have something left."

"If they had it before, surely they would have figured out how to use it already?" Anna asked.

"My dear, we are talking about middle aged men who spend their weekday evenings prancing around in robes. What they lack in physical fitness, and allure to the opposite sex, they lack even more in brains."

Wells tried the door handle to what looked to be a side office. It was locked.

299

"Right children, who fancies having a go at kicking a door in? I'm afraid neither my footwear nor back are suitable for the task at hand."

Anna and Richard exchanged glances.

"Hey, you're meant to be the super army guy..." she said, gesturing with an open palm towards the door.

"True enough, but have you seen this body? I must be 12 stone soaking wet."

Anna looked him up and down and shrugged.

"Looks alright to me."

Oh my Annabelle, behave!

"Anyway, don't you have some sort of super power you can use?" She quickly recovered.

"Yes, it's called a key. Let's spread out, maybe it's stashed in here somewhere..."

"THE SECRETS OF THE ETERNAL FLAME WILL FINALLY BE OURS!!!" A booming voice came from the main doorway. "Relinquish all knowledge, for your time of judgement is at hand!" Keith Cowley, Chapter Head of the Order of The Eternal Flame stood there, robe and all, a heavy chain and padlock in his hands. He was flanked by Terrance, and two other members of The Order, all similarly decked out like rejects from a Lord of The Rings Convention. Wells slid his hands up his face into his hair and sighed.

"You were fairly warned Mister Wells," the man continued theatrically, "Mock the Order at your per..."

"Oh do shut up you tiresome whelp." Wells snapped and started walking towards them. "I've taught three generations of future drug dealers that had more brain cells than your entire gang of costumed cretins put together. I've had post-Guinness morning ablutions that smelt better."

Anna and Richard sidled up behind him, hiding in the eye of the verbal hurricane. The Order members stood there, frozen in place.

"My knees hurt, my lower back is an absolute disgrace and I have had, quite frankly, a deeply stinging case of piles since half term. My patience is thinner than my hairline, and I am standing here in my pyjamas. If you think I'm intimidated by some jumped up Mummy's boy toffs wearing their Grandmother's curtains then let me tell you something." He pointed at each of them in turn. "If you were a fresh shit on my shoe, I wouldn't even bother to take the time out of my day to wipe it off. Now give me the key to that door or by God, I'll tell you all what I *really* think of you." he snarled.

"Hey you can't talk to us like that." one of the slightly younger men said and stepped forward to grab hold of Anna's arm. She shrugged it off, stepped back, and crescent kicked his chin. The man let out a faint whimper, and crumpled to the floor. The other three watched him hit the deck and reflexively held up their hands in surrender.

"Or, we could try that." Wells said with a menacing smile.

The Head of The Order, with the faintest sheen of tears in his eyes, dropped the padlock, and with shaking hands removed his necklace and held it towards Wells. The key, as well as a handful of tacky looking charms were on the chain.

"Right you, get a move on. The rest of you, into the corner."

Richard tied the others to their now vacated chairs, whilst Anna kept a watchful eye on the door. A few moments later Wells emerged, coarsely shoving the thoroughly deflated man ahead of him towards his similarly shamed (or unconscious) cohorts. In Wells' hands was a simple-looking writable DVD and a tattered, scorched Eternal Flame patch.

"Good work Mister Wells. Now we need to get out of here before some more, *competent* threats return." the boy said.

Terrance looked up and scowled behind his thick glasses.

"Indeed. How's about it, young Master Whittaker? Fancy telling Sir if there's another way out of here?" Wells asked curtly.

Terrance turned his head away like a petulant infant trying to avoid being spoon fed. Anna allowed herself a smile at the absurdity of the situation, but it was short lived. The sound of the ground floor door being wrenched back open rattled up the stairwell.

"Someone's coming!" she hissed.

"Right," Richard said, springing into action, "Behind the bar, there's probably a staff entrance." He ushered Anna and Wells towards the far end of the room. As he turned to leave, the Order Chief grabbed Wells' wrist.

"You may mock us, but you have no idea of the world of trouble you've gotten yourself into. The Order is more powerful than you can possibly imagine." he said with a cruel smile.

Wells pulled free and jogged after the others, his confident mood dented ever so slightly. As he reached the bar, the double entrance doors slammed open and The Grey Man flew into the room, his pistol drawn.

Richard dragged Neil Wells through the gap in the bar as the first gunshot rang out. Overhead, a wine glass exploded, raining shards down on the trio as they ducked for cover. A second annihilated a bottle of whiskey suspended behind the bar, and the dust caked mirror behind it. A shard of glass stung his cheek and he looked across, to see the terrified look in Anna's eyes. Richard though, despite the noise and rain of spirits was the picture of composure.

"This way, quick." he said, pointing towards a small door just past the short row of glass-fronted bottle refrigerators.

Another couple of shots splintered the woodwork as he and the girl crouched-walked through and round the corner, with Richard bringing up the rear.

They found themselves inside a dilapidated hallway, the sound of one final shot thudded dully into the thick wall, shaking loose a layer of dust from the flickering, lozenge shaped light fittings. Richard jumped through behind them,

302

slammed the door, slapped across a bolt, and dragged an antique mahogany writing bureau across the doorway.

"That should give us a little breathing space." he said, his eyes darting around the space.

Anna took in the surroundings herself. In the 1950's it was probably the height of moneyed taste. Now it was a dumping ground for dated pub paraphernalia. The patterned carpet runner beneath her feet was barely visible for piles of stained table cloths, beer mats, and stacks of sticky looking crates filled with glass bottles. It was, to her eyes at least, a pretty obvious place to murder someone.

"Where are we?" she asked with a shudder as they crept along.

"It's the flat above the pub. Normally where the landlord who runs it lives." Wells answered, and plucked one of the beer mats from atop a pile of used bar rags. "Oh wow, Higsons' Best! Now there was a lovely drop. The brewery shut down years ago. We used to sneak bottles of this into the teacher's lounge, so we could have a good old swig over lunch break…" His glassy eyed reverie was cut short when he saw the vaguely disgusted look on Anna's face. "What? Oh it was the Eighties! Everyone in that building was plastered half the time." He tossed the mat away. "Ahh, great days…"

"Oh yeah, sounds fab." Anna said, raising an eyebrow, which despite the peril of their situation raised a warm laugh from Richard.

"Okay," he said, composing himself. "Let's head down this way, if we can get down into the pub below, we should be able to find a way out."

The others agreed and followed behind as they continued to shuffle their way along the dimly lit corridor, passing rooms on either side, each filled with more rotten pub crap than the last. Turning another corner they came across the stairway spiralling downstairs. Taking each step with deliberate care, Anna noticed that the art deco design of the

303

flat began to fade into a plainer, more business-like layout. Browning pieces of A4 paper, curling at the corners were blu-tacked to the cream painted walls. Health and safety info, correct lifting practice guide sheets, and cleaning rotas with names illegibly scrawled in black biro. At the bottom of the stairs, a brown and white plastic machine adorned with a broken clock was hung alongside a thin rack containing dozens of clock-in cards. It was the same make and model as the one at the nursing home. Its familiarity gave Anna a modicum of comfort. Beyond the machine, at ground level now, the floor opened out into the blue linoleum floors, and grubby white plastic coated walls of the kitchens.

Richard ran ahead, past a row of stainless steel counters to the door at the far end. Pressing himself up against the wall, he angled himself to look through the circular port-hole window in its centre. Anna and Wells hung back near the distinctly putrid smelling sink, still piled high with unwashed crockery.

Not sure what smells worse, the sink or Mister Wells' dressing gown.

"Okay I think the coast is clear. Keep your wits about you though."

Wells took a relaxed sigh and sidled up alongside to take a look himself.

"Oh yes of course. This is a pretty standard public house layout, this door takes us behind the main bar, from there the main entrance will be across the ways, with fire escapes at either end, and likely a door to the beer garden or car park over to the right. Rather straightforward actually. Come on then kids, let us make haste, Mister Wells needs a cocktail and a lie down." he blustered as he pushed open the door and stepped through. There was a loud 'click-clack' noise and he froze instantly as a gun was placed to his temple.

"Ahh right. Children, we may be caught."

Still on the kitchen side of the doorway, Richard stepped between Anna and Wells. Without taking his eyes off the gun, he waved a hand for her to back up. Despite the cold shock of fear running up her spine, Anna nodded and began to creep away, grabbing a firm hold of a rusty, cast iron skillet from the side as she did. It had a good, comforting heft to it.

Okie dokie, no problem, just more people with guns, coooool beans.

A noise from behind spun her around. There in his freshly pressed suit, The Grey Man lent nonchalantly against the door frame, tapping his gun against his thigh. Anna raised the pan.

"And what are you going to do with that precious? Whip me up a little omelette?" His voice made her skin crawl.

"Eww, are you serious? What are you, like thirty? And with that accent? I bet your mum still does all your cooking anyway. Or is it your nanny?"

The Grey man straightened up, his cocky smile knocked clean off his face.

"Actually yeah, you know what? I will make you that omelette, I'll crack that little pea head of yours to make it!" Anna said and charged towards him, swinging the pan towards his sneering face. The Grey Man, caught flat footed, ducked at the last second, and the pan took a thick chunk of plaster out of the wall behind him. He recovered quickly, and as she lunged again, he caught her wrist, and twisted it sharply. Blinding pain shot up her arm and Anna let out a yelp as the pan fell to the floor with a loud clang.

"Anna, no!" Richard shouted, and sprang away from the doorway. He vaulted the metal counter dividing the room, grabbing and then hurling a plate towards the Grey man in one fluid motion. It struck him on the left shoulder, staggering him enough to release his grip on Anna. Pressing this momentary advantage, Richard used the counter top for leverage and pushed himself into a flying kick, striking his opponent with a glancing blow to the hip. The Grey Man

305

instinctively pulled in his arms to cover up and Richard dove for him, desperate to keep him from bringing the gun in his right hand into play. Wrapped in a bear hug, he tried to squeeze but straight away found himself struggling. The Grey Man, though slenderly built, was pure muscle and Richard, in his puny fifteen year old form, strained to keep him held fast.

"Anna... go... I... can't hold him long."

Nursing her injured wrist, Anna pushed back against the wall to get herself upright again.

Not a chance.

With her left hand she picked up the pan again, raising it to strike. The Grey man saw her movement out of the corner of his eye and planted a short but powerful head butt to the bridge of Richard's nose. Anna heard the crack, as he released his grip and staggered backwards, scattering a rack of metal utensils across the floor. The Grey Man turned towards her, his serpentine smile returning again.

"Right! That's enough of that nonsense." boomed a firm voice from the doorway to the bar. An older gentleman in a tan trenchcoat stepped through. One arm gripped Wells' upper arm, the other kept his pistol pressed firmly into the side of his head. The Detective.

"Put down the frying pan, and get down on your knees or the old fella gets it."

"How dare you, I'm not old, I'm..." The man dug the gun in harder. "Well yes, okay, astute observation. Ahem. Anyway, you were saying?" Well said through gritted teeth.

The Grey Man used the distraction to bring his own gun to bear. Anna looked at Richard. The young man caught her eye as he wiped a stream of dark claret blood from under his nose. Reluctantly he nodded. Anna dropped the pan to the floor with another heavy clang, and slid down to her knees clutching her arm to her chest.

"Out of the frying pan, and into the fire, ey?" Richard

whispered, winked and winced.

A moment of brevity, one Anna prayed would not be her last.

CHAPTER FORTY THREE: RICHIE and THE ETERNAL FLAME SQUAD

The deafening surround sound clash of thirty one guns reverberating off the broken buildings filled his ears, his brain, his consciousness. A hail of bullets descended like a tidal wave of growing pain upon him. The first few tickled, then they began to sting, now each impact felt like a punch. The shots that missed him kicked up broken cobble stone around his feet, the shards of which tore at the loose edges of his uniform, or embedded themselves in walls behind him, chipping away at the plaster and exposing more of the red brick beneath. Where earlier, the bullets had been incinerated before contact, the blue Flames that licked around his body struggled to keep them at bay, and like a barrier being worn down, each shot now grew closer to his skin. The volley of fire staggered him, one struck him on the cheek just below the line of his mask, and Richie reflexively put his hands up to cover his face. As he began to stagger backwards towards the alley, he felt the familiar warm trickle of blood run down to his jawline. Turning his head away from the direction of fire, he saw a doorway, and with no more than survival instinct to guide him, he took three quick steps, and threw himself shoulder first at the wooden door, bashing straight through, losing his balance, and tumbling onto the floor inside. The path of the bullets followed him, splintering the floorboards or pinging off the walls, obliterating an ornate mirror above a fireplace. Richie scrambled around frantically, Will's words on the importance of cover ringing in his head marginally louder than the gunfire around him. He managed to roll around and out of sight, with his back to the wall beside the fractured door.

Bullets continued to rain through, thwipping and thudding into the brickwork behind him. The wall held. The shots began to tail off, and at last Richie could hear his own thoughts again.

Don't have holes, don't have holes, don't have holes.

His breath was shallow and rushed as he ran his hands over his body. A slight feeling of relief arrived when he found himself to be intact. Sore, panicked to all hell, but intact. He put a hand up to his cheek and when he looked at it his fingers were sticky with blood.

Nobody makes me bleed my own blood! Actually, saying that...

Richie chuckled at the mind boggling absurdity of his situation. It was marginally better than bursting into big blubbery baby tears. Marginally. He stretched his long legs out, raised his face to the ceiling and took some slow breaths. The dust motes dancing in the air began to settle back onto the surfaces of what had clearly at some point been a family kitchen.

"COME OUT, COME OUT MISTER MASK MAN!" came a sneeringly playful voice with a thick Germanic accent.

"Yeah, yeah, just give me a minute mate! Just powdering my nose." he said with a tone more confident than he actually felt. The situation he realised, was pretty dire. He looked around the war torn room for something, anything that might help him.

Let's hope the German army's great weakness is broken crockery and a susceptibility to splinters.

From across the room, a face appeared at the small, high window. Green.

"Having a little rest are we?"

Richie looked down at his sprayed legs and smiled back awkwardly.

"Just catching my breath a sec."

"Sure." Green laughed as he popped open the window, and hauled himself through the narrow gap. He landed gracefully on the floor, and clinging to the wall, out of the line of sight of the doorway, edged over towards him.

"Shouldn't you be, you know, kicking their backsides back to Bavaria? You're not, you're not actually *scared* are you?"

Richie scoffed. "Scared? Me? Of course not!"

"Oh good, because…"

"My legs though, yeah they're having a bit of a wobble. And my feet. My Arms… Fingers… Teeth. My teeth are definitely terrified. But apart from that…"

Green chuckled and patted him on the shoulder. "No time for that now chum, by my count there are at least two dozen men out there who seem to be… wait." He cupped a hand to his ear and paused for a moment, straining to listen to something. Richie tried to tune into it too, but couldn't pick up anything out of the ordinary. The relative ordinary at least.

"What.." Richie began.

"Shh… Listen."

"What are you on about?"

"Yes, definitely." Green nodded. "Two dozen silly old Nazis who are literally begging you to go and put your boot up their backsides."

He gave Richie a cheeky smile, who instantly felt his nerves soften.

"Hey, here they are!" Grace whispered from the window.

"Now, quick sharp, on your feet, don't let the Major see you like this.

Richie, quickly clambered back to his feet, as Grace slid into the room, followed by Will.

"MISTER MASK MAN, COME AND PLAAAYY!" came the sneering call once again.

"Good Lord, he needs to shut his face." Richie bristled.

"Is it time Sir?" Green asked.

"I reckon it might be yer know." Will said with a smirk.

"Time?" Richie asked.

"Ohh, I've heard about this." Grace said, stepping backwards and reaching behind her head to tighten her ponytail.

Green grinned as he brought his right hand across to rest on the Flame Squad patch sewn to the upper left arm of his uniform. Will motioned to do this same, before remembering the blood seeping bandage that covered his.

"Hmmff, I guess I'll have to use yours too."

"No problem boss." Green said, shuffling closer so Will could also place the tips of his fingers onto his patch.

"Ready?" Will asked. Green nodded, and Richie was quite taken by the switch in their body language; from playful to supremely focussed and intense in an instant.

"NOT FOR ONESELF BUT FOR ALL." both men chanted in unison. The air crackled and whipped around them, stirring up the brick dust and splinters at their feet. Richie and Grace shielded their faces as blue flames swirled around the men's bodies. Their eyes glowed white, then blue, then back to normal. The maelstrom died down. Will and Green were still stood there, the same, but changed. Richie could feel the energy coming off them, a sense of unity, a connection beyond the physical. It made him feel calmer, stronger.

"What do you say boys?" Grace said with a demure smile. "Got one of those things for me?"

Richie looked around, Will and Green stared back.

"Oh, haha! Does mine do that too?"

God, try to at least sound cool you big nerd.

"It does not. For you to do it, it needs physical contact." Will informed him and nodded to Grace. She took an assertive breath and stepped towards Richie, placing her hand gently on his shoulder. She leant in close and whispered in his ear.

"Be gentle with me big boy."

Richie, who had faced a hundred gunshots and survived, but had never been this close to a woman who wasn't related to him, felt his cheeks flush. Will elbowed Green in the ribs, and the pair laughed.

Grace spoke the words, and kissed him firmly on the lips. Richie felt the rush of power even more acutely this time. When it was done, Grace stepped back, puffed out her cheeks and exhaled slowly.

"Oh my." she exclaimed, blinking in stunned awe.

"Good right?" said Green.

Grace gave Richie's upper arm a long squeeze and shot him a wicked smile as she rejoined the others. "You were fabulous darling."

Richie momentarily felt his skeleton liquify as he turned into a human puddle.

Oh, wow...

Fighting a losing battle to keep the idiots grin from his face, Richie felt suddenly three feet taller.

"Raiight, jaws offt' floor and out t'door gents and lady." Will barked. "We don't have long, so let's make it count. Spread out, stay on't toes, hit hard, move. Understood?"

They all nodded. Even Richie felt ready.

"Flame you take the lead, you are my battering ram."

He grabbed Richie by the shoulders, and looked him squarely in the eyes.

"I won't lie, this might hurt a bit. It actually might hurt a lot. But yer know what? Life hurts. But no battle worth winning ever came wi'out pain an' sacrifice. They want you dead. Us dead. Every thing and every one who doesn't fit their pathetic Master Race vision oft' world, dead. But us here, we've been given a gift. The gift of blood in our veins, breath in our lungs, and bones in our fists. The four of us here are going to get hurt, but my God, we're going to make them hurt more."

"VEE WILL COUNT TO TEN, ZEN WE ARE COMING FOR YOU LITTLE MASK MAN!"

A vein on Will's temple throbbed and he ground his teeth.

"Now go out there an' smash some bloody Nazis!"

Richie gulped.

Wow...

Ten feet taller.

"Raight then. Let's do it."

Richie turned towards the door, let out a primal roar and charged back out into daylight.

"Good speech Skip." Green said, "Can I have one?" he chided.

"Get out there and kill more of them than they kill of you. These plans need to get back to HQ, if we want to win this war we cannot allow that tank to be built."

"Got it boss." he said with a wink and ran out after Richie.

"Wait… What do you mean, stop it being built?" Grace said, but her voice was lost as the bullet storm began to rage once more, and Will charged out of the door. She shook her head, the time for talking was over. Grace took a deep breath, flexed her fists with a satisfied grin, and ran out into the carnage.

Richie's heartbeat pounded in his ears, a raucous cacophony of gunfire and his own blood curdling war cry became the soundtrack to his life as he barrelled head first into the action. Bullets fizzed and evaporated as they struck his trunk, others spattered the stones at his feet, kicking up shards in his wake. Richie Spink has never been in a meaningful fight in his life, had scarcely even thrown a punch, but as he bore down on the Nazi soldiers in their grey uniforms, three deep ahead of him, one crazy, idiotic thought sprang to his mind.

Bowling for Nazis...

Like a crazed idiot he curved his run, and caught one last look at the growing panic on the Platoon leader's face as he lowered his head and raised his left shoulder. "You wanted me mate, well here I am!" he shouted maniacally, as he slammed into the man. The impact knocked him clean out of his polished black boots, sending him pinwheeling backwards through the crowd and into the air, his flailing limbs taking out half a dozen others as he shot past. Richie pushed straight through the crowd, those that he didn't make physical contact with began to separate and scatter away to the sides. He skidded to a stop ten yards past the group and raised his head just in time to see the mouthy barefooted officer hit a wall and fall loose limbed into a pile of putrid hay in the broken down donkey cart below.

"I'd call that a strike biatc-"

Richie was cut off as five others piled on top of him.

"Stop posing and get stuck in!" he heard Will shout from somewhere off to the side.

As more men joined the growing pile on and forced him to his knees, Richie could see Will and Green both embroiled in multi-man scuffles of their own. The weight across his back became heavier and heavier, and with each new body he sank closer to the cobbles. His vision became black, his breaths harder. He strained, and pushed, and wriggled, and finally managed to get one foot back under him, still the pressure grew.

Come on Rich, you can do this. Buckaroo style.

With all his might, he pushed off with his standing foot, powering upwards like a rocket trying to break atmosphere. Throwing his arms back for good measure, the dozen men around him were tossed into the air, like rag dolls. Light flooded his eyes and he heaved a huge, grateful lungful of oxygen as he shook free from the last hanger on.

"Right, that's it! Who wants some? Ey? Do you want some?" Richie looked at one soldier, then another. "How about you mate?"

Several of his assailants looked at each other, nodded and then set upon Richie again.

"Oh come on! Seriously??" he exclaimed as they tried to swamp him again.

314

This time he managed to keep his feet moving, sidestepping the lunge of one, and ducking under the punch of another before a third landed an elbow strike to his cheek. Richie heard the crack of bone and momentarily felt a rush of panic, one that almost instantly vanished as the man cried out in pain and leapt back clutching his limp arm. "Ooh God! Are you okay, that looks like a bad one…" he winced, but was again cut off as another man hit him across the face with the thick wooden stock of his rifle. This one he did feel, and the blow staggered him slightly. Seeing the effect, the man did it again, shattering the stock in the process. Richie fought to keep his balance as the world swirled around him. He shook his head to clear it, and managed to throw up a forearm to block another attack. Reflexively, he kicked out, catching the man full in the gut, folding him into a sleeping heap on the floor. He took two quick steps backwards and put his hand to his cheek, the cut from earlier had reopened, wider this time. Of the dozen men who had piled on him, only five remained. Each held their rifles like clubs, apart from the guy with the broken one, who tossed the barrel to the floor and produced a knife from his hip holster. Richie noticed the cut on his nose and dark bruised circles under both his eyes. It was the escapee.

"You." he growled.

Richie took a deep breath and risked a look to see how his friends were getting on. Though still outnumbered broadly two to one, they each seemed to be holding their own, disarming their combatants and engaging them hand to hand. Or in Grace's case, foot to face as she unleashed a devastating roundhouse kick that sent one man down, like a face propelled rocket into the stone floor.

Yikes. Glad she's on my side.

He saw Will in his boxer-like stance, fists raised, shuffling side to side and throwing jabs almost too fast for the eye to see. Richie tried to mimic the style. He'd seen enough boxing

315

on the telly and had enough play fights with his Dad to at least grasp the basics. He raised his fists, and as the man with the knife slashed forward, he slid to the left. The knife sliced through the side of his tunic, but left his attacker off balance and open, and Richie hit him across the jaw with a left hook. The man flew across the floor and stayed there. His first proper punch.

Oh wow, punching is much easier than I thought it would be, I should just do that everytime.

With a satisfied nod he looked at his fist. Blue flames licked around it. Richie smiled and again adopted the fighter's stance.

Oh wow, yeah that is cool.

"Okay then lads, who's next? Anyone know what 'knuckle sandwich' is in German?"

A fearful look spread over the faces of the remaining four. "Yeah, is right. Fear my flaming fist of terror."

Oh, no, there you go, you ruined it. You dork.

Richie noticed a faint rumble, one that began to grow louder and louder by the moment. The fearful looks of the men before him faded. The rumble became a din, became a roar. A guttural, primal roar that bounced off the battered building walls, and rattled what remained of the window panes.

"RUCKZUG!!" bellowed one of the men. And those still upright broke off from their fights, grabbed their weapons and ran past Richie, out of the square.

"Ruckzug?" Richie mused, as the other three jogged over to his position. "What's that, some sort of German sport?"

"They're falling back." Green shouted.

"Great! Does that mean we win?"

"No, it just means they won't lose here!" Will shouted over the noise. "Standard German military tactics. Strong offence, deep defence. Come on, we need to gerrat 'em before they get dug in. If we can't stop them building the tank from these plans, well, I dread t'think what'll happen."

"Sir, you didn't hear me before." Grace interjected.

"What's that? Come on, we need to get a move on."

She grabbed Will's arm as he went to turn away.

"Sir. Don't you understand? The hanger back in the bunker!?"

"The big empty one that smelled of petrol?" Richie asked.

Grace nodded. "You're too late, the prototype, PzKpfW-VI has already been deployed!" she roared, her voice barely audible above the noise. Something over Richie's shoulder caught her eye, and he watched as the colour drained from her already porcelain face.

"Oh God…"

The others turned. There, rumbling forward, filling the street before them, crushing rubble beneath its tracks, was a metallic beast. It's thick, impenetrable skin painted in a patchwork of greys and brown…

"PzK… What?" Green asked.

Richie gasped as the metallic monstrosity trundled menacingly closer. Recognition hit him. "*The Tiger Tank…*" he said in awe.

"Oof, bloody good name." Green whistled.

"Move! Now!" Will bellowed, taking a firm grip on Grace's collar, hauling her away. To his left, Green scrabbled for traction on the loose shale of broken cobbles beneath his feet.

"GO!" Richie saw him mouth, his voice lost like a leaf in a hurricane.

He saw the wide eyed panic on Grace's delicate features, the veins bulging in Will's hand as his grip on her strained, a circular hatch opening atop the tank as it nosed into the square. A hail of bullets spewing from the machine gun on its front, tearing up the stone in a straight line towards him. The spicks and spacks of the torn up cobbles barely registering

317

above the almighty din. The thick smell of petrol filled his nostrils. The bullets made impact, running a line up his left leg, midriff, shoulder, and fizzing past his ear, like industrial sized mosquitoes. The combined weight of the collisions slapped him back half a step. Blue flames fizzed and sizzled away the worst of it, but with each, another fragment of his uniform was torn away. One of the tank's operators rose from the open hatch, the metallic skull adorning his black hat glinting in the afternoon sun. The man, his jaw set tight, placed one hand to the headphones covering his ears. He barked an order and pointed directly at Richie.

Will, still barely a handful of yards clear, screamed something, but all of Richie's senses were being overrun, devoured. The roar of the engines, the cloying scent of burning fuel, the impact of machine gun ammunition wearing down his defences, the overpowering sight of the metal behemoth filling his vision.

The machine gun ceased its fire.

Richie moved a hand to his shoulder, and touched bare skin. The tank commander's eyes widened and he ducked back inside. Beneath the cacophony of the engine and the sound of splintering stone, Richie was faintly aware of a new metallic clanging sound. He looked down the barrel of its turret cannon; its deep, horrifying black eye looked deep into his soul and found nothing but a scared little boy looking back.

"Get t' cover!!!!" he heard Will scream, but it was no good. The terror had him in its grasp. His spine was ice, his legs were stone, his feet like thickly moulded clay, ran deep into silty earth beneath him. A rising noise, thicker and more concussive than anything Richie had heard in his life grew out from the depths of the gun. Hot, orange fire spewed forth from that all seeing black eye. Windows rattled and shattered. The lethal projectile launched, and Richie knew that this was it. The End. Somewhere in the back of his mind though was a thought, that faintest spark. He felt the heartbeats of the other three, their wills to win, their wills to survive. Escape was impossible, but whilst he had breath there was still a chance, and as the shell reached him, Richie dug his back foot in, threw up his arms and braced himself.

The shell collided. Exploded. Grace, Will, and Green were thrown away by the force, and Richie Spink was enveloped in white light, pain and flame...

CHAPTER FORTY FOUR: ANNA and WELLS

Caught. Again. Closer to freedom by the measure of about two storeys. Further by the measure of the two loaded guns pointed at them, and the competence of the two men who wielded them. Sharp words and bedroom gymnastic karate would not likely be their saviours this time around. Neil Wells and his two young cohorts knelt side by side on the mildly sticky, doubtless dust mite ridden carpet. The effects of the Eternal Flame's power had long since faded, and though it had been gracious enough to take away a hangover thick enough to dig up and re-bury Pompeii, his usual raft of age-related aches and pains were creeping back in. His potential salvation lay in those wondrous "Power Patches", five of which lay spread out on a wooden table nearby, just beyond their captors. Six feet away perhaps. Their relative proximity though was rendered moot by the present situation. These were the men responsible for the death of his father though, and Neil Wells was not prepared to let that lie, he just wasn't sure that there were any favourable options remaining. He'd played Rugby Union to a respectable standard in his youth and Squash in his later years, but age, divorce and alcoholism had put paid to that. There was a chance that he could rush one of the men, maybe the older one? He certainly seemed more sedate than the young buck he'd tackled earlier.

Oh yes, one last charge of the light brigade, take two steps, and get shot to bits. Give the children one last, good old fashioned, mental scarring before they faced their own fate. Bravo Neil.

He risked a sideward glance at them. Anna had her head down, and clutched her right hand to her chest, clearly on the verge of tears, but not willing to give them the satisfaction.

Brave kid.

The boy seemed surprisingly serene. A truly fascinating subject; either a true hero, one blessed with skills and stoicism beyond reproach, or a psychiatric case study for the ages. He placidly took in his surroundings, or at least appeared that way on the surface. Wells had been an educator long enough to spot the smart ones though, and he could see the cogs turning. Perhaps he had a plan. Wells hoped that someone did. If it could happen before the growing agony in his knees became more painful than his considered alternative, that would be splendid.

Anna Harrison stared at the floor and considered the orange, mauve and black swirling patterns that comprised the drink, food and generally life-matted carpet. If something so eye-meltingly hideous could ever have been considered popular enough to cover an entire pub with, then it stood to reason that this seemingly hopeless situation could conceivably still have a positive outcome. Stranger things have happened.

Probably not actually…

To her right she could feel Mister Wells staring at her, from ahead the creepy Man in Grey did the same, but in a way that made her skin crawl.

Might have to start calling him Ick Man…

The other gentleman, the older, broader and generally more composed of the two, kept a watchful eye over proceedings. When he spoke, his tone was measured and relaxed. Anna thought she detected a faint Northern Irish lilt to his rich voice. It was the Detective that had interviewed her at home.

If even the police are actually involved in all this, what hope do we have?

"Okay then. First off, I'd like to thank the three of you. My employer has been somewhat *puritanical* in his search for these things. Trust me when I say that this day has been a

321

long time coming." He stepped backwards towards the table, and ran the back of his hand gently over the patches. "This whole thing has been much more of a messy business than any of us would have liked. However, here we are, approaching the finishing post without too much in the way of collateral damage. A few fixtures and fittings sure, but no bother, this old place is long past due a refurb anyway." he said with an almost cheery tone.

"You killed my father." Wells growled.

"Ahh, yes. That." he replied, twirling his gun around. "Yes, messy business, I'm afraid. Still, at least young Nathaniel here learned a harsh lesson in… respecting his elders."

The Grey Man's lip curled into something between a smile and a sneer. He leant down first in front of Anna, and when she refused to meet his gaze, to Wells. From the corner of her eye she saw the teacher's posture stiffen. Nathaniel ran the side of his pistol down his cheek. Neil Wells had no qualms about meeting his gaze, and held it firmly, but took no further action. Anna, clenched her left fist, ready to intervene, but felt a reassuring hand on her arm.

"Not yet." Richard whispered.

"You see," the man continued, "the Grand Leader has been on the quest for the power of the Eternal Flame for well over half a century now. A quest that has not come cheap, nor has it come without losses. Fortunately, he is a man with deep pockets and a certain, shall we say, perspective, on the value of human life. Some people have value, some people do not. Sometimes people who *do* can outlive that value."

With calm precision, he stepped forward and slammed the handle of his gun down onto the back of the neck of the Grey Man. The younger man went limp and fell face first onto the carpet next to Anna's leg. She let out a startled scream, and looked up at their captor. Richard kept his hand firmly but gently on her arm. In spite of her instinct to jump up, she relented and took a deep breath.

"A wise decision young lady. Your time is coming, no sense in rushing things now."

"What is all this?" Wells asked.

"A good question, a tad broad though. We're in no rush per se, but equally I have a date with destiny and, well, not all things in life need to be savoured."

He quickly turned around, grabbed one of the patches and firmly spoke the words. "Not For Oneself But For All."

Anna watched in wide-eyed astonishment as the Blue Flames cascaded around the man, his tan trench coat whipping open, his finely combed hair briefly standing on edge.

"Incredible." he said looking at his arms and legs, as though seeing them for the first time. He turned around towards the bar, made a fist and slammed it down and straight through the thick, lacquered surface with an almighty crash! A wide, childlike smile spread across his face.

"It's everything he said it would be and more…" he said to himself in wonder.

Anna felt Richard squeeze her arm again. She looked at him.

"When I go, you go." he whispered.

Anna nodded.

"Sixty years! That deluded old fool." he let out a raucous belt of laughter. "And after all that, all we needed was two school kids, and an alcoholic Politics teacher."

"History." Wells said bitterly.

"You will be after today old boy." the man smiled. "You see, the Grand Leader doesn't get out and about much these days, but he doesn't miss a trick either." he said, and gestured the gun over Wells' right shoulder to a small CCTV camera blinking away impassively high in the corner of the room. "Well, unfortunately for him, no amount of recording

323

equipment saw this coming. You see, it occurred to me that money comes and money goes, people fight over it, die for it. But what is it that the people who don't have to worry about money want? What motivates them?"

"Power." Richard said coldly.

"Precisely young man. Precisely. And when one has Money *and* Power?"

"Life."

"Good, excellent. Maybe you're not such a bad teacher after all, ey?" he said and winked at Wells. "Yes, and right now that is the one thing that my employer is sorely short on. Pity." He shrugged. He fired a shot from his gun, and the camera exploded. He then placed the gun down on the table next to the patches.

"So what comes next?" Wells asked.

"Ahh, yes, next. Well, I'm afraid for you and the young lady, next is one for the Religious Studies faculty, or perhaps the Theology Department. It'll be a shame to lose this place, for sure, but the old girl has had her heyday. Better to burn out than fade away wouldn't you say Mister Wells?" He walked towards the doorway behind him. In the gloom, Anna could make out the shape of half a dozen green plastic petrol canisters. He grabbed one, and began pouring its contents over the floor and the bar. The clear liquid ran down the cracks left from his earlier show of strength and began to pool and spread outwards across the terracotta tiled floor that ringed it.

"For the boy though, well it looks like you might have a use a little further beyond that, ey? A bit more than meets the eye to you I reckon." he said, shaking a pair of handcuffs with one hand and patronisingly patting Richard on the head with the other.

The young man sprang to his feet, and putting all his weight into it, landed a thunderous uppercut to the older man's chin. It was a great connection. One that even without superpowers would've likely knocked the other out. If that other was without powers himself. As it was, the blow staggered the Detective slightly. Richard tried to press his fractional advantage, with his fists up in a boxing stance, he threw a left hook, and right jab and followed up with a quick kick to the stomach. The man was knocked back another step, instinctively moving his hands to his midriff. The Eternal Flame stepped forward to strike again, but instead was caught mid stride by a firm boot to the hip. Anna reflexively sidestepped, as Richard flew backwards past her and slammed into the wall. He landed atop a white sheet covered sofa in a plume of dust. Coughing, and unsteady he hauled himself back to his feet.

Anna jumped to hers and ran over to him.

"Oh God, are you okay?"

Richard smiled and coughed again. He gave her arm another gentle squeeze and nodded.

"Stay away from the windows. Be ready." he said in a low voice. "I've got this."

Richard dusted himself down and regained his fighting stance. "I've seen unspeakable horrors from this world and beyond, and few things chill my blood like a man who thinks his life is more valuable than another's, who elevates himself by pushing others down into the mud beneath his heel." He straightened his back and broadened out his chest.

"That's the price of power son." the Detective said arrogantly. "Bold men shape life to their design."

"There's a name for people like you." Richard responded.

"Winners?" the Detective chuckled and gestured nonchalantly around the room.

"Cowards."

The policeman's smile flattened. "Ignorant child. I'll teach you a lesson your idiot teacher here never could." He charged at Richard, who ducked one almighty right handed haymaker, only to be caught under the chin by a short uppercut. The connection threw him up and away again, this time knocking over a set of upturned chairs on a nearby table.

"You talk to me about horrors! Thirty years on the Force, working for elitist toffs and protecting the dregs of society from themselves. Rodents crawling over each other, fighting and cursing and drinking themselves into the filth, then crying pain and poverty. Well no more, that life is beneath me. Today I take the power back."

"What? Is it this power you're talking about 'Old Boy'?" Neil Wells said, as he and Anna stood over the table covered in the Eternal Flame patches.

"No, get away from them, you ignorant souse." he roared, and turned to run, only to find his foot held fast by Richard on the floor. "Silly boy." he spat, and kicked him in the stomach with his other foot, winding him, and breaking free

.

Neil Wells reached down and picked up one of the patches. "Not For Oneself, But For All" he said, with a wicked smile, as the raging Detective closed the gap. This time though the power didn't course through his body. He looked down just in time to register the torn stitching of the fire damaged patch they'd stolen from the Order, as the man reached him.

"Oh you son of a bit…" he swore as he was shoulder tackled. The table went with them, and the patches and DVD scattered across the floor. As the men hit the ground, the flame from the Detective's fist made contact with the petrol soaked carpet. Instantly, thick orange flames flared up and began to spread across the liquid.

Anna Harrison dove for one of the patches that had come to rest in a puddle on the tiled floor. As she grabbed it, the fire rose up, igniting it between her fingers. It incinerated instantly and scolded her fingertips. She yelped and tossed it away, scouring around for another as the policeman and Mister

Wells scuffled behind her. The flames grew quickly, blackening and blistering the wallpaper and climbing the wooden countertop behind the bar. The few remaining liquor bottles, hung with optic spirit pourers, began to pop, shatter and sizzle. Anna felt a shard of glass catch her above the eye, and winced. As she pulled her hand away from the wound, Anna saw another two patches lost to the flames. She cursed and pounded the floor. As her search continued, soundtracked by the sounds of violence, Anna felt the sweat begin to pour down her back as more and more of the room was swallowed up in flame.

Her panic rose, and as it threatened to boil over, she again felt the reassuring hand of Richard on her shoulder. He looked terrible, and yet still somehow at ease with the situation.

"Come on, we need to get you out of here."

"What about Mister Wells?" Anna asked.

"Him too." Richard looked around the inferno, his gaze settling on a raised area as yet untouched by the blaze, with a skylight, walled by windows and a set of double fire escape doors. He nodded in satisfaction.

"There that's it, I think. We need to get him over there."

"Him???" Anna blurted out. "What about us?!"

"Do you trust me?"

"Easy there Aladdin, let's just do what needs to be done."

He smiled back easily, and again Anna felt her anxiety drop, even as the intensity of the heat around her continued to rise.

As acrid smoke began to pool above them, Anna and Richard tried to duck slightly as they approached the two men, who rolled around on the floor between two pool tables. The Detective pinned Wells to the ground again, and reached up to deliver a blow. Before he could, Richard snapped a pool queue over his neck, causing him to arch his back in pain. He turned to growl at the boy, but as he did so, Anna smacked a second pool cue across the front of his face, snapping it in two in a hail of tiny splinters. Blood began to stream from his nose.

"Get an arm." Richard instructed, and both he and Anna grabbed one each, hauling him to his feet, dragging their still dazed assailant across the room. As the windowed area drew closer though, his alertness returned and he struggled free, pushing Anna onto a section of the bar just as a trail of lit spirits crawled towards her. Suddenly there was a firm grip on her collar, and Neil Wells dragged her away from the flames just in time.

"Thanks Sir." she coughed.

Wells, battered and drenched in sweat finally ditched his tattered bathrobe and charged after Richard and the Detective. Anna took a dry swallow, a shallow breath and followed. As she did, a shiny glint caught her eye.

The DVD!

Still in its plastic slip case, beneath which she could just make out the corner of one of the patches too. Anna bent down quickly and scooped them up, shoving both into her back pocket before running back into the fray.

Wells grabbed hold of the man's arm just as he shook Richard free, pushing the boy into a broken Fruit Machine with a hefty sounding crack of glass.

"Up there, quick!" Richard directed the teacher.

Wells, his ageing aches and pains lost in the fiery hustle and bustle of the moment, dragged his opponent onwards, grabbing a fist full of his coat for leverage, and pushing him with all his might towards the open area ahead. The Detective tripped over the two low steps and stumbled into the pool of smoky light cast by the overhead skylight. Anna appeared at his shoulder, dragging Richard alongside, as a wooden ceiling beam behind them collapsed, blocking off the rest of the floor. An academic issue really as the fire had already claimed most of it. The only remaining exit were the two doors behind their captor. Wells' eyes fixed on the thick metal chain and padlock that snaked across them. His heart sank, but his anger remained.

If I'm stuck here, then I'm knocking that twerp down a peg or two before it's too late.

He stepped forward, fists clenched. The time for smart words and snark were long past. But before he could take another step, the boy reached a hand across his chest.

"Let me go, young man. I have a score to settle with this one." Wells said, wiping a stream of sweat from his soot and blood stained cheek.

"Hold on, just a little longer."

"Longer?" Wells spluttered. "Son, I think 'longer' is running a tad short right now. How much *longer* do you mean?"

"A minute. Two tops."

"You're sure?" Anna asked.

"Err… *pretty* sure?" he said and pulled a face.

"Okay. Wait, what?!" Anna exclaimed.

Richard shrugged and stood up straight.

"Time's running out pal!" he shouted as the Detective dragged himself back to standing. "You don't look too good, everything alright?" he asked playfully.

"Fine, more than fine enough to finish off you three misfits." the Detective replied.

"Yeah, maybe. But I'll be honest, that power of yours, looks like it's running a little low, and that over there." He gestured towards the door. "That is a pretty strong-looking chain.

A puzzled look came over the man's beleaguered features. He turned to see the lock in question and scoffed.

"Child's play for one with my power."

Richard smiled. "Well, you see that's the thing. That power, well it's a truly wonderful thing, it has the ability to change lives, to change the course of history in fact. But it comes with a couple of other quirks too. The first, is that though it grants power to anyone passionate enough to claim it, it tends to work better and last longer for those with more, shall we say, *noble* ambitions?"

The Detective looked down at his hands, squeezing them tightly together. Despite the soaring temperatures, Wells could've sworn he saw the colour drain from his face.

"And you see, killing kids and stealing? Not exactly pure of heart stuff." Richard shrugged.

The Policeman's eyes widened in panic. He spun on his heels and bolted towards the locked doors, tugging, twisting and straining at the chain to no avail.

"Now, here's where things get even more interesting." Richard said, and gestured to Anna and Wells to step around to the side. You see the words we use to activate it, they aren't just for effect. It's a code. A clue, even. The power is stronger when it's shared with others, but it's more than that, it also creates a bond between its wielders. A connection, in spirit… and location." he paused, expectantly. A moment passed. Then another.

Anna looked at him. "Erm… Richard?!" she hissed as another part of the ceiling caved in, sending a thick waft of hot, ashy embers floating past them.

The boy laughed awkwardly. "Oh dear, well…"

The doors exploded with an almighty crash! The Detective was smashed backwards as a lime green TVR Cerbera came careening into the building. Glass, wood and bricks were sent flying in all directions. The car came to an abrupt halt atop a pile of rubble, steam leaking from its mangled front grill, chunks of door, wall and window spread across the bonnet. Sunlight from outside poured in around its sleek, if somewhat misshapen frame.

"Is… that *my* car?" Wells said, more in shock than anger. Behind the dust streaked windscreen were the dazed but grinning faces of Marc Townsend and Jackson Sleight. The

330

older man put his grimy hands atop his sweat matted head. "Right!" he barked, "Put it in reverse you two reprobates!"

Marc looked a tad panicked and reached down, the screeching sound of grinding gears filled what was left of the room.

"No, no. Reverse! Put the clutch down fully!"

Second time was the charm, and Marc jerkily backed out over the debris and into the car park again. As it did, Wells noticed Anna laying atop Richard on the far side of the room. Wells shook his head again. "Come on you two, the building's coming down!"

Anna winced and slowly opened her eyes, her face inches away from Richard's. "Hey, you okay?" she asked.

The boy's eyelids fluttered momentarily and then snapped open.

"Hey there, looks like I saved *you* this time, hero." she said with a smile.

Oh what the hell, just do it Annie.

She quickly leant forward and kissed him. Richard's eyes widened in shock.

"NO!" he shouted and sat bolt upright with a start, patting himself all over, and looking around as though seeing this place for the first time.

"What's going on??? The Tiger? Where am I? Where... Anna?" he asked, his fearful babble immediately replaced by flat out confusion. Richard jumped to his feet, and looked down at them, and his hands. He looked so lost that he barely registered the flames engulfing the next room, creeping through the archway towards them.

"How long was I gone? No, never mind that, I need to get back."

Jackson Sleight appeared through the hole. "Hey there you are! Are you guys...?"

"You!" Richard shouted, and taking three steps forward, threw a punch that landed squarely on Sleights' jaw. The acne faced behemoth crumpled to the floor, unconscious.

"What the hell are you doing!?" Anna shouted at him and ran over to Sleight's snoring lump on the floor.

"Wait, what? That's Jackson Sleight, the bully! He's been picking on me for years, I, I…"

"He's just saved us, you idiot!"

"He what? I don't understand. Wait, did you just kiss me?" Richard asked, putting his fingers to his lips.

At that moment, another beam collapsed, and Richard held his hands up to shield his eyes from the backdraft. When he pulled them down again, he seemed different. He shook his head.

"Anna, come on, we've got to get out of here before the building comes down on us." he shouted.

Anna looked at him with a squint.

"What happened to Jackson?" Richard asked.

"You! You happened to him!"

"Oh, right." he winced. "Look, I'll explain later, right now we need to go." he said firmly.

Grabbing an arm each they managed to drag the hefty boy back out into the fresh air, where Neil Wells was chiding Marc and pointing animatedly at the damage to his car. Richard looked at Marc a moment, and Anna was sure she saw a brief change in his expression, but in an instant it was gone.

"Mister Wells, we need to get back in there! We need to try and save those men!" Richard shouted.

Wells thought about protesting, but nodded, and pulling the neck of his shirt up over his mouth, quickly ran back inside behind Richard, as black smoke billowed out of the hole.

Inside, the flames were drawing closer, the heat was nigh on unbearable. Wells tried to stay as low as possible, but the smoke filled his lungs, and made it nearly impossible to see more than a few feet ahead. Richard pushed forward into the burning haze.

"I've found him!" he coughed.

Wells looked down and there was the Detective, his arms and legs splayed at unnatural angles, a deep gash ran from his scalp across his face. Wells checked his pulse and found none.

"He's gone." he said.

Richard nodded, and strained his eyes, looking back to the spot they had been held earlier.

"This is madness, we'll be killed, and for what?? These people wanted us dead." Wells objected.

"They're still people. Come on."

Wells and Richard pushed on, clambering over a collapsed beam. It was only six feet away, but as every impossible step took them deeper into the inferno, Wells' clothes, already weighed down with sweat, began to boil, he felt his skin beginning to blister. A handful of the longest, most painful seconds of his life later they reached the Grey Man, his Grey pinstripe suit turned a dark black by sweat and soot. They began to drag him out. When they finally emerged back into daylight, and reached a safe distance the pair collapsed to the floor, coughing and wheezing to clear the smoke from their barbecued lungs.

Anna and Marc ran over to them.

"Water, car boot." Wells hacked.

Marc scurried away and returned with an armful of plastic water bottles.

Across the car park, the entrance to the function room burst open. Wells watched Terrance and the other members of The Order emerge through the thick black cloud, bickering, coughing and tripping over one another as they did. As Neil Wells gently sipped on the impossibly perfect water, he thought he could hear the sound of sirens in the air, but they

333

were not his concern. His chief concern was letting his head list gently towards the tarmac, and letting the cool breeze wash over him as the embrace of sleep drifted him away.

CHAPTER FORTY FIVE: RICHIE

There was fear. Intense and paralysing. Then came noise. Brain crushing, impossibly loud noise. Then came Light. Unbearable light, heat, and pain that tore at his nerve endings. Then came Impact. Rattling his bones, twisting his bearings, tearing at his skin. Then came Rest. Beautiful rest. A smell of smoke, rising heat, but also a feeling of happiness, contentment. Soft lips upon his. Anna? No, of course it couldn't be. A trick, a nightmare. The Tiger Tank was gone but another terror approached, one from a lifetime ago, or was it days? Sleight. Richie Spink though had faced down hordes, this horror from his past held no fear for him anymore. All his might in one good punch, and the foe is vanquished at last. Victory! But no. This isn't his life. This isn't what he's supposed to be doing now. Is it? An explosion. Heat. Pain.

Yes, I remember. I remember the pain.

Richie opened his eyes to familiar surroundings. He was back in his broken down, bullet riddled kitchen refuge once again. Something had changed though, a new picture hung on the wall, big, broad and jagged. He recognised the artwork… from a history lesson he'd once had? The colours were wrong of course, dark brown and grey and not the sandy colour he knew, and the frame of broken bricks? Well, that seemed a little Tate Modern for his tastes. But the quality! The realism of the Tiger Tank painting was beyond this world.

Exquisite brush strokes my dear, but someone has hung it upside down…

It seemed to change perspective, subtly shifting, the faint wisp of white clouds drifted across the bright blue sky, the Tank growing in size.

Maybe it's not a picture, maybe it's a telly??

He wasn't sure of the name of the show, but it looked pretty surreal, what with its upside-down tanks and skies on floors, and floors on skies. A character walked onto the set. A

335

familiar one. Concerned, panicked, shouting. Richie's ears rang, but he was sure the upside down person was shouting at him. He tilted his head, and both his body, and the whole world flipped 90 degrees. The thick soles of his boots hit the dusty wooden floor with a thud.

Ohhhhh, it's not the telly that's upside down, it's me...

The man stepped out of the wonky brick screen, and slid on his knees in front of him, his voice began to permeate the ringing. At first it sounded like his head was trapped inside a thick cardboard box, it gave the voice a dull, thick, bassy sound.

Hehe, just like the teacher in Snoopy...

Recognition crept in. It was Will. Will was here. Will was shouting. Will was shaking him. Richie wanted very much to go to sleep. Will would not allow it. His Tuba voice became a trumpet, became a French horn, became an angry Yorkshire accent.

"Come on, come on! They're about to fire again!!!" he shouted. His face was red. The tendons in his neck strained. Flecks of saliva flew from his mouth.

"Fire again?" Richie asked sleepily.

"The Tiger! Come on, move, MOVE!"

Over Will's shoulder he focussed on the Tank again. It was bigger. No. It was closer. The roar of its engine, the heavy scent of petrol. The heavy clank of a shell being loaded. Richie's eyes snapped wide.

"Oh God, the Tiger's about to fire again!" he said, scrambling to his feet, leaning onto Will to counter his still shaky balance. His mentor dragged him with all his might, and as Richie again heard the eardrum rattling of the cannon, the pair dove headlong through a side door. The kitchen behind them exploded! What remained of the bullet soaked floor, the wooden dresser, the crockery, the table and chairs, all vaporised in an instant. The pair landed heavily and Richie felt the wind knocked from his lungs.

"Are you okay lad?? Richie? Are you okay?" Will asked, his usually professional demeanour lost to concern.

"Yeah, I'm okay. My head's ringing a bit." He propped himself up against a wall beneath a rickety looking staircase. "And my arms. Whoa." He looked down. His uniform had been completely burned away up to his shoulders, as had much of the front of his tunic. His forearms were scorched, and blistered at the point of impact. His exposed chest throbbed, Richie reaching down to inspect for further damage.

"Oh my God!" he exclaimed.

"What? Are you wounded?" Will asked worriedly.

"I. Am. RIPPED!" he said with a manic smile.

"Wha' is it, shrapnel?" Will flustered, and ripped open more of his shirt to check for an entry point.

"Hey, alright grabby! I meant look at these abs! I'm shredded!" Richie beamed.

Will's concerned face ran through the full range of emotions in a heartbeat before settling back to his customary grump. He punched Richie on the arm. Hard.

"Ow! Hey! Watch it!"

"'Raight you. Up." Will scolded.

Richie did as he was told, albeit gingerly.

"We need t' stop that tank. Now." Will said abruptly.

"Yeah cool, don't suppose you've got a cheeky tactical airstrike, or a nuclear bomb up your sleeve have you? I'd check myself, but…" He looked down at his bare arms. "No sleeves." Richie grinned.

"*Nuclear* bomb?"

"Oh, yeah, nevermind. That's a little while yet I guess."

From outside, the roar of the Tiger's engine grew louder and the rapid rattle of machine gun fire began again. The noise was punctuated by loud individual cracks of rifle fire. Richie closed his eyes and reached out with his senses, feeling for the shared power coursing through his teammates. In his

337

mind's eye he could see Grace and Green out there, feel their grit, their determination, their fear.

"They won't last long out there." Will said.

"Yeah as long as they can stay out of the machine gun range they should be okay. It takes a minute to rotate the turret, which is a bit of a moot point though, because they're not actually allowed to unlock it whilst the drive engine is active." Richie rabbitted. "I mean unless it just runs them over, I guess. I did that in GTA once, pretty gory stu... What?"

Will looked at him in disbelief.

"How d'yer know that? We 'aven't had chance t' check through t' plans yet."

"Eh? Oh, history lesson. The teacher is a decent enough fella, but normally just phones it in. The World War Two stuff really seems to be his bag though. Most of the other kids in class find that stuff pretty boring, but there's something about the tanks I find pretty cool. That out there, the Tiger? Stuff of legend mate." he shrugged, and went back to flexing his abs.

"Where 'as all this been?"

"Oh, yeah sorry sir. I'll be honest a lot of those lessons are just a bunch of kids messing around. I probably need to do more revision before mock exams."

"I don't suppose they happened to teach you how to stop one?"

"Nah not really. Thickest armour, biggest gun. Basically moveable metallic nightmare fuel. Not great in confined spaces though. How would you *normally* take a tank down?"

"Disable the tracks with explosives, get access to the cockpit, take out the crew." Will replied, and Richie could see a plan was forming.

Another gigantic explosion, more distant this time, shook the foundations of the building, coating them in a fresh layer of brick dust. A moment later, Grace came crashing in through another side door.

"Sir, we're running on fumes out here. It's do or die."

"Tell me, is it true that t' crew aren't allowed to turn the turret when it's driving?

Grace looked puzzled. "Well, yes sir. It's a court marshallable offence. Stops the mechanism becoming damaged. But, how did…"

"Nevermind. Where is the armour weakest?" Will asked.

"Sir, the Mark VI is built to withstand even our most powerful anti-tank weapons. The front armour is ten centimetres thick, dual side mounted smoke canister launchers and that gun? The 88mm? Well, you've already seen what that can do. What we've got, well, they're pea shooters by comparison." Grace responded.

"I never asked what *wouldn't* stop it. I asked where it's weakest."

Grace sighed and tucked a loose strand of her rich, red hair behind one ear. "Central mass. Between the turret and the hull. But, it's a long shot sir. Impossible even. Nothing we've got is getting through there, and you'd have to be dead centre to do it. With that gun, anything dead centre is going to be a puddle before they get the shot lined up."

"Maybe. I don't know whether you've met our resident expert in impossible?" Will smiled and presented Richie, who was still lost in his own hunkiness.

"Hi! What? Oh, wait… Me?"

"'Raight, here's the plan."

Richie, it's fair to say, hated the plan. The plan left him somewhere between wetting his pants and running away in terror. But, it was, Will assured him, the only way the four of them were going to leave that square today. Grace had gone, headlong back into the fray. No kiss this time, though he wasn't going to forget the last one in a hurry. Richie could sense her emotions. Trepidation had replaced fear, but strongest of all was a deep sense of resolve. The feeling was shared by Green, and most of all by Will. Richie may have hated the plan, but the people in this with him believed in it, and by proxy, believed in him.

"One more time please sir." Richie said.

Will grinned. "We distract it. You take out one of t' tracks however you want, pull off the wheel plates, melt it, snap it, your decision. When it's immobilised, I want you t' get a good run up, dig deep, focus, and hit t' front of it with every last bit of everything yer've got."

"And before another one of those shells turns me inside out?"

"Exactly."

"Okay." Richie sucked in a deep lungful of dusty air and felt the telltale sting of tears behind his eyes. "Is it going to work Will? I know I've got this power, but I'm not like you guys, and I'm definitely not HIM." Richie nodded down at his body. "I-I don't think I could take another hit like that, Will." He looked at the man, his vision swimming.

Major Will North put two fatherly hands on Richie's broad shoulders and looked him square in the eyes.

"Kid, I'll be honest with you. It might work, it might not. But if you go out there and give it absolutely everything, every last drop and it doesn't? Well then we'll at least go t' next life knowing we did all we could. We cannot control the outcome, we can only control ourselves. Understand?"

Richie nodded, lifted his mask up, wiped his eyes then pulled it back down into place.

"Do or do not, there is no try?"

"Eh?"

"Oh, nothing, just something I heard once."

"I like it, but it's not right. Trying is everything. Everyday could be your last, don't meet your maker with any regrets. We've come this far. Let's go and finish this."

Richie could feel an aura of strength and passion coming off of Will, it washed through him in nourishing waves.

"Okay, let's do this." he said, channeling the resolve he could feel from his teammates to fuel his own.

"Good lad. Smash it's bloody teeth in." Will said and with a final, firm pat on the shoulder he drew his pistol and charged back out through the obliterated kitchen.

"NAH THEN LOVE, LET'S 'AVE A PROPER DANCE SHALL WE??!" he roared.

Richie couldn't help but allow himself to smile. The how's and why's of his situation no-longer mattered. He was here, now, and he would do what he must. He looked down at the body again, and clenched his fists. "Thank God this guy does his sit ups! Right, LET'S HAVE IT!!!"

He pulled back his left arm, and unleashed a powerful blow to the wall in front of him. The bricks exploded outwards and Richie stepped through the gap back into the square.

Okay, okay, just like that, only on a tank, easy peasy.

He already knew the positions of the others, their locations felt like radar pings in his brain, but he was pleased to see that the tank was currently facing away from him. Green fired off a round, then leapt through a doorway on the opposite side of the square as a burst of machine gun fire tore up the ground behind him. The Tiger continued to spin counterclockwise in the general direction of Will. Richie recognised his moment, and broke into a sprint, covering the thirty yard gap in moments. The deafening roar and thick petroleum scent of the beast's powerful engines dominated his senses again. The beast continued spinning in place and Richie stayed on his toes, sidestepping to stay close, trying not to have his feet flattened beneath the wide, jagged metal of the tracks. He reached down and pulled at one of the circular wheel plates, it stayed stuck firm, the rotation nearly dragging his whole hand into the gears behind it. He snapped his arm back and

341

suddenly had a flashback to playing "Crocodile Dentist" with his sister.

It's no good, they are moving too fast for me to get a grip.

Richie felt a sharp spike in Green's sense. Pain, fear, hard; cold and intense. The young man had been downed by a thick shard of wooden shrapnel. The Tiger's rotation brought the path of its machine gun closer and closer. He yanked the blood covered spike out and yelled in anguish. Richie winced.

Oh god, come on, come on!

He reached again for one of the wheel plates, and again failed to get a grip. He let out a frustrated howl.

Across the square, Green hauled himself to his feet, with a pronounced limp and gritted teeth and attempted to move away from the deadly path of bullets. His movements though were too slow, and Richie could feel his rising panic. Green's wounded leg gave way and he fell to the floor again. In a desperation move, he began firing his pistol at the machine gun. The high pitched pings and thumps of impact rising above the din of the engines and crushed cobble.

"Ahhh, screw it." Richie said, pushing Green's fear from his mind, and focussing his thoughts onto his left hand. He shaped it like a knife, planted his feet, and as the rear end of the Tiger rumbled towards him, he brought it down on the track in a chopping motion. It split, cracked, and with a violent whip, came loose from the wheelbase! The loose end slapped Richie across the chest and sent him tumbling backwards as the Tank's rotation slowed, then with an ear splitting sound of grinding metal came to a halt. With its gigantic grey and brown metallic hull blocking his view, Richie quickly reached out again to Green and was greeted with an almost overwhelming feeling of relief. He allowed himself a moment to soak it in, before he heard Will's voice from behind him.

"Phase two! PHASE TWO!" he shouted.

Richie nodded and jumped to his feet and as he did, became aware of another new sound: a repetitive thud/hiss. Before he could question it, a canister landed at his feet and exploded in a thick cloying plume of white smoke. Another landed to his side, and from the opposite side of the marooned vehicle another two. A double clang followed as two of the top hatches were thrown open. The sounds of machine gun fire multiplied.

"This is it! Endgame! Flame, it's on you now son!"

Richie swallowed hard, and began to run away from the tank and its shroud of smoke, circling the village square until he was approximately facing its front end. With the vehicle immobilised, he knew he'd have only a few moments until the crew unlocked the turret. Once it was free to move, the deadly cannon was back in play, and they were effectively back to square one. He took a few steps back, and ground his heel into the cobble stones for purchase. Ahead of him now he could see the muzzle flashes of the machine guns, like sheet lighting inside a thundercloud. On the periphery, Grace and Will darted around, firing individual shots in return, Green had begun to drag himself off the battleground, a torn piece of uniform in his mouth ready to tourniquet his bleeding thigh.

Richie allowed himself one more reach out, sensing the determination of his squad mates. It felt like a cold drink after a long hot day. He felt it permeate his every fibre, nourishing his resolve.

Okay Richie, let's do this…

As he tensed his muscles for acceleration, he noticed that the machine gun fire had died down again. The all too familiar chunk-clang of the Tiger's main cannon being loaded rang around off the chipped and broken brick walls once again.

"NO!" Richie shouted, knowing there was no way he could cover the ground in time. The earth shaking bang came again and another deadly shell erupted from its evil eye, the

343

shockwave pushed the surrounding smoke away, revealing the toothy grin of the Tiger's spare track once more. He watched the projectile's deadly arc, replaying the agony of the last impact through his mind once more. This time though the shot had been taken unsighted, its aim was off, not by much but just enough, and as it reached him, Richie pivoted on his planted back heel, rotated his torso, and brought up his forearms to guard again. The shell hit him at an incredible speed, but his split second change of angle robbed it of the impact to detonate. The speeding shell ricocheted away, slammed through an already broken window and exploded with a calamitous bang! Bricks, shattered window pane and mortar rained down on the spot where Richie had stood. He managed to roll with the blow, using the momentum to spin away just enough to avoid the worst of it. The smaller fragments were incinerated by blue flames as they contacted his body, like the pitter-patter of raindrops on a puddle.

Richie exhaled loudly. Took another deep breath and looked down at his clenched fists, visualising the job at hand. He thought about school, about bullies, about lost bikes and angry German soldiers, about his Mum and Dad's constant rowing, about his inability to talk to girls and, every time he'd forgotten his PE kit. He thought about every single stupid time he'd wanted to speak up for himself, but only found the words when the moment was long past.

No more.

Blue flames sparked from his knuckles, growing in size and ferocity until both hands and forearms were ablaze. It felt good. Natural. Though he could feel the support of Will, Green and Grace, Richie truly knew now that it was his job, and his job alone. One punch to end it all. He looked up at the Tiger, the massive, terrifying, brown and grey monstrosity sitting there, waiting to strike, waiting to end him. He saw the two gunners clamber back out of their holes again, ready to unleash another deadly barrage on his friends.

No more.

He set himself, gritted his teeth and took off like a shot.

His footsteps pounded into the ground beneath him, with each one he felt his power grow. He let out a primal roar!

"NO MORE!!!!" Pouring out his anger and frustrations, pushing them from his heart, to his lungs, his legs, to his flaming fists. The soldiers heard him coming, and with wide eyed panic, withdrew back inside the safety of ten centimetre thick armour. Back inside the great hope of the German infantry, back inside to safety. Richie lowered his left fist, leant forward and as he took his final step sprang upwards with all his might, with every last drop of everything, and drove all of it through his fist. His knuckles hit the spare track on its front, and continued to drive through, onwards, upwards, through the frontal armour plating and machine gun, through the top of the hull, the bottom of the turret, and the base of the deadly, monstrous cannon, carving it apart like a jagged steak knife cutting through a tin can. Somewhere amidst this, Richie was certain he'd seen the terrified face of the tank's commander, but his true focus was only on the power in his fist. His momentum took him up and above the massive body, and as his upward arc ended, he landed behind the turret in a front roll. Tucking his head into his chest, he came off the back of the vehicle, and slammed his fists down on the floor. The blue flames exploded in a powerful, blinding flash, lifting the gargantuan machine off the ground for an instant before it slammed back down to earth!

Richie slowly got to his feet, behind him he heard Will barking at the tank's occupants to surrender as he and Grace closed in with guns drawn. He felt his friend's deep sense of relief and satisfaction, like a warm blanket in front of a roaring fireplace. Richie looked at his fists again, the flames fluttered and faded away. He smiled, a big, wide, wondrous smile. Richie Spink, The Eternal Flame of British Resistance took two more reasonably nonchalant steps with the sunset and the smoking Tiger husk to his back, blew on his hands like an old western gunslinger and promptly collapsed to the floor unconscious…

CHAPTER FORTY SIX: WELLS

He'd been dreaming about his father again, but this time the sun had been shining. The skies were clear, a red gingham picnic blanket lay spread on the freshly cut grass. He felt the warm sun on his face as he ran around the shaded fringes of an ageless, beautiful oak tree in bloom. His mother in a flowing white dress, a beautiful bright smile on her face; his father in a navy double breasted suit, writing thoughtfully in his journal. Wells was younger, happier. They all were. They ate sandwiches and drank homemade lemonade, and as the sunset came his parents exchanged vows beneath the branches and carved names into its thick, weathered trunk. They took off their rings, and handed them to the boy. He looked at them, the sunlight glinting from the polished silver, highlighting the flaming fist emblems engraved on them. Neil, his mother and his father placed their hands together, carefully wrapping the rings in a green cloth, placing them into a small metal box. Neil watched as his Father dug a hole at the base of the tree, his suit jacket hanging from a branch, waving peacefully in the warm early evening breeze. Together they buried the box, and when the job was done, the three packed up the blanket and strolled away hand in hand. A perfect end to a perfect day of childhood contentment.

Neil Wells awoke groggily to the smell of antiseptic, the gentle beeping of a heart rate monitor and a general low level hospital hubbub. He could hear his rasping breath, and reached up to find a rubber oxygen mask covering his mouth and nose. He lifted it off, feeling the tightening of the elastic strand keeping it in place, and tried a breath without it. It was tough to take a deep breath, but it was bearable enough. He removed the strap and tried a few more, each came easier than the last. He felt a spasm in his chest and barked out a quick flurry of coughs. When he took his hand from his mouth, there was a thick, black substance there.

"You can probably expect that for another week or so," said a kindly female voice from the doorway. The doctor, in her late forties, with well-styled white-grey hair walked in holding a clipboard. "You did inhale enough smoke to put Marlboro out of business after all. Maybe next time, don't hang around burning buildings quite so much."

"Given my usual alcohol intake, I'm genuinely stunned that I didn't combust." Wells replied.

"Yes, well, that was my next point. Most of your physical injuries are superficial enough. The cuts and bruises should fade in days. The burns, well on that front you got a little lucky. Given the situation, you're looking at another few weeks, and there's one on your upper arm that we'll need to monitor. If it doesn't improve you may need a skin graft. Anyway, we'll do a few more tests and if your blood/oxygen levels have settled we should be able to discharge you later today. But, and it's a big but, if I let you leave here it will be under the strict proviso that you take it easy. No running into burning buildings, plenty of bed rest and at least a fortnight where your blood alcohol level is more akin to a Boy Scout, than a street corner wino. Understood?" she said firmly, but with the faintest hint of a smile at the corner of her lips.

"I bow to your expertise ma'am." he replied in as debonaire a way as it was possible, for a man who knew he was covered in bandages and likely had no underwear on under his gown.

"Oh that reminds me, you have visitors. Would you like me to send them in?"

"Erm, okay, yes, by all means." Wells said, puzzled and praying that it wasn't his ex-wife.

The rather strikingly attractive doctor left, and a moment later, he heard the sounds of teenage squabbling approach. Anna Harrison poked her head around the door, she had her hands over her eyes.

"Are you decent sir?"

"What? Oh, err… yes." Wells readjusted himself in the bed, pulling the thin white sheet higher up on his chest.

"Thank God," came the thick accent of Jackson Sleight. "We've seen some 'orrible stuff this week, but no-one needs to see old saggy teacher balls. Ey!" he exclaimed as Anna punched him in the arm and wince-smiled awkwardly as she clutched the cast on her wrist.

Last through the door was Marc Townsend, he hung back sheepishly, trying his best not to make eye contact.

"Oh there he is," Wells said, trying to sound as cross as possible. "Joyride Johnny and his sidekick."

"Hey! This little scrote is the sidekick, not me!" Sleight protested.

"Sorry sir, it, well, it seemed like a good idea at the time." Marc said.

"What's the damage then? No, wait, don't tell me I'm sure I'll find out soon enough." He strained in his bed to look beyond the trio. "Where's the other one?"

"Richard, err, Richie?" Anna said, suddenly a little more uncomfortable in her skin. "His mum and dad came to pick him up this morning. He was quite similar to you, bed rest and fluids that kind of thing. They said he should be back to school in a week or two, but we haven't had the chance to speak to him yet."

Behind her, Wells noticed Sleight absentmindedly touching the thick black/blue bruise on his cheek.

"So, pull up some chairs. What did I miss?"

Anna sat in a high backed chair with pale pink plastic cushioning and cleared her throat. Over the course of the hour that followed she broke down the chain of events that had spun out of the incident at the now chargrilled public house.

The Fire brigade and Police had arrived more or less simultaneously. Less, she explained, in that during the sixty second window between the Fire Engine, and a raft of Police Vans arriving, Terrance and the Order had attempted to do a

349

runner. Whether it was smoke inhalation, a general lack of fitness, or (Anna's favourite theory), the difficulty in carrying someone who had been knocked out by her vicious and deadly front kick, she wasn't one hundred percent certain. They did however only make it twenty yards down the road, before being arrested for fleeing the scene of a crime. Wells found his heart warmed by the idea of the podgy men being thrown in the back of a meat wagon, and his heart went near furnace-like when she told him she'd seen the Head of the Order crying like a baby as they did so.

The Grey Man was currently several floors up in this very hospital. Jackson Sleight, ever willing to risk his future chances of employment by adding to his criminal record, had risked a look earlier that morning. He was currently handcuffed to the bed, and connected to a series of machines far beyond the boy's vocabulary level to explain. He'd definitely heard the word 'coma'. Though. Or possibly "Korma". Though, Anna had interjected, the former clearly made more sense given his extensive injuries and smoke/fire exposure.

Information on the fate of the Detective had not been particularly forthcoming. Anna reasoned that gruesome death was not the kind of thing police officers tended to freely discuss with potentially traumatised teenagers at an active crime scene. Marc though claimed to have stumbled upon a leaked news report shared online that referred to the "mysterious death of Police Detective Sandford Kennedy". Within hours of publication though the report had been altered, and the current version on the local paper's website bore no reference to his name or role within the Police.

"And what of the boy? Richard? How is he?"

Anna again shifted uncomfortably in her chair. Sleight crinkled his broad, freckled nose and went back to biting his stubby fingernails.

Marc shrugged, happy to take the spotlight. "Yeah, we think he's okay. His folks and sister Kathy arrived here pretty much the second that we did, and have been with him ever since. We haven't been allowed to see him, but as we said, he was discharged today. He was pretty banged up though. I did see him leave, he gave me a little okay sign as he walked past, so, yeah. I've sent him a text."

"How did you manage to find us? And what happened to the patches?" Wells asked,

"Oh! Well, that's a weird one." Marc perked back up. "You guys got bundled into the car and sped off, and I was just left there on my lonesome. So, I decided to head into your house to see if there was anyone around, or to maybe phone the police or whatever. Nice telly by the way! The plasma!" Marc made a Chef's kiss gesture, and Neil Wells felt a sense of validation that somehow outweighed his outrage at a student poking around his home. "Anyway, yeah, the place was a mess, I spent a while sifting through the wreckage trying to find some clue, *any clue really* to where they'd taken you. And then, just as I was about to give up, well, in runs this big galoot, babbling on about this feeling he had in his head. Telling me he knows where to go.

Jackson Sleight nodded in confirmation. "It was a hot feelin' in me 'ead."

Marc shook his head in consternation. "Yeah, that. Anyway, he wouldn't shut up about it, and seeing as Anna said it was a police car, we couldn't exactly ring them up, just in case. So we…"

"Stole my one hundred and fifty thousand pound car without permission or a valid licence, followed a 'hot feeling' in the head of a bottom set pupil, and drove it through a wall?"

"Well, no, I… yes. Basically."

Wells shrugged again, no sense in crying over it now. "Wait, how did he even have that feeling in the first place?"

351

Anna chimed in. "We think he got a jolt from one of the patches just before he ran off down the street. At the time, him kicking a police car and running off just seemed like, well, normal behaviour. For him anyway."

Sleight shrugged in agreement.

"Which patch was this?"

Anna reached down to the rucksack between her legs and spun it around. There, dead centre in a mass of black marker drawn doodles and logos, was the Eternal Flame Squad patch.

"It belonged to your Father. He gave it to me before he died. I'm so sorry Mister Wells. He was a wonderful man" she said as tears welled in her eyes.

"It's okay, it's okay," he said softly, surprising himself with the softness of his tone. He beckoned her over, and sat up to give her a hug. "He and I never really had a close relationship, I'm glad that you were able to be there for him." He let the hug fade, and Anna stepped back, more composed now, like an unseen weight had been lifted from her shoulders.

"He couldn't remember what year it was most days, but by all accounts he gave the Grey Man a hell of a bloody nose."

Wells laughed. "Yes, he never shared any of his stories with me, but I always knew that if there was trouble, he was the kind of man who would never back down from a fight. He always told me, growing up, that wins could never be guaranteed, so trying with everything you had was everything you could do. It always seemed a tad strange a saying for a man who worked at a museum." He smiled wistfully at the thought. "So that's it then? The last one?"

"Ermm… Not quite." She unzipped the bag, reached in and pulled out a DVD in a slightly melted slip case, and a battle damaged patch with a bullet hole in it. "There's also the matter of who put the Order up to all this. The Detective mentioned a… 'Grand Leader'."

"Yes, and that snivelling toad Cowley, the Head of the Order, he mentioned something to me about the Order being something bigger, more sinister." Wells rubbed his chin. "This right here kids is true, living history. A chapter of British military history lost to both the records and to the history books. It appears that we may have some research ahead… " Wells said, a sense of excitement bubbling inside that he hadn't felt for years.

"Homework?" Jackson Sleight moaned. "Nah, you're alright." He got up abruptly and left, leaving the other three to stare on, bemused in his wake.

"Quite. Anyway for now, I think I'll try my hand at some of that delightful sounding bed rest I've heard so much about."

"Sounds like a good plan sir." Anna smiled, hauling Marc to his feet and ushering him out of the door.

"Thank you Miss Harrison. We couldn't have done any of this without you."

"Thanks sir." she said, "you too."

Wells nodded appreciatively, and the girl took her leave. After a moment he lay back in his bed again, and took some slow breaths. His father had always been a closed book to him, a mystery, but one he assumed stemmed from a form of jaded stoicism or disapproval. But in light of the past week's revelations Wells couldn't help but wonder just how deep his secrets ran. Perhaps there was more to Frank Sebastian Wells than met the eye.

CHAPTER FORTY SEVEN: RICHIE

Richie dipped in and out of consciousness. Tangentially aware of the arrival of nightfall as the light dimmed and the air grew cold. He felt himself hoisted onto some sort of stretcher, caught broken pieces of distant sounding conversation, glimpsed faces of concern, and of celebration. The smell of Will's tobacco, a shock of red hair, a squeeze of his arm, a playful whisper in his ear. He could hear boisterous chatter and the loud, dull thrumming of an engine. The talk was exciting, he wanted desperately to talk to the others about what had happened, but sleep was good too. Better in fact.

At some point later he felt himself drift back to reality, the thrumming, the tobacco and the happy chatter had gone, as had the red hair, sadly. He felt the comforting softness of a pillow beneath his head, and a blanket over him. He reached up to his face and found… face. Not a mask, but actual cheeks, eyes and forehead. He allowed himself a happy sigh and a contented smile as he lay back and waited for his bedside alarm clock to go off.

"Ahh, there he is." Will said.

Richie sat bolt upright, and snapped his head around the room like a hyperactive meerkat. Bare brick walls, half a dozen hospital-style beds with pristine white sheets, and there, whittling a piece of wood with a rather large looking knife was Will. Freshly shaven and wearing a clean white vest above his usual army issue trousers.

"Will?"

"Absolutely."

"But you look so, so… clean."

Will chuckled, "Funny guy."

"Where are we? What happened?"

"Huh? Oh, yer 'course, I forget that you haven't actually been here yet. We are back on home soil, well, of a sort. Temporary base near Dover. Those plans we recovered have been handed off to our science department, as well as some photos and a few bits and pieces we took off the one you killed. One of the lab guys got a little flushed. The Tiger has got 'em buzzing like a beehive. I heard one of them call it the best moment of his life." He smiled. "Anyway, that's for them to sort."

"How did we get here?"

"Now that's a good 'un. Not long after you decided to grab forty winks, the rest of the Squad arrived. Turns out Skinner had gotten wind of their surprise attack, and decided to throw one of their own at their first fall back defence point. Quite clever really, though if you hadn't deflected that second shell, well, they'd have had a hell of a welcome to greet 'em when they got back t' square. Anyway, we rigged up a stretcher, grabbed your sleepy 'ead, and managed to get t' extraction point. Job's a good 'un." Will said as he pulled out his tobacco tin and removed a pre-rolled cigarette. "D'yer mind?" he asked, holding it up.

"Just don't ask me to light it." Richie grinned, holding out a bandaged hand.

"Fair." he replied and held up one of his own.

"Any idea why I'm still here?"

"Therein lies the great ongoing mystery my son." he said and got to his feet, dusting off the loose strands of tobacco as he did. "You did well there kid."

"Thanks Will."

"Don't let it to yer head though, a man's only as good as his next challenge." he said and walked to the doorway. "Hell of a punch though." he chuckled. "Anyway, fancy a walk?"

Richie shrugged, "If you think I can."

"Hop to it lad."

Richie gingerly swung his legs to the side of the bed. He had on a sweatshirt, loose fitting track pants, and white plimsoles. With a little effort he pushed himself to a standing position, wobbled for a moment, then found his balance.

355

Will led him down a narrow corridor, casually puffing away on his cigarette as he did, but making a deliberate effort to blow the smoke away from Richie.

"What is this place?" Richie asked, as an attractive young woman in a pristine white nurses uniform wheeled a metal trolley past them.

"Like I said. Home base."

"Oh... Cool. So, what happens next?"

"Next? The war kid, we fight 'til it's done."

Richie nodded. 1942 meant three more years, he wondered if he would be around to see them. Something else was pressing on his mind though.   "Will?"

"Ye' kid?"

"Who am I? I mean, who is he, where did he come from?" he gestured down at his body.

"Now that is where things *really* get complicated." Will said as they reached a thick metal door, ringed by hefty steel rivets. Clenching the cigarette between his lips, he used both hands to twist open the thick circular handle at its centre. It rotated with a metallic clank and he pushed it open. Richie suddenly felt a cold rush of air, as they stepped into the dazzling bright light outside. As his eyes adjusted, Richie could see nothing but miles and miles of clear blue sky.

"Whoa..."

Will smiled, and stepped towards the grey, cast iron barrier ahead. He flicked the cigarette over the side. Richie stepped forward to watch it go, and immediately felt his jaw drop.

"Oh... *WOW*."

Beyond the barrier, a hundred metres below them lay glistening, choppy, green blue waters that stretched out as far as the eye could see. Excitedly, Richie leaned further over the edge, trying to work out how such a massive structure was seemingly hovering in the middle of the sea. With both hands on the barrier, he craned his neck over as far as possible. Beneath their curved walkway he could see the bottom of two giant, gun metal grey struts. They ran at an angle from the underside of the base and down into the freezing cold waters below. Though he couldn't take in the full scale of the structure, he imagined it to look similar to those water towers they had in small towns in American movies, but more squat, much, much bigger... and, well, in the water. He made a mental note to quiz Will more on it.

So cool...

"Thomas Townsend."

"What?" Richie replied, his question forgotten.

"The Eternal Flame. Thomas Townsend. Submitted himself to be enlisted in the British army in 1941, but between you and me, that's not really where his story started.

Richie watched the water below as a seagull swept gracefully down, and scooped up a fish in its beak before soaring away.

"I first met him two months after."

"What was he like? I bet he's something else."

"I'll be honest, I thought he was an ignorant, arrogant wazzock.

"Oh."

"But there were two things he did that proved me wrong."

Richie turned away from the sea to face Will, pushing his wind blown hair back from his eyes. "Yeah?"

"The first was the day he saved a young kid who ended up on the training range. Threw himself in front of a bandolier of grenades like it were nothing." He shook his head in reverence.

"Wow. That's... amazing. What was the other one?"

Will chuckled. "The other? That was the week before we moved here. The day we nearly lost the whole Squad, Christ, the whole bloody war before we'd even started! It was the day I found out just how deep his power goes, and just how low others would stoop to take it fer themselves." He took a slow breath in through his nose, and out through his mouth. "That

357

was the day I knew I'd die for the Eternal Flame." He said, looking out to sea, his gaze fixed on the endless blue horizon. Richie watched him silently, unsure if Will was done, or about to spill his deepest, darkest secrets. Even in the silence, for the first time Richie felt a real sense of the man behind the soldier.

"Anyway, come on lad," He said, his moment of introspection over, "it's cold, can't have the Eternal Flame catching the bloody sniffles can we?" he laughed and gave Richie a firm pat on the shoulder, "let's get you back inside ey?"

Back in the infirmary, Richie was pleased to see that the bed next to his was now occupied by Green. He was sat up, writing intently in a brown leather journal, his heavily bandaged leg propped up on pillows. When Will and Richie entered, he put the book down and saluted.

"Take it easy lad," Will smiled. "Don't want you to hurt anythin' else."

Green smiled back and picked up the book. "Cheers gaffer. How are you doing Thomas? Or is it Richie still?"

Richie looked at Will, he nodded approval. "Yeah, it's Richie."

"Hell of an uppercut you've got on you pal."

"Yeah, thanks" he replied bashfully.

Will coughed. "Anyway, I've got matters to attend ter, you boys take it easy and get better quick-sharp. This war's not gonna win itself. See yer around kid." he said, patting Richie on the back as he left.

"I guess we've actually not been properly introduced." Green said, putting the journal on his lap.

"Oh yeah I guess so. I'm…" Richie wiped his hand on his sweatshirt. "I'm Richie Spink."

"Nice to meet you Richie, I'm Green. Sebastian Green."

"Cool. What are you writing there?"

"Oh this? I call it 'The Daring Adventures of the Eternal Flame Squad'." he laughed. "I mean, this place, everything we do is so far classified, there's no way on God's green earth they'll ever let me publish it, but you never know. Maybe one day, when all this is over I can sneak it out, show it to the wife, maybe read it as a bedtime story to our kids."

"Yeah," Richie nodded, "That would be great."

The pair stayed there in silence for a moment, the words hanging in the air as Richie wondered whether the book ever did find its way out of the war. "Hey Sebastian?"

"Yes, Rich?"

"Who is Thomas Townsend?"

Green looked at him with a puzzled expression for a moment, before shaking his head. "Why don't you have a look for yourself?" He gestured towards the mirror above a porcelain sink across the room.

Richie felt deathly tired and the muscles in his arms and legs ached from the walk, but he shuffled across the space, using the metal rungs alongside the beds to aid his balance until at last he reached the sink.

Right then matey chops, it's time to get a good look at the man behind the Flames…

He looked up into the mirror, and felt his knees buckle slightly. He grabbed the sink for balance. There, staring back at him was… him.

What the hell?!

He squinted, rubbed his unusually blue eyes and turned his head side to side. From every angle, the face in the mirror was his own. Older certainly. More chiseled and capable of solid stubble growth, absolutely. There was also an unfamiliar scar above his left eye that bisected his eyebrow, but despite all that, Richie was in no doubt that it was him.

"Huh, how about that?" he said, and heard Green chuckle behind him.

"Yep. Wild isn't it?" His friend said.

Somewhere in another part of the building a bell rang, Richie tried to ignore it, but the sound grew louder and louder. His head swam with the impossibility of what lay so clearly before him. The noise rattled his brain against the walls of his skull. He screwed his eyes shut, rubbing his balled fists into them and screamed. Richie's knees gave way and he crumpled to the floor with a thump.

Suddenly a door burst open, and in ran Kathy. The ringing persisted. The concrete floor beneath him was now thinning red carpet. His sister reached over and flicked a switch on the bedside alarm, killing the brain rattling noise instantly. She slid down on the floor next to her brother, their backs propped against the bed frame.

"Kath??"

"It's me Rich. Are you alright?"

Richie shook his head to clear it, and ran his hands up his face. A shot of pain jangled his nerves as he touched a gauze patch above his left eye. He winced. Then he paused. Then he chuckled.

"Yeah... yeah, I'm fine."

They both sat there for a moment. It was his older sister who spoke first.

"Is there anything you want to talk to me about?"

"No Kath, it's cool. Honestly. I'm fine." Richie said, and despite all logic to the contrary, he believed it. He stood up and she rose with him.

"Okay," she said, though her face said otherwise. "If you need to talk, you know you can come to me with anything."

"Thanks Kath," Richie said, quickly stepping forward and wrapping her in a bear hug that nearly knocked the wind right out of her. She hugged him back. When he released it, his sister, so often the family cynic, left with a bemused but happy look on her face. Richie looked around his room, feeling like a lifetime had passed since he was last there. He waited until he heard Kathy's bedroom door close and then

360

crossed the hallway into the bathroom to inspect himself in the mirror.

The face that stared back was his own. Younger again, far less chiseled and with a frustrating lack of consistent stubble growth, for sure, but it was very much his face. He reached up to the thick, white square of badge taped above his left eye, and slowly, painfully peeled it back. Beneath it was a cut that ran through his eyebrow, stapled together by five blood crusted stitches. He prodded it and winced, then he laughed.

"*I am* the Eternal Flame... cool." He shrugged and left the bathroom with a surprising spring in his step.

Richie Spink had absolutely no idea how he could possibly be older yet living in the past. He didn't have the foggiest clue as to why he was using a different name, or why he was jumping into that body. And he *certainly* couldn't even begin to guess how he'd ended up with incredible super powers AND abs that would put the Ultimate Warrior to shame... but he couldn't wait to find out.

CHAPTER FORTY EIGHT: BILL

That evening Bill North sat at the desk in his room and pondered the day's events. His quarters were bigger, and better appointed than The Eternal Flame's, befitting his shift to the rank of Officer. The ornate wooden desk had a green leather top. There was a tall wardrobe and a high backed oxblood leather armchair, more in keeping with the decor of the main house, than the underground facility that housed their super-powered secret weapon. The only things in the way of personal effects were the pull up bar he'd installed above the door frame, a small selection of free weights stacked neatly beneath the desk, and the tobacco tin on the bedside table.

The success of Green's crew had given him a sense of comfort he'd not felt since arriving at the base. Knowing that he had three competent young men for his team was a part of that, a *significant* part of that. That they were able to take down The Eternal Flame was another huge source of encouragement, though even to himself Bill recognised a degree of stupidity in that notion. The Flame was a weapon, and though Bill loved weapons, he knew that they all had uses and limits. Getting a first sense of The Flame's felt significant. When one's life is on the line, a man needed to know where to place his trust. When the crunch moment came, and it always did, that trust needed to be implicit. Split seconds could cost or save lives.

For Bill North that trust began with himself, with his mind and body. They were the only weapons he'd have access to until his dying breath, and his circle of trust in combat extended outwards from there. His weapons came next. Not only had he achieved mastery over each in terms of their use, he knew their component parts as well as the engineer that had designed them. From there came his unit, all of whom he expected to follow the same strict principles. Technical skills were important, but Bill needed more, he needed to be able to look these men in the whites of their eyes and *know* they had the necessary stuff. Today's exercise had been the most revealing one yet. Green, Welsh and Parkinson had proven themselves. The Flame, though clearly willing to risk himself for others, remained a factor unlike any other. Men who think they are unkillable are often the first to die. A fear of death is the ultimate motivator, and it is one that can, and should, never be truly overcome.

He sighed, and sat back, pinching the bridge of his nose. He had two things to do before he could afford himself some sleep. One was a simple fix, the other required some fresh air and clarity of thought. Reaching forward he slid open the bottom drawer of his desk and withdrew an unopened bottle of Brandy. He stood, flipped it 180 degrees, caught it in the opposite hand and walked out of the room.

The night air was cool, but not cold. Bill was dressed in his boots, trousers and a t-shirt, enough that the walk across the campus was the right side of invigorating. In the distance the tops of the woodland carried a peaceful glow by moonlight, but Bill's first stop was closer to home. He passed a guard station, returning the two MP's stationed there's salutes without breaking his brisk stride, and headed towards the barracks. The long, single storey building had a large green door at one end, with the inside broken up into a dozen smaller bedrooms either side of a wide, central corridor. At its peak it could hold close to two hundred fighting men. Right now it housed just the eight remaining potential members of the Squad. Andreo and Marsh were gone, washed out back to where they came from and good riddance. The rest of the personnel on site were based elsewhere, largely depending on rank and/or importance. Bill had been offered the chance to house his men inside the main house, but had flatly declined. He wanted their experience to be as close to the regular army as possible. He wanted his men sharp, and rested but the importance of team camaraderie was high on the list too. Another reason why The Eternal Flame's solitary existence had rankled with him so much, and in turn why his selfless act earlier that day had impressed him so.

As he reached the third door on the left of the barracks he stopped and listened. Inside he could hear the general sounds of merriment, and the muffled melody of a song he couldn't quite discern, but had a beat that suited the mood. He firmly rapped his knuckles on the door, and took mild pleasure in the sounds of panic from within as the men on the other side quickly tried to disguise their 'non-regulation' celebrations. Another encouraging sign.

Bill decided not to wait any longer and barged into the room, chest first and as officiously as possible. The look of panic on Parkinson's face alone, as he frantically tried to hide an armful of cigarette packets, playing cards and what appeared to be a dirty magazine, was priceless. Green and Welsh sat on their bunks straight faced and straight backed. All three froze in place and Bill enjoyed letting the silence hang there for a few extra, awkward moments.

"Do we not salute when senior officers enter rooms anymore, no?" he barked.

Parkinson looked down at the pile of contraband in his clutches and replied, "Sorry sir, yes sir."

Green and Welsh managed the salute but not the speech. Bill's face grew a Cheshire Cat smile. What's up then lads? Laryngitis? I heard that Foxtrot Camp had an outbreak last week. Can't have something nasty like that spreading at such a vital time, probably best to get you both in t' solitary medical confinement ey?"

"Sorry sir, no sir" they responded in unison, each exhaling a thick cloud of cigar smoke.

Bill nodded. "Ahh there we go, raight as rain eh?" He allowed himself a brief smile. "Anyway, good work today gents. That there is yer new standard. Yer can all improve, but

364

I never want to see yer worse than that." He placed the bottle of Brandy down on a chest of drawers next to the door, turned and walked out. As he reached the external door he heard Parkinson drop his cargo, and all three men burst into laughter.

With the easy objective ticked off his list, and enough time to clear his head, Bill headed for his next target. Veering off the pathway he steered clear of the guard station, and away from the floodlights that shone down in sweeping arcs from the roof of the mansion. Avoiding a gravel path, and sticking to whatever shadows he could find, he cut back towards the main building. The Military in battle could roll with the punches, think on its feet, create and change plans on the spot to suit circumstances. Outside the battlefield, it was bureaucracy at its most pure. Someone had ordered one of the weapon crates to be switched out for lethal ordinance. And if someone had ordered it, someone had enacted it, and with every step involved there would be a paper trail. Bill intended to find it.

The main building housed much of the infrastructure of the unit, however everything that related to the Eternal Flame, including the man himself was housed in a bunker to the side, one that ran deep underneath the Mansion itself. It was where General Sutherland had taken him on his first arrival, where he'd first seen the man in action. The files would be held in storage down in Sub-Basement Three. For safety reasons, there were two ways in and out. One was inside the house accessed by the secret doorway in Sutherland's office, and the other was the above-ground entrance outside, which he now stalked towards. The entrance protruded from the ground in a curved arch, with the doorway itself the tallest point.

Pressing himself tight to the exterior wall, he stood and waited, keeping his breathing steady. His chance came just moments later as two members of the science team exited the building, and Bill slipped in behind them before the door could auto-bolt shut.

Despite only having been there once before, Bill had committed all he had seen to memory, and quickly and quietly made his way through the facility. As he reached the end of a raised metal gangway and the lift shaft, he dropped down over the guide rail and down to the concrete floor below. Ahead of him was an access panel which with a swift application of force, popped open. Bill carefully laid it to one side, and began descending the ladder inside. When he reached the hatch marked "B3" he reversed the process, and came out into another similar corridor. A cylindrical concrete chamber with another metal gangway running its length, several feet above his head. The path ahead of him was covered with myriad wires and exposed connections. Bill's expertise did not lay in mechanical or electrical engineering, but he recognised a potential death trap when he saw one.

The hard way it is then...

He sprang up and gripped onto either side of the walkway, and began to climb along. With his knees bent, his boots had just enough clearance space over the wiring. Just. At the opposite end, he swung to one side, and after a few more swings for momentum, flipped himself back up on the top path. The door to the Records Room was unlocked and he gently opened and closed it behind him as he entered.

Inside, the room opened up into a cavernous library. On one side were countless rows of filing cabinets. On the other, were metal racks filled with books, files and documentation. A man could spend a lifetime in this room and not come close to reading everything it contained. Mercifully Bill North knew what he was looking for and had a damn good idea of where to find it.

The filing cabinets were grouped by year, and twenty yards down the row he found the one he was looking for. Inside, ordered again by date was everything from mission reconnaissance reports and intercepted enemy transmission dictations to training exercise evaluation reports and, exactly what he was looking for, equipment requisition forms. He flicked through the masses of paperwork until his nimble fingers fell upon the one from that morning. Bill pulled it out, and under the heavy overhead Tungsten lighting, scanned down the page. There, typed clear as day was his original order, each piece of non-lethal ordinance and any corresponding ammunition or accessory was listed with its unique stock number. The bottom part of the order though had a huge red stamp across it, saying "RECALL". Below, as it should be, was Bill's signature. An additional sheet of paper was paperclipped in place behind the first. Bill flicked to it. There under the heading, MODIFIED ORDINANCE REQUEST was the list of handguns, rifles and grenades that had made their way into the second crate, and very nearly left him with bodies to bury. At the bottom was the information he was looking for, the signature. General Arthur Sutherland. Bill swore under his breath.

God damn it Arthur, what in the blue hell are you playing at?

He folded and pocketed the paper. He wasn't sure what use it would be. If the General was plotting against him, a piece of paper was unlikely to do a great deal. He kept it all the same. Something here was amiss, and finding the so-called smoking gun only served to make that feeling run deeper. Bill slid the drawer back into place and began the stealthy journey back top side. He would have to stay vigilant, not just for dissent and danger on the battlefield, but on the homefront now as well…

367

CHAPTER FORTY NINE: ANNA

"Time is a jet plane,
it moves too fast..."

Bob Dylans' gravely tones filled Anna's ears, his face, hidden behind dark sunglasses, slid in and out of view. A bead of sweat ran down her cheek as she finished the last of her sit up routine at the foot of the bed.

"Oh, but what a shame.
That all we've shared can't last,
And I can change, I swear"

She reached down to wipe her brow with her sleeve, and winced as the coarse shell of the wrist cast scratched against her nose. Annoyed, she placed the fingers of her right hand back to her temple and switched hands.

"Oh, see what you can do,
I can make it through,
You can make it too."

It had been three weeks since the fire, and with a return to school looming, Anna felt pretty good. The frequent coughing fits had faded, taking the, even too goth for her, black phlegm with them. The mild burns to her back and legs had healed, making the cast on her wrist (painted black to match the bulk of her wardrobe) the last outward remaining sign of her ordeal. She'd spent her convalescence binge watching Dawson's Creek, wearing deeper grooves into her Dylan collection, and all the while slowly building up her workout routine. By the time the cast came off, Anna would be stronger than ever. More prepared.

Daily texts from Marc, doorstep visits from the surprisingly (actually, shockingly) sweet Jackson Sleight and a beautifully kind, handwritten letter of thanks and an invitation to Frank's funeral from Mister Wells had been her connection to the outside world. In those three weeks though there had been nothing from Richie.

Or Richard or The Eternal Flame or any other name he fancies calling himself.

Not a call, text, knock, sky written psalm or semaphore. Not. A. Sausage.

"Love is so simple, to quote a phrase,
You've known it all the time,
I'm learnin' it these days,
Oh, I know where I can find you."

Anna had played back the kiss in her head somewhere approaching a zillion times. If the earth had swallowed her whole each time, she'd be doing her situps in Sydney by now. Though the minor details of that afternoon had become twisted in her mind's eye, the look of shock and almost… *fear*… on Richard's face remained crystal clear. It was not her *first* first kiss with someone, but it was certainly her worst. Anna knew. She'd been housebound for three weeks, more than enough time to rank them all. In fact she'd widened the net to *all* kisses she'd had, and then even further to hand holdings, hugs from strangers and those awkward moments brushing past people on the bus. The kiss with Richard? Top One.

Perhaps in the world, of all time…

She'd found an old copy of the Guinness World Records in her brother's room during her hiatus. There wasn't a category for World's Worst First Kisses in the 1989 edition, but that in itself was more than enough proof to cement her claim.

369

With gritted teeth, she finished her set, unhooked her feet from under the bed frame, and stood up. Turning away from her Dylan poster, Anna walked over to the record player. Tomorrow, she would be back to school. Back to the crushing monotony of normal life. The boys would all be there. Maybe she'd bump into him there. Then, like it or not, she could get an answer.

"Oh, in somebody's room,
It's a price I have to pay,
You're a big girl all the w…"

Anna lifted the needle, carefully slipped the LP back into its sleeve and stood on her tiptoes to slide it into its alphabetical place on the shelf. She felt her foot brush against something as she did. It was her back pack. THE backpack, the Flaming Fist patch, still adorned there in its pride of place. Quite possibly the last intact one on Earth. She picked the bag up, studied the stitching. Tomorrow she would get her answers. She'd waited three weeks. Three whole weeks. She could wait one more day.

The worst first kiss ever…

She sighed.

"Ahh, screw it." She said, slinging the bag onto her shoulder, and slipping into a pair of black and silver Adidas shell toes.

Barely five minutes on from finishing her work out, Anna Harrison, hair tied back and full of righteous fury, was setting a ferocious pace to Richie's Spink front door. When she arrived at his squeaky front gate she had no plan in her mind beyond confrontation. When she pressed the rusted doorbell her plan of attack came to her. When a cool looking girl with half blonde, half black dyed hair opened the door, she was ready to take no prisoners.

"Hello?" the awesome looking older girl said.

Come on Anna, take no prisoners.

"Err… Can I speak to Richard please?"

Good lord…

The girl looked her up and down before giving her a sceptical raised eyebrow and a smirk. It was at that point Anna realised that with her hair up in a sweaty ponytail, not a stitch of makeup on her face and wearing her old tracksuit bottoms, she must look like some sort of crazed, sporty vagrant. She tried to put it from her mind. What she looked like wasn't important right now, only that she got to say her piece.

The girl lamented and looked over her shoulder towards the hallway stairs. "*Richard*, oh Richard dear. One has a visitor." she shouted with an exaggeratedly posh accent. She looked back at Anna and smiled. "*Richie* will be down in a sec, love. Wait…" There was the eyebrow again. "You're not *Anna* are you?"

Anna Harrison, whose attention was fixed on her narrow angle view of the worn-carpeted staircase, was caught flat footed by the question.

"What? Oh…" she looked down at herself, and tucked a loose strand of hair behind her ear. "Barely."

"Yeah, I have those days too. I'm Kathy by the way, Lanky's sister." she smiled, pointing a thumb over her shoulder. "*Love* the trainers." she said with an appreciative nod. "Superstars?"

"Absolutely."

"Cool. So, what are your intentions with my little brother?"

"I'm probably going to shout at him for being a bit of a dick."

"Nice. You know what? You might as well just go up. First door on the right."

"Thanks," Anna said, stepping up from the doorstep. "Love your hair by the way."

371

Kathy gave her another nod of appreciation and gestured towards the stairs.

Here, we go…

Richie Spink was sitting at the computer, his face softly illuminated by the shifting glow of the monitor. With night falling behind his already drawn curtains, it was the only source of illumination in the room, and gave his head a disembodied quality. A feeling he related to more nowadays than ever. He listlessly clicked at the mouse and watched as his army's base was overrun, again. "MISSION FAILED" said a faintly robotic feminine voice, and Richie slid his chair backwards into the centre of the room. Beside his keyboard was a pile of textbooks and sheets of printed papers. Homework, catch up tests and general revision. Each untouched since his return to the present day. If gaming couldn't hold his attention, what hope did quadratic equations and French have? He wasn't sure he'd admit it to anyone, but he was beginning to prefer the idea of another Eternal Flame time jump than going back to school. He'd had three weeks in his own company, mulling over his experiences, trying to better himself in ways he felt Will and Sebastian might approve of. He no longer butchered himself when shaving, his hair was slightly better kempt and he could now do an entire fifty push ups without collapsing like an asthmatic squirrel. The hair thing was largely so he could show off his rather cool looking eyebrow scar of course, but nevertheless. The only thing worse than continuing to sit in his own boredom, (*or deep in revision*, in his own boredom) was the idea of going back to school. Back to being boring old, luckless Richie Spink. Whipping boy to the bullies and invisible to girls. Give him German tanks any day of the week. He let out a sigh and spun around on his chair.

God, what I'd give for some excitement in my life…

His bedroom door burst open.

"Jesus Christ!" he exclaimed, falling backwards off the rotating chair, and landing on his backside with a thump. Richie squinted through the gloom, ready to launch a tirade at Kathy. Three weeks of her near constant attempts to jump scare him had grown beyond tiresome. "Oh get lost Kath, it's not…"

"Oi you! Richard, Richie, Eternal Flame, whatever you call yourself." barked the girl who was definitely NOT Kathy.

Who the heck is that? And how does she know about…

"Yeah, you think you're so smart, so smooth, with your 'are you okay Anna's?' and your 'let's take down a corrupt policeman together Anna's' and… and your, 'I'd rather punch Jackson Sleight in the face than be kissed by YOU, Anna's' EURGH! You bloody boys are all the same, selfish, stupid children, too obsessed with your own silly games to think about anyone else. Ohhh, you've got time to play video games and time to… to… spin around on chairs, but no time to even TEXT the girl who helped save your life, AND who gave you, what SHOULD have been, AT WORST a seven out of ten first kiss. AT WORST! But no." She took her first breath. "Well, that's it. That's the first and last one you get from me. Your loss Sonny Jim!" She stomped her foot and turned around to throw open the door. As she did her backpack struck the light switch on the wall, throwing the room into startlingly bright illumination. As she stormed out, Richie's eyes adjusted just in time to see Anna Harrison's face in profile and the Eternal Flame patch glinting under the uncovered tungsten bulb. She slammed the door behind her, rattling the walls as she did.

Anna??? What the hell just happened?

Richie heard the pounding of footsteps, but before his brain could process the verbal beating he'd taken, his door opened again. It was Kathy.

"I like her!" she said with a wide grin.

"What the hell was that???" Richie said, stunned.

373

"I'm not sure, but from what you've told me, that's the most words she's ever said to you."

"She just said she wants nothing to do with me!"

"Eurgh, you boys." she sighed. "No girl storms across town without makeup on and goes into their house just to tell someone that they don't want to see them again."

"But… wait, what?" Richie's head was swimming.

"But, what, nothing. Get after her." She stepped across the room and hauled him to his feet. "Go on, scoot!" she said firmly, making a brushing gesture with her hands. She ushered him to the doorway and down the stairs. "And if she kisses you again, don't do it so horribly this time!".

"Wait, but, what??"

Kathy kicked him across the front doorstep, threw a pair of battered trainers after him and slammed the door shut.

When did she kiss me? Oh…

The memory came flooding back. The Flames, the smoke, Anna nose to nose, Sleight's stupid face. "Oh no…"

Richie quickly put his shoes on, hopping towards the gate as he did so. At the edge of the road he saw her, storming away, hands clenched into fists at her side. He broke into a sprint.

The effect was far less dramatic, and his lungs hurt as darn sight more than his chase through the French woodland, but soon enough he caught her up.

"Anna, wait!"

She looked back, rolled her eyes, shook her head and sped up the pace of her walk. "Leave me alone Richard, I said what I came to say, now I'm going home."

"But wait a second, I just wanted to say…" He reached out for her and only succeeded in getting hold of her bag. Anna tried to shake him off. There was a short ripping sound and she broke free again, but instead of continuing her march, she stopped in her tracks instead. The deep amber glow of the setting sun was bolstered as the streetlight overhead flickered to life, bathing the pair in yellow spotlight.

"What! What could you possibly have to say to me?"

"Erm… Sorry?" Richie said. The word seemed too small for the situation.

"And?"

"And what?"

"Urgh! Impossible!" she said and turned around. As she did there was a faint skittering sound as a small object hit the ground.

They both looked to follow it as the small, pale square came to rest as the foot of the lamppost. Anna looked over her shoulder. Her eyes fell upon the torn stitching around the Eternal Flame patch.

"Look what you've done now!" she shouted, removing the bag from her shoulders for closer inspection. As she did, Richie crouched down to the object on the floor.

When she had received the patch from Frank Wells it had been attached to a rough edged piece of fabric. Later, she'd tidied the edges up, and added both layers- the patch and the khaki to the bag. Now, the dark green material was still in place, but the patch had come away from it. In a panic, she checked the patch itself for damage and breathed a huge sigh of relief when it appeared to be intact.

"Phew… What were you thinking?! Sure YOU of all people should know how important that… Hey! Are you even listening?"

Richie was not listening. Richie had gathered the object, and discovered it to be a tightly folded piece of paper. Carefully he opened it out, it took a few moments but when he was finished, in his hands was a roughly a5 sized sheet of paper, filled with writing, and torn down one side as though it had been ripped out of a book. The handwriting was familiar, but the contents sent a shiver down his spine. As he scanned through it, he muttered fragments from the text.

"...over the horizon appeared the dreaded hulk of Jerry's new super toy, a Tiger Tank! For a brief moment we fell silent and stared agog at this monumental David and Goliath battle. From my position it was hard to tell, but I thought then that I had seen a glimpse of fear cross the features of the masked man..."

Anna, seeing that her furious verbal prodding was going unreturned, sidled over to see what had the boy's attention so rapt.

"What is it?"

"It's… It's me…" he trailed off as he finished reading the page. He held it out and Anna grabbed it from him and read.

"The Allied superman seemed lost, as though he had suddenly lost his bearings! The deafening roar of the Tiger's turret gun broke the silence, as it fired upon him. I closed my eyes in fear of the worst; that our brave "super" soldier had been cut down so soon."

Richie leant against the lamppost. The fatigue of his sprint and the insanity of the situation catching up with him.

"Who wrote this?" Anna asked.

"It was Green… Sebastian Green. This must be from his journal. He is… *was*, one of the Eternal Flame Squad. The thing with the tank? That was me, that's what I was doing when, you err…"

"When I kissed you?"

"Yeah. I didn't even, I had no idea, I mean I didn't even think about what was happening back home. I guess I thought I'd just left this time or something. I never thought about it being a two way thing." He paused and shook his head. "God, imagine swapping World War Two for double Maths..."

"So you honestly have no idea what's been going on here?"

"A bit, Dad told me I'd been in the hospital again, and Marc has sent me a few weird texts, but I didn't dare say anything. How could I? They'd all think I'd gone mad or something."

Anna felt herself softening. The boy in front of her now, with his stooped posture, and 'weight of the world on his shoulders' demeanor, was not the one she had come to know. She read the letter again, the closing lines stuck with her...

And then he was off again, like an Olympic runner, charging straight at it. With force the likes of which I have ...the masked marvel delivered a powerful uppercut to the Tiger's front armour, tearing it apart as though it were wet newspaper. Although the battle was far from over, the belief of victory had been handed to us, and suddenly, we all felt like "super soldiers"...

Anna looked at Richie again and blew out a long blast of air in amazement.

Wow. Not the same boy, but maybe not so different either.

Absently she flipped over the page to study the other side. At first it appeared to contain little but a handful of loose doodlings and markings, like someone trying to test that a pen was still working. Some curved lines, a couple of passable looking little trees beside one large one, a wall, a cross with N, E, S and W on each point.

A... compass marking?

Now it was Richie's turn to get closer. She side eyed him as he did.

"What's up?" he said.

"I think, I think it's a map..."

Richie leant in close, and in her peripheral vision Anna studied his reaction. He traced his slender finger across the paper, over the wall, and past the small trees. Beneath the large one was a thickly marked, black inked, X.

They both looked at each other. "No way."

Anna's eyes lit up. "This is amazing, a secret map! Mister Wells will be buzzing!"

"Yeah! … Wait, who?"

377

"We need to assemble the gang!"

"Gang? What gang? I'm in a gang?!"

"Yeah, of course! Where have you been?"

"1942."

"Oh yeah, hahaha! Well it's Marc, Mister Wells, me, you and Jackson.""Jackson Sleight???"

"Yeah, he's the muscle, Wells' is the sarcastic one, Marc's the handsome one…"

"Marc's the…?

"Richard is, well, you, you're the tactician."

"Oh right. And which one are you?"

"I'm the brains, obviously. Do try and keep up mate." she said excitedly and gave him a playful punch on the arm. Anna began to walk away again, this time with a visible spring in her step.

"Wait, where are you going?"

"Home! We've got school tomorrow!" she said as she bounded away.

"What's the gang called?"

"The Flame Gang!" she shouted. "No wait, that's terrible! Let's add it to the agenda for tomorrow. Pick a better gang name!" she said over her shoulder, raising her index finger to the sky.

"Oh cool, but aren't we going to, well…"

"See you tomorrow Richie!" she shouted as she turned the corner and out of sight."

"… Kiss…?"

Richie's shoulders slumped. He let his head fall back, looked up to the heavens and saw only the thick yellow bulb of the streetlamp shining down on him.

Cheer up Rich, your life might be a mess, but at least it won't be boring. Anna Harrison is speaking to you. You're in a gang, and if Mister Wells is in on it, he might even let you off all the history homework you've missed…

With that mildly uplifting thought, he stood up tall, brushed his hair away from his eyes and walked back home.

"The Flame gang." he chuckled to himself. "God, that really is terrible…"

Anna was vaguely aware that Richie had continued to talk as she moved out of ear shot, but was far too lost in her renewed sense of purpose.

A secret treasure map! I wonder what it leads to! Maybe it's buried treasure, or a lost city, or, or the ark of the covenant. Okay, probably not that, but still! Mister Wells is going to be chuffed!

As she bounced back down the road towards home, a feeling of calm and happiness that she hadn't even noticed had been missing from her life began to spread throughout her body. After weeks of bottling things up it had felt so good to get all that stuff off her chest. Anna couldn't even begin to claim she fully understood Richie's situation, but having had her first proper conversation with the *real* him, one thing was clear. Richie and Richard were two *very* different people. Maybe Richard, The Eternal Flame, would return someday, but she would cross that bridge when it came. For now anyway Richie Spink seemed like a nice enough guy, troubled, but interesting. It would be cool to get to know him properly in time, but her days of chasing boys were over. She would chase treasure and excitement instead, and if the boys wanted to come along for the ride, well, then they'd have to chase her for a change.

If they can keep up.

With her broadest smile in weeks, Anna broke into a run. Tomorrow was going to be a brilliant day, she could feel it.

THE END

EPILOGUE ONE: AFTERMATH

The boy, the teacher and the girl were on their knees facing away towards Detective Kennedy. Slumped on the floor in front of them, the unconscious body of Nathaniel Greystone. Kennedy looked up, his eyes, dark pits of malice, burning through the screen. He raised his gun and fired. The muzzle flashed and the image vanished in a burst of static.

The Grand Leader's lip twitched, he took a shallow, respirator aided breath and moved his frail arm back to the mouse. He clicked it and the footage began playing once again.

"I'm sorry Sir, Mister Kennedy seems to have had this planned all along. We managed to recover this video clip, but it appears that he interfered with the audio somehow."

"A resourceful… asset… to be sure, but not… irreplaceable."

Kessler clenched his fist. "He was a traitor to the cause and everything you, our families, and the Order has built."

The Grand Leader laughed behind his mask. It was cold, croaky and devoid of humour. The action provoked a brief hacking fit of coughs. Kessler stepped towards him, but was waved away by a skeletally thin arm. The Grand Leader rode out the coughing fit with repetitive draws on the oxygen mask.

"One man's treachery… is another's attempt… to bend the future… to their will…" he rasped.

Director Christian Kessler watched over the Leader's shoulder as his gaze turned towards another monitor. This one showed the girl tied to a chair opposite the unconscious teacher and boy. The image fritzed with a burst of interference, and suddenly the three were running towards the camera as Greystone fired shots at them. Behind him, the three conscious members of the Order cowered.

"Did those cretins… have anything… to say for themselves?" The Grand Leader said in a quiet, raspy voice.

"No sir. They are still in the local lockup. They're claiming to be a role-playing society who used the space for rehearsals. Those devoted fools should be under our heel well enough to keep their mouths shut. Past that, there's nothing they know that we don't. The young one though, Whittaker, may be a slight exception, he has a more personal connection with the teacher. He's worth keeping tabs on."

"Tell me more… about these three."

"As you know, the girl came to our attention recently.

She remains of interest. The boy is a new player. Possibly the boyfriend. We checked him out but there's nothing there. Middle of the road student, no military ties in the family. He's nobody. The Teacher though."

"Wells?"

"Indeed. Something interesting came up that we'd missed in our preliminary investigations. It seems that prior to age six, our Mister Wells paperwork is rather peculiar. He has a birth certificate, but it's not an original, looks like it was re-issued several years after he was born. Now, it may be just an oversight. It was the 1950s afterall, post-war Britain, lots of things fell between the cracks. But then we focussed deeper on his parents and found even more irregularities. There's literally nothing on them prior to 1952 when they were registered as married. No birth certificates or job history, they weren't even registered for ration books.

"Is there… a point… to all this?"

"Perhaps. Our sources have uncovered this." Kessler reached past the Grand Leader, through the strong scent of antiseptic, and tapped several keys on the keyboard. On the left hand monitor a scanned image of a photograph came up. The image was badly sun damaged, and had myriad pin holes around the top edge, but a younger Frank Wells could be seen, his sandy blonde hair streaked with grey, his arm around a handsome blonde woman in a green dress. The pair were laughing, cutting a large white frosted cake and surrounded by balloons. Behind them, a long banner with the words 50th Wedding Anniversary, was pinned to the wall. "It was on the staff noticeboard at the museum."

"Charming..." The Grand Leader said sardonically.

"Quite. The head of HR at the museum insists that the picture was taken in 1993."

"Your point?"

"Well sir, if the Wells' were indeed married in 1952, as their marriage certificate suggests, then their 50th Anniversary would not have been until 1999..."

Director Kessler stepped back from the screen. "Again, it could be nothing. Our assumption was that Wells Senior had come into possession of The Eternal Flame materials via his time working at the museum, but perhaps there's more to it. We have our informants following up that pathway. If there are secrets to be found, rest assured they'll find them."

The Grand Leader double clicked the mouse, and the playback on all screens paused. Tapping the stubby black joystick on the arm of his chair, it began to rotate with an electro-mechanical 'whirr' until he faced his long standing assistant. The Leader's wizened features in the dimly lit library were thrown into silhouette by the glare of the screens behind him.

"Ahh, at last... the net begins... to cinch its prey. Keep... an eye on Neil Wells... he has tasted... the power... of the Flame. He won't rest... until he tastes it again... Watch him... If he finds more... we can harvest it... for ourselves."

"As you wish sir." Kessler said. Surveying the monitors, his eyes were drawn to the one in the top right. On it a comatose Nathaniel Greystone lay handcuffed to his hospital bed, the respirator pump beside him monotonously rising and falling.

"Will that be all sir?"

"It will."

"Thank you sir." He bowed slightly, and left the room, closing the heavy mahogany doors behind him.

The Grand Leader rotated his wheelchair back around again, the six monitor screens reflecting in his sharp, dark eyes. Despite his frail frame, those eyes burned with a zeal undimmed by his advanced years. Spread out before him on the desk was a battered purple tin, a rusted lighter, a yellowed letter, a silver ring in two pieces, and the photograph of The Eternal Flame Squad. With his sickly jaundiced fingers, he picked it up, and as he scanned across the smiling faces, a snarl spread across his thin dry lips. He placed it back down and touched the deep, gnarled scar that ran from above his left ear down to his jawline. The Grand Leader thought back to the fateful night that nearly claimed his life, and forever locked him onto this path. Explosions, and screams and blue flame. He picked up the two halves of the silver ring, and clenched them as tightly as he could.

"Not… for oneself… but for all." he hissed, the words spitting from his lips like a curse. He squeezed tighter, and tighter until blood dripped from the folds of his contracted fingers. He let out a pained, rasping breath and opened his hand. In the centre of his bloody palm, the ring was fused together into a formless silver lump.

He looked back down at the photograph, removed his respirator mask and took a long, deep breath, then another. His first unaided ones in years. The Grand Leader of The Order Of Flame gazed intently at the photograph, smiled, and plotted his next steps…

"Soon…"

EPILOGUE TWO: THE WATCHER

Perched high in the corner of the room, nestled on the top shelf of the furthest rack, and hidden between two thick ordinance files, a closed circuit camera watched passively over the Sub-Basement 3 Filing Room. Elsewhere, in a hidden command room inside the Mansion, a huge bay of small, curved screen televisions each displayed a black and white image of a different area of the base. Ainsworth, Turpin and Skinner took turns lifting weights in the gym. Green, Welsh and Parkinson played cards, smoked cigarettes and passed around a bottle of liquor. The Eternal Flame sat straight backed at his desk, looking up and down as he read from a textbook and jotted down notes. A dozen Lab Coat wearing technicians ran tests on the day's field used battle gear. Bill North hurriedly folded a piece of paper, put it into his back pocket, slid closed a filing cabinet and stalked out of the B3 filing room. General Sutherland was perched on the arm of a chair in his private study, a glass tumbler in one hand, the other helping him getting unprofessionally close to his secretary.

Studying all of his pawns with a satisfied smile, Captain Frederick Willerton-Smythe stubbed out a cigarette into an overflowing ashtray and leaned back comfortably in his chair. The power would soon be his, and the world would follow.

About the Author

Paul J. Machin was born and raised in Liverpool. He is the Founder of Redmen TV, the world's first football Fan TV channel, and has appeared at various times on Sky Sports, TNT Sports, BBC and, weirdly, CNN. He also has a smaller, less successful Youtube channel called Maych TV and bad knees. Paul has written and self published four non-fiction books about Liverpool FC, and co-authored, produced and published "The Man Who Stole The World Cup' with his father John J. Machin.

When he is not talking about football on camera, or locked away somewhere trying to squeeze ideas out of his brain into Google docs, he also is Dad to Jack and Penny; and husband to his wonderful wife Charlie.

His favourite movie is Back To The Future (or Shawshank Redemption depending on mood). He read ten years worth of Daredevil comics during Covid, but his favourite superhero is Superman. He once drunkenly told Phil Oakey, lead singer of the Human League, that it was more important to remember *his* name than the other way around because he was "going places". (He cringes about this in the shower at least once a week). His Top 3 Dream Interview List is John Oliver, Mike Myers and James Gunn. His three favourite books are Starman Jones, Slaughterhouse 5 and Going Solo. In 2023 he was inducted into the Football Content Awards 'Hall of Fame' along with Dean who created 442oons and one of the lads from the F2 Freestylers.

He started writing The Eternal Flame in 2008, two years before launching Redmen TV on Youtube. He started writing The Eternal Flame, Book Two in 2025…

For updates, info and general life musings, you can find Paul on all the usual social media sites under the handle @thepaulmachin